OF *Fortune*

LEE DUNNE

Published 2005
by Poolbeg Press Ltd
123 Grange Hill, Baldoyle
Dublin 13, Ireland
E-mail: poolbeg@poolbeg.com

© Lee Dunne 2005

The moral right of the author has been asserted.

Typesetting, layout, design © Poolbeg Press Ltd.

1 3 5 7 9 10 8 6 4 2

A catalogue record for this book is available from the British Library.

ISBN 1-84223-214-2

Typeset by Patricia Hope in Palatino 10/14
Printed by
Nørhaven Paperback, Denmark

www.poolbeg.com

About the Author

Lee Dunne has spent most of his adult life as a writer. He burst to fame in 1965 with his novels *Goodbye To The Hill* and *A Bed In The Sticks* before the final part of the trilogy, *Paddy Maguire is Dead*, was banned by the Irish censor in 1972. By that stage he had long since escaped from a poverty-stricken Dublin background, working as a clerk, actor, singer and cocktail bartender in Jersey before spending one year riding a bicycle around London doing 'The Knowledge' to become a Cabbie so that he would have more time to write.

He has written 18 novels and 10 stage plays. Of his three movies, two were Hollywood productions, including *Paddy* which was adapted by Lee for the screen from his novel *Goodbye To The Hill* and was banned by the Irish film censor in 1970. He has also written a large number of plays for both television and radio and has contributed 2,000 episodes of a radio serial to RTÉ. He has been published as a poet, has written columns for two national papers, and is currently a book critic for the *Sunday Independent*.

Lee also co-adapted and directed a drama based on the writings of Plato for the School of Philosophy in Dublin for six years. He graduated in 2004 with an MA Honours degree in Screenwriting and is currently working on two novels and a screenplay and intent on bringing his long-cherished dream, a musical called *Monto* to realisation.

He lives in Bray with his wife Maura, walks the prom a couple of times almost every day of the year and declares without a blush, "if I knew where the madness came from I'd go back for another basinful." Lee turned 70 in December 2004 and is looking forward to middle age, while agreeing with Hubie Blake that "had I known I was going to live this long I'd have taken better care of myself."

Also by the author

Acknowledgements

Again for Helen Quinn, and for Eileen Pearson and Elva Oglanby.

*For my wife, Maura, all time best-friend,
with all my love.*

Part One

1

Dublin

June 30th 1902

The bank teller's name was Eilish Whitmore and she smiled with pleasure at the latest compliment to her appearance from Mr Sweet. Not that she had any romantic interest in him, but he was more than just another customer. She thought him a gentleman even though he was a Jew, and she felt at ease when they conversed through the grill between them as he withdrew the wages and business expenses for his small building company every Friday. She did not always get the chance to serve him, of course, but she felt admiration for him while admitting to herself that he was surely the handsomest man she had ever seen.

He wore the same suit every Friday morning but it was always freshly pressed. A six-button jacket over a white shirt, a plain red tie, with a tiny diamond-studded pin at its centre, something that to her mind marked him out as a man conscious of his own worth and likely to make great headway in his life. She continued to believe this despite having heard the rumour that the business community of all persuasions had eschewed him. She found it hard to imagine that such a gentle, well-mannered man could have behaved in a manner likely to warrant such punishment.

As Sam Sweet left the bank, he was about to put his wallet into the back pocket of his pants but was deprived of the chance to do so by a shaven-headed sprite of perhaps fourteen years, who whipped it from his hand and took off along Sackville Street.

"Stop him, stop that lad!" Sam yelled, as he hared after the street lad. "Somebody, stop that boy!"

Running as fast as he could, Sam gained some yardage on the young thief who seemed to skip and hop in pain for a moment, before he took off again. Seeing blood on the footpath, Sam guessed he had trodden on a piece of glass that had cut into his foot. He wasn't unhappy about this. He needed all the help he could get if he was ever going to get his wallet back.

Charging along towards the bridge over the river, Sam felt he was getting closer to the bullet-headed youth. He lost ground then as he had to swerve around a fat woman stepping out of a doorway with a birdcage clasped to her voluminous girth. He saw his target make the turn onto Bachelor's Walk, losing faith in his chance of recovering his wallet. He pressed on regardless, pushing himself all the way to the corner.

On Bachelor's Walk Victoria Brewer was standing on the edge of a large crowd gathered about a fire-and-brimstone preacher. The large bearded evangelist possessed a powerful booming voice, and he was so powerfully built that he reminded Vicky of one of the great shire horses that hauled Arthur's stout and beer all over the city and its environs. The preacher had charisma, and had totally captured the crowd that was now blocking off the width of the street running parallel to the river.

Victoria's attention was suddenly diverted when a pencil-thin boy almost knocked her off her feet as he went hurtling around the riverside edge of the preacher's audience.

Behind her, Victoria heard a man's voice yell, "Stop that boy!" At the same time, she found herself quite unable to take her eyes off the young lad as he jumped up onto the wall that ran along the river.

A man of startling good looks was now running towards the youth on the wall. As he flashed past her, she was aware that his dark wavy hair shone in the noon sun. She heard his strangled voice again cry out for someone to "Stop that boy!"

The man was now getting closer to the street boy who was trying to use the river wall like a tightrope, to get beyond the crowd. This would bar the way of his pursuer, unless he too decided to walk the wall above the choppy surface of the water below.

Victoria cried out in horror as she saw the lad lose his footing. She heard his cry of fear as he tumbled into the sea-going current some fifteen feet below. In the moment, she saw the man in the tweed suit throw his jacket to the ground, rip off his shoes and jump up onto the wall. He paused just long enough to take a deep breath before he plunged head first into the rushing waters of the Liffey.

Victoria could scarcely believe her eyes, and she was certain that never before had she witnessed anything so brave. Running to the wall, like many of the preacher's audience, she saw the man swimming with powerful strokes towards the boy being swept away by the outgoing tide.

Calling to Seamus to bring the carriage, Victoria ran as fast as her full-length skirt would allow. She flew across the tram-lined roadway at the northern shoulder of the bridge, hoping that the pair in the river might be saved.

Sam Sweet thought his heart would explode as he made another grab at the drowning pickpocket. This time he got a grip on the kid, and started to haul him towards the ladder on the wall just below Sackville Bridge.

The kid was unconscious, and Sam was already feeling exhausted, but there was something he had to do before they were dragged all the way to Dublin Bay at the mouth of the river.

Using his free hand he plucked his wallet from inside the flimsy jumper the young cur was wearing. He yelled in satisfaction, swallowing a mouthful of foul water in the process. For several moments he thought he was going to choke. He jerked his legs to maintain buoyancy, found the next breath, and stashed the leather wallet into the back pocket of his pants. When his breathing became normal again, he turned on his back and held the boy's head above the mean, choppy surface of the water. He felt somewhat in control now, as he allowed the ebb tide to take them down river, using his hand like a rudder to take them to the wall ladder. After what seemed like half his lifetime, Sam exhaled in sheer relief when he knew his life wasn't going to end in the impersonal embrace of the Liffey.

Seamus Byrne was halfway down the ladder, his free hand held out in offering to Sam Sweet. A rope tumbled down, and the goat-faced man wrapped it around Sam's wrist. Then, with surprising strength, he hefted the inert lad and transferred the slim figure to the waiting arms of the men above.

Sam found himself deeply moved by the knowledge that he was not going to die, allowing himself to be drawn upwards by the powerful little man in the brown derby hat. Moments later, he was on the quayside, retching up the foul water of the Liffey.

"It tastes even worse on the way back up!" Sam said, wondering if anybody had brought his shoes and his jacket. Nobody had. He felt a bit aggrieved, sure and certain that his belongings would have been stolen by now.

As he shook his head in disgust, his eye fell upon the loveliest girl he had ever seen. And this beautiful young lady was on her knees, attempting to revive the lad who was surely dead. She turned her head now to address her servant, tears in her wounded blue eyes, and Sam heard her say, "I'm afraid the poor boy is dead, Seamus."

The man-servant drew her to her feet, as a fat-faced fruit dealer called out to one and all, "Ah Jesus help us all, he's dead, morto! The Liffey's gone an' drownded him, the heartless whore."

Victoria moved to one side, and Sam saw her wipe away her tears. Wearily he leaned on the wall, trying to find the will to go and look for his jacket and his shoes. He heard the servant urge his mistress to leave.

"There's nothing more we can do here, Miss Victoria."

Shaking her head, the young woman moved to where Sam leaned heavily on the river wall. She touched his arm with her gloved hand, and he turned to face her. As their eyes met for the first time he was enraptured again by her stunning beauty and he couldn't even try to hide how her nearness was affecting him.

"My dear sir," Victoria's eyes were bright with tears, "I salute your heroic effort to save the boy."

Sam could see she was genuinely distressed, and was more than surprised to find he had taken her gloved hands in his own.

"And I thank you for your effort to revive him. He shipped too much water, before I could get to him."

Victoria had to avert her eyes. She was stunned by the impact this exotic-looking stranger was having on her, but not unaware that she was having a similar effect on him. She found a wan smile, using the moment to retrieve her hand and remove her glove, before taking Sam's hand again. He looked surprised by the firmness of her grip, while she tried to get her own response to this man into perspective. His eyes were black, his mouth quite perfect under the neat blue-black moustache.

"He might be better off, ma'am," Sam suggested with a shrug of his powerful shoulders. "Now, if you'll excuse me, I have to go and see if my jacket is where I left it." He bit his tongue to stop himself saying, "Some hopes!"

"Seamus," Victoria spoke without taking her eyes from Sam's face, "would you fetch this gentleman's jacket? He dropped it on Bachelor's Walk before plunging into the river."

"And my shoes, if you please?" Sam grabbed the man-servant's hand. "And thanks for pulling me out of there. You've an almighty grip on you."

The man-servant smiled, his flinty agate eyes registering gratitude for a moment, before he left on what he knew would be a wild goose chase. The streets were alive with Dubs who'd take the eye out of your head, and come back for the eyelash.

Glancing back, a slight frown creased his forehead. He moved on, hoping Miss Vicky wasn't going to put this fellow on a pedestal because he had tried to save the life of a street-arab. He found himself grinning at the picture of a Jew saving an Arab of the streets, a kid who was most likely the mistake of a Monto whore, thrown onto the by-ways of life to fend for himself as soon as he could run fast enough to stay out of the clutches of the law.

The cause of his concern, Victoria Brewer, wasn't quite sure what she was doing, but she had no doubt that her life at this moment was exactly where it should be. Willing to sound calm and collected, she told Sam her name, offering him her ungloved hand again. He shook it with some care; by now he was almost incapable of taking his eyes from her lovely face.

"How do you do, Miss Brewer, I'm Sam Sweet."

"May I be of some assistance to you, Mister Sweet? My carriage is nearby and I'd be happy to offer you transport."

"That's more than civil of you," Sam was even more impressed. "Thank you all the same, but I can manage," he smiled ruefully, charmed by the absence of any suggestion that she was above him in any way.

Victoria saw that he was worn out by his ordeal in the river so she said firmly, "I insist on giving you a ride to your destination." She finally let go of his hand, wanting to know more about him. "If you feel it is in some way inappropriate, my driver could take me home, and take you on from there."

"I'm not only soaking wet," Sam conceded, "I'm exhausted after the unexpected swim, and the loss of the lad is hard, even though I didn't know him at all."

The man-servant returned empty-handed. Sam shrugged, but he found no philosophical response to accompany the gesture. 'Not only my good jacket,' he fumed inwardly, 'but the only bloody good jacket I had.'

"That settles the matter then," Victoria said, taking Sam by the arm. "We can't have you walking the streets barefoot." She smiled, pleased as she saw he was unlikely to give her an argument.

Sam made no bones about the excitement he felt at being in the company of someone he would never have expected, not in his wildest dreams, to be speaking to on a one-to-one basis. He thought her wonderful, and he was happily surprised to find her so nice – a young lady to the manner born. In the same moment he was scoffing inside at his outlaw thinking which had considered, if only for a moment, the notion of taking her in his arms.

Of course, he knew who she was. Everybody who could read knew that the Brewers were one of the wealthiest families in the British Empire. They were from old money, and Sam knew that the brother of this young woman was the head buck at the famous Brewers Brewery, chief competitor to the Guinness organisation.

Sam knew that BB stout was already a thriving success, the expanding company operating from a huge complex on the banks of the Liffey on the western edge of Dublin city.

As they walked towards the carriage he recalled reading about her personal success, her acclaimed talent as a painter and sculptor, with an exhibition of her work showing in the National Gallery at the present time.

He found himself smiling in wonder at the way in which a day could insert a situation into your life, a day suddenly enriched by moments you could never have envisaged, not even under the influence of alcohol. He chuckled now in his mind, imagining someone telling him that morning that he would be riding with Miss

Victoria Brewer in her personal carriage, with her own driver holding the reins. He would have laughed out loud. Yet, here he was in the middle of that unimaginable happening, tantalised by the idea that his life might never be the same again.

In the carriage, Sam was shaking himself out of any further wishful thinking, while Victoria opened a silver cigarette case, and held it out to him. "You're an unusual man, Mister Sweet, with, if you'll pardon my candour, an unusual name."

The carriage moved off, and Sam leaned forward, holding her hand steady as she touched a sulphur match to his cigarette. When she saw him draw smoke into his lungs, she lit her own, inhaling deeply, before she settled back on her seat to face him.

"I changed my name when my father died," Sam told her. "We weren't what you'd call close, Miss Brewer." He was grateful for the cigarette in his hand, glad of the allowed ritual. You said something and you took a moment to inhale, before it was necessary to carry on, while you thought again that she was the most attractive woman you had ever seen. Yes, he was all for smoking!

"My father's name was Greenblatt, which he shortened to Green. My given name was Herschel. I didn't like my father, and I didn't like his name." Sam stopped talking and started smoking again defensively. Victoria sensed that he had not meant to say quite so much.

"I have a mother I feel like that about, Mister

12

Sweet," she said in an effort to diminish his unease. "The Pater, Daddy, not a bad old stick as they say, likes his plonk and is a demon for the damsels! Not a mean bone in his body." Victoria drew on her cigarette. "It was in our house that Oscar first said, 'Children begin by loving their parents, as they grow up they judge them, sometimes they forgive them,' or words to that effect."

"I'm a great admirer of Wilde," Sam said, his senses under her spell. "That he came to your house – forgive me, I find it amazing. And you an even greater wonder."

He wondered had he overstepped the mark. There was nothing in her lovely face to suggest this, while he lowered the window and flicked the cigarette ash onto the street, in an effort to cover his relief. He chuckled, confessing instantly, "And I'm wondering what my mother would think if she could see me now!"

"How wonderful," Victoria chortled. "Even as you spoke I was picturing my mother's colour rising! That lady would be appalled, believe me!"

She savoured the sight of him, delighted with his forthright manner, which in time she would come to cherish as one of his most appealing virtues. "May I call you Sam?"

"You certainly may," he said, without guile.

"On one condition," she insisted. "That you call me Victoria."

His protest was genuine. "That seems just a bit beyond me at this moment."

Victoria playfully held out her hand and waited until he set about shaking it gently. Then she said in a loud stage voice, "Ay am delayted to make your acquaintance, Mister Sweet!"

He exploded into laughter and Victoria joined him until something rendered them mute. They both sank back onto their seat. There was nothing more to be said for now, but to go on saturating their eyes with each other's image.

After a while Victoria said with some vehemence. "I reject all the pomp and pomposity, all the images and the taboos that the class structure has created. I reject it, Sam. Will you reject it with me? Can we be the kind of friends who can be totally honest with each other?" She waited for his answer, while he was struck silent by the enormity of her suggestion.

"Let me tell you," Victoria said, her voice filled with meaning, "I have never seen anything more wonderful than the sight of you hurling yourself into the Liffey after that poor boy. You will always shine in my eyes for that magnificent moment."

He seemed to be sitting way behind his voice as he heard himself saying, "You bless my eyes. You sit there, a fantasy in the middle of a working day. And I'm insane enough to ask you . . . am I totally mad to hope that there may be more to what is happening here?"

"You're not the least bit mad. I'm so glad to hear you say it," she laughed a short dry sound. "In honesty, I feel I deserve that much."

He saw the truth. It was there to be seen in the blue eyes, the tilt of her chin and in the easy set of her splendid mouth. He had already fantasised kissing that wonderful mouth, touching with a fingertip the perfect Roman nose, planting breathy kisses on the sculpted ears like beautiful seashells beneath golden hair tied up under the low-crowned, wide-brimmed hat.

"My only concern is that I may send you running because I am not, and cannot, and will not, play coy," she said. "You are the first man in five years to send my blood racing. I'm sorry, but I'm not going to allow you to pass by like a ship in the night without at least letting you know of the effect you are having on me." She stopped at this point. If she went on she might actually admit that she wanted to make love to him, right there in the carriage.

Sam was dumbstruck for a moment, wishing he had a cigarette between his fingers, needing the ritual of smoking to help him remain calm. He wanted to take her in his arms and make love to her. He took a deep breath, and several moments passed before he could speak.

"I'm flattered, overwhelmed. I want to be your friend. I want whatever you might want with us. But first I need to tell you some things I want you to know."

Victoria nodded her head, and willing him to be as intimate as he dared, she said, "Some moments ago while I was trying to gather myself, not wanting to say too much too soon and send you running for your life, I tried to ask you about your life, your mother . . ." She ran out of words since his eyes remained on hers. She felt transparent, and delightedly so, and she simply had to stop talking because once again she wanted to say too much, too soon.

Sam smiled, and as though taking charge, he leaned forward and touched her hand with his gentle fingers. His hands were very large with many scars, testaments to the way of his work, hard and demanding for the last five years since he had been blacklisted by virtually all of the business community of the city.

"My mother's called Esther, and as she herself says, we rub along. I like her for her guts, if you'll pardon the expression. She was driven out of Germany by Jew haters. Esther walked a long walk across Europe, to end up in Ireland," Sam smiled grimly. "She didn't like my father much, either. She's gone back to her maiden name, Levy. I like her for that, too. I get my rebelliousness from her. My father had no fight in him, which is why he died."

Victoria had lit two cigarettes, passing one to Sam. She exhaled smoke, using the diaphanous veil for a moment to savour his appearance again without being too obvious about it. When she spoke, she smiled in a knowing way.

"When I first saw you I wondered where you got your looks from. One doesn't see that many exotic-looking men in Ireland."

"That's a fact," Sam conceded, laughing unashamedly at his own vanity. "But even in what you might call our community, Esther and I are thought of as decidedly odd."

"That's something we have in common," Victoria said lightly.

"I'm not against anybody, what they believe, once

16

they don't interfere with me. I've no time for tradition, ritual, that kind of thing. Dublin's Jews consider me a lost cause, and that suits me, really."

"We sound like kindred spirits," Victoria smiled. "My mother thinks I should be locked away to save any further scandal to our family's name. I'm privileged, of that class I mean. I did nothing to be born into a wealthy family. It's useful, and I do enjoy all that money can provide. We never talk about money, of course. It is bad form, Papa has been heard to say."

She laughed shortly, wanting to put her lips to his rueful smile. Then she said, "Sam, I am the bane of mother's life, and I have to confess that it rather pleases me that I am."

He allowed his gaze to linger on her face, particularly her mouth. She was clearly pleased that he found her so attractive, and she smiled as she said, "I have a twin brother, Arthur. He's a wonderful chap, and not at all brazen like me. We are alike in many ways, for better or for worse. Our feelings for each other are forged on an anvil of dislike for our mother. Some day I will tell you the whole story. Arthur and I, we share the same feelings. Since we were twelve years old we became a team to battle mother, with a lot of help from Seamus, the gent currently driving us towards Leinster Road in Rathmines."

Sam inclined his head in appreciation of her memory, and she preened under his gaze. She drew deeply on her cigarette.

"I would die for Arthur," she said quietly. "He is just

17

the best chap alive. And though you and I have just met, I know I want you to meet him. Have him meet you. He needs the friendship of a real man. Just as I do, but, of course, I want to be much more than your friend. So there! I've said it, and I can but hope you won't flee from my boldness."

"Believe one thing, Victoria," he laughed shyly as he used her name for the first time. "I will never run from you. I have strong feelings about you, even in so short a time."

Sam had to pause since he was unsure, having trouble with the part of him that could not believe what he was hearing, doubting even yet what this amazing woman had just said to him, though her words and what they meant were surely burned indelibly onto his mind.

Victoria gave him the time to gather his thoughts. She was still reeling from her own brashness though feeling better that she had shared the truth about how she was feeling. As she waited for Sam to continue, she went on allowing her gaze to confirm her sheer appreciation of him. She longed to touch his skin, to openly admire the exotic quality his birthright had added to his features, as she was keen to know someone who could so boldly risk his life. She knew she would willingly have put her fingers into the mass of jet-black hair, swept back now in dampness to reveal the perfect broad forehead and the dark, liquid eyes. Those eyes shone now, in their deep setting, as Victoria basked in the warmth of the smile lingering on his mouth. She knew it had everything to do with their being together like this.

Suddenly his expression changed, his mind taken for a moment by something that clearly bothered him. She saw his lips compress into a tight line, giving her a glance at the determination that defined Sam Sweet's character.

"Something is troubling you?" Victoria heard the tremor in her voice, wondering could he hear the muted excitement he had engendered.

"There's something I must tell you." Lines of concern lay snaked across his forehead. "I have to tell you, Victoria," he smiled tentatively, nervously, though his eyes expressed relief now that he'd breached the first hurdle. "It's about the lad that drowned . . ."

He felt further relief at the lack of judgment in her eyes as she said, "You were pursuing him, am I right?"

"Indeed I was. He had stolen my wallet as I left the bank. I had to get it back. My four workmen, their wages were in it." Sam looked into her eyes, and she felt a wave of fascination disturb her concentration. "So you see, it wasn't all that noble, my going into the Liffey after him. I went in to get my wallet back." His expression was an abject apology and she felt the need to defend him against his own judgment of himself.

"You tried to save him. I watched you bring him out of the water, when nobody would have blamed you had you left him to save your own life." She leaned forward, touching his face, somehow resisting the urge to kiss his mouth. "You were wonderful, Sam. Never forget that. And thank you for telling me."

2

Wicklow, Ireland

June 21st 1885

Molly Harney rose from her sacks-and-rags bed, sipping the day's first drink of water slowly into her toothless mouth, using her tongue to spread the liquid across her dry lips. She dipped her forefinger into the tin mug to touch the corners of each eye with drops of water to relieve the crusty dryness.

She fell then to her knees, her hands clasped together as the prayer tumbled off her tongue.

"Oh, heavenly Father, I place all my trust in thee! Thy will be done, of course. At the same time I make no bones about the longing inside me for the moment you take me to rest at last in the peace of your bosom."

Her failing sight reached out to the rough-hewn chimney breast, her eyes coming to rest on the wooden cross long ago carved from a chunk of bog oak which gained purchase on her attention as it did each and every morning of the year. She made the sign of the cross on herself. "'Tis a weary worrold, brethren. God keep us in it."

A litany of devotion and gratitude poured now from her deserted mouth, a gently spoken hymn to her faith in an almighty God who had given lodging to her life since she was a small child learning to pray at her mother's side. Since that time she had been host to a faith strong enough to help her deal with the pains and the vagaries of the hardest life, supporting her as she survived the lung disease that had robbed her of her only sister, Deirdre, and her brother-in-law, Tom, leaving her as guardian to their baby daughter, Lizzie.

Her eyes dropped to the fire well banked up with peat mould. She paused in her praying to give it a poke and set it breathing. Lizzie, hurrying out earlier in a rush and running to stand still while she hunted for a rabbit, hadn't bothered to give the embers a moment's notice.

Molly's face wore the withered skin of a life lived in poverty and deprivation, a straggled moustache of stained hair concealing the collapse of her upper lip. Old knitted gloves that left the fingertips free hid her hands, old woman's hands, long beaten and abused by the labour of staying alive, or as she thought of it, keeping body and soul together. Her beaten body was a testament to the long days of the spring and summer work, the hardest work of keeping the walls and the roof of the cabin from falling down around them. The hours planting and tending her winter vegetables and digging spuds out of the lazy beds without the aid of a spade came naturally to herself and Lizzie, but to hold the derelict cabin together ensured the winter night's sleep came highly priced.

Even when the work was done for another while, her hands seemed to relive the strain of stirring earth and water, and ground potatoes into the mix as a binder, to cover the death mask of the structure that was hearth and home to herself and the orphan girl. She climbing the ladder Tom had, made, Lizzie handing her the mixture on a tinker's tin plate, she forcing grass and the mud and potatoes in among the thatch that was working beyond its time, the ladder not strong enough to support Lizzie's weight.

That she remained positive most of the time was, as she saw it, another great gift from God. Molly thought of the prayers that she had to say in order to just keep going, as the bonus to her life. While she was developing her devotion to God through the heartfelt ejaculations of love, she was free of the thousand-and-one questions that seemed to add up to just one word. Why?

A worn cotton shift was her only garment, covering her slender shoulders that were a source of regular pain, shoulders pushed forward by the curvature of her spine. Molly never complained, never thought much about herself once she stuck with the prayers.

She possessed no mirror so she had not seen the wreckage in her face and her eyes, the ravages of time and trouble that marked her down as an old woman though on this June morning in the year 1885, she was just forty-seven years old.

Usually, she washed her face and hands and drank half a cup of milk before she knelt to pray on the dirt floor of the cabin. Here on the same spot she placed her life into the care of Almighty God on a daily basis. On this morning she felt she had to get on with the praying first, before she lost her nerve.

"I haven't the fear of dyin', Lord. Knowin' I'll be in your safe keepin' the minute these eyes close for the last time. Forgive me. Badly in need of your help so I am. I need you to show me what to do about Lizzie. She's gettin' on, y'see, no denyin' that Lord. An' only the other day didn't I hear an ugly cur in the town below, and him sayin' she'd want to get a move on them hipsa hers or she'd soon be beyond the bearin' of a child. 'Tis a lie, Father, but she is pushin' hard to thirty years, not that a brute like that'd see the good in her, the decency of her nature."

Pausing only to gather her breathing, Molly pressed on. "A great lassie is Lizzie. Looks for the best in everythin', the good in her inherited from my sister Deirdre and her husband Tom, the pair of them gone. When the great hunger that tore the living from the land after turnin' the spuds foul was losin' its grip, they had no strength to fight the cursed ailment that robbed them of their lungs, so t'was said.

"Nobody hereabout is worth the tips of her spit, Lord, and this feeling is growing up inside me, that she should go up to the city, go to Dublin. A while back I got the parish priest in Wicklow town, Father O'Byrne, to write off for me. He was after showing me an advertisement in the paper for a domestic servant in a place called Ballsbridge. That's in Dublin so the PP said. I never heard of it, never gettin' north of Wicklow town, or the odd time I went to Arklow, when we'd a pony alive and kickin'.

"We got no word back even though Father O'Byrne gave Lizzie a good character in the letter he wrote. Now there's an urge on me to send Lizzie up to Dublin. Let her go and present herself at the house of the folk that put the advertisement into the newspaper. Sure when the people take a look at her, the big strong lassie she is, when they hear how willin' she is to work all the hours you send in the day, surely they'll take her in? If ye hear my prayer, dear God, send me a sign, show me in some way what I'm to do about Lizzie? Guide me in every action I make this day. Spare me the agony of offending you. Most Sacred Heart, I place all my trust in thee!"

Molly made the sign of the cross by touching her forehead and her chest, her left and right shoulders, joined her hands once more and bowed her head before struggling up off her knees.

She brushed the earth and peat mould from the front of her shift before wiping her face with the cloth floating in the worn basin Lizzie had rinsed in earlier. She dried her face and taking the basin she went out of the one-roomed cabin, throwing the water across one of the vegetable patches she had torn and wrenched from the rocky land close by. A pair of hens ran squawking before the sudden shower as Molly cast her eyes over the potatoes growing in the lazy beds. The spuds looked game-ball at the minute, she sighed gratefully, and whispered, "Thanks be to God."

Peering beyond the vegetable patch, her eyes registered the buzzing hedgerows down the lane leading to the spine of roadway into the town. She frowned at the fanciful notion that the trees on either side of her plot were beckoning her to keep going, to be sure and see this through. She offered a silent prayer to the belief that God would protect Lizzie. Sure he had to mind her. There was nobody else.

Going back inside the cabin she gave the fire a bit of attention and found herself touching the black cauldron she referred to as Deirdre's pot. 'The only thing poor Deirdre had to leave behind her, if you ignore Lizzie,' she'd say to herself from time to time.

Despite the built-in sadness that lodged in her heart over her sister's passing, Molly never failed to experience the wisp of a smile when she thought of Deirdre's courage, the way she fought to live for her unborn. Even with her lung trouble she might have held on. It was the fifty-two hour labour to deliver Lizzie that had been too much to survive, a demand too far on her wasted body as ongoing hunger went on turning the country into a mass grave for the bones of the poor and the dispossessed.

Gentle Deirdre and the most decent skin, Tom, gone to a pauper's grave. Molly surviving somehow, spared she supposed, to look after poor Lizzie. Which she did with a good heart, feeding her goats' milk because the cow had died the previous winter, keeping the child alive to sleep in her arms as they lay under sacks and rags, dried grass, and bits of hay gathered after the harvesting of a nearby farm. This farm was managed for an English landlord who had never seen the land, by a Scotsman who wouldn't give so much as a greeting to the paupers existing on the rim of his property.

Molly had held slivers of offal to Lizzie's tiny mouth, feeling her heart move as the child sucked the nourishment into herself like someone fighting to hold onto life. Each and every time Molly had a penny to spend in the town she bought some morsel of nourishment for the baby girl. Every so often she would barter a scarf or a pair of gloves that she had knitted for a half-pound of calf's liver or the heart of a lamb. When she earned from a day's work labouring at harvest time, she'd buy the head of a pig or the trotters she herself loved above all else. And thanks to the will of God they had survived. She sighed and thought it time to eat something.

While she added water to the stirabout in the black hanging pot over the embers glowing in the bed of warm ash, Molly wondered would she get a sign from God. And if she did, if there was a sign, would she recognise it? The Indian oatmeal had cooked gently through the night over the low heat from the banked-up peat and mould. It was ready now for the table, simple grub you could trot a mouse on. Leaning now across the half door Molly began yelling to Lizzie as the sun slanted across her face into the room behind her. The lower part of the door kept the wee pig she had at the minute, and the few hens, mice and rats, outside where they belonged.

Molly spooned the porridge into a pair of wooden bowls, the sunlight disappearing for some seconds as Lizzie bustled into the cabin.

"You'd want to mind me, Aunt Molly." Lizzie sat down carefully at the old pine table, well aware that it was too dilapidated to handle any part of her weight. "If Eamon Coyle comes near me again with his hands, I'll cut the legs off him with the hook after I cut his ballocks off."

Molly was already bending to retrieve the long-handled hook Lizzie had thrown on the floor. She hung the treacherous curved blade on the wooden dowel fixed into the diseased birch-wood dresser to one side of the door.

Throwing open the cabin's single window, she glanced at the valley of Cullen Lower below, while further down the sea like a silver blue silk scarf caressed the east coast. 'Peace by the shore, Lord,' she prayed in her mind, 'but fear here in the heart. Dear God, I have to get Lizzie away from this place. Help me! Please help me to know how to do it.'

"Me mind you, gerrel!" Molly snorted, affecting disdain. "I can hardly mind meself."

Lizzie drank water, the tin mug wrapped in her hand. "I was scarcely breathin' by Doran's stile, willing them rabbits to be still. Oh! I dropped them outside." She was gone for a second, returning to throw the brace on the floor inside the door. "I was lucky. They didn't stir. So whack! One two! And that pair went to rest in peace. While I'm bendin' to pick them up, there's dirty Eamon. He's there, touchin' me, wantin' to kiss me, tryin' to paw me, get at my chest. Rubbin' against me, his weapon stiff as a fence post. He wouldn't quit, so I hit him a kick, eased his urgency very rapid." Lizzie ate the porridge with a little milk. "He was hurtin' real badly from the kick he got, didn't stop him swearin' he'd have me on my back before long. I told him he'd have to kill me first."

"The apple doesn't fall far from the tree!" Molly expelled a snort of derision. "His oul' father's the same, a drunkard and a womaniser. If there was ever a decent Coyle born in these parts they must have thrown out the baby and kept the after-birth."

Lizzie went outside with the pan of ashes from the fireplace. Molly's eyes were drawn upward by some invisible force. 'You're surely tellin' me to get her away from here, Father. In my heart of hearts, I believe you're giving me the answer to this mornin's prayer for sure and certain!'

"I warned him so I did." Lizzie was back with a bundle of sticks. "But nothin' stops him comin' back in the same sorry state of wantin'." Lizzie shook herself free of the revulsion she had felt. "I told him, 'I castrated a mongrel hound a year ago, and I'll cut you too, Eamon Coyle, if you don't leave me be'."

"You can stop frettin' about that dirty-lookin' go-be-the-wall!" Molly moved as though to close the window. Taking a wet rag she wiped the frame, hiding her face from Lizzie, knowing she couldn't look at her while she told, what she hoped would be, the whitest white lie in the history of the world.

"You've a position ready and waitin' for you up in Dublin city so you have."

Lizzie stopped the skinning of the rabbit, the hazel pupils of her eyes filling with confusion and disbelief. She felt a rush of excitement for a moment before guilt came sliding in behind the joyous thumping in her chest. She felt shame that she could even think of leaving Aunt Molly. But she had thought it, was still thinking it, and she felt a thrill shoot through her. And for the first time that she could remember, Lizzie didn't know what to say. She had no idea how to respond to her aunt.

She went back to skinning the rabbit, feeling even guiltier as the memory pictures of their life together took her mind by the hand. The crystal-clear images were old friends. Aunt Molly supporting her as she climbed over a stile for the first time; she must have been about three years old. Us picking potatoes, me in my skin, running through the lazy beds, my only item of clothing drying on the line. Aunt Molly had just washed the pig slurry out of it in the stream; me after skidding in the last delivery from the wild young sow we never managed to catch.

Lizzie remembered the lessons. Aunt Molly called them "the essentials – the three R's for reading, writing and 'rithmetic". Lizzie took her time coming to understand that one. She remained a willing student, growing quite tall, who never tired of Molly's company. In the fields that were her classrooms they picked and saved the apples growing across the nearby fields, exchanging them in the town for whatever they needed to get through another day. They gathered the berries from the hedgerows as August was going home for another year, bartering these for an axe to help them get in a stock of firewood to warm the open hearth of the long winter evenings, and Lizzie sang out the answers to the questions that Molly directed at her. Molly made her write composition with a nib pen and ink, having fired the child's imagination with the stories she herself had heard at the feet of a hedge teacher, an itinerant tutor who did what he could to deny illiteracy to as many children as he could on his travels about the countryside. Lizzie's essays took their time coming to life on the blank page of the copy book in the light of an ancient paraffin tilly lamp, but breathe they did to the delight of the woman who had nurtured the imagination and the penmanship of the awkwardly growing lassie with the strength of a man, and the gentle heart of an earthbound angel.

Molly's teacher had possessed a nose like the blade of an axe and a whiskey breath to burn rust off a gate. He came to the area every few weeks to plant his stories of ancient Ireland into the minds of his young students. How many times had Molly heard the tales of the Fianna and Cuchulain and all the other heroes gone before, men and women whose achievements fired the eyes and the heart of the teacher and his young charges.

They were the spawn of the best of men, they must do all they could to honour that tradition, they must be the best they could be, and they must pass the word and the stories onto the next generation. The stories ought never be allowed to die. That was the only sin the teacher ever mentioned. The gravest sin on earth, he said, would be to let the tales of our forebears atrophy through indifference.

The songs of Molly's childhood and her early life, heirlooms of the heart her aunt called them, were burned indelibly into Lizzie's mind. They had been sung to her in her baby shawl and heard by her consciously from the age of about five. Words and melodies living and breathing alongside her private picture gallery where she could find woman and child singing and laughing on the river bank of the early summer evenings as they fished for their dinner. In Lizzie's eyes her aunt was some kind of genius at catching trout with a bit of a stick, a length of hemp found by the roadside and, scarcely believable, a bit of a hook that looked like a bent pin.

"Have you nothin' to say, gerrel?" Molly poked the fire, giving her back to the girl standing still over the rabbits now readied for the pot. Lizzie turned her head to look at Molly, hardly recognising her own voice, hearing some kind of fear, something more than surprise as she asked, "How could I have a position waitin' for me anywhere, never mind in Dublin city?"

"By the end of the week you'll be in Ballsbridge, Dublin. Gentry – so Father O'Byrne told me. You'll be workin' in a grand house with lovely people who had an advertisement in the newspaper. He asked me would you work as a domestic servant for decent people. She'll work the long day through, Father, said I. Anythin' to give her a halfway decent start in life, I said to the PP. For our Lizzie there has to be something better than this."

"I can't believe it, Aunt Molly," Lizzie felt tears come close.

"The PP said it'd be best to start callin' yourself Elizabeth. He said it sounds better to the gentry than Lizzie." Molly, taken by the emotion in her niece, was trying to hold onto her own tears. "You'll be gone, child," she assured Lizzie. "Safe and sound before that sleeveen Coyle has his way with you if you don't take his life first."

Their life together changed from that moment though neither of them could have said how or why. It was as though their hearts could only cast odd glances in the other's direction, some kind of fear preventing them from saying what they truly felt about their imminent parting. The words describing the feelings present in the air threatened more pain than they could deal with in the ongoing numbness of what might well be their last hours together.

Two days later, Molly was taking Lizzie into the town of Wicklow on a flat two-wheeled cart drawn by a donkey, an animal that showered hatred at the world and his wife, and refused to go quietly into the soft good heat of the June morning.

'Ye're one cantankerous beast, so y'are!' Molly

admonished the donkey in her mind. 'Ye've no right to wear the cross of our Lord Jesus. Ye've a mean nature and how you feel about your lot is the last thing botherin' my mind at this minute.'

Molly's heart felt like a great stone-bruise inside her. To be parting from Lizzie was fierce altogether, to be sending her off like this? Good God! Standing by the train at the railway station wearing a plain well-worn grey wool coat, bought for a few pence at a fair, Lizzie hugged her aunt so fiercely that Molly gasped audibly. The young woman let her aunt go and kissed her face, unaware of her own strength, her size not in any way diminishing her sense of her femininity.

"As soon as I'm in the door in Ballsbridge I'll write a couple of lines to let you know I'm all right, Aunt Molly. You know yourself now that I'll do that right away."

In that moment, Molly was more than ever grateful she had taught her niece all she herself had gathered, and could remember, at the hands of the man she thought of every time she chopped a block of wood with the hatchet.

"You're gettin' on a railway train, gerrel," Molly chortled above the tears in her voice. "More than I ever did in this lifetime." Carefully now, she embraced Lizzie. "Get up there for God's sake." Molly threw the words out in a show of bravery, a rent-like grief spreading over her chest. "Go on, gerrel, or they'll leave you behind so they will."

As the steam locomotive pulled out of the station,

Lizzie wept openly, hung in the frame of the carriage door, tears flowing as she waved goodbye to the woman who had been everything to her for as long as she had been aware of anything. The whistle and the belching steam gave Molly a start but her eyes remained on Lizzie as the crocodile of carriages pulled away from the station.

As the outline of her niece began to fade in the near distance Molly allowed her tears the freedom they had been denied. 'All her days by my side, in a matter of seconds she is already out of my life.' Molly held onto the cast-iron rail that divided the platform from the roadway; the pain of parting from Lizzie had, for the moment, made walking difficult. She shut her eyes fiercely, unwilling to give houseroom to what she called the poor-me's.

"She has a great heart. She'll be grand so she will." Mumbling the words, Molly forced herself to shuffle out to the cart, dismissing the ache in her left knee with the thought, "I don't like ye, but what's that got to do with anything!" Aboard the cart she knew that in the heel of the hunt nothing mattered except the will of God. When she was there, behaving as though God was right by her side, all was well with the world even if what was in front of you gave you pain.

"I know you'll mind her, Lord, the big child," Molly cackled briefly through the remnants of her tears. "Twenty-eight years old, Lord, a child in many ways. Her heart as big as her body! Her mother's daughter, so her heart is golden." Molly gave the donkey a good larrup, just for the hell of it. "Ye've a very cushy life, so ye have. So behave yerself or I'll give ye 'sally come home in the dark!'"

She was on the road into the town, a longing on her for the taste of a pork chop, a couple of beefy sausages, but she'd have to wait. Her last coins were gone on the train with Lizzie, her only regret that she hadn't a pound note to give her, in case things didn't work out ideally.

Molly cut that line of thinking, admonishing herself for the slack manner of her mind. Imagine allowing ingratitude to darken the dream she had forged on the anvil of her desperation over Lizzie and the blackguard with the surname of Coyle. Hadn't God himself given the answer to the predicament? She felt better in herself as she once more prayed in her own way.

"All will go well for her, Lord, given a tiny fragment of your care." She pushed the ass on with a few more lashes from the sally switch, trying not to give any more power to what surely had to be, the last great loss she would have to endure.

3

Lithuania

June 21st 1885

Half a world away from Dublin, Rebecca Moses hauled her loaded handcart as she trekked westward from Lithuania. In her uncertain world she was feeling certain that no matter how hard life might turn out to be in Europe, it would be a better life than the one being left behind.

She'd had to make the journey. No Jew was safe at the present time, since their Gentile neighbours only came to call when they had enough vodka inside them to rape and plunder those who were less fortunate than themselves. Rebecca had escaped the latest attack just a few days before by hiding under the raised wood floor of the cabin she shared with her father. Terrified, and at the same time angry enough to kill any man attempting to violate her, she had lain still under the cabin with a finely-honed knife in her hand.

The next morning, nineteen-year-old Rebecca Moses

told her father Mendel, "I'm leaving, Father. I'll be gone from here within a few days." She let the words sit, giving him time to hear the implication, 'with or without you!'

She was not surprised that within seventy-two hours many in the *shtetl* were of the same mind. As she loaded the cart that would carry the simple possessions of her father and herself, many others were doing the same thing. She was not the only one who had been through enough.

Her father Mendel, a Talmudic scholar whose advice and counsel were sought on many subjects, had responded to his daughter's ultimatum with a willingness that surprised her.

"Our torturers are tortured by the madness of the Russias and I will not ask you to endure it any longer. To hate as they hate the Jew is enough to drive them to mayhem, rape and pillage. The authorities turn a blind eye as the lower classes labour in the industry of ethnic destruction and murder. We will leave the homeland before they butcher any more of us."

Rebecca knew immense relief since she had expected him to deny her the right to leave, but he was not a fool and knew she had only just survived many nomadic seasons of insecurity and fear. It hadn't mattered in which village, which *shtetl* the Jews attempted to settle in, they had been violated and butchered by faceless Cossacks revering the Romanov Tsar while they wallowed in their addiction to the ongoing expulsion policy.

The authorities claimed absolute ignorance of such

goings-on, causing Rebecca to think how very convenient it was for the chosen few to ignore the stench of the festering injustice that was currently thriving wherever a Jew lay down his head. She pulled the cart with an angry strength. The same power she had used to load it, doing all the work herself because the very life-force that had made her father such a teacher seemed to be draining out of him. He had agreed to leave but then began ranting and raving on the day after her revelation, becoming silent then and seemingly lost. He had long blamed the Tsar for not giving the Jews protection, now he had nothing to say as his daughter's impatience threatened to boil over. Once more she decided that men talk a lot, a lot of the time, with little to show for all the gasbagging. Rebecca carried no guilt about this since Mendel would talk the long night through with his captive audience, leaving the chore of keeping the samovar topped up to his only daughter.

"I have no choice," Rebecca said to Sarah Elkins.

"Nor I," Sarah, mortified, confided in a hoarse whisper.

The younger woman's eyes opened in horror. "Sarah?"

"Two of them, Rebecca. I told them, 'I am sixty years old'. They didn't listen. They had their way," Sarah shuddered, her tears flowing. "Will I ever feel clean again?" She moved closer, afraid of being overheard. "I told Nathan I had hidden. What's the use of him knowing this? We'll surely die on the journey."

"We don't have to die, Sarah, on the walk west. If I

had stayed," she shuddered, "I would kill any man putting a hand on me, or he would kill me. I feel for my father but why did he not leave here, take us out of it years ago? For us, living in this bloody land belonging to the Tsar has been a miserable and wretched existence. So let the Tsar go to Hell, where he belongs."

She remembered the several times she had escaped pogrom-rape thanks to the lack of pride in her looks, and some sixth sense that warned her of imminent danger and kept her safe from harm. She had covered her face with a scarf over her features, bending, her body stooped as she walked to ensure she looked older than her years. She painted carmine spots on her face and her hands, not washing for days before the imminent attacks in the hope of causing the Cossacks to believe she was diseased. She had hidden herself when she could, her knife at the ready as the White Russians had their sport. She hated them, and she cursed them in her heart as they left the smell of hatred and burning and the stench of their damned souls in their wake. She was revolted by the manner in which they surrendered their group conscience and their inherent humanity, drowning decency in vodka that set them free to dance to the balalaika and sing their stupid songs. Anything would be better than enduring such vileness even one more time.

Rebecca accepted that the endless trudge westward would make huge demands on young and old alike. But overall she believed she would survive, felt this in her breast, as she pulled out of the village without so much as a glance backwards.

An hour before leaving, Rebecca had a visit from Ezra Babel. He put a simple pine coffin on the cart. "Your father paid already. Sit for a moment. I can secure it on the cart."

The sun was on Rebecca's back as she hauled herself and the cart westward. Now her father was yelling behind the cart, "Why? Why?" His voice was an old open wound festering now as the disease of fear spread deeper into it, fouling the entire body as it systematically corroded the scholar's once brilliant mind.

He sounded like a man believing that his very soul had been ripped from him by the creeping madness of the men who had stolen land and liberty from people who had paid for their plot and obeyed the laws of the land. The Cossacks came and they plundered and robbed the vast oceans of wheat the land was allowed to bear. And they did as they wished with the people who had worked there for many generations, asking only to be left alone to practise their way of life.

Rebecca pressed on against the morning, letting her father be, allowing him to unload the grief that was tormenting him. She wondered was he preparing for death. Was he willing death to come for him, sooner rather than later? Why else the coffin, why else the burial robe?

"Why so much pain, such endless injustice heaped on us? How can we allow it to continue year after year after year, the degradation heaped upon my people?"

Hearing this blasphemy tear itself out of his heart, Rebecca knew he was losing his mind entirely. In her wildest imaginings she could never have expected to hear him address God in this way. He yelled again like someone expecting to be heard, his fury driving him to distraction.

"We go where we must," Mendel shouted. "Always, we go in peace. But, I cannot go on and on accepting your will. I am sick and tired of being sick and tired, weary of being wearied by the abuse and the persecution you send us year after year. Death can be but a release, yet you created in us the instinct to go on living. I do not understand. Is it your will that I cannot understand you?"

Rebecca took the cart out of the crocodile. Sarah Elkins, behind her, hearing Mendel's demented outbursts, followed suit as the two women had agreed to look out for each other. Mendel's emotions had worn him out and things got worse as his daughter realised he was unaware of what he had just been through. Taking a damp cloth she wiped her father's eyes and mouth, and cleaned spittle from his beard. He didn't respond, and she choked back tears as she realised just how broken was his beautiful mind.

Mendel sat by the roadside, unaware of the endless line of carts trundling past, looking at his beloved land with eyes that couldn't see. His powerful, craggy face was embalmed in emptiness, the usually animated countenance was a death mask, a face condemned to die stateless and homeless, without one single breath of say in the matter.

Minutes later, Rebecca was dumbfounded as her

father's mind returned to the present moment, taking a sip of water before hauling himself up onto his feet. She wanted to protest when he gripped the shafts of the cart. She let it go. How many will survive the journey, anyway? Mendel Moses heaved and the cart moved. When they finally stopped as the light began to fade, her father was still there between the shafts.

He ate very little but he seemed peaceful enough to Rebecca as she sang softly, strumming the guitar, as he drifted into sleep. Mendel had sung to her from the day she was born, and she felt the balm of gratitude rest on her heart as she accepted the role of parent to her father as he slept.

The next afternoon while she was pushing from behind, Rebecca was asking herself, 'What if the Jews said no? What if they gathered their skills and their courage and their education, and their knowledge and their will to live and their devotion to God, and allied this powerful group to concerted action? No more subjugating those skills and qualities to what they called the will of God. What would happen if they stood up, one mass of people, and collectively yelled, No!'?

Now, the cacophony of many pots and pans hanging and rattling on a train of carts and handcarts across the endless days gate-crashed once more on Rebecca's interior monologue. It was as if she was being warned not to think too much. She snorted at the fanciful notion. What else was there to do when you were taking a walk of several thousand miles?

4

Lough Bray, County Wicklow

June 21st 1885

Seamus Byrne brought the horses to a standstill and the
wheels of the brougham stopped turning on the
lakeside road leading to Lough Bray House, which lay
half a mile in from the road to Sally Gap, the gateway to
West Wicklow and County Kildare.

Some ten miles south of Dublin city lay the
Featherbed with its vast bogs undulating to the hamlet
of Glencree and beyond to the shooting lodge on the
shore of Lough Bray. This was one of many homes
owned by the Brewer dynasty. The vast estates included
more than fourteen thousand acres of the peat bog, a
thousand years a-growing, on top of the timbered hills
overlooking the city down in the valley on either side of
the Liffey.

Here was wealth vast enough for royalty, the Victorian
lodge a model of its kind with deer and grouse and
partridge, pheasant, fox and rabbit to have the hunters

salivating as they tied the laces of their fine boots, prepared for the day's sport.

The house was cared for by seven servants and retainers residing in their own grace-and-favour cottages on the land. Two full-time gardeners planted and harvested the vegetables needed for the family, their visitors and the servants. All excess produce was sold at the weekly market in Enniskerry village six miles down the mountain, on the road to the seaside town of Bray.

All over the estate, paths of broken granite and limestone had been laid, so that the family and guests could traverse the rollercoaster terrain around and up and beyond the lake on the far side of the water, and in the areas regarded as prime spots for hunting.

The mix of mountain and meadow, river, and stream – with the corrie lake and its many moods housing huge numbers of small trout – brought animals from all over the mountain and helped fill the sky with predatory falcons, and seagulls when the winds and the cold drove them inland to seek fish for dinner.

Seamus Byrne smiled slyly to himself, his posture erect, very much the coachman in livery and a brown derby hat, yet secretly amused as he went on turning a deaf ear to his mistress seated behind, a lady with murder on her mind.

Constance Brewer took several deep breaths to distract her need to direct her fury against the goat-faced creature holding the reins, the man-for-all seasons to her husband, Arthur Shane Brewer. Her desire to simply take a whip to the wretch almost overwhelmed her but reason prevailed and she simmered down. She had enough to deal with on this morning and she would need all her energy to ensure that the situation received every shred of her attention.

Nonetheless, the moment the wheels of the carriage stopped, she heard herself say: "I have been ordering you to stop since we came through the gate. Have you lost your hearing, man?"

Constance found herself gripped again momentarily by the need to explode, to give this wretch a blistering, even though she had to accept that it wouldn't do any good. The cretin was her husband's very own servant, allowed to drive her or the children only when the Master didn't have need of his service.

"I'm sorry, ma'am." He lied blandly. "The hearing suffered all right, the hours coming up the mountain'll do that when you're on the driving seat." At the same time thinking sorely, 'I've the mother-and-father-of-the-night-befores, due to imbibing a pig's feed of Galway poteen, or I'd chuckle so I would.' He extended his arm for the missus, turning away to hide the derision in his eyes.

Constance averted her own gaze as she allowed him to help her from the brougham, unable to bear the sight of the whiskey-marked face. Stepping down, she immediately moved away from him, distancing herself from the body odour threatening to make her nauseous even in the chilled air of the mid-morning mountain. Seamus grimaced in satisfaction. She hadn't liked his answer. Well, to Hell and back with her. He knew she wouldn't dare give him the sack, just as he knew she

45

had wanted to do so from the day they had first laid eyes on each other.

"The wind ma'm'd turn a body deaf as a corpse at Christmas," he said, twisting the knife. He didn't think of this as a lie, since his face and head were smarting busily after the long, slow drive up the mountain road. Even with a brace of high-class nags, it took ages to climb from the main Brewer country house, five miles below at Woodtown on the Dublin road.

While he waited for the next crack of her whip, Seamus heard his inner voice assure the lady, 'You can kiss my arse, ma'am!' A small evil grin burst in his chest, his secret sound singing wickedly down the canyons of his resentment.

Constance gave him a look that would melt snow. "You will remain here by the carriage until I return." She allowed time for this to sink in. "Or until I send someone to fetch you." She paused, using all the force of her position to make this dolt pay attention. "Do you understand clearly what I am saying to you?"

"The horses need water and rest, ma'am, after hauling us up them hills." Seamus ladled mock sincerity all over his voice, spitting inside at the idea that anybody could care about a bloody horse. He knew his overture was bouncing off the woman's ears turned deaf. Constance Brewer wanted to keep him away from the house for the minute. He felt like smiling. She was bloody naïve if she hadn't guessed he already knew the reason for her early morning mission up the mountain, blast her anyway!

·"I have no need of your opinion as to the state of the horses," she snorted in fury.

Seamus lowered his head to hide the thought, 'She whinnies like a bloody horse, too, when she's up to ninety'!

"Should one or even both of the animals drop dead, you will remain here. Have I made myself clear?" Constance insisted, knowing that she would willingly whip this cretin to within an inch of his life.

"Oh, you have, madam, yes indeed you have!" Seamus, refusing to surrender to her authority, hit the words with a mallet.

At the same time he touched the rim of his brown derby, knowing he had gone as far as he dare. He tried to present a contrite expression, play the game, but his flint-filled eyes undermined his intended pose. Even when he tried, he simply couldn't take Constance Brewer half as seriously as she took herself.

Constance turned and began walking quickly along the driveway towards the shooting lodge, the brooding corrie lake and the damson mountain to her left. She would not, as yet, see the lodge built into the hillside beyond a great curving mask of pine trees towering like sentries over hillocks of rhododendrons.

By the carriage, Seamus sipped more of the cognac, chuckled as the spirit hit his innards, recalling the pain and the glory of the exchange with her ladyship some hours earlier.

"I might wella sneaked a lie-in this morning had she not woken me at five o'clock, if you don't bloody mind!" Seamus cast his reflections to the mountain and the billy leading his herd down along the invisible damson trail of an underground stream, to the lake and a noonday drink. "The cursa Christ on whoever sneaked to her about the master diggin' the furrow here in Lough Bray!"

He'd been deeply into a nightmare. One where Constance bellowed at him as though he were dead, and deaf with it! Then as he began slowly to surface, he thought he was seeing Constance towering over him in the bed.

Before reality dawned, Seamus formed the opinion that if a fellow drank enough of last night's poteen he could well die there on the spot. Not that Angela hadn't reminded him that he had an early start! To judge by the sounds coming from the kitchen, it was no longer early. He came up from under the blanket. That was when he knew it was going to be a hell-sent day.

For herself to come downstairs, she was demented about something. Seamus sighed heavily, knowing too bloody well exactly what that something was.

Risking a quick glance through a half-open eye, rolling momentarily towards the wall, he farted with all the strength he could find. His willingness to aggravate Constance further worked splendidly, and he had to clamp down hard on a gargoyle chortle as he enjoyed the sight of her recoiling in horror, backing away across the basement room.

On the mountain Seamus had more cognac from the flask, filled earlier from the dining room decanter at

Woodtown House. "No wonder they call it the nectar of the gods!" he said to the nearest horse.

He was beginning to feel good again. The brandy was doing the job and Constance had disappeared from the picture. 'The hell with it!' he said to himself, finishing off the cognac. Standing still, he let the golden bounty flow all the way down. He waited until he felt the change that sent all the pain of last night into some dark hole, never to return. Until the next time!

As his mood and his condition generally felt the benefit of his alcoholic intake, he decided that Constance was all wind and piss. She was here on the mountain to take the boss to task. She'd never do it. By the time she got up to the house and gave the servants a piece of her mind over anything that occurred to her, she'd come to her senses. Feeling no pain at all now, he was free to enjoy himself, which he would do, when the high and mighty bitch had to climb down off her high horse. Take on Arthur Shane Brewer? Not bloody likely!

Dumping his livery coat onto the back seat, he clambered down along the rocks between the driveway and the water's edge, the small freshwater waves only inches from his boots.

As he reached the first great clump of rhododendrons, fading fast now in June, he muttered venomously, "Oh boys of boys! Like yourselves lads, the peace of the morning is on its last legs!"

He was about fifty yards from the lodge when he had to stop. He was puffing and blowing after his scurry along the lake edge. His heart seemed to be jumping a bit. He smiled grimly. 'You get enough of the cognac, sooner or later it'll get all of you!' He chuckled: 'To hell with it!'

Seamus bent and scooped water into his mouth, hoping Lisa was working in the kitchen. The pinpoint of wishful thinking shattered in the face of reason. 'Lisa'll be too occupied above stairs to be helping get the lunch ready'd be my guess.'

Directly below the shooting lodge by the lake's edge, he took a ladder from the outside wall of the boathouse. He was hidden from the view of anybody inside the lodge, unless they stood on the balcony outside the master bedroom, "and then," said Seamus to himself, "they wouldn't be inside, would they!"

He carried the ladder up the narrow granite steps tiered into the slope rising from the lake to the house. He propped it against the great lone beech tree, close to one corner of the rambling Victorian pile.

In the heart of the beech tree, Seamus cursed himself for killing all the brandy. He found himself see-sawing about the missus. He'd always thought she was a touch cracked. Perhaps she was daft enough to actually go up against the guv'nor. Not that she really cared about what he was up to. There was no great love between the boss and the missus. Madam was seething only because she was being made to look foolish in the eyes of the servants and retainers.

Reason had to come into it, he argued. Surely with all her training to play the games the crust played, surely she wasn't about to confront the boss. She couldn't be that stupid? He wasn't so sure. Her pride went before her like an evil-smelling perfume. And that same pride could unravel both the common sense she'd been born with, and the ambition she had nurtured and developed until she ultimately married one of the most famous and wealthiest men in the land.

Constance had ignored her husband's years of philandering, since it suited her that her husband went elsewhere for his pleasure. Discomfort and disgust had been her only sensations in the marriage bed, the verbal ranting of her husband during intercourse causing her some concern about the quality of his mind.

This latest episode was simply too much to bear. To hear of it through the whispering of the servants at the Merrion Square house was something she simply could not ignore.

Unable to decide well enough to place a bet on it, Seamus returned to the fact that Constance Brewer stank with pride, pride powerful enough to unravel any plain, ordinary, neurotic woman like herself! And, be the hokey! If that happened! Boys of boys! There'd be wigs on the green!

On the landing, Constance froze, her common sense telling her to turn back, let it go, release the need to bring this ridiculous liaison to an end. The sounds inside the bedroom held her rooted to the spot. The pounding of the bed and the animal-like ululations of the girl repulsed her. She found the will to turn, to get out of the lodge, to leave Arthur to his wretchedness.

In that precise moment, Arthur Shane Brewer was

rocked by the power of his orgasm. But, even as his yell of triumph slithered into a whine of satisfaction, he found a yell from somewhere, so that the words "I adore you, Lisa," reached the ears of Constance on the landing, shattering her determination to do the proper thing.

"I adore you, Lisa!" Arthur Shane now cried passionately. "I love you, girl. I cannot live without you. You are my will to live, darling, darling."

In that moment Constance actually screamed in fury, so blinded by her anger, completely mindless to the urging of her common sense, that she, quite literally, blundered into the room.

Seamus had just positioned himself perfectly in the beech tree when he saw the bedroom door slam inwards. It happened so suddenly, he almost lost his footing.

"Sweet Jesus, she's taken a brainstorm, thrown the head completely!"

Constance would have been horrified to see her beautiful features distorted by the tirade of abuse ripping from her shattered mouth while Arthur Shane Brewer rolled off Lisa's body, the girl turning quickly to lie on her side, tugging at a bed sheet to cover her nakedness.

Seamus saw the boss drawing on his hunting breeches, a tall well-built man of fifty-five years, his large spaniel eyes, the weak line of mouth endorsing his overall helplessness, evidenced in the slump of his shoulders and the hanging of his head under the lash of contempt wielded by the woman who had vowed at the altar to love, honour and obey him.

Constance was turning her attention to the servant girl who lay mute, knowing what was to come. Seamus caught Lisa's glance in the direction of Arthur Shane Brewer. He was now dressed, ignoring her presence, and he left the room without a glance at either woman. Lisa immediately rose from the bed to stand naked before the woman who was dismissing her on the spot.

Hooking the ladder back onto the boathouse wall, pausing at the cry of a kestrel hovering high over the lake, Seamus returned along the shore to the carriage, beset now by concern for a lad called Arthur.

Unless the boss could stamp on the missus, make her realise she was out of order, there could be very serious consequences. If this pimple was given its head, allowed to turn into a boil, it'd be the lad would go under the lance of the parents' festering ways.

Thankfully, Victoria was as tough as teak, so she'd be all right. But Arthur, her twin, whose only constants for the past five years had been his sister, and Lisa, and Seamus . . . he was a different proposition altogether.

The girl was gone for sure, Seamus thought in disgust. Tough enough on the lass, ejected from the life of the lad she'd mothered during the years his mother had been honing her skills as a social butterfly. But Seamus knew there were rougher days ahead for the Brewer heir.

Within the hour Lisa came down the drive, head held high, the one bag she carried no bother to her, her cape draped over one arm, a plain, brown wool dress emphasising her beautiful figure.

Seamus shuffled to shift his interest, taking her bag, holding her arm, not surprised she was coping well with the violent change in her situation.

"You're to take me into Dublin. She forbids me to ever see young Arthur ever again." Lisa was close to tears. "I have nowhere to go."

"Everything's taken care of lass. When we get you somewhere to stay in town, I'll tell you what the boss has ordered."

"He hasn't deserted me then, Seamus?"

"Arthur Shane will never desert you, Lisa. I promise you that."

Just minutes after the debacle in the master bedroom, Arthur Shane had come to Seamus by the carriage, his eyes belonging to a wounded spaniel. He gave Seamus a wad of banknotes. "Look after Lisa. Bring me her address. She will not be forgotten. I must get back. My wife has lost her reason. Divorce! How very bourgeois! Unthinkable! Collect me first thing in the morning." He flipped his eyebrows. "And never get caught with your pants down!"

Before Seamus could say a word about young Arthur's welfare, the boss scurried back up along the lakeside towards the shooting lodge. And without a backward glance, the master of the Brewer dynasty, one of the country's wealthiest scions, a man who dined with kings and queens, a man who was himself regarded as near royalty, disappeared from sight like a wicked, frightened schoolboy.

Seamus deposited Lisa at a rooming house he knew in the city. The girl was now in tears.

"What will happen to young Arthur? If it hadn't been for you and Victoria and me, the poor mite would have killed himself."

Lisa made no mention of her own situation. Seamus was impressed that her main concern was for the boy, and willingly offered to put the word out about a new situation for her.

Before he took his leave, Seamus sat Lisa down. He poured her a small glass of brandy, purchased as soon as he crossed the canal bridge at Harold's Cross.

He touched her glass with his own and told her of his instructions from Arthur Shane. He gave her the wad of notes, and allowed her see that he had written down her new address in a precise line of block letters. He knew the address by heart anyway, since the landlady and her husband were drinking pals he'd known for years. He was trying to give Lisa something to remember, just a small thing really, but knowing that her lover would actually be handed her right and proper address might help the lass get through the early days of her unhappy new circumstances.

"The boss will be in to see you shortly, count on that. And I'll be in myself as soon as I get word of a job for you. You'll be making your own enquiries about work, no doubt."

"I'll be fine once I get over the shock," Lisa assured him, her cheeks flushed slightly from the drink and the heat from the peat and coal fire in the grate. "I know

Arthur Shane will come to me. He meant what he said to me. I know he did."

"Don't build your hopes up too high now, Lisa. The boss is a public figure. Times his life is not his own," Seamus urged carefully, hoping that her hopes would be realised, that the boss would live up to his lakeside concern for Lisa. However, having served the great man in the twilight world of various Monto bawdy houses he frequented, the manservant knew that out-of-sight out-of-mind lurked just below the surface of Arthur Shane's very good intentions.

"I don't expect to end up marrying him, even if that awful woman does divorce him." Lisa held her glass out for another drink. "I may not be educated, Seamus, but I'm not stupid. And I've no interest in married life, not after what I've seen in the places I've worked."

"Have you any idea what you'll do? You've a sister in America, haven't you?"

Lisa nodded, a tender smile softening her mouth. "Rose. She's three years older than me. I could go to her, of course, but I need a bit of time to consider things. You understand?"

Lisa sipped the amber nectar, offering Seamus a cigarette. They lit up and sat smoking for a moment.

"Best I don't say anything, 'til I talk to Arthur Shane. Just in case talking about it might be bad luck," she said.

"No matter what happens, Lisa, I'll always be your friend."

"I'll never forget your kindness to me, Seamus, and

the way you care for the children." Sensing his need to leave, she kissed his face. "Tell Angela I asked after her," she said just before she closed the door after him.

Outside Seamus stood by the horses, making a commitment to himself that if things didn't work out by way of the boss looking after her, he would do all he could for the girl. She was behaving beyond the call of duty, despite the demands being made on her young mind, not forgetting her open heart. All of that being allowed, Seamus knew he was more concerned about the great young lad yet to be told that Lisa O'Brien was no longer going to be a part of his life.

"The lad's going to need me more than ever," Seamus groaned, seriously bothered by the thoughts of what lay ahead.

Deciding to try and look for a bright side to all this, he gave the nearest horse a friendly puck. "At this minute, friend, I only know one thing for certain. And that is, I know nothin'."

5

Dublin City

June 21st 1885

Ten minutes after leaving Lisa in her new abode, Seamus was sipping tea laced with whiskey at Martin Murphy's stall in Westland Row, while he prepared himself mentally for his night in the empty bed, since he'd sleep over at the Merrion Square mews. Off again then in the morning, all the way back up to Lough Bray to pick up the boss. He quickly lit up a cigarette, preparing himself right now for a tale of woe. Pat Doyle had just pulled up his nag and had indicated to him that he needed a word.

Seamus, who was attracted to strapping women, liked the look of Pat's female passenger, although she looked taller than he liked his women to be. The right size for Pat Doyle though, he thought, nearly afraid to consider the noise the pair would make if they ever got to the conjugal stage. He smiled to himself. If that were even a possibility, the lassie'd want to know her stuff, since Seamus knew for a fact that the big Dublin born jarvey was a prick virgin. He watched Pat go to the tea wagon to fetch a sandwich and a cup of tea for the woman on the sidecar. A few minutes later Seamus felt his ear was beginning to bend as Pat related a strange tale of the job that was not there when the young woman, fresh off the Wicklow train, turned up expecting to start work as a skivvy at a house in Herbert Park where they already had a pot-walloper, and no need of another one. Pat's dilemma was fairly straightforward.

"What am I to do with the lassie, Seamus?"

Seamus blessed the God that sent him the right answer, or at the very least the answer that landed well and indeed, sat well, on the mind of the big jarvey.

"Take her home to the Ma in Peter Street, Pat. What else would you do, and you about as handy around women as a one-armed banjo player."

Seamus allowed himself another cup of tea, and another snifter of whiskey to give it muscles, as he watched Pat Doyle take the sidecar away at an urgent lick. It clattered down Westland Row, turned left along Great Brunswick Street to head for home and his oul' Ma in the Liberties. Seamus had a special feeling for the Liberties, an area of the city where the Protestant Huguenot and the Jew, and many another, were given the liberty to live by the people of Dublin, who knew all about oppression and all that the word implied.

On board the sidecar, Lizzie held onto the safety-rail, giving Pat much of her attention as he told her something about the goat-faced man in the brown derby hat. She had watched them talking while she ate her sandwich of ham and drank the tea Pat had brought to her from the first tea stall she had ever seen in her life.

"A decent enough skin, though he'd drink Lough Erin dry," Pat said, with more than a hint of judgment in his tone. He felt elated in himself, talking more than he normally did, free of the shyness that could turn him mute at times. "He's well-in with one of the richest families in Europe." Pat went on, chatting with ease in a fashion that would have surprised many who considered him a misery guts and lugubrious to a fault. "The Brewers had money when it first came out! Like the Guinness family, and that's saying something!" He told Lizzie of a visit Seamus had made to the Doyle home in Peter St. "I'd told him a few bits and pieces about the mother, and he wanted to meet her and he wouldn't take no for an answer." Chuckling at the memory, Pat shook his head in amusement, while Lizzie thought that all her birthdays had come together in the best possible way. "From the minute I told him the mother lived on potatoes drenched in butter and pepper, and that she drank only tea and the odd drop of whiskey, and that she hadn't been downstairs for over twenty years, he'd settle for nothing less than a sit-down chat with her by the fireside."

"I ate nothing else, Seamus," Pat mimicked his mother, marvelling at his own boldness and the ease he felt in the company of this welcome stranger. "The mother provided the pair of us with a rasher of bacon, plentiful floury spuds, the butter melting on the top under the pepper. I never saw anyone so taken with anything, and not a word out of him unless it was another question about herself and where she came from and the like"

"Used t'ate the porridge of a mornin', Seamus," Pat was flying now as he continued the story. "No need of it now. The spuds do me grand, so they do."

"Wasn't it just great that the pair of them got along so well, Pat?" Lizzie felt bathed by the warmth of the story, her expression one of delighted incredulity.

"He liked the mother more than I could have believed. And the same man's been back to see her on a fairly regular basis, whether I was there or not. And always the drop of whiskey brought without mention or fuss." Pat sounded appreciative before his response to the generosity of the Kerryman erupted into a raucous laugh he had not anticipated. "I didn't think Seamus was capable of being surprised, Lizzie, but as sure as God made little apples, he was downright amazed so he was when the mother lit the clay pipe that was never out of her mouth the rest of the evening, unless she was putting grub in."

Pat wallowed in the memory and Lizzie preened in the nearness of such happy recall, already more than fond of the big man. For his part the jarvey was convinced that his mother would put out the welcome mat for the young woman from Wicklow. He certainly hoped she would.

He brought the nag to a halt at the Westmorland Street corner so that the horse-tram from Rathmines could pass by on its way into Sackville Street. Lizzie's mouth dropped open when she saw the grandeur of the parliament building at College Green, just across the street from Trinity College.

She shook her head in mock denial, disbelief etched into her handsome face at the scale of the magnificent building.

Seeing that his passenger was more than impressed, Pat said as off-handedly as he could. "It'd be based on Greek architecture, Elizabeth. Those pillars now would be Ionic."

He had read this recently and taken the time to memorise it – this kind of thing went down well with people from the country who had never seen such a building before. Lizzie nodded her head unsure of what to say to that, and remained silent.

Pat went on, "It's a structure worthy to be the seat of government, the house of parliament, and a fitting companion to the classical, hallowed entrance arch of Trinity College, which the English queen, Elizabeth the first created in the seventeenth century."

"Living in this city must be a very exciting thing altogether, Patrick," Lizzie said, her eyes stretched in the sunshine of the June day she would remember all the days of her life.

"If ye can earn a shilling at all, it's no bad place to be. But, many can't and there's poverty that's shameful." Pat let the subject die there, not wanting to dampen the spirits of his passenger and she only off the Wicklow train.

Lizzie fell in love with the horse-drawn tramcars, while she was gasping at the sheer variety of carriages and the number of jarvey-driven vehicles, some of them barrelling along quite recklessly, others stopping here and there to pick up or to set passengers down. Then there were the delivery carts and floats, and box-vans sitting on top of two-wheeled and four-wheeled drays, single-horse light-vans, with the larger ones drawn by a pair of sturdy-looking animals that were not in any way bothered by the noise, the hustle and bustle of the city. She gasped at it all, the likes of which she had never expected to see with her own eyes. Aunt Molly had told her of great cities like Dublin and London, places she had read about where large numbers of people somehow lived side-by-side, without killing each other by the new time.

Lizzie was drinking in the panorama that rolled across her line of vision, something she had been incapable of earlier as Patrick had ferried her from the station. She had recovered her nerve, losing the fear and anger that had fuelled her assault on the degenerate who had tried to lure her from the station platform. Pat had been very kind, reassuring her that he had been on his way to deal with the Monto Ponce – whatever that meant. Once she was seated on the sidecar she had managed to hide her real feelings, not allow him to see that she felt daunted by the sheer size and swell, and the smells of the city of his birth. In remembering what had happened at the station she again felt repelled that the slimy individual had put his hand on her as he attempted to take her bag out of her hand while pretending to be concerned for her welfare. She knew now he had reminded her of Eamon Coyle, his intent so obvious that the pair were twinned in her eyes. So she had been lashing out at her rapacious Wicklow tormentor, as well as the worm she had knocked unconscious.

Just now she felt nurtured in her heart, her eyes resting on Patrick's face. 'Thank you, Lord, that not all men are the same.'

For a moment she wondered was her face glowing from the excitement generated by the extravaganza of people passing by, ordinary people most of them, but generally better dressed than she was used to in Wicklow town, or had it more to do with Patrick and the way he was looking after her. She smiled at the idea that the people passing – it was like they were parading before her, many of them, men and women, seeming to dance for her as they glided by. She held her breath on the wonderful thought 'this is just part of living in the city of Dublin'.

Moments later she was gasping in sheer delight as her vision was filled by three young women.

"They're demonstrating the joy of cycle riding," Pat informed her. "It's got a lot of people excited. It's the future is what they're saying."

As the three young women pedalled what he called Penny-Farthings, Lizzie wondered how they didn't fall over since the wheels seemed so narrow. The cycling machines, Pat had called them, had a large wheel at the front under the seat on which the rider sat holding the handlebars, with a smaller wheel at the back. Lizzie admired the young women as they merrily rode between the delivery drays and the hackney carriages, and indeed, between the tramlines, and not a bother on any of their smiling faces. She was in awe of their bravery. To do what they were doing with such traffic about, and so many people looking at you! She loved the decorated straw hats the ladies wore, their wonderfully white blouses, each with a dark necktie tumbling down the chest to a tight-waisted skirt, their buttoned boots shining on the bicycle pedals.

She sighed, feeling very downtrodden in her gingham shift under the grey coat, with her feet complaining in the too-small worn shoes long past their best. But as the lady cyclists rode away she found a smile at their boldness, a little prayer that surprised her arising in her mind, 'Lord if y'ever bless me with a daughter, let her be as sure of herself as those three young ladies'.

The flow continued passing, men and women, gentlemen and ladies, a stream of people moving along so easily, people who were clearly familiar with the streets and the rules of the streets. She imagined that city rules needed to be obeyed so that things could happen as smoothly as they seemed to do at the minute.

She saw workers heavily dressed considering the warmth of the June day. Many men wore cotton shirts with tweed waistcoats and jackets over homespun trousers and corduroys, with boots the norm except for the gentry going about their business on foot. Just about everybody wore some form of headgear to keep the top of the head warm. She saw quite a few men riding bicycles.

She gasped audibly as a sidecar went flying by, rocking from the weight of too many passengers who were rocking themselves from too much grog. Lizzie envied them their joyous laughter.

Pat drove across a break in the traffic that was heading for Sackville Bridge. In the same moment Lizzie saw an exotic-looking lad push a handcart across the road. She was literally stunned by his beauty, knowing that somehow he was different to the men she had seen passing by in the last minute or so.

Pat called out a greeting to the lad who responded with a wave of his hand, a huge smile on his perfect, sculpted mouth.

"Hello, Mister Doyle." Sam Sweet's grin revealed teeth so white and so beautifully-formed that Lizzie could hardly believe it. Her own teeth were a lot of trouble and Aunt Molly's gums had been empty since the famine days.

"Who'll be a rich man by the time he's thirty years old!" Pat Doyle laughed, impressed yet again by the haul of articles the young dealer had on the cart.

Then, with a friendly wave of his hand, he drove the horse towards Dame Street, chuckling as Sam yelled, "It's not going to take that long, Mister Doyle!"

"Isn't he only beautiful?" Lizzie sighed openly.

"He's a Jew." Pat said. "From up north Germany

somewhere. His parents like. He was born here in Little Jerusalem. He's a great lad, even though he's a Jew. He never stops working and bright as the evening star."

Pat sniffed, his chagrin bordering on respect. "The Jews have the gift. They know how to make the shillings." He grimaced like a man whose innards were disquieted. "It's like God himself taught them how to hold on to them."

Sam Sweet kept an eye on Pat Doyle's swaying sidecar and as he heaved between the shafts of his own cart, came back to the question of a pony and dray as part of his equation.

"I could do with a nag myself instead of mullocking this yoke like an ox." He dug deeper against the shafts, pressing on in the wake of the sidecar. "A great day's tot all the same, two good chairs, a lick of glue and a varnish and they'll fetch a couple of bob each. The rest of the tot will sell well, as well. The books alone will earn what I paid for the lot."

He smiled about the books. There was no end of reading before he sold them in one's and two's, or as a job lot. Wonderful, when he considered that the morning had been a total write-off. He smiled, remembering the words of Four-Fingered Louie, "The day starts lousy, go with it. It can only get better!" Louie usually spoke German to Sam who had the language due to his mother's industry in that department. Sam smiled as Louie slipped into Yiddish which he also had thanks to Esther, his mother. He thought Louie's accent funny, and this, coupled with the man's continual philosophical insights, created in Sam the wish for more of his company, and so a casual bond existed between them. The truth was that his mother and the German-born peddler were the only people he felt in any way close to.

His mother would fly through the books even before Sam himself got around to them. This was the one thing in her life for which she could admit gratitude to his grey shadow of a father, who had never recovered from the pain of having to leave his homeland. Esther had accepted her fate and, to her surprise, had come to like the way of life in Dublin, the living being easier since she had quit caring that her husband hadn't a word to throw to a dog.

"If your father hadn't been too miserable to talk to me, I might never have started regular reading. So he gave me two blessings. He gave me you, and he drove me to the books. So, to your father I'll always be grateful. He was so generous with his misery he forced me to find escape in the books you bring home. You and me, we discuss the stories and the history and whatever, we talk with each other. If you ever feel the need to make my life complete, find a nice Jewish girl and make me a grandchild, four or five even."

Sam pushed on. He would be home in Clanbrassil Street within an hour, to hot food cooked by his mother on a wood fire. Tonight she was preparing halibut marinated for hours and cooked in parsley and garlic, lemon juice and fresh apricots. This was his favourite dish and he had given her some extra housekeeping that morning to make sure she would have enough for all the right ingredients.

For a few moments Sam felt weak, his mouth watering, and he remembered how tired he was. As he turned into South Great George's Street, he dropped the shafts, needing to take a short rest.

As he leaned against the cart, he saw a pair of street urchins on the other side of the roadway. Lads his own age, their tight tenement faces coated in anger, their eyes malevolent, youths prepared to be dangerous in their hunting.

Sam wished he hadn't decided to take a break but George's St was always a trial, not steep, but with enough incline to guarantee the cart pusher plenty of sweat on a summer's day. He stood up straight and kept his eyes on the street-arabs. They crossed the roadway, close enough to each be the shadow of the other, their sense of urgency a harbinger of the violence they wore like a second skin, their bare feet making no sound.

Feeling lucky that he knew they were coming, Sam picked up the three-foot length of four-by-two teak he had fashioned into a club, and stood there, waiting.

He gave them his 'just you try it' stare, tapping the club on the wheel of the cart. He used this route so often coming home from the east of the city, that many in the area knew him by sight. Fortunately, this group included one half of the terrible twins!

"Hold on, Wire!" The youth held the other back "Stay away from yer man. He's a bleedin' Jewboy! Mad so he is. You'd have to kill him to get away with an'thin' offa that handcart!"

Sam stood his ground, silently daring them to come near him. He hit the wheel very hard with the club, like someone steaming for a fight. He saw them hesitate, hold, begin to withdraw. He watched them go back across the street. Then he began the long push towards home, hunger and relief coursing through him like life's chemicals, the cobbles protesting under the wheels of the cart.

6

Woodtown House, County Dublin

June 22nd 1885

In the stable-yard of Woodtown House, some six miles down the mountain road from the shooting lodge, Seamus Byrne closed the door of the horse box with an unnecessary heave, before striding out into the waning sunlight like a man badly in need of a good fist-fight.

Angela had opened the kitchen door as her lover stormed across the cobbled yard. She ignored his anger, standing with her hands on her hips. She thrust her breasts forward, her legs wide apart. As he came nearer she said, "Instead of giving you your dinner and a glass of whiskey, I know what I'd like to give you this minute."

She knew this would make him forget whatever was turning his beautiful lecherous eyes into dollops of death-dark coal. He stopped in front of her, releasing a sigh that took years off his face, and allowed Angela to give him a hug. "You feel those beauties against the wall of your chest and tell me you shouldn't be feeling good, you devil." She released him and found him smiling before her. He gave her a kiss on the lips and he said, "How the hell did I not go entirely mad before you took advantage of me and made me your bloody slave?"

"Come in out of the wet with your flannel feet!" Angela said with a laugh, glad to have him back safe-and-sound. It had been a long couple of days for him up and down the mountain roads. Any day without a glimpse of him was a long day to Angela. She took his arm and they walked towards the kitchen. The June evening was dry, almost balmy in the foothills of the mountains to the south, as she said to him with a laugh in her voice, "I've got a plate of rare beef with your name on it. Never mind lead, it'll put steel in your pencil, so it will."

Angela sat and sipped a glass of punch as she watched Seamus devour a ploughman's dinner and several smacks of the punch, which was fairly lethal since she herself had made it. He didn't speak until he had wiped the last smear of her gravy up with a crust of her home-made bread.

"The Brewers'll rue yesterday's madness as sure as God made little apples." He put down the glass down on the table, more relaxed now as the food and the drink did their work. "Between them, Angela, the boss and his cow of a wife – Lisa's the only mother the lad's ever known. To just rip her out of his life and her so devoted to him – they've put paid to whatever chance young Arthur had of a normal life. I only hope to God he doesn't kill himself."

Angela poured him another drink, squeezing his hand. So that was it. Her bloody ladyship had heard about the boss shafting Lisa up at the lodge.

"Jesus!" she exclaimed in disbelief. "Wouldn't you think she'd have more cop-on? A woman born and reared to be a wife to someone like Arthur Shane Brewer . . ." She rose from the table and moved the kettle onto the hottest plate on the cooker. "I'm awful sorry to hear Lisa's gone. And, please God, Seamus, the lad won't take it as badly as you think. Is she going to be looked after?"

"She is. I gave her my word, the boss after giving his to me. And he better live up to it. I'm going to take Arthur to see Lisa in a few days. I only hope it'll be enough. It'll be like a death to him, the only mother he's ever known in the real sense. Jesus! What a bloody farce!" He downed the fresh drink and lit up a cigarette. "Did her ladyship come in here yesterday on her way down from the lodge?"

"Oh indeed she did." Angela was wetting tea. "Thomas had to go up with the coach and four. She was in a foul mood, warning everyone that if we so much as talked to Lisa, we'd get our walking papers."

"I'd like to give her as a gift to a ship's crew heading into the Arctic for about eighteen months," Seamus said vehemently.

"Be too good for her," Angela said casually. "With her heart the size of a walnut, all those lovely sailors'd

73

be wasted on the likes of her. Now, if it was me . . ." she bantered teasingly.

She exploded with laughter as he turned abruptly on his chair. "He loves me, he loves me true." She chortled to the ceiling as she came to the table with the teapot. "I made a bread-and-butter pudding that'll charm the cockles of your heart." She kissed the top of his head. "Don't spend the evening fretting about the boy. Whatever happens, we'll deal with it, the way we deal with everything."

He sighed and nodded his head. "I only hope Pat Doyle had a better end to the day than young Arthur and Lisa. You know that Constance will have told the lad Lisa got sacked for stealing."

"May her back-passage fester, the rotten bitch," Angela was angry, her concern for Seamus, and two glasses of punch she'd taken, scratching at her mind, so that her great hazel eyes shone with a wild light that hinted at the madness within. She hadn't slept well last night, her discomfort caused by thinking of Seamus lying in the bloody loft over the stable at Merrion Square.

"Let's hope Pat Doyle and that big woman from Wicklow come to something. It'd take some of the sinful smell off yesterday."

Angela gave him an old-fashioned look. "I know I taught you to read, but don't start expecting me to read your mind."

"Let me get these boots off and I'll tell you the story of the day." He allowed a rueful grin to adorn his mouth. "You're in good health, aren't you?"

Angela let go of her ire, relieved to find him simmering down. When he got himself up to ninety he could stay there for days at a time. "It must have been some day for you to come back to me in flitters."

"Don't be talking," he said with a sigh. "From the time herself threw the jug of cold water over me yesterday morning to get me up out of the scratcher, 'til I sent Pat Doyle home to his Ma with a fine woman, you could write a book about it so you could. And that's without mentioning the flop in the loft over the stable. The fleas there had hobnailed boots on." He threw his own boot on the floor, and a cackle of laughter stuttered from his throat. "I'll tell you one thing though, Angela. I'd have given a right few shillin's to be a fly on the wall at the Doyles' place when Bridie Doyle set her eyes on the woman from Wicklow, a lassie that could take Pat off the list of eligible bachelors, in the sweet whore of a city we call Dublin."

On the previous day, in the bosom of that sweet whore of a city, in the Doyles' living-room just down the road from the Huguenot cemetery and the Adelaide Hospital on Peter St, Lizzie was eating floury potatoes smothered in butter. Alongside her at the old table, Pat was devouring what could have been called 'a right feed of spuds', while his mother fried another couple of bacon slices in a deep, black pan of goose fat over the open fire in the huge tenement room.

Bridie was sixty-five years old but she kept her age

a secret. She liked a bit of mystery. Not even Pat's father, Eddie Doyle, a cattle jobber with a thirst that killed him, had ever discovered her right and proper age.

"I'm as fit as a brace of stays!" Bridie could announce of a sudden, for no reason at all. Sudden pronouncements were a part of Bridie's input to daily life, and those who knew her rarely showed surprise at anything she said. Some, including her only son, Pat, thought Bridie 'a fair bit mad' but she was generally regarded as the decent, rather odd, ageing woman she was. Her decision, taken two decades earlier, to live out her days by the fireside in her own home had raised an eyebrow or two and caused an index finger or more to be tapped against the temple of the person hearing the news. Bridie didn't mind. If anything she enjoyed being thought *a bit quare*, and she was happy with her lot, wanting nothing but God's gift of a grandchild to hold in her arms.

"A couple more spuds, while yer waitin' for the rasher, Lizzie." Bridie scooped the potatoes onto Lizzie's plate.

"I could eat spuds till the cows come home, Missus Doyle." She was smiling up at the old woman. Out of the blue, she shared the thought that had captured her mind. "Wasn't God just great, making sure there was no job for me in Ballsbridge."

Pat's attention was stolen from the last spud on his plate. He was already feeling good, secretly pleased by his mother's welcome for the young woman he'd brought home. Then, in the next moment, he was more than surprised to hear himself say, "Amen to that, Elizabeth."

"Just think," he said as he recovered from the initial shock, "if you'd got the job, you'd never have tasted the mother's French cooking!"

Bridie exploded into a huge laugh, while Lizzie knew that she was having the time of her life.

"And I'd never have met you the way I did, Patrick. I'd have paid you the fare from Amiens St station, and never have got the chance to know you, the chance for you to help me," Lizzie spoke disarmingly and laughed again, surprised by the magical happening of her good fortune.

Bridie felt a lump in her throat, and she took a deep breath as she saw Lizzie as the answer to her prayers. Even though she had met the girl little more than an hour earlier, she believed she was a gift from God, surely sent to them as a wife for her son, a mother to his childer, her grandchilder. 'God! Imagine childer around the place,' she thought. Her mind wanted to soar on the possibility. 'And here was a lassie with hips on her to breed a regiment, and the dairies to suckle them through the early years when so many get taken by one thing or another. And shure she, God love her, needs us as much as we need her. Not a stitch, only the shift she's dressed in, and them shoes must be cuttin' the feet off the poor lass.'

"Get them shoes off you, Lizzie, and I'll know you're really taking me at my word to make yourself at home."

Bridie was dolling out more of the thick bacon slices Aggie Mac brought her. Her niece, Aggie Mac, had a right leg of the butcher on the Coombe. She got the best of off-cuts and though they never discussed it, Bridie knew that the beef hearts, and the hocks, and the tripe herself and Aggie cooked on a daily basis weren't the only meat your man slipped to her niece. She was easy with this arrangement, admiring Aggie Mac who had turned widowhood into a better life than many of the moaning minnies around the place. Most of them did nothing but pray, and drink stout in the snugs on Wexford St. And for all the Holy Communions, they came out of the chapel ready to rip into a tirade of gossip against anyone interesting enough to provide them with a target.

As she ate, the old woman chatted about the city, the good and the bad points of living in such a very big town. At other moments, she returned to a silent prayer that God would give Pat the shove he needed, to make this girl his own. As far as Bridie knew, he had never been with a woman. Maybe that's why, for all his decency, he's more times miserable than not, she reflected. He's not short of money to live. He's a saver, and he has the way of someone you'd expect to end up doing very well for himself.

Bridie could see they were made for each other. Shure, y'only had to see the way they kept stealing glances, to know that they were in the grip of the madness that led people to stand before the altar and say "I do". She believed this was so even now, as Pat and the girl became caught on each other's eyes, scarcely able to look away. She sighed, not sure she ever felt that way about her husband. She'd given in to his passionate pleadings and she was four months in the club when they got married, and if there was a better reason than that to tie the knot, it hadn't come into the realm of her personal experience. So, she'd do all she could here to help them to the altar, but she wouldn't interfere. She wouldn't try to organise things and bring them all the way together. She'd let God get on with that part of things. Well, as long as he got a move on! Elizabeth was a sweetheart of a lassie. But, she was no spring chicken!

At the same time, and just a mile away from the Liberties, at the Brewer family's townhouse on Merrion Square, twelve-year-old Vicky embraced her brother in a mothering way, willing him to freedom from the pain of Lisa's going which according to her mother was because of stealing.

Neither she nor Arthur believed this, nor any other word ushering from Constance, no more than they paid attention to her continual orders and demands as she went on trying to assert herself whenever her husband was not in residence. This was due to their father who, in order to expiate his own guilt for being such a flop as a parent, countermanded every order Constance issued to Arthur and Victoria, assuring them that he would always be on their side, having no desire that they should pay for his great mistake.

The implication that he had married the wrong person was not lost on his bright young children. They felt not a shred of loyalty, or filial devotion to the woman who had given birth to them. She had virtually abandoned them to the nursery, and a long line of nannies and nurses, under the watchful eye of a medical doctor, Patrick Lote, who had been through school with Arthur Shane Brewer. He was a gifted and caring medical practitioner and gave young master Brewer, as he called the boy, four in-depth examinations each year, since he was concerned not only with Arthur's physical condition but his emotional vulnerability. Constance considered that all this attention merely fed her son's self-absorption. Her husband would have none of it hence she had no influence in the matter. When he felt it was needed, Arthur Shane Brewer put Constance in her place, without any hint of emotion in his admonitions.

"You were given every chance to be a caring mother, old girl. This role did not require that you tend to the children's every need, that you spend all day in the nursery, but, since it's a matter on record that you never once entered it, that the twins were wet-nursed because you could not bear the trauma of breast-feeding, I ask you to be reasonable. Desist, old girl, from any further display of your belated need to show motherly concern for our children."

When Constance actually became aware of the indifference shown towards her by her children, she never once considered that she was paying another sliver off the debt that her behaviour had incurred. Far from any show of contriteness, she reacted resentfully rather than philosophically, entrenched in her ignorance of the rule governing the universal law of book-keeping, which ensured that no debt went unpaid.

The twins were naturally intelligent and worked diligently with their tutors in the library at the Merrion Square house. Thanks to the fact that their father had hated every second of his life at places such as Eton and Oxford, he had decided he would never inflict the ritual of school-going education on his children. Constance had been appalled, but since her opinion went unheard, the twins studied at home, and as they approached their fourteenth birthday were both well up to speed with their studies. However, Arthur's education would suffer as the direct result of his soul-mother, his title for Lisa O'Brien, being ripped from his everyday life.

"We'll get the true story from Seamus in the morning," Vicky said in her matter-of-fact way, relieved that Arthur's need to weep seemed to have come to an end. The following morning he was so utterly withdrawn that Victoria had the family doctor, Patrick Lote, call to the house. After the most cursory examination he gave the boy a sedative. He then enquired of Victoria if she knew of any reason why Arthur might be shutting out the world? Vicky told him that Lisa had been dismissed and sent away without even a chance to talk to her twin. The doctor shook his head in a show of mute regret. As he made to leave, he assured Victoria he would return later in the day.

"Thank you, doctor," Victoria said quietly, worry etched into her face.

"We would all do well to allow our concern to surface, Victoria. Your brother finds this present situation unbearable. Hopefully, we can help him come out from under this. He has no interest in anything else. But there are severe days ahead of us, and I want you to prepare yourself for them. You and Seamus Byrne may well be Arthur's only hope of overcoming this dreadful ordeal."

Victoria went down the back garden and let herself out into the laneway. She found her great friend in the stable harnessing the pair he had driven up and down the mountain the day before. As usual, he was willing to tell her everything that had happened at Lough Bray.

Well, almost everything – what had happened in the master bedroom at the lodge was not for the ears of a twelve-year-old girl, Seamus decided.

7

The Long Walk West

1885-1886

Rebecca found herself dismissing the accepted notion of 'God's will in all things', and felt no remorse. She allowed her free thinking to stake its claim to her attention, and she granted the same to the radical poems and songs that had been writing themselves out of her heart and her experience, like a built-in defence system against pointless wishful-thinking and self-pity.

She had only ever expressed her doubts about God's bounty in the security of her own mind, never uttering a word likely to disturb her father in any way. But she neither received nor wanted any respite from the inner voice that refused to lie still. It seemed to insist that she go on and on regurgitating the truth of the injustice to her people.

She found herself crying out to her father in the secret apartment of her mind, 'The Jews have lived too long with the sickness of the Russias. I'll shed no tear for the life we leave. How could I? How could I, when, like you, and your grandfather before my grandfather, like every Jew gone before us under Russian skies, I will never be allowed to own an acre of land in the land of the Tsar! My God! How we must terrify them.'

Later in the day, as she relieved her father between the shafts, Rebecca recycled her anger to empower her effort to keep up with the carts ahead. She looked down at her feet. The home-made sandals wouldn't last very long.

'There has to a better life for us all in some other place. There has to be!' She pulled harder against the weight behind her to still the drift into the kind of wishful-thinking she hated and feared. 'There must be people who treat justice with respect, people who allow a manner of living to balance things out for everyone.'

Rebecca held onto this notion before and behind the cart. She kept it close through endless rain-soaked, sun-drenched miles. She admired each heart in that growing river of souls, was herself inspired by the way ordinary people as a force could contribute by their will, strength and movement to the torrent of over two million people as with wind-burned eyes, their minds holding onto some life-saving dream, they shuffled westward, resembling at times a vast herd of people shunted away like diseased cattle.

"They won't kill me," she vowed passionately. "No matter what happens, I will be there till we reach civilisation. I will hold on!" And hold on she did, Rebecca Moses, nineteen years old who found the wisdom of a grandmother to help her cope with the comings and goings of her father's mind. She never knew from one hour to the next how he was going to be, but on the seventh day, after she had written her daily notes into her journal, she thought she felt a shift in Mendel's energy level. Rebecca couldn't explain it to herself but it seemed that her own heart had gauged, assessed and registered the withdrawal of the power in her father's jaded pump.

It was a warm night and she played the guitar, singing gently for a few minutes to the old man as he surrendered to the arms of Morpheus. Sarah Elkins sat with Rebecca, her husband already snoring where he slept under their cart. By this time the two women were like mother and daughter, drawn together by the spirit of understanding that wasn't there in the men they lived with.

Rebecca sent her father to sleep on the words of his favourite song, 'I Rest In Your Love'. She knew that he was referring to the Lord God Almighty when he sang the lyrics to her from the time she was a small girl. Did he still feel he was singing to God, she wondered. Since his difficulties with his faith after their voluntary expulsion, she thought it unlikely. Perhaps he was thinking now of her mother, Rachel, who had died when Rebecca was ten years old. As she sang, she felt him become peaceful, and soon he was sleeping.

"I rest in your love,
I feel the welcome warmth of your embrace,
There is no other resting place for me,
I pray you'll always be,
Forever here with me,
That I may rest in your love."

As she finished singing Rebecca saw that Sarah was weeping, her tears copious but silent as distant raindrops. She knelt beside her friend and put her arms around her. The woman embraced her, sniffed back a further flow as Rebecca said, "I'm so sorry, Rebecca. I didn't mean to make you sad."

"Oh, you didn't. You didn't at all, child." Sarah pulled back to hold Rebecca by her upper arms, her eyes invisible even though there was a moon. Then she said in a very quiet voice, "I believe your father has passed over."

In moments Rebecca knew that Sarah was right. Her father had died while she had been singing. She wept brokenly for some little time, bothered by sadness for what might have been. She felt the other woman's hand take her fingers in a gesture of support as she dealt with the dart of guilt arriving on the coat-tails of her relief, the compassionate relief that he was no longer trapped by the injustice of his earthly circumstance. Her father was now free to talk and discuss, and argue and get as fiery as he wished in a polemic with his Maker. Perhaps he would finally get some answers to the mysteries of a life that somehow got away from him, turning him to an angry, frustrated old man who, though he was equipped to deal with whatever life presented, ultimately found himself bereft of the heart for the fight to survive.

Had her father died just days earlier she would have honoured the funeral rites, the ritual that meant so much to him. She would have torn off the silk fringe of Mendel's tallith. Had her mother been alive they would have sat morning and evening for a week, ideally with ten men coming to the house to make their mourner's prayer, the Kaddish, for the deceased. On the endless road west Rebecca simply called to mind the words of the mourner's prayer her father had taught her.

"And hereafter, when all shall have ceased,
He tremendous, alone shall reign; who was and is,
And ever will be in glory,
He is without beginning, without end,
To him belong majesty and dominion."

Mendel was buried at once. The marker of his roadside grave would soon be torn from the earth by the wind, or washed away by the rain or burned up by the sun scorching the vast oceans of land. In time he would be returned to dust like so many more in the crocodile. This number would soon include Sarah Elkins, whose caring heart gave up the ghost soon after her husband had wandered off during a night that was just like any other.

"Israel is gone, gone on a long walk of his own," Sarah said through her quiet tears, while they shared a drink of morning tea. "At least it's a walk he chose to take for himself."

Sarah passed over within days, and a weeping Rebecca was helped in the digging of the shallow grave by a bearded man she had never seen before. She left a slip of paper bearing Rebecca's name and the date of her death in the pocket of the old cotton dress her friend had lived in, and died in.

The bearded man was Peter Stein. He was on the run from the Russian authorities. If he were caught he would be found guilty and executed. "I objected to being manhandled by a pair of drunken soldiers threatening to take me into custody unless I gave them money," he explained to Rebecca after a couple of days in each other's company, Peter now doing the bulk of the hauling while she pushed the cart from behind.

"I had to leave St Petersburg with all haste. Agents of the police, you know the kind of scavengers, men that would sell their children if there was money in it."

"Did you kill them?" Rebecca asked as they sat close in the light of a campfire shared with others who were parked close by for the night.

"I had to kill one." He laughed shortly, defensively. "Nothing to be proud of, I know. I would sooner die than go to prison. I was born in St Petersburg. My parents are buried there. My father was cut down by a drunken hussar as he was walking home to his evening meal," said Peter through gritted teeth. "A cutlass in the hands of a hussar is allowed to cut down a Jew. My mother simply withered away, died of a broken heart. I had to get out, get away from the sickness of that city. By putting a price on my head, they made my decision for me, the first service I have experienced at the hands of mother Russia."

Rebecca felt just as bitter and she didn't hide it from him. "Rapists and murderers made my decision for me. The arrangements I made myself on behalf of my father and me. God blast the Russias and all who serve the Tsar!" She smiled ruefully. "Bitterness is bad for the digestion. I keep trying to let it go. So, with that in mind, tell me, Peter, do you know where you want to go? Have you anywhere particular in mind? Assuming we manage to survive the walk?"

"We will survive. We will come through," he looked intently into her eyes. "I am going to Ireland."

She could see that he wanted to say more and she waited, but he rested on the moment and she did not press him. She found him to be a wonderful man and she wanted him to say more but she allowed that one of the things they were not short of was time. Later they had drifted back into the question of destinations – who dreamed of going where. "And it is to be Ireland for you, Peter? Why there?" Rebecca felt close to him as she spoke.

"Ireland has a great cultural history. That alone makes me want to live there. A friend of mine is living there. He assures me that in three years he has never been abused or persecuted in any way for being a Jew. I am ready and I am most willing to have that experience. And, in truth, the further I am from Russia, the more I will like it."

In this manner they began life as a couple, Rebecca willing to share in his hopes and his dreams since she had none of her own. She began walking beside him by the shafts of the cart as he told her all that he had learned about the small island on the western edge of Europe.

"We have to get there, Rebecca. It's been called 'the land of saints and scholars', and I can feel the peace of it even now reaching out to me with open arms."

She loved the dreamer in him and she willingly surrendered the cynicism that had soured her view of life in the last few months. As a relief she allowed Ireland to become the focus of her own hopes; she willingly succumbed to the idea of a land where peace was the norm, which gave her added strength to share the burden of hauling the cart across Lithuania and on into Romania.

In Romania they found that kindness was in short supply, the fear-filled peasants readily prepared to be violent, abusing them, warning them to keep on moving, that this was no resting place for them. Some gave them a little food and water as a bribe to keep on passing by. Others sold bread and water, milk and vegetables at exorbitant prices. One thing above all else became all too clear all too quickly – nobody wanted this flood of unwashed, ill-kempt, half-starved exiles camping on their doorstep. Nobody wanted the wandering Jews.

The Romanians, who hardly differed from themselves, had seen it all before. God alone knew how many Jews had been expelled down the last several decades, and this lot was no different to any that had gone before, or to those whose bodies littered the land. There were hundreds of unmarked shallow graves, foreign plots that had failed to hold the remains of the fallen when the wild dogs of the plains came calling hungry in the night.

Almost a year later, having spent two months on the

Italian shore of the Adriatic, Peter Stein married Rebecca Moses in a registry office at Bevis Marks in London. During the eight-week period in Italy they had both worked hard to earn enough money for the fare to England. They had no complaints about the heavy toil, the twelve-hour working days like a holiday after what they had been through since leaving Lithuania.

The laughing couple, with little or no money, needed nothing but each other as they went to their wedding night in their rented room off Aldgate. Early in the morning after the first long night of their love-making, Rebecca knew that she was pregnant, knew it as surely as if she was close to her time of delivery. She wept a little as she looked down on Peter asleep still in the rented bed, and she wished with all her heart that their first child be a girl.

Much as they wanted to go directly to Ireland they accepted that they had to stay in London to try and earn money to live, with hopefully some small part left over to save towards the boat journey to a new life in the Land of Saints and Scholars.

Rebecca did sewing by hand for a Jew who ran sweatshops in London's East End. She worked at home in the tiny room, singing the songs that continued to create themselves in her mind. She recited the psalms learned in childhood, thinking of them as poetry rather than some kind of religious text, and she prayed for guidance every day though she had no set philosophical concept of a God. Times she wondered if there was a God. Why not have two Gods, she asked herself, male and female? It seemed to make sense – God the Father and God the Mother, each feeding every person with its own special qualities.

Peter was working as a clerk at a meat market by Brick Lane. He was paid nine shillings a week, which with the three shillings and coppers Rebecca earned, allowed them to live well enough. The rent was paid on time, they ate well, even managing to save one and sixpence every payday, which they had hidden under the mattress of the bed in which they made their first child.

Rebecca suffered the morning sickness in silence, feeling that Peter had enough to cope with at his job. Ten-hour days were the norm, no work on Sundays touted as a bonus. He was responsible for all produce in and out of the factory market. He produced the inventories, invoices and accounts, but recently he'd started to worry that serious pilfering was taking place right under the noses of his superiors. It didn't take Peter long to see what was going on. He knew quickly why there was a discrepancy between his figures and the monetary returns.

A couple of vendors came three times each day to take away the offal from the animals slaughtered on the premises. When the horse-drawn drays were loaded with the drums of offal, they were quickly driven away without anybody checking what was being taken from the market.

Peter concluded that only the top half of each drum was filled with the offal, this being used to conceal half a drum of prime cuts. This meant that at least nine full drums of top class meat were being pilfered six days a week. Little wonder the figures didn't balance out.

That evening Peter saw the market manager about the situation. He launched nervously into a description of what he thought was going on. George Davis held up his hand apologetically and spoke to Peter carefully, avuncular in his approach.

"Don't worry," he said. "We'll sort it out."

Later that night as Rebecca finished sewing for the day, a neighbour living downstairs in the house called up to Peter. There was a man from his workplace to see him at the front door. Peter had told Rebecca of his earlier meeting with his boss. He had gone on to tell her of his suspicions, feeling better now that the situation was to be dealt with. Rebecca had misgivings about him taking the risk involved.

"If people are stealing all that meat, there has to be quite a lot of money made from the sale of it. That could make it very dangerous for you to expose whatever is going on. Perhaps we should think about it, Peter, before you take it any further."

"But I am paid to do a job. It is my responsibility to balance the books. This can't be done in light of what is going on. How can I ignore something that prevents me doing what I am paid to do? Don't you see?"

"I see it all very clearly. But I am afraid of what might happen to you."

"You're not suggesting I should let it go on, ignore the stealing from my employers?"

"You might consider getting a job somewhere else. If you leave the market, this situation will be behind us."

"Finding another job could prove to be very difficult, Rebecca. You know how lucky I was to find employment in the market, much as I detested having to work on a Saturday."

"All I ask is that you think about what I'm saying."

"Of course, I will, I always do. But, Rebecca, I have to do what I feel is right. Now let me see if it is Mister Davis come with some word for me." Peter left the room while Rebecca went to the window to look out.

Her uneasiness increased when she saw that there were two men below. She could not see their faces since the street was barely lit by a light from the brothel across the way. In a moment she saw Peter join the waiting men. One of them instantly pulled him forward while the other appeared to drive his fist several times into Peter's stomach. She realised that her husband was making no effort to fight back and so, choking on her fear-filled breathing, Rebecca went down the wooden stairs as fast as she dare.

When she got to the street, a peeler was responding to cries for help from a middle-aged couple afraid to get involved as Peter was being attacked.

Rebecca fell to her knees by her husband, lifted his head onto her thighs, her mind almost deserting her when she saw the blood that had pumped from Peter's stomach. The policeman had blown his whistle. She heard words like "done for, cut to pieces" as she found some semblance of voice.

"Peter, my love, can you hear me?" Her heart had dropped to the pit of her stomach. The blows she had thought to be punches had been stab wounds through which his very life was draining out of him. He opened his eyes, appearing to see her from a great distance. "Ireland, Rebecca. Promise me you'll go, take our child to live in Ireland."

She nodded her head, blinded by tears she didn't want to shed all over him.

"Say it, Rebecca. Say it, please."

"I promise you, I will take our child to Ireland."

She was beyond civility, consideration, her heart cleft in two by what had happened. She tried to wipe blood away, her eyes pouring her pain down her face and onto Peter's beard, her grieving cries of utter desolation terrifying the bystanders.

Rebecca saw the light fade in Peter's eyes and heard the death-rattle as his mouth eschewed his last cough of blood. She held him close in the numbness, the denial of her loss. She heard his voice again in her mind as he sought her promise, her own voice then saying, "I promise you I will take our daughter to Ireland if it's the last thing I ever do."

Rebecca allowed some local residents to bring Peter's body into the house but she could not have said who they were. She was too desolate to speak and had little or no memory of how her beloved husband came to be lying on the bed they had come to from their marriage vows.

Next morning she found her journal open by the

chair in which she had drifted into a fitful sleep. She had some trouble reading her own writing but she managed to decipher the erratic scrawl and felt no surprise when she read the words. 'Were it not for the unborn child in my womb, I would now lie dead beside my husband. This black day is the sixth day of September 1888.'

8

London

June 30th 1905

"Take your time, Mama," Gloria said reassuringly, the agitation in her violet eyes at odds with the calm quality of her voice.

Rebecca grimaced in pain, leaning heavily on the girl. "We must get the train, put some distance between ourselves and Jem Riley."

Gloria kissed her mother's face, knowing the positive tone was being forced through the wall of pain mirrored in Mama's eyes.

She was virtually carrying her mother as they reached Euston station, and she was sweating under the poncho she wore. It had been an old blanket until she had tailored it a bit, adding some stitch-on-cloth flowers in an effort to make it more presentable. It had helped save her freezing to death during part of last winter. On this June day as the sun was blistering everything, it was like a sweatbox. She also wore the one heavy skirt she possessed, and the much-mended jumper that seemed to weigh a ton at the minute. She had worn the same garments throughout the past winter, as did most of the people who lived and slept on the city streets of London and Westminster. Many of them were just ordinary people like herself and her mother Rebecca, people who could die from the cold during the seemingly endless winter nights. The spring nights too took their toll on the dispossessed, and, far too often, many lost the will to live during the midnight hours of summer and autumn. They were forced to sleep rough, condemned to lie down or huddle together, as she and her mother often did, in the doorways of run-down shops and factory sheds, their clothing stuffed with old newspapers, the nearness of each other's bodies often the salient need that kept them alive.

To add to their intolerable situation, this last winter had been the one in which they were destined to meet Jem Riley, the accursed Irishman from Liverpool, who had now become the primary reason why they needed desperately to get out of London.

Gloria glanced back along the Euston Road, terrified she would see Jem coming after them. Thank God, no sign of the dreaded creature who had turned their manageable existence into a living Hell.

She gave her mother all her strength now, fully supporting her as she struggled to get her breath. Rebecca couldn't move but then Gloria heard her mother's whispered prayer, a weary, pain-filled ululation, the voice of someone remembering a long-forgotten friend.

"The King saved us from the hands of our enemies."

Gloria prepared to move on as she felt her mother discover, yet again, the will to take another step towards the train, and her heart beat faster with every step taken towards safety. Suddenly, some inner terror was telling her they wouldn't make it, that Jem Riley would get his hands on them again. Gloria forced the voice from her mind, supporting her mother with all her strength, keeping them on the move, forcing herself to be strong on this the last stretch of their slow walk away from Hell.

As they finally got into the station, Gloria was almost carrying Rebecca, who was very pregnant and bleeding again. This had made it so painfully difficult for the girl to keep her mother on the move. How Mama coped with the endless pain – Gloria could hardly believe it was possible. At times the only thing between the girl and total despair was the hope in her heart that she had killed the man who had inflicted his evil nature upon her beloved mother. The hatred she felt for Riley tasted like a poisonous liquid in her mouth, and she used this to support the surging hope that she really had left him dead on the floor of the King's Cross doss-house. She believed he deserved to die slowly and painfully, and she prayed that his demise had been so. Let him suffer the pains of Hell.

Gloria had been washing herself in the room, when Jem Riley had returned from the alehouse that same afternoon. She pulled her vest on quickly, trying to ignore the effect her naked breasts had on his eyes. She donned her jumper in an instant, her attention going to her mother, who seemed to revive a little at the sound of her lover's footsteps on the stairs. Rebecca was stretched out on a foul mattress under the gaping window of the flophouse room. She was enduring appalling suffering, close to losing the baby she carried for Riley, who was drunk and clearly had just one thing on his mind.

"For God's sake, Jem," Rebecca pleaded, "keep your eyes off my girl. Is nothing sacred to you?"

Gloria moved quickly to her mother, helping her to sit up on a wooden box, the only chair in the disgusting hovel. She pleaded with her eyes, 'Please don't annoy him, Mama'. She knew from bitter experience what a madman he could be when he had drink taken.

"Shut yer mouth, ye Jew cow, or I'll break it for ye!" Riley vowed fiercely, in the half-Irish accent of the Liverpool streets where he had been dumped, the unwanted child of a prostitute. "This one's good and ready." He looked at Gloria, like a farmer appraising a heifer. "Yeh, she's ready, and drippin' for a good shaftin'! Them tits on her, like ripe fruit they are, fruit I'm goin' to pluck, me bein' the very bloke to help her get rid of her useless maidenhead!"

Despite her pain and her hugely pregnant belly, Rebecca reacted before Gloria could stop her, somehow hurling herself at Riley as he let his foul overcoat drop to the floor.

Drunk though he was, he twisted, avoiding the punch Rebecca threw at his face. Then he knocked her down with a stunning blow to the brow and, despite Gloria's screams, he kicked her mother brutally several times. Then, as though he was coming out of a memory lapse, he rounded on Gloria, slapping her face hard enough to bring her screams to a stop. She tried to scream again, and he hit her once more, a stinging blow that cut off her ability to make any sound at all.

"Shut it, Gloria. Move so much as an eyelash, and I'll kill you stone dead!"

He stepped close, held his hand to her face, before he fondled her breasts. Horrified, Gloria closed her eyes, stifled her sobs, afraid that her mother might try doing something that would bring even more pain to them both.

"You know who's the boss around here, don't you!" His breath was foul, his breathing strained, his hand up under her vest. She wanted to collapse in horror as she felt a finger touch the base of her stomach, caressing the slope where it touched her thighs. Now his calloused fingers were doing whatever they wanted with her, while she choked on the viscous bile of her own helplessness.

With his other hand, Riley, as though needing to reinforce his sense of power, squeezed one of her nipples so hard that the girl almost cried out. Somehow she held down her reaction to the pain, afraid of fuelling her mother's pointless resistance to Riley's strength and viciousness. She let her silence feed the fast-growing, violent anger inside her, and for a moment she no longer felt quite as powerless.

"It's time, girl," he said loudly enough for Rebecca to hear. He pulled Gloria against him, taking her hand and pressing it against his rampant erection. "See what Jem has for ye, sweetheart! Jem has a right handle for ye, so he has!" His tone changed, leaving no room for argument. "Now get that skirt off ye, and the knickers too. No messin' now."

Gloria didn't move, and he slammed his groin against her as a final warning. "Do what I tell you, Gloria, or I'll rip the gear off you, so I will!"

A groan of pain-filled despair ripped from Rebecca, and Gloria wanted to get to her to save her from another beating. Riley turned on a sixpence, and he struck the ailing woman an open-handed blow, moving to her to grab her throat in his other hand.

Gloria's response came from beyond her mind and her conscious resolve, her anger finding its voice in a demented yell echoing down the canyons of a mind turned demonic. She seemed to move in slow motion as Riley, bent over Mama's struggling body, turned his face back to her in shock. Gloria was so calm that she seemed removed from what was happening. With all the strength that her body and her will could muster she lashed out. She seemed to be watching, as the ball of her right foot powered against the side of Riley's shaven head. The impact sent a shock wave along the right side of her body, before she sank unconscious to the floor.

A sickening smell greeted Gloria's climb back to consciousness. In a moment, she remembered what had happened. As she clambered to her feet, she found herself looking into the eyes of her mother. She gasped in muted terror. Rebecca's eyes were distorted by something that seemed to have bent her mind out of shape.

Gloria took her mother by her upper arms and held her firm, willing her own new-found resolve into Rebecca's battered heart. She pressed harder, so moved that they were both still alive and that they were free for the moment. She needed to weep but she forced the tears off. This was no time for that.

Riley was lying in his own foul mess, like a dead man, on the floor. Gloria was tempted by a very strong, violent urge to find a weapon of some kind and beat him to a pulp. Had her mother not been standing close, she felt she might well have done just that. She bit her lip to gain purchase on her ability to focus, terrified that if she allowed one scream to tear out of her heart she might never again stop wailing.

Not knowing what else to do, she shook Rebecca. "Mama, can you hear me?" She held her breath, terrified that her mother had been driven all the way over the edge. "Mama, we can't stay here. We have to get out of here. Can you walk at all?" Gloria waited, willing her words, and the powerful sense of urgency in her voice, to reach her mother. "Mama, we have to move out, in case . . ."

She couldn't finish the thought. If Rebecca could hear, understand anything, she would know what he would do to them both, should he ever get the chance.

Again she felt herself nudged by the thought that she could make sure that never happened – some inner voice urging her, 'Take Mama downstairs, leave her a moment, come back to the room and slit his gullet'.

With wings of panic tearing like hungry birds at her sanity, Gloria dismissed the notion, and got on with the task of getting her mother out of the room. They were on the first floor. She sighed heavily, shouldering as much of Rebecca's weight as she could cope with, and slowly, very slowly, they began the mountainous climb down the stairs to the street.

Euston Road, the main artery from Marylebone to north-east London, was a busy mass of vehicles. Broughams and carrioles, sidecars and hackneys, vehicles of every known design fought for the space in which to speed on their way, the electric trams adding their own particular sound. The added clatter of the commercial traffic drowned the cracking of whips, and the bawdy ribaldry from many of the drivers, to any female catching the eye of the rascal holding the whip.

Gloria heard the raucous whistle of a train, gritting her teeth against the complaints her body was making. She felt her mother respond to the shrill screech of the whistle, and together they found the will and the strength they needed to press on with the main business of the day, staying alive.

Rebecca pressed a small purse into her daughter's hand. "Your grandfather's sovereigns," she whispered, her voice choking on the cusp of memory. "He saved a penny here, a penny there, a hundred pennies to make one rouble. Imagine the time it took for him to save one sovereign."

Gloria had the train tickets to Holyhead in her hand. Mama leaned against the wall by the ticket grille, relying on her daughter's shoulder as the girl put the change into the pocket of her skirt.

As they stuttered along the platform towards the train, Rebecca found the strength to wonder would she live long enough to get to Ireland. Whatever else happened, she wanted to keep her promise to her beloved husband, father to Gloria, taken so young and so brutally, because he was an honest man. He would be thirty-nine now had he lived. How he would have loved seeing his daughter become such a beautiful, gifted young woman.

"Ireland, Rebecca," the words had been among the last he ever uttered, she responding to his need of her promise, knowing that had she not been carrying his child, she would have died by her own hand from grief along with him in the East End of London.

The train journey from Euston to Holyhead seemed endless to Gloria. She knew they had to get to north Wales to take a ship across to Ireland, a small country that had been called *the land of saints and scholars*. Gloria was not in the least impressed by the idea. The man who had destroyed their lives had never stopped bragging that he was Irish, hating anybody that dared point out he was an Englishman, since he'd been born in Liverpool.

As the train bored a hole in the distance, punching

north-west through England, great streamers of steam and smoke billowing around it, Gloria helped Mama to the lavatory. She washed her as best she could, with all the care she could find, her every heartbeat willing her mother to hold onto life. She was appalled when she saw how much blood Mama was losing, but held her nerve that she might ease Rebecca's discomfort as best she could.

Later, when she had settled her mother into her seat, she choked back burning tears as Rebecca said in a hoarse whisper, "Forgive me failing you so." Stifling her own need to weep, holding the girl close, as though fearful of letting her go, Rebecca was too ill, too tired and beaten to feel any concern as other passengers reacted in discomfort. "You deserved a better mother, a mother that didn't lie down with a dog. Forgive me, girl."

Gloria clung to her mother, literally choking on emotion, never wanting to let go of Mama. "You're my whole world, Mama. I love you more than my life. We will survive and come through this terrible time together."

She forgave herself the lie, trying not to think or she would instantly scream from fear. She caressed her mother's face, believing that her own fingers would turn lifeless if her mother died. If Mama were taken from her, what would be the point of trying to go on living?

They dozed fitfully, holding onto each other, the girl keeping an eye on Rebecca's every move, an ear on each and every sound Mama made. Finally in the early hours of the morning, they emerged from the train. Rebecca was losing blood still, struggling bravely to respond to Gloria's unselfish efforts to protect her, shield her from the jostling crowd of people hurrying to get on the steam packet to Ireland.

Aboard the ship, Gloria knew that the first priority was to find a place for her mother to lie down. At Euston station she had been told that for third class passengers it was first-come first-served. In one corner of the crowded saloon a bunch of people tuned up musical instruments, clearly preparing to have a jolly time on the voyage. Gloria picked out a large, curly-headed man as the leader of this party. He was a man used to giving orders, his baritone voice and his demeanour suggesting he was a man of the world, not someone to trifle with. He responded in some surprise when Gloria spoke to him. She was well aware of her down-at-heel appearance, understanding his reaction as she spoke to him in perfect English, with just a hint of Eastern Europe on the edge of her accent.

"Forgive me troubling you, sir, but I wonder if you could spare one of those seats for my mother? She is rather unwell."

"My dear young lady, you may have as many seats as you need, though you seem to be alone." His accent was borderline gentry, but Gloria, after some years surviving on the London streets, detected the peal of Bow Bells, and felt very grateful for his cockney smile and his generous air.

"My mother is ill, sir, resting on deck. Would you help me to bring her here?" Gloria dropped her guard. This was no time for pride, Mama so desperately in need of help.

Big Bill Boswell hurried out of the saloon behind Gloria, calling to his wife Emily, and beckoning to a couple of his men to follow him. Taking control, he created a passage for them, as if by magic.

Rebecca, barely conscious, was slumped against the ship's rail. Emily Boswell glanced knowingly at her husband, who, with a nod of his head lifted Rebecca up in his arms. Gloria allowed the older woman to take her arm and lead her along behind the man bearing her mother. They began to descend an iron staircase. The lower deck of the ship was given over to all kinds of vehicles, including four wagons bearing the legend Big Bill Boswell's Bohemian Band in large multi-coloured lettering. The horses, resting between the shafts of the four-wheeled wagons, were munching away inside their nosebags.

Bill Boswell, displaying gentleness surprising in such a big man, laid Rebecca down on the bed in his caravan. Emily held a damp cloth to her forehead, a teaspoon of cognac to her lips, shielding what she felt from the girl with the violet eyes and the tumbling mass of blue-black hair.

Bill stood back, quietly insisting that Gloria sip a little brandy. "It won't hurt you one bit, my dear."

She allowed him to press the glass into her hand, gasping as the cognac created a burning sensation in her throat. In a few moments she somehow put her heart pain aside, and gave her mind to the task of willing Mama to live, denying room to the fear that it was already too late.

Oblivious to her whereabouts, Rebecca could hear voices softly sounding. Papa was there. Sarah, dear Sarah Elkins was there too, along with Papa. Papa was smiling, beckoning to her, telling her it was good where he was, a safe place to be. He was beckoning to her. Come home. She wanted to speak, needing to say something, hearing a whisper escape her throat on the words, "Gloria, I love you." The pain's weight was lighter, oh, gradually, yes, even lighter still. Oh relief, blessed relief, the pressure easing-going-going-lighter than ever before, no longer weary, going to rest gladly, easily, going home, coming, Papa.

Gloria choked on a broken cry, shocked mute for a moment as she saw the light fade from her mother's eyes, scarcely feeling Emily's arm encircle her shoulders, barely hearing her voice, laden with care, "You are not alone, child. Your dear mother would be very proud of you."

The brandy glass slipped from Gloria's fingers. She bent over and almost fell onto the bed. She lifted her mother up into her arms, choking on the denial that scorched her throat. 'No, no, no! No!!!!!! This cannot be. Mama! Mama! Open your eyes please, Mama, please!!!!!' She held down the need to scream until her mind lost its reason and she knew nothing, hearing only this pitiful screeching. It was a young girl's voice trying to empty pain from a heart that could no longer endure.

"Mama, Mama, I can't go on. How can I live without you? You are my rock. You can't be taken from me."

Gloria rocked her mother like a baby in her arms, powerless to stop the animal-like sounds of denial tearing from her throat. Emily stood quietly by, letting the girl go on with her ritual, knowing how necessary the keening was as it tumbled through the flood of tears from the heart-broken girl, while the ship's siren moaned its dry, lonely warning over the waters of St George's Channel, and Gloria kissed her mother's face for the last time.

Agony had deafened the young woman. She was too demented to hear her own despair, her heart tearing itself against the jagged walls of anger and loss, and the hatred of Riley that choked her yet and imprisoned her spirit.

Bill Boswell allowed the stricken girl to unleash the pain as he held his weeping wife against his chest. "Let the lass weep till the tears run dry," he whispered. "Let her weep and wail until the unacceptable is no longer turned away at the gate." He kissed his wife's forehead, reminded yet again by life, that death was always hardest on loved ones left behind.

Emily dropped to her knees now, praying that this unbearable loss would not scar the girl permanently. "Lord, Lord, help this poor child in her hour of desolation."

Her husband stood there by the bed, observing the

peace granted in the passing over as it turned Rebecca's death mask into the face of a younger woman. He sighed, not unmoved by his witnessing of the woman's going. But he was more concerned as to what to do about the girl – there was no point in him taking any of the grief on board. He would need all his energy for things that afflicted the living, so he would reserve his strength that he might give the girl the help she was certainly going to need.

Gloria couldn't pray. She was mindless now to any belief she might have held. Her grief was so powerful that the years of nourishing, loving tuition by her mother counted for nothing. All of Rebecca's devotion to truth and love, it was all torn asunder, rent from the seventeen-year-old heart, the first flowering of her womanhood violated by the robbery of the one life on earth she cherished more than her own.

Her mind began to clear but her anger remained on its hind legs, a wild horse of fury lashing out blindly in the face of such immense loss. Gloria, who had learned scripture and the psalms, spat her defiance into the face of God.

"Do it to me! Take me, I dare you! Mama was the finest lady ever to grace this earth. She was all and everything to me. She was entitled to peace and love after all she had come through. She walked from tyranny pulling a cart. Mama buried her own father by a roadside in Lithuania. My own father was ripped from her life while she was carrying me. My father, the love of her heart, he was butchered by mindless men, too rotten to be called animals. He was murdered simply because he was an honest man obeying the law. You know what happened to him. Why bring them together, two beautiful, loving people, why do that, then allow my papa be killed, gutted before my mother's eyes? And now you rob me as you robbed my mother. I will never forgive you for what you have done to Mama and me this day."

Strong hands drew Gloria to her feet in the caravan. She didn't resist, allowing Bill to sit her down at the table where Emily had tea ready to drink. The older woman looked into the girl's eyes as she said, "I want you to have a good wash while I find you something to wear." Gloria shook her head, dismissing the impossible, dissolving into another flood of tears.

"And then," Emily pressed on firmly in the same tone, "you and I will attend to your dear mother." She sniffed back her own tears. "I realise no words can help you at this time. But we will, you and I, attend to your mother's corpse. It's only proper. I know your mother would wish you to go on. How she would hate it if her passing was to deprive you of the will to live."

Over the years Emily had played nurse and confidante to many of Bill's strolling players, nursed any number of broken hearts, calmed many an angry soul, salved a lot of pain, heard many secrets. Now she pressed on with her no-nonsense approach, knowing this was what was needed. And Emily was right. Gloria was so shattered by grief she needed to be told what to do. Bill left things to Emily, knowing that if he was needed in the rescue of the girl's will to live, his wife would let him know.

He had plenty to occupy his mind. He was breaking in a new character actor who was very trying to his patience, writing a couple of one-hour melodramas for the season ahead in Ireland, and he was learning new material he had written for his comedy turn in the variety section of his touring show. He was also keeping a close eye on his juvenile lead, whose good looks had gone to his head since the last tour in the north of England.

The funeral ritual always seemed theatrical to Bill Boswell. He was fond of the manner in which the grief of loss, and the celebration for a life well lived could bring people together. The next day he stood at the funeral by Gloria's side, in the Jewish cemetery at Ballybough on the north side of Dublin city. Emily stood on the other side of the girl, holding Gloria's arm as though she was her own daughter. It was Emily who encouraged her to read the few lines she had written down as her last words to her mother.

"Release us all from hatred, Lord. The King has delivered us from the hands of our enemies. He rescued us from the Philistines."

Emily knew the girl had served the moment well, using words taught her by her departed parent. "Your mother is not alone, child. Her spirit is with God, her body surrounded by your own race."

Gloria nodded, wishing she could show more gratitude to Emily. She stayed for a while, wanting to be there with her mother and the other men, women and children – people from Russia, Germany, Poland, France, as well as in Portugal and Spain – that had been laid to rest alongside their Irish brothers and sisters in the plot of sacred ground belonging to Dublin's small Jewish community since the early part of the eighteenth century.

On the way back to Kingsbridge where Bill Boswell had parked the touring wagons on the southside bank of the river, Emily took Gloria's hand.

"As you have no relations or friends here in Ireland, will you consider staying on with Bill and me? We'd love it if you would, if you think it would be good for you."

Gloria hugged the buxom woman, while she sniffed back another threat of tears. "What would I have done without you both?" she buried her face in Emily's broad shoulder. "If you'll bear with me until I can harness my sadness, I'll work hard to pay my way."

"Good," Emily smiled, her expressive eyes brightening in relief. "We'll find a place for you in the company, and you can earn your keep. You have too much spirit to want it any other way."

"I am a singer," Gloria said quietly. "I can play string instruments as Mama could. I have our songs to sing. I won't let you down."

"I know that, my dear. Both Bill and I felt you were someone very special, right from the moment we laid eyes on you. We will look after you. We have all known the loss of a loved one."

The next day Emily dressed Gloria in a black taffeta frock with a red trim she had added when she bought the garment. It revealed enough of the girl's honey-coloured skin at the shoulder and breast, to have the young men of any town come back again and again to see her onstage.

Gloria was not only beautiful, she was exotic-looking, and she had already displayed her gifted musicianship on the guitar for Bill and Emily, singing songs written by herself and her mother.

"These are some of the songs Mama and I busked on the streets of London," Gloria said simply, trying to discard the thought 'until death came to call in the shape of Jem Riley'.

One week later, Big Bill Boswell's Bohemian Band opened the first night of the Irish tour in County Westmeath, and Gloria had to sing one encore after another in the variety half of the evening's entertainment. The Boswells had taught her a couple of Irish ballads, both of them being very impressed, not only by her instant recall of words and melody, but by the way she used her personal sadness to help her sell the song that she was singing.

"She was made for this business," Bill said emphatically.

Emily smiled, disinclined to disagree with her husband.

9

Dunbla, County Dublin

July 5th 1902

At Dunbla House, some seven miles south-east of the city, Seamus is on duty in the master's bathroom, the clock hand moving toward the noon hour. At the moment he is adding a large pot of boiling water to Arthur Brewer's bath. The man himself, to the relief of his man-servant, appears to be coming back to life.

Arthur, no longer referred to as young Arthur, since his father retired to France with an enchanting mistress, is recovering from his hangover sufficiently enough to cause his temporary state of paralysis to consider departing from his mind and body.

Up to this moment, the twenty-nine-year-old master of the Brewer dynasty has not yet been capable of viewing the morning from his recently-built personal home lying on the east coast between Dalkey and the bay of Killiney, which just now compares favourably with its Italian twin at Naples. In such fashion, Ireland dons her golden coat under the ocean of sky above the silver sea, presenting a morning fit to make you gasp in such delight that you might allow the greater glory of a beneficent god.

The young man in the bathtub of piping hot water is now capable of raising his hand to take the flute of Veuve Cliquot provided by his goat-faced servant. The same man, himself bereft of any sliver of pain, having vetted several glasses of the bubbly just to be certain it is right and ready, is waiting on his master's pleasure.

Seamus feels chirpy since no pain lingers from last night – it might well have done had he not been intelligent enough to down a full bottle of the champers before trusting himself to attend to the needs of his master. He grimaces for a few moments in sympathy as Arthur drinks his flute down the hatch. His mouth becomes a moue as his master convulses for several seconds into a shuddering ritual, which, since he is shedding water left and right over the bathroom floor, might well remind a person of an Afghan hound leaving a river and divesting itself of the water in its coat. As the gasping and the shuddering ceases, the re-born man's devoted retainer smiles grandly to himself in relief, on behalf of them both.

'You're the two ends of a whore, so y'are, Mister Arthur, when you're on the tear!' Seamus reflected privately in his own affectionate way, carefully adding another great jug of freshly-boiled uisce to the bath turned tepid while he'd been nipping out to the top floor pantry for another glass of the VC. The goaty man from Cahirciveen in the county of Kerry, to which, in the privacy of the bed he shared with Angela, he often referred to as 'the arsehole of Ireland', would admit with his natural candour that this particular sipping was for the sheer joy of drinking the blessed nectar since yesterday's toll on the system has already been relieved by the most agreeable healing fuel.

Putting the jug back on top of the great bathroom stove, Seamus glances out of a huge Georgian window. His vision captures the sea and the curve of Killiney bay in time to see a steam train disappear from sight as it enters the tunnel through the mountain on the way to Wicklow town and Arklow and beyond. He shakes his head in wonderment. How they made a locomotive move at such speed, and how the hell they had ever bored a tunnel through all that rock . . . Well, awesome was the only word for it.

He now pours another flute of champagne for Arthur Brewer, and wonders would his young master ever quit drinking quite so much. He allows that he himself can bend the elbow with the best, but, ah, what was the use in speculating. His hopes for the man he has cherished in his heart since he laid eyes on him twenty-two years ago had not been realised.

Unfortunately, to the manservant's mind, Arthur was his father's son, a drop off the old sweat. The son of the father spent too many nights drinking in hotels and the fancier fancy-houses of Monto.

This leaning towards the dark, seamier side of Dublin night-town – the company of tarts and whores and madams and pimps and criminals, and gents that were not gentlemanly in this milieu, this penchant for the late, late night-time where politicians seeking something other than your vote, and lawyers only too willing to break the law in search of sensation – was the norm. It seemed to have been passed on to Arthur, as part of the inheritance that made him one of the richest men in the British Empire.

Seamus's mind ruminated on Arthur's lifestyle. 'Consortin' with whores'd rob yer wallet, their ponces ready to pounce if you make a sound, not touchin' him though for fear of me comin' down on them with my own team of heavy-handed lads from the Kingdom. Jesus help any that ever tried to hurt Mister Arthur. He has his faults but he's one of the best and most decent skins ever drew breath. But God, I'd give my life to see him settled with a good woman'd give him the comfort he'll never find in the bed of a whore, I don't care how hard she's willing to pleasure him to earn the rent. I doubt he'll ever get married, and I often think it's because he doesn't feel entitled to a decent woman.'

Seamus cut the speculation with a sigh of chagrin and the silent chastisement, 'Ah, shure. What do I know about anything? He could outlive me since I haven't minded myself as well as I might have done, only thanks to Angela the liver still works, and who the hell is goin' to take care of him when I'm providin' dinner for the worms in the bloody cemetery?'

He found for the moment that his concern was fuelling ongoing words he had no need to hear yet again. 'The work could save him for a good while, I suppose. He works like a dog when he's workin' and his heart stays good. The plans he drew up as a twelve-year-old already making his ideas heard by myself and Victoria and Lisa, plans for the benefit of the brewery workers, some of his ideas were now in operation and causin' the fear of Christ to rise up in many a business heart in Dublin. A little genius, that young lad. Ongoing so he is in that department, he wants to share the business with the men who do the work. Just let the bankers and the people in the business community try and stop him. He'll go the whole hog so he will, the workers will be shareholders in the brewery and its cousins, the other companies he's getting involved in all the time. He's going to be a blessing in the lives of a lot of people, if not in his own.'

He found himself remembering things long forgotten. 'The poor mite was so ill for so long. God! The days of agony when just a handful of us were there, wondering would he even survive the horror that Constance cast into his life the day she threw Lisa out of Lough Bray.'

He took a fresh bottle of champagne from the water bucket, the magnum in danger of sticking to his flesh. For a moment he pressed the chilled bottle against his forehead. He felt very hot and very bothered. Too much wine, he allowed, as he let the cork press itself out of the bottle's neck, reining it in when it might have exploded across the bathroom. As he poured the sparkling wine into Arthur's glass he licked his lips. Another glass or two, and I won't call the queen me aunt. He shook off all the thoughts that were queuing up to invade his mind. He had to attend to the needs of the boss.

Arthur accepted the fresh glass and unceremoniously dumped it down the hatch. He burped, bright enough now to make conversation.

"Sweet, you say, Seamus?"

Seamus smiled, and shook his head to himself. Arthur Brewer could come out of a hangover you could hang your coat on and go right into a conversation you'd been having the day before. The strange thing was that although he would pick up something already spoken – as he had just done in remembering the name of Victoria's new friend – he might not remember anything more. But then again, he could surprise you.

Seamus poured again for Arthur and quietly filled a glass for himself. He felt it slide all the way down, like a prayer answered with love.

"Unusual name, Mister Arthur. By all accounts he is an unusual man."

Seamus had donned the role of being major-domo to Arthur on the attainment of the young man's majority as the age of twenty-five. This was five years earlier than usual at the insistence of his father, who had retired from public life to devote all his time and energy to a stunning nubile mistress of dubious character. Since that day Seamus had made a point of never slipping into the role of friend; those days were behind them.

"Yes, sir," he continued, since he knew that Arthur

was waiting to hear more. "He's a Jew, born in Dublin. His parents came here from Germany. He's a forceful character, regarded as dashing by the ladies, but not brash or what you might call vulgar. I understand that he's always been a hard worker and by all accounts, a man intent on becoming independent. Not someone to trifle with is my impression. I've been asking questions since Miss Victoria and I made his acquaintance, courtesy of Anna Livia Plurabelle."

"Oh, yes. I remember now," Arthur held up his empty flute and Seamus poured. "Indeed, a brave fellow. Am I remembering the story correctly? He did attempt to rescue a street boy from the Liffey." He felt sure he had heard the story from Victoria, too. He smiled philosophically, and tried to recall whether he believed Vicky had been talking like a woman in love, or like someone about to be in love. Arthur was unconcerned. However it worked out, nothing would change Vicky. He couldn't think of anything that would change anything that mattered about his gifted twin. As nothing would ever change how they were with each other, not ever.

"He arranged for the unfortunate boy to have a funeral, you say?" Arthur seemed to be reading the words off the wall of his memory.

"Yes, sir. The lad got a proper burial at Glasnevin cemetery." Feeling quite moved by the combination of memory and the bubbly he'd been downing by the new time, Seamus went on, "Just the three of us at the graveside, of course. Rotten sad, really! Mister Sweet handled the whole thing. And he looked after Miss

Vicky. She took a weakness as the coffin went into the ground. They seem to care for each other a great deal, Mister Arthur. I'm sure you'd want to know."

He made no mention of the fact that Vicky had been quite ill as they left the morgue at Amiens Street, the day before the funeral. Or that she had allowed Sam Sweet to support her, one arm about her waist, her gloveless hand held faithfully by this new man in her life. To Seamus, these were signposts to a passionate affair. He kept his counsel, deciding to let sleeping dogs lie. In the event he was right, the barking would begin soon enough. He had observed Victoria's interest in the man Sweet from the moment she laid eyes on him by the Liffey.

The following morning as he held the carriage door for her, he saw immediately that infatuation had already moved in and got its feet under the table. In recent weeks she had been dressing down, not interested apparently in looking as good as she could when she paid more attention to her ensemble, and to whatever toiletries she used to enhance her God-given beauty.

"Sweet won't be able to take his eyes off her, so he won't," Seamus thought, as he took in the dove-grey skirt and matching jacket over a blouse of warm pink silk. Her hair, golden in the morning sun, a simple sapphire brooch at her throat . . . of course, Sweet had found her enchanting.

Had it been possible for Seamus to observe Sam Sweet, as he sat facing Victoria in the carriage on the way to the morgue at Amiens Street, he would have chuckled aloud. He would have known Sam was trying to ignore his dry throat, caused by his inability to ignore the swell of her breasts under the beautifully-cut jacket. He would have gathered in an instant that the poor Jew felt pretty helpless in relation to the power of her presence, embraced as he was by the fragrance of her nearness. Practised observer that he was, the manservant would have commented to himself that the man was completely in the grip of an unrelenting desire, one that had nothing to do with ensuring the Christian burial of the drowned urchin.

"Is something wrong, Sam?" Victoria asked ingenuously, as they were heading back to her home at Fitzwilliam, while she somehow hid her delight that he was so clearly taken with her.

"Forgive me staring." Sam smiled self-consciously, wondering if she could read his lecherous thoughts. "I'm not used to riding in carriages with beautiful women." He shrugged his face into a smile, helpless to put it any other way. "I feel a bit disarmed, I have to admit."

"Being with you is disarmingly pleasant for me too," she said frankly. "And I thank you again for your support at the morgue. You were right. It was far beyond my idea of how it would be. Had I thought about it, I might have concluded I shouldn't go there." She opened the silver case – they were both smoking within moments. "That being said, I'm glad I was there with you, if only to experience how wonderful it is to have a real man at one's side. To see how you dealt with it all." She exhaled a smoke ring, smiling as the breeze through the open carriage window quickly swallowed it. To his credit, he certainly had warned her against going with him to make the funeral arrangements.

"This morgue, it's not a place for you," he had spoken carefully. "I've been there before. Let me deal with it. You join me for the funeral."

"Please, Sam, don't be concerned." She resisted the urge to touch his hand, she had removed her gloves just in case this was to happen. "I've lived in and painted in the slums of London and Paris, so have no fear for my sensibilities. I'll be fine." She smiled at his look of disbelief. "I'm serious, Sam. I have slept on the streets of Paris, spent nights in the opium dens of London's East End. I paint every aspect of life without judgment."

Her assurance had drained out of her when the morgue attendant in Amiens Street said to Sam, "Which one, mister?"

Sam's eyes flicked from the tired-looking little man to Victoria. She tried to express reassurance, let him know that she was all right. She failed miserably.

He shrugged and said to her quietly, "We have to look at more than one."

Victoria was dismayed at her own squeamishness and she had held onto his arm impulsively, seeking steadiness, aware at the same time that the ever-devoted Seamus was taking it all in. Not that she minded this. She had very few secrets from the Kerry man, who had been a rock to Arthur and herself.

They followed the attendant along a passage, Sam allowing that he was excited since Victoria was now entrusting her hand to him. For God's sake! What man's heart wouldn't beat like a drum at the thought of holding her hand! Never mind having the experience.

The attendant opened a door, and a distinct odour made Sam want to vomit. He glanced at Victoria. Her lips were pressed tight. Seamus took her other arm as they followed the man into a large room.

"We got four in the last few nights," the little Dubliner said in his lifeless monotone. "Take a gander for yourself, sir. One's been asked after, the other three are paupers."

The large gloomy room housed many slabs. Mercifully, Sam found the remains of the young pickpocket under the first grey sheet. He heard Victoria's intake of breath, and put his arm around her. "Let Seamus take you out of here, while I make the arrangements."

She exhaled volubly, "I'm all right, really."

"Be quicklime for him," the attendant nodded impartially, his rheumy eyes like harbingers of a fatal disease. "There was nothing on it, the body, when it was brought in here. Not a coin a medal, scrappa paper, nothing. The mother a Monto whore, most likely."

Sam caught the man's eye, a blade of warning in his own. The Dub held his breath and looked uneasy, inclining his head by way of apology.

"Saving your presence, lady," he shrugged at Sam. "Monto – the women throw them out on the street the minute they can walk. Then they're old enough to beg and rob," he peered at Sam. "I can tell you're not related, sir. What's your interest, if you don't mind me asking?"

"I want him to have a decent burial," Sam answered, wanting to slap the attendant. "He's not going into any quicklime!"

"I'll look after it for you, sir. I'll bring in an undertaker." The little Dubliner sensed there could be something in it for him. "Any way I can be a help, sir, you only have to ask."

Sam gave him a half crown, "Attend to it. I'll see you right! Nothing fancy, but decent. I want him buried tomorrow at Glasnevin. I'll pay the undertaker at the grave. Fix it for eleven o'clock tomorrow."

In the bathroom at Dunbla House, Arthur asked for one last glass of champagne before he left the bathtub, and his manservant returned to the present. He decided against having any more of the bubbly himself. He had to help the boss get ready for the trip to England, and he was feeling a tad wobbly even now.

"Be interesting to see what you make of Miss Vicky's friend, sir." He thrust logs into the flat-topped wood-burning stove, installed to provide constant hot water for the upper floors of the shoreside house. Arthur Brewer liked his premises to be warm, and to be maintained free of the dampness that is part and parcel of living by the ocean.

LEE DUNNE

"Did you tell me he's already working on the renovations to Vicky's place at Fitzwilliam? The moment I return from this trip I'm going to lunch to meet the man himself." Arthur sounded as though he was looking forward to it. He had been impressed by the Liffey story, Seamus reflected, so it was a dot on the card he'd want to meet the hero of Victoria's heart.

A month later, on the day before Arthur was due to come to meet Sam, Vicky knew she was in love with the man from Little Jerusalem. The previous day, all the renovation work on her new home had been finished, and she and Sam had decided to go to the Shelbourne for a celebration dinner.

Vicky felt good about her newly-decorated house. She had been impressed from the inception of the renovations by the sterling quality of the workmanship, and the fact that Sam made certain everything was perfect.

This attention to detail had carried right through to the cleaning work at the end, which had left the house spotless as a new pin after six weeks of renovation, rebuilding and decoration. Before they left to go for dinner, Victoria proposed a toast. "To us, Sam." They touched glasses and sipped the champagne, their eyes fixed on each other. "To our wonderful friendship, honesty between us, at all times."

Sam responded with a tiny bow of his head, a disarming smile on the mouth she wanted so badly to kiss. "If I don't wake up to discover that this was all a wonderful dream, I might just allow that there is a God," he said, his smile broadening, his sound light-hearted. They were then standing close enough that Vicky felt she could see her own deep feelings for him, mirrored in his midnight eyes.

"I don't frighten you by drinking to honesty and openness between us?" she asked.

He shook his head in answer to her question, his eyes filled with all that was there between them. She went to him and he stood awestruck as he realised she was about to kiss him. Their lips touched for the first time and his champagne glass fell to the carpet. Her arms were about him, the length of her body vulcanised to him. They locked into an embrace that could only be the prelude to the love-making they had been aching to know since they first laid eyes on each other.

Dinner was instantly forgotten in the heat of their power and their passion for each other, and within minutes they were welded together on one of the vast couches at the marble fireplace. Without a word they had come to this sharing – all of the moves and the shedding of garments happened as if by magic. In a matter of moments, he completely captured her by the force of his passion, and the power of his comings and goings. Moments later, the thrusting ceased, his gentleness took her by surprise, his tenderness so lyrical, so unexpected that she soon wept in wonder. Here was the first man ever to make love to her as though he was there to serve her needs and her every desire, rather than simply drive towards his own release. Her heart pounded to its own music, as he took her on his blessed ride, and she heard her voice praising and urging, her ears turning deaf then as she fought to be there along with him when he went tumbling from the height they had climbed together.

His unselfishness allowed her to give to him in kind, which she did so willingly. At the same time she found herself wallowing blissfully in the sheer physical beauty of his body, while he soared like an eagle with the most wonderful lover he had ever had.

In this way, they began to discover each other beyond what had been in the days gone before. This night neither of them was concerned about bricks and mortar, plaster and paint, plumbing and papering. They were out of sight, lost to the debits and credits of day-to-day living. The wish that had landed on their lives in the early startling moments was coming true with its own sweet melody.

Some days later Arthur came to lunch to meet Sam Sweet. Vicky had borrowed the services of the second cook and an upstairs maid from his new home at Dunbla House. Seamus had driven the staff into her house at Fitzwilliam Square, before going to Stephen's Green to collect Arthur at his club where he had spent the night on his return from England. Coming through the front door for the first time, Arthur was delighted to find Vicky glowing with a sparkling and he thought rude happiness as she presented Sam as 'my good friend and confidant'.

Arthur Brewer, tall, slightly-built, with a gentle handshake and a shy smile, stood some inches taller than Sam, his shoulders pointing forward slightly, his self-consciousness about his six feet three inches in height never far away.

"It's an honour to meet you, sir," Sam said without a qualm. To shake the hand of such a man, a captain of industry, master of such vast wealth, a powerhouse behind his diffident social manner, was a moment he expected to remember for a long time.

Over lunch the two men enjoyed the time in Victoria's new home. Arthur was relaxed, and she was not disturbed by her belief that he had been drinking during the morning. It was just Arthur. That was how he needed to be sometimes.

She knew that he liked Sam, which pleased her in a separate way. Sam was clearly taken with him. This was something she had hoped for, having decided that her new man was the right man to be a good friend to Arthur. She felt sure about this, knowing that she would trust Sam with her life. That was how she had to feel, to consider him for the role of friend to her beloved twin. She was all too aware that Arthur had no man he could trust. Seamus was the exception to this, but of course that was in a different context. Arthur had no real friend among his own class any more than she could name one that she would take for a lover, never mind a husband. They had friendly acquaintances, people of their own kidney and in business Arthur had colleagues and contacts, but no man he considered a genuine friend.

Victoria knew that in Sam he would find a loyal person who sought no favour. She was sure of this and felt good about the way the meeting developed. The warmth between the two men was a good beginning, one that would before long benefit both, while she would be part of the sharing of happier times that lay ahead.

Just one week after her house at Fitzwilliam was free of the smell of fresh paint, Victoria gave a small dinner party. In truth, she was so in love with Sam, so happy to be his woman that she wanted to show him off, drive some of her acquaintances mad with jealousy. But this was not going to be that kind of dinner party. Sam was too special to be waved in people's faces like a trophy. She chuckled gleefully, like a happy schoolgirl, when she remembered yet again that he was the first man that had ever left her satiated and smiling, and in need of sleep. So their first dinner party was to be shared with just one very special person.

When Sam arrived to attend the first formal dinner party of his life, he was surprised to find that the only other guest was Arthur. Neither of the men commented on the fact that there were only three of them, and Vicky seemed totally relaxed as they once again hit if off in a casual, easy-going way. They had both admitted liking each other, something she had hoped for from the moment she knew that Sam was going to play an important part in her life. And she was not just thinking romance or marriage, knowing somewhere deep inside that there would be much more to their relationship than any of that.

"Surprise is allowed, Sam," Arthur, 'a tad tipsy' according to Victoria, opened the conversation. "My doing, really, since I asked Vicky if we could have just the three of us."

Victoria allowed this, though as far as she could remember, she hadn't mentioned dinner for three to her brother. Sometimes Arthur forgot what had taken place the night before, and there was the odd time when he would take credit for something not of his doing, without realising that this was happening. What did it matter? She smiled inwardly as her mind suggested, yet again, that he might be a little bit crackers. So what? She asked herself. Anybody interesting she had met in her life had been some kind of bonkers, and she made no bones about including herself in this view. The fact that Sam had changed his name at the age of seventeen, and eschewed Judaism while still so young, meant that he was entitled to be a member of the same club.

Arthur smiled ruefully, "I have a proposition to offer you, Sam, and I rather wanted to speak of it just between the three of us, provided you have no objection to discussing a little business over dinner?"

Sam felt his pulse quicken and he returned Vicky's squeezing of his hand on the tablecloth. "I'm at your service, Arthur."

"You'll understand, I'm sure, when I tell you I have

made enquiries about you. This would be in the way of protecting Vicky, and I believe that as you truly care for her, you will be glad of my interest in her welfare."

"Absolutely," Sam nodded.

Arthur sipped his glass of Beaujolais before continuing. "The excellent reports I received, to one side, let me say that your workmanship is *par excellence*, first rate, and the speed at which it was carried out here tremendous! So one can safely say you run a tight ship. You know your stuff."

"The right way is the only way," Sam said, with a glance at Victoria.

"At this time," Arthur's words flowed effortlessly, the wine ensuring that there was no hint of insecurity in his normally diffident manner, "at this time, I am about to build a major extension to the brewery. I am not happy with the people who expect to be involved. As I've suggested, my agents have informed me that you deliver first-class work, that you are totally honourable which, incidentally, makes you something of a rare commodity." Arthur sipped his wine before continuing. "In the event you are interested, that you would take on the extension work, I'd be happy to offer the contract to you."

Sam was speechless for several moments before he said quietly, "I'm flattered, Arthur, and my immediate answer would be yes, of course. But . . ."

Arthur raised his hand, "Any problems relating to finance, any and all of that can be dealt with without any great difficulty. I give you my personal guarantee of that. Does that eliminate your reservations?"

"Yes, it does. And I thank you for the opportunity." Sam glanced at Victoria. "Young lady, you look like the proverbial Cheshire cat."

"Oh, I'm so happy," she exclaimed tipsily, raising her glass in an impromptu toast. "Great days ahead of us, oh yes."

There was no more talk of business that evening. Sam agreed to be at Arthur's town office the next day at noon. Arthur wanted to go to work on the logistical plan for the operation without delay.

Arthur left around ten o'clock and Vicky sat down, a glow of satisfaction about her. She faced Sam on the other side of the marble fireplace. Her hair was golden in the soft light from the oil lamp on the occasional table beside her.

"I want you tell me why you have been held down by the business community of this city. You are not the kind of man who bumbles through life, working hard without results. The situation – it doesn't fit with the man I've come to know. I've heard a rumour, even though one tries not to listen to that kind of gossip. I'd like to hear your version of the story. If you feel you can tell me."

"I'll tell you the story," he said, dismissing his initial reluctance. "First let me assure you that I have never taken a liberty with any man in my life. I have never struck the first blow in any fight I've had; never stolen from a man; I have never robbed another man's wife. You know I employ four men on a permanent basis, bring in extra hands when I need them?"

She nodded and he smoked as he began the story. "A few years back I had two men working alongside me, a lot of small work, graduating to bigger jobs, my prices lower than some other builders because of my low overheads. Understand," Sam continued behind a ribbon of cigarette smoke, "being in the building game is like being a bandit – you take what you can get when you can get it, or before long you disappear. I was taking small wages myself, trying to develop a business. I worked harder than others did. I had no offices, no big yard with workers hiding rather than earning their pay. These are just some of the reasons I could offer such reasonable rates. It was paying off, bigger jobs coming in, with me bringing in extra workers as I needed them. So I kept my expenses pared to the absolute minimum. I'd work out that I needed a plasterer for three days, and I made sure he did the job in that time. I thought of it as running a tight ship, just as Arthur said.

"Certain people in Dublin didn't see it quite like that. Two brothers called Foran – two big rough-and-ready Corkmen – they said I was undercutting their rates. They were guys who wouldn't have known what being anti-Semitic meant, but they were expert Jew haters. 'You Jews are all the same,' they spat at me. This was the gist of it. They were glaring at me like fellas begging for a fight. 'Wherever you Jews go, you work for less, and you sleep and shit in the same place, and you take the bread out of the mouths of Irishmen and you better quit, or you will be a very sorry jew man'."

Victoria rose to replenish Sam's glass. He indicated he'd had enough. She admired his in-built discipline, still surprised that this quality didn't annoy her. Sam never apologised for the fact that he didn't drink more than two glasses of wine at any one time.

"I didn't concern myself with the threats they made. A lot of Irishmen threaten you when they have drink on board. They can be decent skins the next time you meet them sober. I made a mistake by putting the Foran brothers into that category. I carried on as I'd been going, working around the clock, getting a week's pay to keep myself and my mother alive, paying my workmen and generally minding my own business.

"One night as I was walking home from Harold's Cross, I was only a few hundred yards from home when someone stepped out of a garden as I passed by and clattered me on the head with a wooden batten. Even as I fell down, I realised that whoever hit me had been watching me, checking when I came and went, which route I took coming and going.

"I was close to unconscious, when one of them pulled me up off my back so that my face was level with his. The face belonged to Dinny Foran, the older brother, and he made a big mistake in picking a night to down me when the moon was full. I often thought afterwards that the brothers had to be half-mad, in the grip of the moon madness, to do what they did. It was all very strange, like lunacy, the gift of the moon giving them the craziness. At the same time the pale-faced lady let them down. She did this by lighting Dinny up so well that I could see who he was. There was the cure for a hangover on his breath as he shook me hard. He was half-demented with anger and the need to do me serious damage. His brother stood back. He'd already hit me so hard in the ribs, I thought he'd broken one or two.

"Dinny told me as though he was using a four-pound hammer to pound the warning into my brain, 'Jew boy,' says he, 'this is your last warning. You quit your way of doing business, you quit it now, or I'll put you into the ground. No more warnings, Jew boy. I swear to the Lord Jesus, you cross us again and I'll have your rotten life.' Those were his last words to me, just before he knocked me unconscious, with a fist the size of a ham!"

Victoria face was a missal of denial, her eyes welded to Sam's face, her hands shaking as she lit a cigarette. "It's incredible," she said hoarsely.

"It takes hard men to work hard on a regular basis," he said in a philosophical tone. "Now and then, hard men need to find out just how hard they are. Fights are commonplace on building sites – the Foran brothers had a fearsome name as brawlers. People said that if you crossed them, you might as well emigrate." Sam was looking at the Persian carpet. He drew on the cigarette, wishing he hadn't got into this, finding that he was reliving the memory emotionally, tasting again what it felt like back then. He knew he had to finish the story, that Victoria wouldn't settle for anything less. He vowed to himself this would be the last time, hating the feeling of being sucked back into the quagmire of black emotions that accompanied the repetition of the tale.

"This is really a lovely room now, isn't it?" He was playing with her for a moment, hoping it would take some of the sting out of what was to come.

As though reading his mind, Vicky said, playing sweet, "The rest of the story, Mister Sweet. I'm all agog!"

Sam lit a fresh cigarette. "I was renting a room at an old house on Charlemont Street. I'd moved out from my parents' place in Little Jerusalem, so I went to my pal, Four-Fingered Louie. He had a room in the same tenement. Between the pair of us we bound up my ribs. He used carbolic soap to clean up my cuts and bruises and he put melted lard on the cut to my scalp. He made me strong tea and lashed rum into it to help ease one or two of my aches and pains."

He looked at Victoria, knowing that what he said next was likely to put her feelings for him to the test. Could she hear the rest of the story and still see the man who was now before her? Or would she simply see him as a vengeful animal?

He pressed on. "I had my pony stabled in a lane near Charlemont Street Bridge. I took my time walking up there. I was sort of testing myself out to see if I was fit enough to do what I had in mind. I drove the pony up to the village of Ranelagh. This was where the Forans' property was. I cut the lock off the main gate, went inside, and I did what I had to do. I'd brought with me most of what I needed, finding the rest of it in the complex.

"About half an hour later I drove the pony back across the canal bridge, heading to a site on Richmond Street where I had a job on that day. It was early morning still, so there weren't many people about. I stopped on the bridge to look back towards the village behind me. There was a long swirling cone of smoke so thick and viscous that it might have been raining black mucous. The Forans' place was burning itself to extinction in the biting wind of that March morning.

"By the time the Forans reached their property the buildings no longer existed. I got the story later from one of the fire brigade fellas. Burned-out shells is all that was left of their workshops and storage units, years of work gone up in smoke.

"Shamey Foran broke down, cried like a baby. Dinny went in search of strong drink. The fire brigade officer could tell him nothing of any value, but then he said something that seemed to cut into the big Corkman's heart. 'I would have guessed the fire was set deliberately, Mister Foran. Except that the gate was chained and locked when we got here. There was no sign, like, that somebody broke in to do the damage,' he shrugged. 'We have to keep looking till we find the exact spot where the fire started. It'll be hard, huge damage has been done to the main buildings, all stock and supplies destroyed. It'll have to be built again from scratch.'"

Sam paused and inhaled deeply, wanting to give Vicky time to take it all in. He determined to give her just the facts, not dress the story up to make himself look good. It was a tough and dirty story and he was part of it and it was only fair to allow her see the warts and all.

"The fireman spoke in a matter-of-fact way, but as I would learn later from the mouth of Dinny Foran himself, the man's voice was like a broken bottle ripping into his brain. 'No sign like, that somebody broke in to do the damage.' Those words scorched his mind, while frustration and savage anger mingled with the grime on his face. 'The Jew! The fucking Jew!' Dinny swore out loud to the fireman. 'I shudda killed the kike bastard, when I had him at my mercy.' He picked up a brick and banged it against a wall. 'Only a Jew would think up something like that.' This thought drove Dinny to the main gate. He found the lock and chain I had cut off the gate. It was lying on the grass verge. He saw that a link in the chain had been severed, by a man that knew what he was doing.

"When he gave attention to the lock, Dinny saw right away it was the same lock he had turned the key in when he was closing up last night. He knew I had brought a lock and chain of my own. He yelled at the fireman who told me all this. 'Oh Jesus! I am going to kill this bastard Jew, if it's the last thing I ever do. Dinny Foran swore my life away. The fireman said to me that it frightened him just being so close to such insane anger.

"Meanwhile, I arrived at Richmond Street and set my men to work. I bought a bottle of Red Biddy from the brothel next door to the job. This is wine that you wouldn't drink unless you were in serious pain or addicted to the stuff. I was hurting enough to pour it into myself. I had to be in some kind of shape to deal with the storm that was coming my way from the Forans. And I had to see my pal, Louie. I needed him to help me stay alive when the Corkmen came to call. I got to the tenement in Charlemont Street in time to catch Louie before he set out with his tray of trinkets and pins, and anything else he could sell to help him stay alive another day. He was drinking tea in his room. I gave him the small dark loaf I'd bought from the kosher bakery on Richmond Street, and I drank some of his rum. I gave him a ten bob note, while I told him what I had in mind.

"'You're contemplating a premature demise?' Louie said blithely, not really believing me.

"'Just you remember that when you've done what I've told you to do, you're to slip into your room and stay there till the place is like a tomb or I knock on your door, all right?'

"'I'm not all right! The situation is not all right! The friend, Herschel Green, who is now known as Sam Sweet, is not all right! But, all right!' Louie finished his tea, reacting to my look of get a move on with, 'all right, all right, I'm no longer here, all right?' Then he went outside to sit on the steps leading up to the hall door from the street. His job was to wait there for the brothers to find him.

"When they arrived, Louie was scribbling a few lines into a small copybook. As the brothers loomed over him he looked up in appreciation, 'The twin sons of Gargantua!' he said, as though it were a fact of life, remembering the moment well, just in case I came through alive and wanted to know what had happened.

"'The Jew Sweet – he lives here, right?' Dinny leaned over Louie. 'His breath, Sam, was what you might expect to find in an alligator with a chronic dose of indigestion,' was how Louie described it to me later.

"'Not a nice person,' Louie said to Dinny. 'He has the room behind mine. Second door on the left as you go in.'

"'Show me,' Dinny said, not expecting any argument as he pushed Louie up the granite steps, following him into the dark hallway of the tenement.

"'This is my room. Sweet is in there,' Louie said.

"Dinny Foran threw him aside. 'Get outa here. Find a hole and crawl into it.' As the brothers tiptoed forward, Louie closed the hall door, stepped into his room and turned the key in the lock. As he leaned against the door he heard me say, 'Good morning, men. I imagine you're here to see me.' The brothers turned around, more than surprised to see me step out from behind the hall door.

"'You stinking Jew!' Dinny's diatribe stopped in mid-sentence, as I smashed his left kneecap with this club I made a long time ago from a piece of Indonesian teak. Teak matches steel for hardness and durability. Dinny yelled and fell down, and I stepped forward and smacked Shamey on the side of the head. He keeled over without a sound. Dinny pulled himself up onto his right leg, dislodging a length of the banister rail with one hand. Before he could even think of using it, I punched him in the groin with the club. He tumbled back through the worn rail supports and ended up sitting on the stairs with pain and fury, and God knows what else, bursting out of his eyes. 'I'm going to kill you, Jew,' he swore, looking more demented by the second. I hit him again, carefully this time, on the side of the head. I didn't want to knock him out. I needed to shut him up for a minute.

"'One more threat and I'll kill you stone dead,' I assured him and for one moment, I meant it. 'And I'll do the same for your brother. So shut up and listen. I could kill you right now, and nobody would give a damn. This morning made us even for what you pair did to me last night. I want you to believe you're only living because I don't want your deaths on my conscience. The problem is I live in this city and I intend to go on living in this city. Your problem is that it's not big enough for us all. So you and Shamey, you're going to have to leave Dublin and go back where you came from.' Dinny started to protest. I gave him another poke in the crown jewels with the club. He groaned a bit and I told him the rest of the good news. 'If I ever see either of you in this town again, I'll commit murder. You leave by six o'clock this evening, or I'll do what I say. I swear it on my mother's life.'

"Dinny crumbled, and I called Louie from his room. In moments he was throwing cold water over the brother. Shamey opened his eyes and sat up. He wasn't happy when he saw me the club in my hands. 'Help your brother up,' I told him, 'and get him out of here. He is leaving Dublin by six o'clock this evening and you are leaving with him. If I ever see you again I'll kill you stone dead. Do you understand me?'

"I followed them down the steps to the footpath, and I hailed a passing hackney carriage. 'I shudda killed you last night,' Dinny said to me, with a lot of regret in his voice.

"'Yes, you should,' I agreed. 'If I see you again in this town you'll come to know that I keep my promises. Take it away driver.'

"I stood there as the horse cab moved down the street. Louie stood beside me, and he seemed taller than before, a smile suggesting he was tickled about something.

"'Mazzel Tof!' he said to me.

"'I couldn't have done it without you,' I told him.

"Louie nodded, delighted in himself. 'If anybody ever asks, Sam, you can say I'm your friend!'

"'I'll keep that in mind, Louie,' I told him. 'Now, come on. I'm going to buy you something to eat. I'm starved myself.' And there you have it, Vicky. When the story got around in the trade, I was turned into an outcast by the Jew haters, and a lot of Jews weren't far behind. They were ashamed of me. I don't give a damn but, by definition, the Catholics are anti-Semitic. The Prods are just as bad. And with my own crowd throwing their hat into that particular ring, I had to look to other small builders, people I had done a turn for in the past, to help me get my hands on enough supplies for me to make some kind of a living."

Victoria sat still as Sam finished speaking, sobered somewhat by the story. She might have been seeing him in a darker hue, but he was the one she wanted and she was grateful that there was nothing frivolous about him. His colours were vivid, and yes, violent, but she could admit that she felt for him something beyond being in love, in lust, and she wanted to find out where this would take them. Besides, he was the right man to be there for Arthur, who had need of a real friend. And the beauty of it was, Sam needed Arthur just as much as her twin needed him.

"I'm surprised that firms wouldn't supply you with materials. I mean, whatever happened to 'business is business'?"

"You have to understand. They sold to Forans, a huge firm by comparison to a jobbing builder such as myself. I'd wiped out that serious business concern. I'd cost them a lot of money. Apart from which, I'm a Jew, Vicky. I am an outsider! The fact that I was born here, that doesn't seem to matter. And in hurting two of them, I frightened all of them in a powerful way. I had scared the Forans – that made me a scary fella. They just didn't want to have anything to do with me."

"Was Louie the only Jew who was proud of you?"

Sam nodded his head. "And he's a sort of outsider too. A right pair, you could say!" he grinned ruefully. "So there's the story you insisted on hearing."

"I understand," Vicky said.

She went to him and she kissed him then with a passionate strength that burst from inside her. His arms encircled her as he buried his face in her breasts and she pressed him closer in her wanting, secure in the feeling that for the first time she embraced a man strong enough to hold her, and to satisfy so many of her needs.

10

Dublin City

August 1906

Deirdre Doyle waved goodbye to her father with a sigh of relief. She was standing on the steps of the converted Georgian tenement he had helped turn into one of Dublin's up-and-coming fashion establishments. Two of the floors above the basement were now busy as a tailoring and dress-making business, with a design studio that housed a display and reception area, and back-up facilities for alterations and ironing.

As Pat drove away from the door he sat proudly on the brightly-painted four-wheeled dray that bore his name and the legend – Hackney Transport, Haulage, Retail Food Shops, Clothing Emporiums and Wholesale Wine Supplies, on its sideboards and tailboard – a testament to two decades of hard work and dedication to the prosperity he had set out to earn for himself and his family.

He used the fancy cart, as he called it, to personally

haul materials and other goods for Deirdre's business, from one or other of the city's railway stations or the docks on every other Thursday. He performed this ritual to help her build on the initial success of her business as a fashion designer and dressmaker. This was how Pat saw it anyway, though, like her mother, Deirdre knew it was his need to keep an eye on her and make sure she wasn't doing anything stupid.

Deirdre granted him some leeway, since his money had given her this bright start in business quite soon after her graduation from the City College of Design the year before. But, she knew it was just him, just the way her father was, with his need to control her along with the rest of his family.

She was in her twentieth year, a handsome young woman, her hair in auburn sheaves tumbling to her slender shoulders. She was quite tall and had a resolute nature, her emerald-green eyes unwavering, her perfect, thrusting nose suggesting that nothing was going to stop her moving ahead in life.

Deirdre waited until her father had turned left onto Gardiner Street before she attended to the day that was in it. It was such a glorious summer afternoon, the sky an azure blue, a whisper of breeze wafting the perfume of the flowers in the huge communal garden across the street in her direction. She loved the garden, and had been inspired to some of her best colour creations by time spent in what she thought of as her oasis in the square.

As she turned to go back in to the studio, she

reflected again on how lucky she had been to have her mother's total backing for her business project. Her father was such a conservative man that anything smacking of different simply hijacked his reason. As he viewed it, Deirdre, having been educated by the nuns at Loreto until she was sixteen, should have been seeking a post in a well-run ladies' shop, or as a junior clerk in an insurance office.

"Don't you mind him, Dee," Elizabeth Doyle had settled the matter, while they were alone together. "You know what he's like. We'll just go ahead, and tackle what we have to do to get you the training you need. That's the first step. Don't fret. You're not going to finish up in a haberdashery or an office, not as long as my name is Lizzie."

From the time she was fourteen, Deirdre had been sketching all manner of things, and nobody doubted her artistic flair. It was Elizabeth who noticed that when she produced a drawing of a lady, the clothes were much more interesting and alive than the female figure. It was through this recognition of Dee's specialist talent that the dream to be a fashion designer was born. Her father knew nothing of this until the day his wife enrolled Deirdre in the College of Design at the age of seventeen.

That this happened was entirely due to her mother's energy and her influence over her husband, who deferred everything relating to the girls to his wife. Years earlier Elizabeth had taken back the reins from the children's grandmother Bridie, an old woman now and no longer able to care for them. Bridie was content to surrender the reins – her dream had been realised when the lanky, awkward girl from County Wicklow had arrived into her living-room without a pair of decent shoes to her name. Elizabeth had proved to be the answer to her prayers, as a God-sent provider of grandchildren, and she had given her thanks to God by serving the children well, while their parents were working around the clock to create a solid financial future for all of them.

Deirdre spent two years at the College of Design, graduating with honours and a growing sense of her own worth, her ambition to be her own employer now coupled with a strong desire to be a person of value to society. This sliver of altruism had come to her through Elizabeth, and her daily exposure to the views held by some of her student friends. Going to college had opened up a whole new perspective for Dee, and she shared her awakening with her mother, who thought – another secret held from her husband – that Ireland should be free of English rule.

Dee had been attracted to this notion through her mother's heartfelt wish that it would one day come to pass. Her mother had sworn her to silence on the matter since her husband, through the twenty-one years of their marriage, knew nothing of his wife's wish for Ireland – Pat had never asked Elizabeth what she thought about anything but the upbringing of the children.

Pat was a status-quo man who didn't want anything

to change in case it cost him money. Devoted as she was to him, Elizabeth did not share Pat's love of money. Neither did she admire his view that the country should stand still because that would be more convenient for him.

Throughout her married life, Elizabeth had been educating herself through reading books and the writing of endless compositions. And she somehow made a little time each working day to spend with the children and their schoolbooks, keeping pace with their progress, though not, to their delight, always. They loved being able to provide the answer to a question by their mother on grammar, delighted when Elizabeth could demonstrate what she had learned from the child in question. In this way, her ongoing studies had helped her be close to her children even though she worked full-time with Pat down the early years. Elizabeth thought of her scribbling into copybooks as talking to herself, and she burned the books as she filled them, her mind returning often to the ways and the days of Aunt Molly teaching her the three R's, while they scratched and scraped to stay alive. Times of scarcity and lack for sure, but she felt warm every time she revisited the memory of how close she and her aunt had been from the recall of her earliest yesterdays.

Through her husband's inherent decency, she and Pat had been able to improve Aunt Molly's lot – he had rebuilt the cabin at Cullen Lower – though no amount of reason or argument could make the old woman agree to leave the spot where she had reared Lizzie.

"All my good memories are here," she said one day, with a finality that closed that particular chapter for once and for all. Molly was more interested in having her niece read from the works of Shakespeare – Elizabeth knew many of his sonnets off by heart. She was too a devotee of Dickens and Galsworthy and Trollope and a host of others, while she never tired of reading about *Oisin* and *Tir na Nog,* and the other legendary characters of Irish history and myth. Two decades later her thirst for knowledge was as unquenchable as her need to understand everything that left her facing any kind of question.

Most of the books had been rented to her for a few coppers a week by the lad she had first seen pushing his cart on her very own first day in the city. Sam Sweet was 'the first foreigner I ever saw in my life' she remembered. She laughed at her own innocence, and in time had shared the story with the young man himself. He gave her a present each Christmas of a book she pined to own, and later still they would discuss – as Sam and his mother did – their views on what they had read.

So Deirdre had been reared in a home where being read to by her mother before sleep was commonplace, where contentment was regarded as normal, her parents being never less than good friends.

The young Dee and her three siblings Mary, Cormac and Paddy, were also granted the bonus of their wonderful, half-mad Granny. Bridie filled their heads with her own verbal tales of the ancient heroes of

Ireland, never differentiating between historical fact and legend on the principle that you should never allow truth to interfere with a good story. For the two boys she churned out her own version of the various fights for independence, drawing garish, highly-coloured versions from the well of her memories, unintentionally engendering in the mind of the quiet boys a growing hatred of all things English.

Deirdre gathered herself, drawing her attention away from the vivid reverie of her early life at Grandma Bridie's knee. She heard the old woman's voice retreating to a whisper whenever her son arrived home. His mother thought Pat was a real stick-in-the-mud, a man afraid of change and she had little to say to him any more. Not that he noticed.

Checking the time, Deirdre decided it would be an hour before Victoria arrived. With an appreciative glance at the garden, she smiled and went indoors to the studio. The final check on her latest creation was the first item on her must-do list.

Inside the principal changing area, Crissie Cole heard Deirdre's Cuban heels make their mark on the polished wooden floor of Reception. With a big smile on her provocative mouth, Crissie pulled the curtain aside and made an entry. She was wearing the newest creation by Deirdre, flouncing dreamily, almost playfully, into a pirouette for her employer, her large manic eyes alight with the joy felt by wearing such a gown. Deirdre twirled her finger and the girl continued to waltz with an imaginary partner. She moved with grace and flair around the large open area, in which the space used to design and display materials was combined, with dressing-rooms close by, all of it having as its focal point a pot-bellied stove in a circle of seating for patrons with a chill in their bones.

Crissie had been blessed with the same measurements as the Brewer heiress and she was already in love with the evening dress. "It's only beautiful, Miss Doyle. Your best work yet, I'd say."

The gown was cut in a deep décolletage, but since Victoria had the poise and the flair – not forgetting her magnificent, highly-set breasts – Deirdre knew she would wear the new creation with great style. Crissie departed to remove the gown and Deirdre moved to the nearest full-length mirror to tidy her appearance. She pulled the abundant reddish-brown waves back on either side of her splendid emerald-green eyes, adding a hint of carmine to her full lips.

She straightened her shoulders, conscious of her height. She was her mother's daughter, taller than many men and tending to lean forward at times, without being aware that she was doing it. All through the in-between years, the crushingly awkward times she had experienced on her way to womanhood, she had cosseted herself against the reality of her height, by dreaming of a fair-haired man with blue eyes and a gentle way, a natural-born gentleman who was taller than she was. To her continuing astonishment and delight, nine months ago her dream man had been brought into her life by Sam Sweet and Victoria.

Arthur Brewer was the twin of her friend Victoria, and though she had not yet admitted it to Vicky or Sam Sweet, Deirdre had dreamed the impossible dream of a life with the brother of the young woman she admired more than any other she had ever met.

Thinking of Arthur, Deirdre found she was nervous again – this came about whenever her ideal man came into her mind. She went to her drawing-table looking for something to help her gather her attention, and added a wisp of flair to a design needing the touch of an inspired person. At this moment she knew she didn't fit the bill. She lapsed into thought, feeling silly, allowing that a woman did feel a bit stupid when she dreamed of things that were so impossible they simply could not happen.

And yet, something had happened – for just one moment Arthur had looked at her in a certain way – did that really happen or had she imagined it out of her driving need to be with him? Oh, it was impossible! She knew this, knew that it was just ridiculous to give room to such a fanciful and unlikely picture.

But still. If Grand-Aunt Molly hadn't been a wild dreamer and believed in fairies and angels and God above all, mammy would never have come to Dublin on the train after a job that never was. 'And I wouldn't have been born, there's no denying that. So, sometimes miracles can happen, even for ordinary people like me.'

She smiled now as she usually did when she was thinking of her mother, Lizzie Dillon, now Elizabeth Doyle, born to a mother dying as she gave birth. The child, reared in a hovel by a woman grown old before her time, emigrating from County Wicklow at the behest of this eccentric aunt who feared her niece would be violated by a local blackguard, or that she would take his life if she didn't get her out of the locality before it was too late.

In this manner, her mother had taken the first train journey of her life, washed in her own tears but without a word of complaint. Deirdre believed her mother had got that sense of acceptance from the little woman who had put her on the train on that eventful day. She blushed with pride that Lizzie from Cullen Lower in County Wicklow was her mother, admiring the way she allowed her father to believe that he ran the ship, that he made all the decisions. She had smiled many times as Elizabeth steered her father in the direction she wanted him to go, Pat having no inkling that he was being handled with care. No matter how she led him around by the nose, she ensured his children grew up respecting him.

She had devoted her life to the family business for years, turning then full time to the family, which included her mother-in-law Bridie and Aunt Molly. Thanks to Bridie she had been able to work side-by-side with her man, allowing him give the orders. She had quietly nudged him this way and that when he needed help but couldn't ask for it, and she smiled thinking of how they had never had a cross word while she then wondered how many women knew just how much power they had when it really came down to it.

Deirdre had a working relationship with her father but, overall, he was too dogmatic for her liking, and she couldn't have said she loved him. She had respect for the way he had coped with his life up to now and she was the first to acknowledge how good he had been to Aunt Molly Harney, for which she would have forgiven him almost anything.

Returning her attention to the mirror, she used a wide elastic band, another of her own designs, to hold the russet brown tresses in place and give the effect of a horse's tail behind. Applying face powder, she brushed the shoulders of her working cotton dress, wanting to look more than presentable when Vicky arrived, just in case she brought Arthur along for a visit.

"Would you bring me a cup of tea, please, Brendan?" Deirdre called to a youth at the far end of the workshop. The long room gave lodging to four sewing machines, and two cutting tables. Between the huge Georgian windows overlooking the rear garden, deep-pine shelving sat on the wall, erected by Deirdre's father. Pat had virtually remade the workshop. His shelves now supported rolls of material including American cotton, Indian silk, wool, and exceptional cotton from Yorkshire in England. Belfast linen was displayed alongside several racks of home-grown wool that Deirdre bought from a family firm of weavers in the town of Cork, and a splendid array of Nottingham lace.

Giving her hair one final touch with a comb, Deirdre sipped the strong tea Brendan provided. She liked the young Dubliner, convinced quietly in her own mind that he was an important man in the making. She smiled, thinking of Sam Sweet. She wondered would he come with Vicky to see the dress she had applauded at her last fitting. Was it, could it be even remotely possible that he would bring Arthur with him? Or that Vicky would?

She dropped the wishful picture from her mind and fell into some memories of Sam. What a friend he had been ever since she fell in love with his startling good looks when he came to the cottage in Long Lane to fix a window for her mother. That was just after the move from Peter Street – the Doyles' tenement rooms being part of a row of houses to be knocked down to make way for Jacob's Biscuit factory. She could remember still the first time she had seen Sam even though she had been just four years old.

"Isn't it well for some people?"

Hearing his voice now, Deirdre shook her head at the sheer coincidence of it, so that she was already chuckling as she turned to find Sam, his buttocks perched against the reception desk.

"Great to be the boss, drink tea when you like, ay!" He smiled and she understood yet again why women would always be captivated by her oldest friend.

He made a mock bow, delighted to see Deirdre. He was, as always, taken by the earthy beauty of her, and his feeling that beneath her natural charm there was a core of steel.

Every time he saw Dee, the same question arose in his mind. How could Pat Doyle and big Lizzie have produced such a handsome woman? The heart and the guts, yes. Even without any input from Pat, Lizzie had an abundance of both, but when it came down to the overall look, there had to be a God in there somewhere. To Sam, her hair shone like burnished nickel under light and he wondered how eyes could be so clear and truthful looking in a world of secrets and masquerading.

'I'm glad you're so out of the ordinary.' The thought arrived unsought – she was a woman so out of the ordinary that he had no qualms about the proposition he was here to make to her.

"I'm glad you got here first, Sam," she confessed. "I'm in a right dither. It's silly, I know, but, and you're not to say this, today I found myself dreaming and fantasising about Arthur and me. I had to be very firm to stop myself wallowing in such an impossible dream." She felt safe sharing her disconcertion with him. He was the best of men. He now delivered one of his golden grins and she wondered had he heard her right. The very last thing she expected was that he would be amused by her restless state of mind.

"It's not so impossible, not any more."

Deirdre was already speaking defensively. "And look at you dressed like a prince, if you don't mind. Silly me, thinking you'd be up to your armpits in bricks and mortar and all the rest of it at the brewery in Kilmainham." Her voice trailed off somewhat, her eyes registering doubt as she wondered had she heard him right.

Sam removed his brown derby hat and shed his

cashmere overcoat. He was not surprised that his words might have sent Deirdre into shock. He responded playfully to her jibe that he had become a gentleman builder by tapping his forehead playfully as he said, "up here for brains," pointing now at his feet, "down there for dancing!"

Deirdre went to him and gave him her cheek, pretending to swoon as he placed a gentle kiss there. "You're getting very bold since you started making dresses for the upper crust," he chided her with a grin, enjoying the exchange as he hung his coat by the door.

Admiring the perfect dark-blue suit he wore, she commented, "That has the look of Savile Row about it."

Sam chuckled. She had an eye like a hawk, the gift of observation being second-nature to her. He nodded in confirmation. "There's no tailor in this city makes clothes to your standards. Someday, maybe you'll make me a suit. Then I wouldn't have to go to London for my gear!"

She gave him a searching look, and Sam said to his reflection in a nearby mirror. "Watch out, Sam! You're being measured for a sales pitch, or something!"

"I think you could make a fortune selling popular lines in ladies' frocks and dresses," Deirdre said, her off-handedness a mockery as she stifled the rising need to ask him what he had meant just now with the words 'not so impossible, not any more'. "Someone else doing the selling for you of course, you being so busy and so powerful these days. We're coming out of the caves. There's going to be a lot of money in ladies' fashions."

She threw this away as an afterthought. He came and took her by the hand. She allowed him to lead her to a seat by the pot-bellied stove. When he sat down beside her, he looked into her eyes. "Vicky has talked to Arthur about you two."

Deirdre had to look away for fear that she would burst into tears.

"Tell me this, and tell me no more." He asked lightly, smiling to help Dee Relax. "Have you thought any more, seriously, I mean, about yourself and Arthur? I don't mean fantasising, Dee. I mean, really."

She was blushing to the roots of her hair, trying to recover her composure.

Sam said, "It's been almost a year since you met. He likes you tremendously. Vicky's told you this herself, so it's not just my opinion."

She looked directly into his eyes, knew he was being serious. She had known anyway that he was speaking from the heart, but that nagging doubt had returned like a chill breeze to freeze her hope.

Seeing that she was in some difficulty, Sam took a silver cigarette case from his pocket. By the time he was smoking, she was able to say. "I've never tried to hide it from you, how I feel about Arthur. But it all seems, no not seems, it all is, utterly, totally impossible."

Even as she said this, her insecurity seemed to be pushed aside. In the instant she was again infused by Molly Harney's madness, the part that allowed her to put Lizzie on the train to Dublin. She had risked so much in the belief that her only living relative being hooshed off to the big city in a hurry would pan out all right.

But, in back of the romance and even Sam's willingness to help her dream come true, Deirdre knew there was no way to escape the dark cloud of her father's rigidity sitting there like a judging magistrate, ready and waiting to rain all over her hopes.

Sam said, "What I can tell you is that when Vicky mentioned marriage as a possibility to Arthur, he was more than happy to allow the pair of us to talk to you about it."

"A couple of days ago at lunch, Vicky and me, we talked about nothing else," Deirdre laughed nervously. "Sam, I think I might expire if I ever came to believe that myself and Arthur . . ." She felt an unexpected bout of shyness, but she found herself saying with real energy. "I would marry Arthur tomorrow. I would give up everything to be his wife." She shook her head, awed by the fact she could say the words out loud. "Even if he felt the same way, it doesn't alter the fact that it's impossible."

A thoughtful expression creased Sam's brow. "I know what you're thinking, girl. Remember, I knew your da before you did, since I was a lad. I'm well aware that he's set like cement. No man in his right mind would argue on that. But, if I carried the banner for you, perhaps, between my charm and my wit and the length of our friendship, not forgetting your desire, we might somehow just get you what you want. This last eighteen months, ever since Vicky's become a client of yours, I've noticed a shift in how Pat talks about the Brewers." Sam's eyebrows flicked up and down, like question marks. He lit another cigarette.

"Victoria's not stopped." Dee allowed. "Each time we've met for lunch or coffee, whenever she is in for a fitting, however we meet, she has been filling my head with impossible pictures." She wished she could smoke a cigarette, not quite knowing why. "Bless her, she is dear, so good, so kind to me. Oh, Sam! Please. Tell me from your heart. Do you really think there's even a remote possibility my father might allow this miracle to happen?" Her facial expression was severely at odds with the sliver of hope lacing her voice.

"There's one way to find out," Sam said. "Let me be your matchmaker. With a devious *shadchen* such as me on the job, we might be able to swing it."

"A *shadchen*?" Deirdre asked. "That's a matchmaker?"

Sam laughed shortly, tapping his cigarette into an ashtray. "As a rule though the *shadchen*, he or she, finds a girl, one with a big dowry for some fellow regarded as a great catch! The idea being that the bride brings with her the money for him to start up a business. He brings the natural equipment to pump children into her. So young lady, you better start coining the *scheckels*." He rubbed his thumbs against his forefingers, parodying the stereotypical Jew.

Deirdre laughed in relief. "I wouldn't bring much of a dowry, but at least I could provide my own trousseau!"

At that moment, Victoria breezed in, and having

greeted Sam with a hardy kiss, she embraced Deirdre. In the instant many heads rose up in unison, work ceasing for the moment as her workers gaped at such openness. She smiled, accepting that this was how it was when Vicky walked into a room, any room, anywhere.

As Deirdre beckoned to Crissie Cole to bring the new gown, she took Victoria inside the dressing area. The sunlight shining through the nearest Georgian window bounced golden off Vicky's hair, the friends sharing a giggle as they drew the masking curtain.

At that moment, Brendan O'Connor arrived to place an enamel mug of hot sweet tea in Sam's hand, not surprised as he received a sixpenny coin in reward. The mug was Sam's own. He had brought it to the showroom on the opening day of Deirdre's business. "Thank you, Mister Sweet." Brendan said, in a voice deep enough to be a bonus should he ever become a public speaker.

"Don't spend it all in the one shop!" Sam slipped him a cigarette. Brendan placed this behind his right ear and went back down the room.

Helping Victoria into the new dress, Dee was remembering how Arthur had come into her life for the first time. So typical of Vicky, to bring him here, that he might meet me in my place of work, no frills of any kind, she just being her honest-to-God self and allowing me to be the same.

Soon after that memorable day, Deirdre knew very quickly that she was in love with the tall, slender twin of the young lady who was now eulogising about her latest creation. "It's beautiful, Dee, magnificent. What a gift you have." She kissed Deirdre's face, her eyes sparkling wickedly. "I'll certainly be showing off my beauties, won't I?" Vicky twirled, affecting casualness as she said, "Arthur's meeting us at the Shelbourne at five. Can you be free then?"

Deirdre laughed shortly in delight. "I'm not religious, but I've been doing novenas for this moment to happen."

Removing the gown, Vicky said: "This is the most perfect gown I have ever seen." She glanced casually at her naked breasts in the mirror. "I'm very vain about my beauties. I'm not sure it's a good thing."

"If they were mine, I'd be vain about them too." Deirdre said without guile.

Vicky chortled, "You great ninny, I'm trying to distract you, stop you looking so serious." She slipped into the skirt of her pale pink two-piece suit. "Sam's told you about my latest chat with Arthur?"

Deirdre held the jacket and Victoria slipped her arms into the sleeves. "Why do you think I'm in a dither? That Arthur could consider marrying me. Have you any idea what that could do to a person?"

"If you could see yourself through my eyes, you'd not be worrying." Vicky embraced her, holding her close for a few moments. "Let's enjoy whatever happens later at the Shelbourne. And for heaven's sake, let me see one of your sunshine smiles."

Vicky fretted with her hair for a moment before the

giant mirror. "And let's you and I have lunch tomorrow, if you can leave the studio for a few hours. There are things I want to tell you, things you should know before you make any commitment. And we have to talk to Sam about a plan of campaign to bring your father around to our way of thinking."

Deirdre said nothing, knowing that it would take a copper-bottomed miracle to shift her father. He was a religious man, a committed Roman Catholic, and she had lived long enough in the environs of his bigotry to know he would never countenance her marriage to a Protestant.

Sam Sweet too was fully aware of the fortress that Pat Doyle's intransigence on the religion issue would be. Pat had always been something of a Holy Joe, and a man who doffed his cap to the establishment. For someone born on the fringe of poverty, he was almost unnaturally conservative, a man to whom money and power and prestige meant everything. Sam had hopes that this might be the area where Pat could be manipulated in relation to the possible marriage of Arthur and Deirdre. It wasn't every day of the week that the daughter of a poor-born man was offered marriage by one of the richest gentlemen in the land.

At lunch the following day, Vicky told Deirdre that Arthur would marry her. "He has cared for you for months. What I had to overcome is his inability to believe that he is fit to deserve such a prize. He's shy as you know but he has a good heart, and he does care deeply for you, I promise you that. He is a heavy drinker, and that's unlikely to change all that much, though when you have children and a settled home life he might well prefer the fireside to his club. In my heart I believe he will make a good and loving husband."

Victoria raised her hand and a waiter appeared as if from nowhere to take her order for another bottle of wine.

"The question is, Dee, are you ready to let go of your business, give up working, to be a wife and mother? That life is not for me. I'm far too selfish. You are successful and your reputation as a gifted designer is running before you. You would be sacrificing a lot to be Arthur's wife."

Deirdre nodded her head without a qualm, her immediate response being the answer. Thinking it through, even in the early days when the impossible dream was setting up house in her mind, she realised that she could walk away from the business world to be Arthur's wife. Her ability and talent would go with her, and when she felt the urge she could design again. She might even make a start at gratifying her inclination to help the less fortunate, the poor and the downtrodden that lived with the suffering and deprivation she witnessed each day as she rode her bicycle across the city to Mountjoy Square.

Dee saw for herself, week in week out, that poverty was rampant in Dublin city. Around the docklands north of the Liffey – she had been appalled at first by the foul and stinking tenements that festered within a stone's throw of Carton's magnificent Customs House.

Dee found it unacceptable that the spires of many churches in and around the Liberties stood alongside brothels and drinking holes that never closed – hovels that should long since have been burned to the ground since they were active lazy-beds of disease and violence and all that was sad and reprehensible about the human condition.

She realised there was little could be done for the men who were already lost in the grip of booze and opium, or the many women who seemed doomed to die in degradation, but she ached to help the legions of decent mothers, women without food to feed their children – women that had to be helped that they might have a halfway decent life, and rear the children of tomorrow in a city where the infant mortality rate was a national scandal. Too many mites were dying by the age of five because of neglect and the filth in which they existed. It was in this area where Dee felt she might be of service, knowing that as soon as she possibly could she would find a way to help those who had survived thus far at the coalface of their wretched circumstances. Above all, she wanted to help them help themselves toward another level of day-to-day living.

Within days, Vicky invited Dee and the two men to meet her at the Shelbourne, the occasion being what she called a moment to celebrate simply being alive. When she and Deirdre arrived at the hotel, Vicky suggested they drink a couple of Gin Noir. "Or even three," she chortled wickedly. "Gin mixed with blackberry cordial. Blackberry is deep of flavour, you can hardly taste the gin.

My idea of a lady's best friend, especially when one is under strain or stress. Or," she cocked her head and cackled a hag's laugh, "in those dark moments when you need to keep the wretched world at bay for a little while."

Deirdre was excited enough to agree to anything and joined Vicky at a small table in the bar. Within minutes she was complimenting her. "It's so easy to drink and makes you feel better in no time." She chuckled, surprised at her own wickedness, the ease with which she blissfully allowed herself to be led astray.

"Three, the power of three, and you will feel as though you're floating on air as we head in to dinner," Vicky assured her as she indicated another round of drinks.

As they were leaving to join the men in the dining-room, Dee did feel as though she was floating, while she wondered had she had three of those wonderful drinks, or was it four?

Deirdre was ravenously hungry and more than a tad light-headed as they began to eat dinner. She found she had stopped being nervous, and that her remarks and quips had her companions laughing their heads off. She found too, that she had the courage to look directly at Arthur from time to time, and her heart swelled in those moments. She was more than ever convinced that she would die for him. Her heart beat faster when she remembered how Sam has talked to her father about the time she was spending with Victoria Brewer – how he had smoothed the way for this celebration at the Shelbourne.

"What would I do without Sam?" she asked herself, not for the first time.

At some stage between the main course and dessert, Dee found herself on her feet with a glass in her hand, while a tipsy voice that sounded rather like her own proposed a toast to Arthur and Deirdre – not the slightest sense of embarrassment or remorse anywhere to be seen. "I toast them and I pray that all the fences between them and their marriage will be hurdled without too much difficulty. They deserve to be happy together; they are made for each other."

Some time later she found Vicky caring for her when she came back to awareness in the ladies' room at the hotel. She was seated on a fine Chippendale chair with Vicky holding a cold face cloth to her forehead. Dee felt relief that Vicky was smiling happily, shaking her head in appreciation. "You're a true original!"

Deirdre didn't understand. "What?"

"Arthur considers your toast as a marriage proposal, and as he will tell you himself, when we return to the table, he has accepted. Isn't it wonderful?"

Fifteen minutes later, having had a cold compress on the back of her neck – the backs of her wrists almost frozen from the cold water tap running on them for what seemed like ages, followed by an overhaul of her make-up – Deirdre followed Vicky back to the dining-room. Both men kissed her, Sam with a wry expression on his handsome face, Arthur more diffidently but with sincerity.

"Please accept my apology," Dee said as she sat

down. "Vicky's told me what happened. I can only put it down to the Gin Noir."

"It's the cordial that does you in," Sam said.

"What a brilliant drink," Vicky's mouth formed a sweet smile. "I should have thought of it ages ago – you two might be engaged by now."

Sam sat back in his chair, smoking a black cigarette with a gold band. "I might feel a bit let down if it was me, Arthur. This woman here on my right, she's saying she's sorry for asking you to marry her!"

Arthur, having quaffed a glass of champagne, found this amusing. "Spare a chap's feelings, Dee. I was quite looking forward to a state of married bliss."

"It's not fair making fun of me." Deirdre was blushing. "I'm not used to hotels, and drinks with funny names, any of it. But I will tell you," she warned, "I love it, I love it all." The laugh that followed was like an eruption of relief, and she drank from the champagne glass in front of her. "Now, Arthur, I apologise for apologising. I will now spare your feelings by asking you again, here and now before two people I would give my life for, will you marry me?"

She burst out laughing at the effect her monologue had produced. All three of them sat as though frozen before they exploded into laughter. Then they were hand-clapping, rising to come to her to kiss and hug her and tell her how wonderful she was. All the while she nodded in agreement, determining to remember that whenever she had to make a speech, or, for some reason or another, be brilliant, she must make sure to have several tipples of Gin Noir before she opened her mouth.

Arthur now raised his glass in her direction. "I toast you, Deirdre, and with great joy, I accept your proposal. I'd be honoured to become your husband!"

Deirdre sniffed back her tears, held her hand out to him across the table. Arthur bent over her hand and she felt his lips on her flesh for the first time, "My dear lady."

"I love you," Deirdre heard herself saying.

Sam Sweet drew so deeply on his foreign cigarette that he thought his ears would explode, while Vicky simply allowed her tears to flow while grinning like a circus clown who couldn't stop.

Arthur, about to sit down again, stopped and stood very straight. "Sam suggested, while you were away from the table, that you and he should go and talk with your father on my behalf. I did agree, but I've had a change of heart. I hope Sam might arrange that I pay a visit to your father, Sam joining me, of course, in order that I may seek permission to make you my wife. If that's agreeable to you, Deirdre, I will make myself available at any time, to suit your family."

In the ladies' room, Deirdre and Victoria stood side-by-side as they washed their hands. The occasional smile touching her friend's mouth caused Dee to blurt out, "If ever a person could look like the cat that got the cream!" They both laughed, before Victoria said, "I'm sorry if I've been pushy, a bit overt, Deirdre. But someone had to put you pair together. It wasn't taking place organically." She pressed her lips together, looked satisfied with the repairs she had carried out. "I'll never forget hearing dear Arthur asking you, formally, to marry him. He was wonderful – and you!" Laughing shortly, she pressed on, "You, you trollop, you asking him to marry you. I could have hugged you to death. You were simply incredible, and I shall never stop being grateful that I was present when you came out of your box to amaze the entire company!"

Deirdre's face turned serious and she sank onto a chair.

"What is it, darling?" Victoria was bothered by the sudden change.

"I'm just afraid, that's all," Deirdre said honestly. "Part of me believes in miracles, but my father's pragmatic ways have rubbed off too. I'm afraid to believe in the impossible dream. And really, you and I, we have to find a way to let it all happen at a less heady pace. It will take time before Sam and Arthur can talk to my father."

"Do you think time will help? Is he likely to be any the less rigid in six months or a year?"

"Quite honestly, Vicky, I doubt it."

"Well, you know how I hate the waste of time, the waste of our precious life's time, pretending that other people's rules matter? Well, they don't. They don't matter." Vicky's fingers tightened on Deirdre's hand. With a quiet passion, she said, "Arthur cares for you, Deirdre. In his own shy way he is taken, I can see it. He's good, a truly good man, he deserves all your goodness. He wants it now. So, I urge you let them beard the lion in his den, right away. Do you understand me?"

11

Athlone, Ireland

August 1906

On the edge of the town of Athlone, some sixty miles west of Dublin city, Gloria wept tears that burned her eyelids. Twelve months on from the death of her mother, the young woman had found no way yet to heal her broken heart. Nor did she feel that her mind had repaired itself. Times she felt she had been fractured beyond repair by the violence, and the madness of the times in which she had to live, her memory facility, of total recall, denying her the luxury of forgetfulness.

Not that she ever wanted to lose the memory of her mother, even in death. The burial was so vivid that it might have happened only yesterday. She could see the plain pine box go into the earth, her heart tumbling into the gaping hole of Rebecca's resting place. She could see herself, the girl twisted in pain, not hearing a word whispered in compassion, because somewhere deep inside her other self was screaming at some God somewhere, why, why, why, did Mama have to die? Why did she have to die when the Promised Land – the land she had promised to live in for my father on his death breath – was there before her, if only she could have seen it, as her life ebbed away across the waters of St George's Channel?

Sitting in her caravan home, on the fringe of the town, Gloria laid down her pen. The lined book on the tiny table bore her penmanship, the record – all that she could remember – about the life she and her mother had led. This was the closest she had come to some sliver of relief from the pain imprisoning her willingness to live. For the odd minute she seemed free, before, inevitably, tears flowed again with little or no lessening of force, the deep hurt remaining, wrapped like a tight band of rust about her heart.

She turned back a page or two, and read once more of the ordeal of taking her mother's corpse from the ferryboat – the slow journey from the harbour of Kingstown, the early morning sun doing nothing to relieve the gloom darkening her spirit. Her mind gathered fleeting glimpses of elegant Georgian houses, no more than shadows flickering across her tear-filled vision, her breathing periodically ruptured by the painful irony that her mother's dream of coming to Ireland had turned into the nightmare of her premature death.

She brushed away the tears, reading today's words by the light of the tilly lamp hanging from the ceiling over her seat.

'The words are not helping today, Mama. Twelve

months on from the violation of your passing, the pain thrives in its command of me. Only the other life, the play-acting, helps me cling on to my precarious sanity. Even the beautiful words of the great prophet, words you taught me, they bring no relief from the grief I feel, the anger that will not let me go.

'Out of the depths, have I cried to thee, O Lord
Lord, hear my voice: let thine ears be attentive to
the voice of my supplications,
O Lord, who shall stand?
But there is forgiveness with thee,
That thou mayest be feared.
I wait for the Lord, my soul doth wait,
And in his word, do I hope.
My soul waiteth for the Lord more than
They that watch for the morning: I say, more
Than they that watch for the morning.
Let Israel hope in the Lord: for with the
Lord there is mercy, and with him is
Plenteous redemption.
And he shall redeem Israel from
All iniquities.'

'All the fine words in the world, they find no place in my heart. I remain bereft.'

Gloria turned from the page, as for a moment she remembered Emily Boswell helping her to her feet by the graveside in the tiny Jewish cemetery. "Your mother is not alone, child," she whispered, allowing her own tears to fall. "She is with God, while her body is here now, lying in the company of your own people."

Gloria was too numbed to show anything like gratitude, though she was aware of the kindness of Emily, her husband Bill, and indeed the other strangers in the theatrical touring company, and the rabbi that made up the funeral party.

The rabbi understood all too well the depth of sadness keeping the girl rooted to the spot by her mother's graveside. He nodded to Emily Boswell, a silent 'let her be, let her grieve', before he finally took Gloria by the arm and guided her from the cemetery, followed by the troupe of strolling players.

Once the company was on the road, journeying to towns they played in year after year, Gloria followed the directions of Bill and Emily Boswell. With something approximating to relief, she took on the severe rehearsal schedule, putting everything she had to give toward the work that the production of any professional entertainment demanded. This helped her resist the effort of her own mind to tear her apart. She threw herself into the work, taking some time to get over her astonishment that the company presented a completely different, two-and-a-half-hour production, seven nights each week, for the duration of the tour.

The format was billed as 'two shows for the price of one' since the entertainment began with a full-bodied variety show of singing and dancing and comedy sketches, with several novelty turns, including a good, fast-moving marionette item, rationed out over the week.

The interval was occupied by a raffle for a small sum of money, or a novelty item such as a blanket, or a pair of inexpensive cotton sheets, or even a bottle of whiskey. Whatever novelty prize Bill handed out to the lucky winner, this had been bought wholesale, by either Emily or himself, the profit from the raffle going towards the wage bill and the expenses that such a show incurred, no matter how hard the Boswells tried to keep the costs down.

The second half of the night's offering was a play, a melodrama, a tear-jerker. This was followed by a comedy sketch – whenever possible, it paid to leave the punters laughing.

Big Bill Boswell's Bohemian Band was one of the better touring companies travelling the circuit of small towns and villages, around the British Isles. The success of the show depended on not merely attracting townspeople, but those who were willing to walk, or drive a cart drawn by a pony or a donkey, for a distance of five miles, or even more. In addition, the company had to attract those people night after night after night, since the countryside was sparsely populated, while public transport was virtually non-existent.

The better-off country folk were beginning to appear on bicycles, something not seen that often in the Irish countryside, the rudimentary roads often turning the riding of a pedal cycle into a near hazardous experience. Not that this, or anything else, stopped many people from going to the show! It was accepted that some people saved their pennies the year around, so that they could afford to attend each night's performance by the touring company.

Fun and laughter had been as scarce as charity, to the people of the land of saints and scholars, and since the touring show, and the circus, were the only form of entertainment available in the broad countryside, the entertainers were always welcomed back.

Gloria quickly realised that poverty was rife in Ireland, and despite the ever-present hatred of Jem Riley, she identified with the sad plight of so many people. At times they seemed to be like Jews, treated like foreigners in the country of their birth. She also became aware of just how repressed were the Irish by the English establishment, while its puppets in residence ran the country, and were well-rewarded with land not theirs and positions of power and prestige for doing so. She felt a rising sense of injustice in relation to how things seemed to be, but she didn't dwell on anything for long – the pain in her heart saw to that, staking its claim on her with its relentless power.

On stage, she was the star of every production. This violet-eyed girl with the voluptuous figure had more than lived up to the expectations of the Boswells. They had agreed she was 'made for this business' and, as Emily had expected, young men came back night after night to feast their senses on her 'foreigner's' beauty. She was like someone from another world, a place where her charm and her full-breasted voluptuousness, might well have been the norm. Not so in the day-to-day living of Irish countrymen, who thought her a goddess. Others came to listen to the magnificent singing voice of Gloria Rose, the 'Princess of Song' as the advertising handbills boldly declared – while women often wept through the songs she sang as though the pain had been driven into the words by her own personal experience.

Gloria felt life's blood coursing through her when she was performing. She simply sparkled onstage, her presence and her built-in acting talent lighting up the run-of-the-mill melodramas that the company served up to those that might never get to a legitimate theatre. Some of these old chestnuts, such as *East Lynn* by Mrs Henry Wood or *She Died for Love*, were a must during every visit by the touring show. *She Died for Love* was the story of an Irish heroine, forced to leave home by starvation, and dying in America even as her confederate officer husband-to-be returns to make her his wife. A couple of songs were introduced as an excuse to use Gloria's singing voice as much as possible.

She had written lyrics suitable to several of the melodramas, so she might well be found in the light of a tilly lamp in upper-class England, or as far away as the banks of the Mississippi river. As if by magic, she would have a guitar on her knee, her superb soprano creating in the audience the kind of silence that some thought of as spiritual, before applause and loud expressions of vocal gratitude erupted to embrace lovingly the final moments of her singing.

Off-stage, she rehearsed with relentless energy, at times annoying the seasoned professionals who knew all the plays by heart. Gloria, being a perfectionist sometimes sought extra rehearsals from Bill or Emily, who though they knew the plays inside out, were delighted by her enthusiasm and her ongoing desire to achieve perfection. Some of the others players didn't take kindly to her spontaneous criticism of a bad performance, even though they believed she had the welfare of the company at heart. Sometimes, behind the scenes, Bill and Emily cosseted the wounded egos of their older players – some of them had been part of the Bohemian Band for years. In time, it was the consistency of her ongoing performances in roles that the actors had seen played to death that earned Gloria friendship with some members of the company.

Gloria hardly cared, while Emily, who had been here before with young actresses who'd lost a parent or a lover, allowed that grief had to be given its head, for a time. But only for a time, and then it was time to put an end to overt suffering of the kind crippling Gloria as a woman.

One afternoon as Gloria was talking about her mother again, Emily suggested it was time to stop doing it. Gloria caught her breath, stunned to the point where she simply couldn't speak. "What I mean, my dear," Emily waxed forcefully in her own careful way, "when I used to talk of my heart-rend over and over again, I found it was as if, it was like I was reopening the wound, sticking the knife in myself, day after day, without even knowing I was doing it."

Their relationship had grown steadily the past year, but in the silence that followed, Emily wondered would they survive her latest no-holds-barred response to Gloria's need to wallow in grief and anger, and though she didn't dare say it, self-pity.

"I'm sorry, Emily," Gloria spoke so politely that Emily instantly knew she was in a huff.

"Now, now, don't be like that. I'm trying to help. I only ever have your welfare at heart. Like my own daughter you are. I'm trying to encourage you to think about the future, leave the past where it belongs. It doesn't mean you're going to forget your dear mother, good heavens, no!"

"That couldn't happen, Emily. I would die first."

"I understand, my dear, as you will when you have your own children."

"That is not likely to happen, since I have no interest in acquiring a husband," Gloria's resentment wavered in the face of Emily's matter-of-fact way.

"Oh, give it time, dear. Someday, a man will appear and sweep you off your feet. I only hope I'll be there, to help you prepare for your wedding day."

With a lightning flash of anger, Gloria retorted, "All the pain in my life, Emily, all the brutality and the cruelty, the murder of my father, all of it was caused by men. Why would I have anything to do with any man?"

Gloria bit down on the need to say Gentile man, since she didn't wish to give offence. At the same time she accepted that it was there, this hatred of Gentile men. It sat like a disease waiting to drop from her lips. She often felt it was irrational, but at those times her emotions overrode reason, and this deep hatred of all Gentiles flourished in her mind and in her feelings. She hated them for what their kind had done to her mother and to her father and to herself, and to Jews everywhere down the flickering, bloodied pages of her people's history.

Emily was shaken by Gloria's outburst, but she didn't stir from her point of view. "I would have thought," she said respectfully, "you being a Jewess, that a husband and family would be the priority in your life."

"It seems I have little influence in relation to what happens to me in life," Gloria said, failing to hide the anger flaring like twin torches in her violet eyes.

Emily went to her and held her arms open. In a moment, Gloria responded with a fierce embrace, and a flash-flood of tears. Then over the next minute or so, silently, they released whatever hurt or pain they might have caused to the other. Emily sighed with relief. At the same time she vowed to herself to take the risk again, by having another honest chat with Gloria before long.

Meanwhile, the touring show was gaining popularity above and beyond anything it had never known before. Bill and Emily, and most of the company, admitted it was due to the talent of Gloria Rose. Week after week, business rose from good to wonderful – word of mouth being the best advertising. The show played to large audiences at every venue, so that it was only a matter of time before the competition sat up and took notice.

Several times recently, Boswell's main rival on the tour circuit, Daniel George, had written to Gloria through his solicitor, making her an offer far in excess of what she was currently earning. Gloria was not interested in working for someone else – it had never crossed her mind that she would work with anybody but the Boswells. These were the people who had rescued her when she was in the deepest need of her life and she knew she would never forget that, as she would never allow anything to get in the way of their friendship. Meanwhile, she dismissed the offer from Daniel George by ignoring it.

During one week in August, the man returned three nights in a row to the hall in Arklow town where the Bohemian Band was booked in for the week. On the third night, Gloria found a beautiful bouquet of roses waiting for her when she got to the hall. There was a note asking if the writer might have a word with her after the evening's entertainment ended. When she considered the tone of the request she felt she could not avoid meeting the man, and this meant that it was time to tell the Boswells.

Gloria insisted that the Boswells be present during the meeting with Daniel George, since she had no wish to be alone with any man, least of all a middle-aged Gentile. The meeting ended rather suddenly when the man insisted – financial considerations apart – that Gloria's talent would be better served by his company, since it performed at a much higher standard than the Boswells'.

Having just poured a large whiskey for his rival, Bill responded by handing this to Emily, while he thumped the impressario hard enough to knock him out of Gloria's dressing-room into the passage. George lay there unconscious, while Bill drank a toast to Gloria,

Emily and his company, before he carried his rival out to where his coach and horses waited.

A week later, Emily brought an agreement, drawn up by a leading solicitor, which in effect gave Gloria a one third share of the profits in Big Bill Boswell's Bohemian Band, without her being in any way responsible for any shortfall, or any debts that might at any time be incurred by the company. Gloria protested, she was more than satisfied with the current arrangement. Emily insisted on behalf of herself and Bill: "You're the star, my dear. You are the reason we are doing such wonderful business everywhere we go. You must share in the profits. It's what Bill and I want. Apart from which, it is only fair."

Gloria finally signed the piece of paper, without any feeling in relation to the financial dividend it would bring, but when some days later, Bill presented her with the gift of her own caravan home, this touched her more than she would have imagined possible. Tingling with joy and excitement, she was soon hugging the Boswells, vowing she would never work with any other company. As they left her to get accustomed to her new home on wheels, she gave Bill another hug, and Emily smiled as she witnessed the effect it had on her husband. Later, he commented to her, "A kiss on the cheek from that lady and a man needs to adjust his dress!"

Gloria came to love the quiet of her late-night caravan home. She was glad of every busy week, of course, as the touring company journeyed to another nearby town or village, but her late-night retreat had become everything to her. She literally loved living in her wagon and within weeks she insisted on driving herself, easier now in the business of horse management, actually enjoying the work that went into the care of the roan Mendel, named in memory of her grandfather who had died pulling a cart westward across Lithuania. The chestnut was just three years old, standing fifteen hands. He had a docile nature, and Gloria was soon glad of his welcoming snicker when she returned from the performance each night. His reaction to her arrival kindled a hint of something good in her heart, the odd whinny he presented, as she wrote by her late-night oil lamp, made her feel safe and helped her to be easier in herself. As she continued to feel better, she talked less about her mother and the awful things that had been inflicted on their lives. Emily noticed this, silently caring, never needing to say I told you so. The girl having touched her deeply, she was glad to feel that the life force coursing through Gloria had begun to outshine the pain.

A short time after the metamorphosis began, Gloria opened up to the idea of writing something other than the words she shared with her journal every night. She began her effort at authorship by writing the thinly-disguised version of her life as a touring actor, giving it the working title 'Strolling Players', wondering was she not being a little pretentious. A couple of days later she decided there was no harm in it, particularly since nobody else was ever going to read it anyway. A few weeks later she was telling Emily that the story was coming along, not being in the least surprised when her friend said she'd like to read it.

"A friend of mine suggested," Gloria murmured, tongue-in-cheek, "she suggested I leave the past where it belongs. Naturally, I resented her honesty, the very last thing I wanted to hear. This dear and brave and caring lady, my friend, she pressed on with her unwanted advice. She may just have saved my life."

They embraced, shedding a few tears, and for the first time since she had clapped eyes on the dark-haired beauty, Emily believed she was witnessing something very special as the violet-eyed girl allowed her tears, tears of release and joy, to flow.

Some weeks later, before the final performance in the seaboard town of Wicklow, a tall, well-dressed woman helped an old lady into her seat at one end of the front row. The performers, playing to another full house, simply sparkled right through the evening's work, and when the extended performance finally ended Elizabeth Doyle helped her aunt, Molly Harney, to walk backstage to meet the players, and above all to shake the hand of her heroine, Gloria Rose.

Aunt Molly had seen the young actress a year before, driving herself through the summer's evening, the four miles from her cabin at Cullen Lower. The old woman had no worries about getting home since the pony Pat Doyle had given her had a halfway decent nature, and could canter at a fair lick, once you kept reminding him you held the whip. Molly had read about the actress, Gloria Rose, in the newspaper Lizzie had brought on her last visit. When she heard the lovely girl sing Molly was transported in her feelings, and like those around her in the audience she had clapped for more and more until her hands were giving her gyp. The aches and pains disappeared as she gasped at Gloria's portrayal of Lady Isabelle in *East Lynn*. From that night on, Molly had talked of little else during Elizabeth's monthly visits, the journey to see the show being the reward for her aunt's persistent enthusiasm.

"Lizzie, she'd sing the birds off the bushes, the same lady. You have to be there with me when she comes again. She must be the greatest woman ever drew breath to sing a note."

Tickled by her aunt's praise for the singer, she promised she would take her to Wicklow to see the show. The thought caused Elizabeth to reflect that there had been precious little to enthuse about during their life together during the poverty years at Cullen Lower. Aunt Molly's life was better now in that she had a home with a roof that didn't leak, and she had bedding and clothing and all the food she wanted, but Lizzie knew she would never pass up a chance to do anything that would brighten Molly's life, if only for a few hours.

In her eyes, the older woman was some kind of paragon, an unsung saint in some ways, the niece more than grateful that the old woman's faith in God was unshakeable. Molly believed, no, *she knew*, that when she passed on she would be, within minutes, 'in God's pocket'. For the moment though, the visit to once again enjoy the wonder of Gloria Rose was about as close to heaven as the little woman could get.

12

Greystones, County Wicklow

July 1907

When Bill Boswell brought his touring company to Greystones in County Wicklow, he pitched his summer tent in the same field he'd hired from Sam Sweeney for the last eight years. Bill wasn't mad about working under canvas, but since there was no hall available in the town he had no choice. Sweeney's five-acre plot formed a promontory with direct access from the road winding along the coastline, south of Bray. This field was separated from the sea down below by a fifteen feet bank, and a wide beach where the handmade wooden boats of the local fishermen lay like great sleeping slugs in the scutch grass planted by the local authority, to bind the sand to some small degree.

Bill usually enjoyed himself during the Greystones visit even though he had to pay his touring players something extra since they erected and took down the tent, under his guidance. He would fish and swim and rest in the sunshine, and when he had made love to Emily for two or three nights in a row and she opined in a sleepy voice, "The air here is certainly very bracing!" – he felt gratified that he had done the right thing in returning.

Bill reckoned it was one of the few towns on the tour where you got an almost even mix of Catholic and Protestant, where farm hand, tenant and landlord could watch the same show at the same time as the resident West Brits, who ran the establishment. A mixed bag, Bill repeated to Emily, not that he cared once the punters could pay their sixpence at the door, and buy a raffle ticket or two during the interval.

He was feeling particularly good as he sat by the sea this noontime. He had just received at the railway station a telegraphed booking for six seats for tonight's opening performance. Since this was the first telegraphed booking he had ever had for a show, he looked on it as a good omen for the week ahead. He happily reserved six seats in the front row, and six more in row three, just in case these particular punters didn't want to sit looking up the noses of the performers for two-and-a-half hours.

Casting his heavily-weighted fishing line, smiling as it hit the water some thirty yards from where he stood, Bill waited until the bait had sunk down deep. And it was deep out there, when you moved beyond the shelf of sand at beach level. He was content now to leave the line. With a bit of luck, he'd land another fine plaice to go on the pan for dinner. He stuck the handle of the long rod into the tube buried up to its neck in the sand, walked up to join Emily who sat with her back against the sandy wall of the field up above and behind her. She lowered her book, meeting his approach with a smile.

"Two glorious plaice so far, my dear," he said, flopping on the sand.

"When you grin like that you're always thinking of grub, so how come you look like a chap just found a pound note?" Emily chortled. "There was a time food wasn't always foremost on your mind, nor money neither. Hmmph! How things change while you're waiting for the tram!"

As he told her about the booking, her eyes followed Shane Malone who was dashing down the sand to throw himself into the sea. Bill turned to admire his new leading man. Born of Irish parents, Shane was a tall, golden-haired American blessed with good looks and a great physique and, lo and behold, genuine talent as an actor. Shane had told Bill he was in Ireland to visit his aunt Lisa, a widow living in Dublin. In a bar frequented by the theatrical profession, he learned that Bill Boswell needed a leading man.

"I know I can do a good job for you, Mister Boswell." Those had been Shane's first words to Bill, who appreciated all that the young man had to offer. The lad was a born leading-man, Bill reckoned, with a wonderful baritone voice, and the bearing of someone well-born and bred. Someone had spent love and time and money to turn this young man into an exciting, finished article. He could well be sensational on the stage, Bill allowed, and even as he offered Shane the job, he was seeing him play opposite Gloria Rose in melodrama. Moments later the picture of the pair of them singing romantic duets in variety made Bill chortle and he told himself aloud, as he rubbed his hands in glee, that 'some days are good days'. Bill's was even happier when he discovered that Shane was an accomplished pianist and guitarist.

"Got my heart set on a stage career, Mister Boswell, and I'm going for it. If I have to, I'll work my teeth to the gums to make the grade."

Bill welcomed Shane's enthusiasm, but even so he decided against informing him right away of certain things about his new job. There was plenty of time to tell him that he would also feature at the piano, that at times he would virtually be the orchestra, when the other actor-musicians were getting ready for their next onstage entrance. Bill also delayed mentioning that Shane would be a master of ceremonies, and since he was a brand-new face on the tour circuit, he would before long be worked into some comedy routines with himself.

Naturally, Shane would be the juvenile lead in the plays. Sometimes when he was free for a little while, he would have to take the money at the door, ensuring that none of the local lads bunked into the show without paying. He would also be called upon to sell tickets for the raffle during the interval. Bill smiled at the busy times Shane was going to enjoy thinking, 'He wants experience. He'll need it to become a star – working for me, he's going to get it in bucketfuls'.

Bill was unconcerned that Shane might find his

workload a tad heavy. By the time he realised all that he was doing for minimum pay, he would be in love with Gloria, ergo unlikely to leave the show unless he did so by dropping dead from working too hard. Which was hardly likely, him being a fine strapping American lad and in the best of good health.

Shane said his parents were Irish, living in New Jersey where he'd been reared. His Aunt Lisa lived at Sandymount, by the sea, just outside the city of Dublin, and was the younger sister of his mother Rose. Almost from the time he was born, Aunt Lisa had made regular trips to New Jersey to visit her only nephew.

In Bill's eyes, Shane was a nice lad, and this was important on long tours. With a team of actors dressing and undressing in a small space every night of the week, you couldn't afford to have even one malcontent in the company. Bill also felt that Shane would be popular from the beginning. In this he proved to be right, the young Yank being a great draw where women were concerned. On this pleasant thought Bill dozed off by the shore, wondering about the punters that had sent the telegram booking for six seats.

Sam Sweet had no interest in theatre, so the idea of sitting in the front-row of a theatrical tent in Greystones made him laugh out loud.

'But here you are old son,' he told himself with a wry smile. 'It's about time fellas like you got wise enough to never say never. You just never know.'

He was surprised to find that he was enjoying himself, soaking up the atmosphere that filled the long tent. 'And why wouldn't I be? Am I not here with my lovely Vicky?' he thought. 'And are we not here with Deirdre and Arthur, two of the very few people I am always happy to see and be with? And is not my heart's delight, big Lizzie – now called Elizabeth, he reminded himself – not here too, along with her wonderful, half-mad aunt that sent her for a wild-goose-chase job in Dublin, so she could meet Pat Doyle, have a child who is about to become the wife to one of the richest men in the British Isles.' He shook his head in disbelief, saying to himself, 'Somebody should write a play about that!' The fact that the bride's father would not be attending the wedding came as no surprise to Sam, and he remained hopeful that time might well effect the change necessary to alter that situation.

Sam felt Vicky touch his hand. He turned and gave her a crooked grin, whispering, "It never ceases to amaze me how you light me up, just by being beside me. Isn't that daft?"

Victoria patted his face as though he was somewhat unwell. "You poor love! It's awful to see you afflicted with mush-mush, the latest disease known to mankind," she chuckled, and he turned to respond to something Elizabeth Doyle has just said to him. Holding onto his hand, Victoria thought again about what she had to say to him in the next week or so. How would he react? Would he be able to honour their agreement that honesty between them was a priority?

Arthur, who was sitting next to her, seemed eager as

a child for the performance to start. Beside him, her hand in his, Deirdre was thrilled that the birthday treat for her great-aunt Molly Harney had worked out so well. She had been keeping an eye on her all evening, and she had no doubt that when they got to the hotel for supper after the show, the old woman from Cullen Lower would be as wide-awake and as eager to enjoy herself as anyone had the right to be.

Deirdre was happy for being seated alongside the people that were so very important in her life. Since she had become engaged to Arthur, nothing had interfered with her sense of well-being. She knew she was shining inside.

It would have been even better had her father allowed that she had a life to live, and that she was entitled to live it according to her own lights. But that was not the way of Pat Doyle, a man who expected a return on everything that he gave.

Deirdre expected he would have been surprised had she ever said to him that she was her mother's daughter, too. In fact, it went beyond this. She was her mother's daughter first and last, having seen very little of her father in her formative years. His obsession with business and the making of money had even deprived her of her mother at times, but it was Elizabeth who had defined the mould that formed her, doing everything in her power to inculcate a sense of her own worth into her first-born child, never having forgotten the vow she made to herself by Trinity College when she saw the Penny Farthing girls, on her first day in Dublin.

Someone began tinkling a piano behind the black masking curtain that created the backstage area. Sam caught Deirdre's eye checking that all was well with her. She smiled and nodded her head, her mouth shaping the word 'thanks'.

Backstage, someone hit a cymbal hard, this being followed by a heavy hand on the piano keyboard to produce the cue chord for the opening chorus. The curtains opened and slid sideways as six performers began singing and dancing and for a few moments, Sam enjoyed the snappy opening. The performers were attractively dressed but in an instant, five of the figures simply disappeared as his eyes registered the sixth, a young woman who had to be the most beautiful creature he had ever seen. She was a raven-haired girl with a startlingly, voluptuous figure and she seemed to illuminate the dimly-lit stage with the glow of her personality.

"My God, what a magnificent creature," Victoria whispered urgently to Sam. He glanced over, and saw that Arthur and Deirdre were likewise taken by the young woman on the stage. Looking quickly left, he thought for a second that Molly Harney was about to fly her seat.

Victoria put her hand on Sam's thigh and he knew she wanted to say something. When he turned to her, she whispered, "I believe we're looking at the Jewish girl of your dreams." She smiled wantonly and he gave her a grin – a promise made for later that night. She held his gaze and leaned closer still. "You will marry someday, and your bride will be a Jewess. I think we were brought here tonight that you might see this lady."

Sam resisted his need to dismiss this, turning back to the opening chorus. He was sore, hurting, knowing that their vow to be totally honest with each other meant more to Vicky than it did to him. She had warned him never to think of marriage between them, and he had again acquiesced, being just as dishonest as he was now being. In his own way, he loved Victoria, knowing that she didn't run that deep about anyone but Arthur. And for the second time in a week, he had the uneasy feeling that Vicky was telling him something, something, he guessed, that he would not want to hear.

As the performers filed off stage, a tall good-looking young man with an American accent introduced himself as Shane Malone and extended a hearty welcome to one and all. He then invited them to sit back and enjoy the talent . . . He got no further, because Big Bill Boswell erupted onto the stage, leaving nobody in any doubt that he was here to make them laugh. And laugh they did, from the start of his patter routine, with Shane Malone playing straight man.

As Sam sat there laughing along with the rest of the audience, he felt more than surprised for the second time that evening. Gloria Rose had been a revelation and to find Shane Malone performing in the same company astonished him so much that Vicky felt it in the semi-darkness. "What is it, Sam? Are you all right?" He nodded without speaking and she misread him, saying, "It's all right for *moi* to find him delicious. I trust that's not the reason for your discomfort?"

"I'll tell you later," he whispered, still shaken by seeing the young American on the stage in front of him. He saw then that Shane had recognised him. Hardly surprising, he allowed, since I'm sitting just three feet from the apron of the stage. 'That's torn it,' he thought, 'now there isn't any way I can avoid telling Vicky what I know.'

During the interval, Sam and Arthur drank champagne with Vicky. They were standing by the motor coach hired for the occasion, while Deirdre sipped a cup of hot tea sold to them by a local woman with an eye for a penny. In both groups, virtually all of the conversation consisted of gushing praise for the young woman billed as Gloria Rose, while Victoria, for fun, made a point of saying how much she appreciated the attributes of Shane Malone. A few moments later she openly pondered – completely out of the blue – the possibility that the young man called Shane was one of her father's children, born the wrong side of the blanket. Sam was grateful he was exhaling tobacco smoke – had the reverse been happening, he might have choked.

Arthur chuckled at his sister's ribald joke, before he paused and nodded his head. "Shane is an unusual name," he allowed, as Sam held a match to his cigarette. "Wouldn't that be one for the book, what?"

At that moment, Deirdre joined them and Sam used her presence as an excuse to go and have a chat with Lizzie and her aunt, who was still gushing volubly about Gloria Rose.

The young woman had performed several spots in the first half, singing different types of songs with a change of costume on her hour-glass figure. Gloria had no vanity about how she looked, but she knew that when you earned your living on the stage, you had to use everything in your repertoire to win over an audience.

As she waited for the second half to begin, Gloria was peering through her personal eyehole in the masking curtain. Already dressed for her part in *East Lynn*, she was free to enjoy the miniature view as the punters returned to settle down for the play. The late arrivals were now getting into the front-row seats Bill had reserved for them. Gentry in the main, she thought. The tough-looking little old woman who had been to the show before and the tall person helping her didn't seem to be of the same class as the quartet accompanying them.

A lovely young woman with an abundance of auburn hair seemed to be satisfying herself that the other two women were comfortable, before she turned to share a laugh with the tall man beside her.

She was exquisitely dressed, the men also, though the taller of the two didn't seem to fit his clothes with anything like the style of the last member of the party. He was an exotic-looking individual, his white teeth flashing as he threw away a quip. Gloria's eyes lingered on his intense good looks, until she heard Bill intone, "Places, everyone!"

As she took up her position, Gloria could see the dark-haired man in her mind's eye. Perhaps he was

Italian, Greek? He could be a Jew. He was something of a dandy, a very attractive dandy, his cream shirt-front sporting ruffled lace under a floppy maroon bow, pierced by a diamond pin she'd seen sparkle once or twice as he turned in the soft glow of the tilly lamp set close to the front row. He wore another diamond on the third finger of his right hand, waving at the tall fair-haired man, a dashing smile, quick as his flashing eyes under blue-black hair, the gesture accompanying a quip, Gloria supposed, since both men laughed as he sat down. Their ease with each other suggested they were close so she reasoned that the exotic one was hardly a Jew since the gentry were known to be anti-Semitic.

She now dropped her images of him and everything else from her mind as Emily's forceful dramatic piano chord sequence set the tone for the opening scene of the play. The story of Lady Isabelle Vane – divorced by her husband because of a misunderstanding and forced to leave her baby son, little Willie – had always been what was called a tear-jerker, and within a short time Sam could feel the tightening of the audience's collective throat, including his own.

Having been sent away from her home, Isabelle is seduced by the handsome and ruthless roué, Sir Francis Levinson, before finally returning to her old home as governess to her dying son. The death of the child in his mother's arms, she wearing dark glasses and a veil to hide her appearance, was unashamedly melodramatic. Sam found it fairly nauseating, particularly the delivery of the immortal line, "Dead, dead, and never called me mother!" which, to his mind bordered on the incredible, and it was at this point in the story that his mind drifted back to his first meeting with the American actor, Shane Malone.

13

Greystones

June 1907

A little over three weeks earlier, Sam Sweet had been visiting his friend Lisa O'Brien at her house in Sandymount when she introduced Shane Malone as her nephew. Lisa was now well-established in the role of a demure middle-aged widow, doing nothing to attract attention to herself. By night she used the name of Molly Stafford. In this role she wore a red wig, her costume and the make-up appropriate to one of Dublin's more famous brothel-keepers. She was a woman of resource who went on paying the police well to help her preserve her separate identities, her separate lives.

When Shane had left his aunt's house to go and meet some people in the city, Lisa told Sam that the young American was her son by Arthur Shane Brewer. Feeling intuitively that she was telling the truth, Sam said, "I take it Arthur and Victoria know nothing about this."

"Not from me. And Arthur Shane never said anything he didn't have to say. He may have written it down, for it to come out after he dies. My son thinks my sister Rose is his mother, and I want to keep it that way, for now."

"He could be entitled to a whole pile of money if Arthur Shane has any balls. And he had to have, to look after you the way he did," said Sam.

Some years back, Lisa had told him of the substantial settlement her lover had granted her before he left Ireland, to live between Europe and America.

Sam and Lisa had known each other since he had renovated the first of a number of houses she had bought in and around Monto, Dublin's notorious brothel area. At this time, Sam was blacklisted by Dublin's building suppliers, and Lisa, having listened to his story of his run-in with the Foran brothers, had bought the materials he needed to carry out the work on her house. Their friendship had grown from there. The outsiders had formed a brother and sister relationship, sex between them never entering the equation, he having no qualms about taking the help she offered, while she admired the humility that allowed him to admit he was in need of a helping hand.

Lisa had been delighted when Sam secured his first contract with the Brewer organisation, and when later she learned that he was the lover of Victoria she was delighted for him. When he needed Lisa, she was there to help him through a disturbing circumstance that was not of his making. Recalling that time, Sam was infused with mixed feelings. Joy that at last, thanks to Victoria and Arthur, he was getting a much-needed break in his business life, sadness and regret at the memory of the man intent on destroying him.

Roger Ashmore was a man Arthur had inherited along with one of two other board members, when his father handed over the reins of the business to his son when he celebrated his twenty-fifth birthday. Ashmore had been a business acquaintance of Arthur's father for years. His many interests included his sole ownership of one of Dublin's largest suppliers of building materials to the trade. When he heard that Arthur, whom he regarded as wet behind the ears, was intent on giving the brewery extension contract to Sam Sweet, the man became apoplectic, unleashing a tirade of invective that left none of the board members in any doubt as to the strength of his anti-Semitism. He also joined forces with Constance Brewer – she had already heard about Victoria's affair *with that Jew*. In this climate this rather odd couple set about creating an uncomfortable climate for Arthur, and Sam went to him offering to set him free of any obligation sealed through their handshake. Arthur would have none of it, asking Sam to be patient while he found a way to disarm Ashmore and his mother without harming either of them publicly.

That same evening, Sam was working at one of Lisa's houses in Monto and she sensed that he had something problematic on his mind. Sam told her the story about Ashmore's interference and Lisa invited Sam to join her at her main house on the following evening, laughing as she said, "Tomorrow is Thursday, isn't it?" When Sam confirmed that indeed it was, she gave him a reassuring pat on the cheek. "Tomorrow night, all will be revealed and you and my dear Arthur will be free to get on with signing your contract."

On Thursday evening, Sam and a photographer called Harry Prior, stood in Lisa's private viewing room watching Roger Ashmore through a two-way mirror. The diminutive figure of the financier was bent over as he drew on the silk stockings of a prostitute called Nelly Weaver. He now attached the suspenders hanging from the belt around his lower waist to the stocking tops, before slipping into the prostitute's shoes while she brushed out a wig for him to wear.

Harry Prior, a weedy little man with shiny pomaded hair checked that he had positioned his camera perfectly. When he was satisfied, he nodded to Lisa. Sam stood there smoking a cigarette, shaking his head in disbelief as Ashmore straightened the seams of his black stockings before putting on the wig Nelly had prepared for him.

Ashmore now raised his face to the woman. It was made up in the overdone style of a prostitute so that he now looked like a singularly unattractive little woman with a flat chest and enough red hair to stuff the average mattress. As he faced the heavy-breasted woman, Sam saw that he was sporting a more than respectable erection for such a little man.

Nellie stepped close to him now. Supporting a great breast with one hand, she allowed Ashmore to guzzle at her nipple. She dropped her other hand to grip him fiercely down below. As she enclosed him in a vice-like grip he cried out. The woman knew what he wanted and without lessening the force of her grip she began to work her hand furiously back and forth. Ashmore writhed and squirmed in painful ecstasy while Harry Prior put his head under the black cloth of his camera and snapped the first of a series of pictures.

Two days later, Sam Sweet entered a gentleman's club on Stephen's Green. In moments, he was shown into the reading-room where Ashmore, sitting in a wing-backed leather chair that quite dwarfed him, gaped in discomfort as Sam approached him.

Leaning over the man Sam whispered, "I won't make problems for you if you don't make problems for me." Slipping a foolscap envelope from his briefcase, he placed it in Ashmore's lap before he walked quietly from the room.

The next day, early to the brewery and despite much work to do, Sam joined Arthur – it was seven o'clock – for the express purpose of seeing his friend's great shire horses come from the loading bays. Arthur wanted Sam to see them hauling the great wagons in a trot up the cobbled incline to the outside world, their giant hoofs sending sparks shooting either side of their path.

It was a stimulating sight and one that Arthur never tired of showing to those people he valued. The great beasts, behemoths of beauty and grace and strength, towed the drays loaded with barrels of Brewer's stout so easily they might have been pulling nothing more than a second tail behind.

Sam laughed out loud in the sheer delight of witnessing such marvels of nature as they went about their work, understanding right away Arthur's love for the magnificent shires. Minutes later, as they strolled among the stables built especially for the wonderful horses, they came upon the hanging body of a man dangling from a rafter. It was Roger Ashmore. For a moment, the taller man seemed stunned enough to fall over, Sam grabbing him about the waist to make sure this didn't happen.

Victoria's touch on his arm brought Sam back to the last moments of the melodrama *East Lynn*. As he turned his head to look into her eyes, he could see large numbers of handkerchiefs all around the tent, hearing now the sobs and the voice of weeping throughout the place. He leaned toward Vicky who clearly wanted to say something, relieved to note that she was not moved in the least by the play. "As I said earlier, I believe we may have stumbled across that nice Jewish girl you're going to marry some day." She was smiling, flickering fireflies of light from the nearest tilly lamp like dark diamonds dancing in her golden hair.

"I'm not sure she'd tolerate the presence of a beauty named Victoria Brewer in her husband's life, 'til death does them part!" Sam said in an ardent, hushed whisper.

Her smile deepened, she touched his fingers, her

muted laugh short and sexual. "I feel like a shiny apple."

As the audience all around him rose as one person, the sound of their collective applause astonishing him, Sam saw that Deirdre and her mother and her old aunt were sniffling back their tears, even as they pounded their hands together for the performance of Gloria Rose as Isabelle Carlisle.

Deirdre leaned across Arthur and touched Sam on the arm. "Do you think you could arrange for us to meet her? I'd love to shake her hand, she's fascinating." Sam gave her a smile and a nod of his head: "You know there's not a thing I wouldn't do for you."

"You can arrange anything. You always could." Dee's eyes shone.

"You're having a good time, right, Dee?"

She nodded enthusiastically, and he saw her hand squeeze Arthur's. He had watched her as the play began. Her eyes were wide from the opening moments in the flickering light from the paraffin lamps, adding to the atmosphere Bill Boswell had intended to create, with a fairly rudimentary replication of a Victorian drawing-room. Yes, at times the players, in moving about the stage for dramatic effect were in shadow for a moment or two, but this didn't harm the production in any way. It had been well acted too, by players who knew precisely how to draw a laugh or a tear, when the moment called for it. So, though Sam didn't care for the play itself, he could appreciate the professionalism that had gone into the staging and the overall effect. He left his seat before the sketch that had been promised by Bill Boswell 'to send you home with a smile instead of a tear' – he wanted to find Shane Malone.

Gloria had not forgotten the old woman with her helmet of white hair. She was reminded yet again of a porcelain figure by Bustelli, seen in Paris by her mother's side, as a child. Her heart had been touched when she was brought backstage on a previous occasion. She remembered well the clear appreciation shining in her time-beaten eyes, the gentle touch of her hand. She remembered her name, not a usual occurrence for her. Molly, Miss Molly Harney. She had a vague recollection of the old lady's companion that night – it was the same tall woman supporting her now as they came together into the hotel for the after-show supper.

Sam had smoked a cigarette while he went looking for Shane. He paused for a few moments, drew smoke into his lungs, feeling he could walk along the corridor of pale cream that the moon had painted onto the pond-like sea. Finding the young actor having a quiet cigarette he asked Shane to invite the entire company to supper as his guests at the local hotel. Lisa O'Brien's son by Arthur Shane Brewer had hurried away to make what he considered an exciting invitation to Bill and Emily, and the band of strolling players. "The company has never been invited to supper before, Mister Sweet – I'm sure they'll be delighted to accept your offer."

Sam then spent some time by the sea, glad to be alone for a few minutes. He needed the silence as he wondered about some of the feelings buried down deep where the light didn't shine. He now heard laughter coming from the tent and he moved closer to the water to be free of the sound. Something had happened to him and he needed to tease it out, see what it was all about. To his astonishment, he had thought of Passover in the early part of the variety show, and he felt it was because of a beautiful Jewish girl called Gloria Rose. Long-forgotten words surfaced like darts that hurt him, little arrows that seemed to wake him up to he knew not what. It was as if some invisible force was attempting to harness his attention. He had no idea what all this was about, and he found it awesome. The words were still there like legends painted along the wall inside his forehead.

"After the ninth plague, Moses said to God-what now? And God said-Let all Hebrews in Egypt prepare quickly food for a hasty journey." This was how the unleavened bread – matzoh – had come into being. "Anoint your door with the blood of the lamb, so that it may be not hit." The first-born sons of Egypt were hit – "The angel of death will pass over. And bitter herbs symbolise, for the Hebrew, slavery, and shank bone is for the strong arm of God."

As random, isolated words and phrases filled Sam's mind, he stood through the silent harmony of the moon's music over the benign ocean, his thinking confused by the sudden demands that the past seemed to be making on him. He stood on the butt of his cigarette, wondering what was going on. Was it the girl's beautiful singing, or was he fantasising about making love to her, while he dressed it up as something else? Confused sufficiently that he was willing to shrug all of it away like dust brushed from a jacket sleeve, he rejoined his party as Bill Boswell was introducing them to the members of his company. There was jollity in the air, much talking and hand-shaking and words of congratulations but he felt estranged from all the good will until Gloria came through the masking curtain to meet them.

She shook hands, making a point of repeating everybody's name so that she might remember them all. Once the introductions were out of the way, and she had agreed to join them at the hotel for supper, she gave most of her attention to Molly Harney and to Elizabeth Doyle.

The old lady with the snow-white hair seemed to be in a state of mild shock from the moment the actress kissed her on both cheeks, but once she relaxed she had the young actress laughing heartily at some of the things she said. Observing this, Deirdre thought highly of the manner in which Gloria Rose attended to Aunt Molly. It said something for the young woman's character, and perhaps her heart, that she could be bothered with an old woman when their party consisted of such attractive people as Arthur and Sam and Victoria.

Gloria wore a cream-coloured silk dress that highlighted her violet eyes. It was worn without any frills, the actress not wearing jewels of any kind. Her dark hair was loose and tumbling onto her shoulders covered by a plain grey shawl resting on her arms.

Exotic-demure, Sam thought, even more astonished by her beauty now that she was up close. Scenting her perfume, he smiled to himself. Forget demure, he thought – in a nun's habit this lady would be exotic.

Gloria had shaken hands warmly with Deirdre, checking that she was the daughter of Elizabeth, repeating some things that she might remember the details. What did become very clear to all of them was that *family* was very important to the young actress.

Dee noticed she had this way of giving all of her eyes to the person she was talking to while Vicky wondered was this a gift of nature or something Gloria had worked into her offstage act. She wondered further, was the lady in some way smitten with Arthur? Yes, her inner-voice agreed; she held old Arthur's hand as you held Sam's that long ago day by the Liffey.

Arthur had not been looking for anything when his eyes met Gloria's. However, in the minute or two when they were free to respond silently to each other, he couldn't deny an intimately-connected moment and to his surprise discovered a surge of pleasure that it had happened.

Gloria suffered somewhat through her mixed feelings in those same early moments. That a Gentile could affect her in this way left her feeling uncomfortable. Meanwhile, the man himself hid his attraction to her by bringing Sam alongside him to meet her again.

"Shane Malone mentioned that you two have met before, Mister Sweet," Gloria said, almost biting her tongue in an effort not to sound so trivial.

"Oh yes," Sam smiled easily, almost overcome by the desire to kiss her. "His mother's sister and I are long-time friends."

Gloria found him attractive and sensed that he was a powerful man. "I was wondering, Mister Sweet," she said with a smile, "if I may sit by Miss Molly Harney during supper."

The party at the Le Basque hotel was a gay affair. Sam ate lobster and drank wine from the Rhineland, casually observing that Vicky was drinking rather a lot. Several times he was very conscious of how effortlessly Gloria Rose fitted into the company. There was nothing actressy in her manner and he liked that about her. She seemed a genuinely nice young woman – the fact that she was gorgeous enough to turn the head of a statue seemed to have passed her by. Another plus, Sam thought.

Gloria gave most of her attention to Molly Harney, occasionally speaking to Deirdre and to Sam and Arthur. Without being able to put his finger on why he felt so, Sam formed the impression that the actress was very taken with Arthur. He admitted to himself he could be wrong – once in a while his instinct did let him down.

Why not? Sam said to himself. The Brewer name was famous the length and breadth of Ireland and Arthur, one of nature's own gentlemen, was affable and hearty and frequently very amusing when he'd had a few drinks. When he had taken more than a few, well, you had to take what you got. When he had been drinking a lot, anything was possible. He would remember this philosophical thought later in the evening, since part of the birthday treat for Molly Harney was that she would spend the night at the hotel, a first for the old woman who was relishing the prospect.

Shortly after Elizabeth had taken her aunt up to bed, Sam heard Gloria openly admire Deirdre's engagement ring. Hearing this, Sam got a nudge from within suggesting that she was actually checking out who it was that Dee was engaged to marry. By way of an answer, Deirdre took hold of Arthur's hand. Gloria wished the couple all the good luck in the world. They thanked her for the good wishes before Arthur indicated to a waitress to replenish glasses all around.

Sam turned to Shane Malone to congratulate him on his evening's work. "You have a lot of talent, Shane. I was really impressed. You and Gloria, surely you can go all the way – the London stage, New York, wherever you want to go."

Shane smiled, gesturing to the actress who remained modestly silent. "You're right about Gloria, Mister Sweet. I'm not so sure about me. But tell it to Aunt Lisa when you see her again. She can tell my parents, put my mother's doubts to rest." His easy smile revealed sparkling white teeth, but Sam noticed that his eyes lacked warmth. At the same time, he actually heard Victoria's intake of breath and he avoided eye contact with her. Earlier, she had jokingly postulated the proposition that the actor called Shane might be one of her father's wrong-side-of-the-blanket children. Having just heard Shane speak of 'his Aunt Lisa', Vicky would have concluded that coincidence could stretch only so far.

"You've chosen the stage as a career," Sam filled what might well have been an uneasy silence. "It's your life. Go for the rainbow, Shane. Give it say five years. If it isn't working out like you want it to, you can always change your mind. You'd still be a very young man."

Shane tore his eyes away from Gloria, Sam aware that the young actor was hoist on the hinges of unrequited love. "I guess I'll go back to America, when I feel I'm good enough," Shane said quietly. "I know one thing, I've got to give it a real shot. Being onstage is the most exciting thing."

Sam passed him a business card. "I'll be making trips to America. I'd like us to stay in touch. If I can help you any time, please let me know. I happen to have a very soft spot for your aunt." Sam gave him a nod, raising his glass in a silent toast. "I'd bet good money that you're going to be very famous one day. You mark my words well, young Shane."

By one o'clock in the morning, the players had departed. Arthur had turned in looking the worse for wear – his drinking had become very heavy during the last hour at the table. Deirdre and Victoria were sharing a small suite. Sam and Vicky had decided against sleeping together in deference to the presence of his friend, Elizabeth, whom he had known long before she became Dee's mother. He retired to his room to sink happily into the feather bed. His sigh of gratitude was short-lived since he didn't get to sleep right away, that last glass of wine over his normal three being an unwise choice.

His mother arrived in a fitful dream along with people he knew in Little Jerusalem. All of them were going on at him. Loudly they were urging him to do his duty concerning propagation of the race, the absolute need for children, and children, and more children. Some of them were shouting at him – then, coming awake in a sweat, Sam realised that someone was shouting on the landing outside his door.

He knew instantly it was Arthur's voice and he hauled himself out of the bed quicker than he would have thought possible. As he slipped on his pants, he was glad he had left the hanging oil lamp burning. He opened the door to find Arthur was right there in front of him on the landing. He was stark-naked, wrestling with some invisible opponent. Hearing the door open he swung around to face Sam.

The pale blue eyes were slates of pain belonging to a demented man. A demented, angry man who was throwing empty blows at some unseen posse of demons.

"Arthur, for God's sake," Sam grabbed him by the arms, anxious to avoid the disturbance this wild fit could cause. For Lizzie to discover that the man Dee was going to marry could behave like this would cause all manner of unnecessary suffering. And as Lizzie often said, she had suffered enough.

Arthur grabbed Sam by the throat. Taken by surprise Sam didn't move for a few moments but as the pressure on his windpipe increased he knew he had to do something to stop this carry-on.

"Sorry, Arthur," he mumbled, bringing his knee up into Arthur's genitals with real force. The hands dropped off his throat as Arthur stumbled back a pace. Sam shifted his balance to hit his best friend with a short right-hand punch to the jaw. Arthur sagged like a bag of hay, unconscious even as Sam grabbed him and hauled him over his shoulder in one deft movement. Stepping back into his room, he laid Arthur on the spare bed and covered him with the eiderdown. Satisfied the big man would do no more shouting tonight he got back into bed and before long felt himself dozing off. As the need for sleep claimed him, he regretted it had been necessary to punch the best friend any man ever had. He shrugged away his concern. If ever there was an appropriate time to knock Arthur unconscious, that moment on the landing had been it. He smiled ruefully, allowing that he would give his life for his friend. For all the madness that could erupt when Arthur had too much booze on board, Sam believed him to be the finest of the fine. His mind drifted to a more pleasant picture – he was coming out of a passionate embrace with the beautiful Gloria. She had just accepted his proposal of marriage. This was followed by the look of surprise on Arthur's face as Sam asked him to be his best man.

The bride-to-be of Sam's fantasy was not sleeping at all, nor was there a smile about her lovely mouth as she sipped water, her pen poised over writing paper. Gloria had sat down with a need to write and yet the words had turned in for the night.

She picked up one of the books she had filled with her penmanship during her time with the show. She flicked through several pages, wondering if a word or a phrase would reawaken her slumbering thoughts. She felt confused. It seemed her power to reason had somehow dozed off. Why has this happened? Had her mind become unbalanced by meeting two civilized men? Or was it the fact that she had found herself drawn, unbelievably, to the Gentile, a tall, gentle man who was, by all accounts, one of the richest men in the British Isles. Or was she so flattered by the attentions of the other, a Dublin-born Jew no less, who would make any woman a fine husband, since, according to Bill Boswell, he was a major building contractor in Dublin.

She thought of Shane. The poor boy was so in love though she had done nothing to encourage him. He had been like a big golden-haired puppy dog lapping about her from the moment he had arrived. But he was not for her since she knew that she would need a man older than herself, a man of substance, someone with a proven character, if she were ever to even think about getting married. She found herself looking at a page written in her early days with the Bohemian Band, and she took the risk of reading it. She knew that the words might make her sad, but she had to get over the pain of loss that had diminished her for so long. She began to read: 'Mama, as I watched you become emotionally involved with Jem Riley I became frightened. So very quickly, you seemed to need him as though he were some kind of opiate. He quickly came to know the power he had over you, and over me, and I began to fear that before long he would do just as he wanted, with both of us.

'In no time at all, our working hours were the only time he wasn't there to rule the roost, though he found us on the streets when he wanted money. He didn't work since we kept him in money for drink. I tried talking to you, suggesting it was time Jem Riley moved on. For the first time in my life you stepped back from me, your eyes dilated in dismay, even fear. 'Please don't ask me that,' was all you could say to me, your eye such a wounded window that I felt that I had already been brutalised.

'Some nights later, I had drifted off to sleep to the private sounds that I hated so to witness. In the night, I found you cuddling me. I had been weeping copiously. Mama, you wiped my face, whispering to me that the cost was too great, that you would speak to Jem and tell him it was time to go.

'In the morning, I was tying up my boots when I heard you plead for his understanding. You needed your time to devote to me, you said. I was growing up and needed all the help you could provide in this topsy-turvy world. We could not go on supporting him since we were hard-put to earn what we needed to keep body and soul together. As I listened to the innocence in your voice, Mama, as I heard the childlike expectancy that this man, because he had shared your bed, would agree, acquiesce, be reasonable and understand your need, I became fearful.

'I saw him hit you with such force that he knocked you off your feet. I was so shocked that for a moment I couldn't move, my eyes fixed on his cruel mouth and on the ferocity of the anger flaring in his black eyes. I moved to help you, Mama, and he slapped me so hard I almost lost consciousness.

'His message was short and to the point. He came and he went as he saw fit and we would accept that. He undid his leather belt, and while I sat there, my face numb from his blow, he whipped you, Mama, about the thighs and buttocks. I was almost deaf in one ear but I could hear you whimper through the beating you took before he stopped swinging the belt and ordered you to your feet.

'He made you undress, forced you to take every stitch of clothing from your body. I remember how he assured you that your precious daughter was going to get a lesson in what was to come for her before too long. She was about to see a real man take a woman, he said, and, if you didn't obey him, he would beat you to a bleeding pulp. I heard a prayer for help run through my heart and up out of me and away to a God unknown, with little hope in the after-moment that anybody would understand the silent words, distorted as they were by the terror imprisoning me.

'At that moment, Mama, you unleashed a cry of utter despair, a tearing sound rent from a heart that could take no more. It was as though the very flesh of your soul was being ripped out of your being, a wail of such agony that death needed no further proof of welcome.

'Our cocoon of suffering and madness burst open

when the door of the room slammed inwards, the landlord standing there with a wooden mallet in his hand, his voice a warning against argument, as he ordered us out before he handed us over to the police.

'Later that day we followed Jem Riley to a doss-house room that was truly unfit for anyone to live in. I saw Riley fall to his knees before you, his arms encircling your thighs, his sobs of regret so palpable that he seemed to be choking on them.

'I saw your hand move to his head like metal drawn to a magnet. I saw your tears fall down your face, and I turned away. There was nothing I could do, Mama. You were making a pact with a devil that could turn on the charm and produce his pain-filled regret with the same facility that empowered him to become a madman capable of killing us both.

'Some days after that you told me you were twelve weeks pregnant. Oh, Mama! I could not speak. For the first time ever, I could find no word to say to you. I stumbled away, and I seriously considered ending my life in the river Thames. I wanted to die, Mama, until I thought of what that would do to you. So, as I had acquiesced when you returned to his arms, I let go of my death-wish. And so the degenerate life, the dirt and the filth and the pain and the drunken madness of Jem Riley, hung about us like a poisonous cloud that would surely engulf us entirely before too long. This thought no longer terrified me, Mama. In fact, it was like the toll of a distant bell that promised relief from our Hell upon earth.'

14

Dublin

May 1st 1908

During the months that followed the meeting of Gloria and what she thought of as the Brewer contingent, Sam Sweet drove his motoring car from Dublin several times to see her, always behaving as a gentleman might be expected to do. She appreciated this, though she half expected him to make some kind of physical advance. When he did not try to kiss her, she felt that he respected her as a woman and she quit thinking of him as brash in his 'I know what I'm talking about' kind of way.

Since the night of the after-show supper she had been comparing Sam Sweet to Arthur Brewer, who somehow glowed in a quiet, diffident way that much appealed to her. This confused her since Arthur was a Gentile. A year earlier he might well have featured on the top of her hate list. In fact, he had beguiled her. This had come about because he practically ignored her, though he covertly sought her eyes over the rim of his drinking glass, and later, when he had become tipsy, by naïvely allowing her see his several surreptitious glances at her breasts. But Sam Sweet had come-a-calling and she had to admit she looked forward to his visits.

Sam wasn't quite sure why he was drawn back into the countryside to see the lovely, dark-browed girl, who was more than gracious when he paid a visit. He made a point to spend time with the Boswells on each occasion, having become friendly with the couple, enjoying Bill's stories about the business, respecting Emily for her folksy wisdom and philosophy and for the fact that she talked about Gloria as though she were her own much-loved daughter.

Shane was no longer touring with the company, true to his word about trying to match himself with those performers who were making it on the New York stage. Sam was aware that Shane was back in America since the young actor had written to him from Manhattan to stay in contact. Sam smiled to himself when Emily talked of Shane's broken heart.

"He fell in love with Gloria the moment he clapped eyes on her. Most men do, present company excepted," she said smartly, "though I'm not sure you drive all this way to see myself and Bill." Emily took a further risk before Bill could come in with one of his stories. "Gloria dreams of a home and a family. She's been through enough hard times. Married to an actor, can you imagine?"

"Ah, Samuel," Bill intoned in mock mournfulness,

"they soon forget that a man with sterling qualities, such as my own, is worth all the security and middle-class values on earth."

"I did say present company excluded," Emily chortled. "I know better than to cast Cistercians on you as a husband and provider. Gloria was never going to get serious about a penniless actor, not even an uncomplicated, gorgeous one such as dear Shane."

Sam smiled at the malapropism, thinking, 'If only you knew. The same penniless actor could be a multi-millionaire once Arthur Shane Brewer goes for his tea!'

Later as he sat with Gloria in her caravan, Sam allowed that she had staked a claim on a portion of his mind from the moment he had first seen her onstage. Yet, Emily had been right when she excluded him from the line of admirers that had fallen in love at first sight, though he had several times found he was actually wondering what sort of wife the young actress would make. At first he had laughed it off, putting it down to the fact that she exuded a powerful sexuality, and the disarming habit of looking directly into his eyes when she was speaking to him. This combination was very potent, being all the more enticing since she had no notion that she did this. Or so he believed.

He reckoned he was not in love with Gloria, since his feelings for her were not the familiar shades of the love and lust he knew with Vicky who continued to captivate him. Yet, just a few nights after his most recent visit to the countryside, the violet-eyed girl with the incredible breasts was very much in his thoughts as he shared an

LEE DUNNE

evening of passionate love-making with Vicky. Not that he was imagining having sex with Gloria – but Gloria seemed to be there watching him as he groaned through the ecstasy of orgasm as his beautiful mistress yelled, "I'm coming. I can't stop!" in her own inimitable way.

Later, Vicky commented that while he had been ferocious in their love-making, "At times you seemed to be elsewhere, unless I'm going dotty from too much plonk," she allowed. "I'm not complaining, since even now I'm waiting for the rest of my bits and pieces to fall back into place." She presented him with a playful bow of her head. "Nobody plunders quite like you do."

He denied that his mind had wandered, denied it to such a point that it was all too clear she had been right. It was then she decided to tell him of her plans. "I'm going to Paris some time next week." Anticipating his offer to accompany her, she raised her hand. "No, please, darling, hear me out." Her tone suggested that this was not easy for her, while he, already feeling it was not going to be easy for him either, lit cigarettes for them both. She understood, knowing things about Sam he hadn't yet discovered about himself.

"I need to be away from Dublin, Ireland, and, darling, I simply have to get away from you for a while. I have been dilettanting in my studio, happily talking about getting down to some serious work, while really, all I have wanted to do is drink wine, smoke cigarettes and jump into bed with you at every conceivable moment, if you'll pardon the pun."

Willing to be light about this despite the feeling in

the pit of his stomach, Sam said, "Speaking of conceivable moments, may I ask what you do in that area. How is it that you haven't become pregnant?"

Victoria simply burst out laughing, reaching out to hug him for a moment. "It's my secret, but since I can't keep anything from you, I'll tell you. Tissue paper."

Sam stared at her, his incredulous expression fuelling another burst of her most musical laughter. "Tissue paper?" he gasped.

"Yes, my darling. I stuff the old boiler with tissue paper." She beamed as though she was bathing in gratitude. "Been using cartloads of the stuff since you came into my life. You're not bothered, are you? I mean, you and I, we were never going to get into all that domestic stuff." Vicky's eyebrows shot up, as though it suddenly occurred that Sam thought their relationship had deepened beyond what they had agreed upon when they decided to be lovers. "You didn't want me up the duff, did you, Sam?"

"Of course not, we laid out the ground rules." He meant it as he said it but despite this he wondered what would have happened had Vicky conceived their child. The instant answer – he would have married her 'with a heart and a half'. He believed too that he would have agreed to whatever her terms were, just for the sheer joy of sharing his life with such a great, wild, unpredictable woman.

"I have to go, Sam. There's another part of me, the part that has nothing to do with you and I, us, and it is staking its claim to my time and my work."

She said this in a tone that suggested it was only fair to honour this need, even though she was entirely happy with their relationship. He knew that what was being presented was a *fait accompli*, and so he resisted the urge to at least attempt to talk her round. He smiled and tried to show her that he felt all right about things, the truth being something else.

"Of course, you must go." He knew his smile was diplomatic – he lit a fresh cigarette, so preoccupied with his mixed feelings that he didn't think to light one for her. "If you need me, or you want to see me at any time, you only have to let me know. How long will you be gone for?" He drew smoke deep, wishing he hadn't needed to ask the question.

"I don't know. I'll come back for the wedding, of course, since I am to be Dee's matron of honour. By that time I'll have a better idea as to how long I will stay in Paris." She took a cigarette and he hastened to hold a light to it. She smiled her thanks through the waft of smoke as she exhaled. "My not being here for a while, it will give you time to get to know Gloria. She would make you a fine wife, Sam. And, even if you haven't faced it in yourself, I know, or I believe I know, that you need the kind of prize mare Gloria is to bear your children."

Sam poured wine for them both, catching his breath at her description of Gloria. It wasn't out of character – Vicky liked to apply amusing labels to people, sometimes pejoratively. As he sipped the wine he wasn't sure whether she was merely making a joke that, for him, misfired, or simply being anti-Semitic. He smiled inwardly at the somewhat fanciful notion that – even though she waxed enthusiastic about the romantic possibilities for him and Gloria – she was jealous of the young singer? He dismissed both caveats as fanciful. Vicky was never less than honest. But then, she believed him to be the same. In truth, this was not always so – he had rarely told her a downright lie, but he did indulge sometimes in what a wily barrister might call 'concealment of material fact'. Would Vicky do that kind of thing? Not that it mattered. Vicky was going away and, by the sound of her, she was going for quite some time. This created a dart of discomfort in Sam. The wedding would not be happening until Easter, some months away. He feared that coming back for the wedding was a duty she would perform with love, but it sounded to him that she would return to Paris when the nuptials had been put to bed.

During the early weeks following Victoria's departure, Sam threw himself into his business life with a renewed energy. After about a week, Arthur was urging him to slow down – his own late-night drinking ensuring that mornings were sometimes the very devil to deal with – but Sam went on working on plans for another building at the brewery, even when his friend had begged off to go and have a liquid lunch at the Shelbourne.

Meanwhile, Sam had a team of artisans working on the house in Leinster Road, which he now owned. He was involved in talks with a Kilkenny businessman with a fleet of canal boats for sale. The builders' provider's yard, which he had recently bought by Portobello Harbour, he trusted to Brendan O'Connor, the ginger-haired lad who used to bring him a mug filled with strong tea when he worked for Deirdre. Sam smiled in his ongoing admiration for Dee – how she had asked him if he would give Brendan a job in his expanding business since his role in her employ was not worthy of his genuine ability in so many areas. She had been proved right since Carrots – as Sam called the fiery young Dubliner – had the mind of someone destined for a bright future in business. He also possessed self-belief enough to assure Sam that if he made him manager at Portobello complex, he would not regret it.

Six months on, Brendan had proved he was as good as his word. He had many gifts but above all he got along with people, customers, employees and anybody else that he had to deal with – his gentle generosity to his workers evoked a sense of trust in even the hardest of the labourers, and Sam soon allowed him to know he had an important role to play in his future plans. Brendan accepted this compliment and that same week found that he had been given a rise in pay. This was something that Sam felt was right and fair, especially as Carrots hadn't asked for it. Meanwhile Sam and Arthur had to deal with the recalcitrance of Pat Doyle.

The one-time Dublin jarvey was now a man of substance, a serious performer in the business community of his native city. He was currently running retail shops, a couple of offices that bought, sold and rented property in Dublin and the surrounding countryside, and a large fleet of hackney cabs. He owned the premises and the yards where his horses were stabled, and had a full-time blacksmith employed to keep his animals properly shod and the wheels of his vehicles maintained to a high standard.

Sam was not surprised when Pat turned on him when he broached the subject of marriage between Deirdre and Arthur Brewer. "That could only happen over my dead body, Sam. Understand me. No daughter of mine will never marry a Protestant and I don't care who he is." Before Sam could get another word in, Pat went to the door and called for Deirdre to come to him in the room he used as an office.

She arrived, her eyes wary. "I want you to tell me here and now, Deirdre, here and now in front of Sam Sweet, that you will dismiss immediately any notion you might have been holding that you are going to marry Arthur Brewer." Pat was standing as he unleashed this demand, a tall powerful figure, not above using every inch of his height in his need to dominate his daughter.

Deirdre stood tall, her shoulders straight, and Sam was moved by her quiet, respectful attitude. "Daddy, I have never disobeyed you when I felt you were entitled to order me about, tell me how I should live my life. In my opinion, that situation no longer exists, and though I mean no disrespect to you, I can't possibly give you the assurance you're looking for."

Pat's eyes were wide in disbelief. Sam saw his fists

clench, hoped that his old friend wasn't about to physically attack her. He moved on his seat, prepared to spring between them, should that be necessary.

Finally, Pat, breathing down his nose like a confused bull, said in the flat adenoidal tones of his native city. "Hear me now, young woman, and hear me real good. I'm telling you now, just this once, that unless you promise, promise me here and now, that you will do as I say, I want you out of this house this very minute."

Sam was shocked by the finality in Pat's voice and the rigidity of his demeanour. He was like a large rock that had been dumped in the middle of his office. 'No arguing with that,' he thought.

Deirdre looked at Sam. "Will you wait and take me with you?"

He nodded his head. "Of course, I will."

She left the room and Pat Doyle turned to face Sam. "She would never have met these people if it hadn't been for you. That you, of all people, have brought the Brewers into our lives? You're a Jew. You're part of a race that disowns them that marry out of their faith. Could you not have put the boot into this madness, before I even needed to hear about it?"

"Times are changing, Pat." Sam felt sorry for him, "None of us have the right to tell someone else how to live their life. Not even a son or a daughter. Deirdre is the finest of the fine, and whether you believe it or not, Arthur Brewer is worthy of her and needs her and loves her. They will grow further together and I'm only sorry that you feel so strongly against it."

"He's a bloody Protestant, Sam. She is a Roman Catholic. The two do not go together, especially since he's high up in the establishment. This family will be the ridicule of everyone that knows us. Is there nothing you can do to make her change her mind? We go back a long way. Can't you help me here?"

While Sam tried to get Pat Doyle to see reason, "We're talking about a young woman of twenty-one years of age, Pat. You can't legislate for her life, not any more," Deirdre was in the kitchen embracing her mother, grateful for Elizabeth's whispered support.

"Between now and Easter, girl, I'll try and get him down off his high horse. If he'd met Arthur, if he knew him even as little as I do, he mightn't be so set. But, set he is, like cement at the minute, so it's best to let him be. You meet me for a cup of tea tomorrow and we'll talk without having to whisper."

Thanks to this exchange with her mother, Deirdre left home in better heart than she might have expected to, remembering a not-too-distant evening when she had told Vicky that this banishment would most likely be her father's reaction. Vicky had hugged her, dismissing her concern. "You can live with me, Dee. I'd love it. And if by some chance I'm not in Ireland, you can have the house all to yourself, and, of course, Arthur too, should you decide to sleep together between now and the nuptials . . ."

Deirdre had laughed somewhat nervously, but was delighted to accept Vicky's offer, amused by her effervescent incorrigibility but, above all, intrigued by the implication that her friend might be away. Scarcely able to hide her feelings, she asked Vicky, "Are you and Sam planning to go somewhere?"

Vicky shook her head. "I'm going alone. I need to go and work. And, to tell you and you alone, I've heard from a woman I love that she is lonely for my company. So I'm going to Paris to work hard, and help a dear friend get over an unhappy affair. This is between you and *moi*, as I have yet to tell Sam the details of my plans."

As they drove away from her family home, Dee was surprised that she felt relief, but thinking about it, it made sense – better that the situation was out in the open. She felt comforted in knowing that she could cope with her father as long as she and her mother remained as close as they had always been. She reminded herself that she also had Sam and Arthur and Vicky on her side, quite a strong supporting team, she allowed, with a smile of gratitude.

She moved into Vicky's house at Fitzwilliam Square, to find that she had a cook, and a butler who was a general factotum, ready to drive her and attend to her needs as required. Arthur came to the house several evenings a week and they ate dinner. He generally left by eleven, and though they kissed intimately there was never any suggestion that he would stay the night. Deirdre knew that had he asked to sleep with her, she would have agreed, although she felt no pressing urge to consummate things before they were married. Still dealing with the pain of leaving her family home, she was perfectly happy with the romantic nature of their gentle courtship.

Sam dropped in regularly, delighted but not surprised, to find Dee reading a pamphlet about midwifery. He gathered that she wasn't ready to talk about this new interest and said only that he had come to invite her out. He was very off-the-cuff in personal matters, and today, on the spur-of-the-moment he had decided to drive her off to Rathmines to visit his mother. This happened several more times in the early months after Vicky had gone to France, and Dee was more than happy to be in Sam's company. The more she listened to Esther, the more she liked her. The old woman radiated contentment since she was, according to herself, now living in luxury in the house on Leinster Road. Esther enjoyed these visits, and though she took her time, she would come to think the world of Deirdre, even if she was *goyim*.

Month by month Bill Boswell's current tour was taking the company further from Dublin, and Sam found it interesting on his weekend visits to Gloria, that the further he had to go to drive to see her, the closer they seemed to be when he got there, which made him feel good.

On one occasion she kissed him on the lips as he was about to get into his car. He was so surprised, she burst out laughing.

"Sam, I had no idea you would be startled." Her head was thrown back in the laughing and he wanted to crush his mouth against her throat, put his lips to her breasts. Instead he stood his ground and held his arms open to her. For a moment she seemed perplexed, then she came and allowed him put his arms about her. Without any word of explanation, she helped him realise that her simple kiss had been in some way a gesture of gratitude, rather than an overt move towards bed. Though he imagined he burned where her breasts touched his shirt, his instinct told him this was not the time to take the situation any further.

"I would like you to know that you are the only man I have ever kissed," she said quietly into his shoulder. "The first with whom I have embraced."

By early June, the touring company had returned to County Wicklow. This came about because Deirdre hired Big Bill Boswell's Bohemian Band to perform at Dunbla House for the official party to celebrate her engagement to Arthur. She called it a Stags and Hens night, and arranged that it would take place on June the twenty-first. In no time Dee was checking that every detail was being attended to, a happy gleam in her eyes in the days beforehand. Even Arthur, who was notoriously shy about any fuss, was won over by Dee's enthusiasm and Sam's support for the idea.

Arthur knew they were obliged to have a gathering, where all his long-time friends and acquaintances would be wined and dined, and "What better way to entertain the buggers than by giving them the show, before a late dinner and music to waltz to – if they aren't all too drunk by then," he said with a rare smile.

The offhand reminder about how drunk Arthur and

most of his old friends could get on occasion, caused Sam to remember the night in the Greystones Hotel. He smiled in mild disbelief – it was like something that really couldn't have happened – Sam wondering if Arthur had ever worked out what happened on the landing outside his bedroom door. He smiled as he remembered how Arthur had been rubbing his jaw on the journey back to Dunbla the next day. Every so often Arthur would utter, yet again, his intention to see his dentist since his gum was giving him all kinds of gyp. 'Serves you right, you rascal,' Sam had said to himself, his smile one of relief that he had been on hand to tame the wild man on the stairs.

Driving his latest motorcar, the first of its kind ever seen in Ireland, Sam watched the speedometer needle move beyond the twenty-five mile an hour mark. He laughed out loud at the very idea – the open road was ensuring his ride was a bumpy one but he didn't care. He was simply flabbergasted to be moving so fast, aware that he missed Vicky and her incorrigible wishful way to have every experience allowed, speed being close to the top of her list of fun things. He laughed again, wondering how she was. Dear Vicky, a true original. He loved her still but enjoyed the relief of having overcome the suffering her leaving had engendered. He eased back on the throttle as he neared Dunbla House, looking forward to the party for Arthur and Dee. Now he found himself smiling as he thought about Gloria and decided that it wasn't impossible to be in love with two women at the same time, especially when one of them was far away and not likely to be returning to his bed for some time to come. The bonus was that he had nothing to feel guilty about since his main lady, Vicky, had actively encouraged him to woo the other while she was in Paris painting, and he guessed, making a lot of sexual love with her fellow bohemians, male and female.

He slowed down before turning into the driveway to Dunbla House, which overlooked the sea half a mile in from the road. He sighed at the thought that he would have to leave the party at midnight but there was nothing else for it. He had to drive to town for a secret, early meeting with a Dublin Corporation official. This man was to give him, for a price, information that would make him a lot of money in the next several years. He had to meet the man at the ungodly hour of three o'clock since his informant was paranoid about being seen with one of the bidders for the land sale he was handling for the Corporation.

This particular sale was for open land on the edge of the city. When it had first been advertised for sale, Sam's instinctive nose for a good deal had made him look into the situation. But was it just an idea at the advertising stage, or had the decision to sell the land been reached? Corporation bureaucracy was a joke in the eyes of the business community, and sometimes it was possible to cash in on its ineptitude. All you needed was a man who, for a price, could give you the full picture, which would give you an advantage over your opposition. Should the land be zoned for a housing project, you could make some serious money if you got your hands on it without the housing caveat being acknowledged by the selling department. It was commonplace for different departments in the Corporation not to know what the other was up to. One might be selling land, the other planning to buy that land some time in the future. A speculator could buy from one, and then sell to the other in a couple of years, for anywhere between ten and a hundred times the price he had paid for the land in the first place. This was where information at a price was literally invaluable.

Sam turned off the engine of the car and got out to stretch his legs for a minute or two. He would like to have stayed all night at the party – to spend that much time with Gloria in a disarmingly social situation – who knew what could happen. He smiled at the thought but he knew he would go back to town. He was not just unwilling, but, he ruefully admitted, he was simply unable to resist the chance to pluck a deal from the grasp of the competition that had once eschewed him.

15

Dunbla House

June 21st 1908

Sam accepted a glass of champagne while Deirdre was making a final check that everything was in place for the evening's fun. Arthur was in good form and Sam sensed that he was genuinely happy about solidifying his engagement to Dee.

"Of course, Sam, I'm a most fortunate chap, a lucky fella. But, it has to be allowed that something is missing." Arthur spoke quietly like someone thinking aloud. "If only we could find a way to mollify her father's anger. Dee is her mother's girl really, but it would be the icing on the wedding cake, if Pat could be defrosted." Arthur chuckled, "I say, the old bubbly is making me wax rather poetically, wouldn't you say?" He was tipsy, Sam allowed, letting go of the thought 'as usual', while he found himself grinning at Arthur's appreciation of his own wit.

Sam drew on his cigarette. "No guarantees, but I

may have come up with an idea that could work the oracle. We won't discuss it right now, but in a few days, let's talk about it. Is that all right with you?"

"I've been hoping for something of the kind. You're so adept in dealing with people and their feelings. I'm not a complete oaf in the boardroom and I get along with my staff, but when it comes to anything like emotional intercourse, I'm baffled as to what to do or say," Arthur shrugged. "Keep an eye on me tonight, won't you? To you alone I admit, that while I feel happy for all that I possess, for Dee's love for me, so much for which to be grateful, a part of me, something, somewhere behind the good man I would wish to be, it stalks uneasily about." Arthur quaffed his drink. "Disregard me, Sam. The plonk talking."

"I'll keep an eye on you while I'm here. I have a meeting at three o'clock. Unless you absolutely need me to stay, it's an opportunity I would like to avail of."

"Please, Sam, forgive my self-indulgence. I'll be fine. I never intend to get into mischief. Sometimes though, when the champagne flows and bubbles in my blood, well . . ." Arthur grimaced, self-effacingly. "You keep your appointment and may it work out to your advantage. By the way, word today from Vicky. According to her latest missive she is painting like a fury on legs, her words, not mine." Arthur exhaled a ribbon of smoke, "You're not troubled by her being gone for what might well be quite a while?"

"We have a great understanding, Arthur. She's been encouraging me to talk to Gloria about marriage." They

241

stood beneath an awning above trestle tables under white linen tablecloths, from which Sam took a bottle and poured more wine for both of them. "As you confide in me, I say to you, even marriage would not come between Vicky and me, in any real sense." He sipped the sparkling wine, "But as I get older, I find the idea of wife and family taking up more of my thinking. It sounds so Jewish it's like a joke told against oneself. Nonetheless, I'm going to talk to Gloria, see how she feels about the idea of having me for a husband."

"That's wonderful news," Arthur clasped his hand. "My dear friend, one of the few wishes I hold dear is that you will have a happy life. You have been the best friend any chap could ever wish for. And as for Vicky, well, you somehow got her to settle down for several years, something I could not have envisaged. She was the wildest young thing ever until she met you. So, just between you and I, let me tell you, I hope that Gloria has the good sense to jump at you."

"If she does, Arthur, will you be my best man?"

Touched by the compliment, Arthur put a hand on Sam's shoulder. "I'd be honoured. No other word for it." He shook Sam's hand again, breathing deeply to allay the possibility that his tearful eyes would let him down.

Deirdre had ferried her mother and Molly Harney to Dunbla House for the party, and was now happily seated between them as Bill Boswell presented his full touring production – one hour of singing and dancing and comedy sketches, followed by *East Lynne* especially requested by Deirdre since it was Molly Harney's favourite play. All of this, followed by a comedy sketch that had the audience in stitches of laughter for a full minute after the final curtain.

A short time later, a hot and cold buffet supper was served by a team of servants and local people hired for the night, all of them under the direction of Seamus Byrne and Angela, living permanently now in their own home on the estate overlooking Killiney Bay.

The members of the touring company had been invited to join the guests for supper and drinks. Gradually, once they had removed their make-up, and out of their costumes, the players mingled easily and were soon having a good time.

Deirdre had ensured that Gloria should use a guest cottage in which to spend the night. It was close to the main house, making it easier for her to make her costume changes for her various entrances during the evening's entertainment. The one-bedroom guest cottage was tucked away behind rose bushes forming a screen between it and its surroundings, so she had total privacy for her overnight stay.

Gloria was actually on her way there to hang up her dresses after the show, when Sam found her. Offering to carry the gowns, he decided as he walked beside her to come to the point.

"I wonder have you ever considered the possibility of being my wife, Gloria." He was fairly calm, having decided to simply keep his mind on what he had to say.

His matter-of-fact tone took Gloria's breath away. As she remained silent, a growing wall of music began to build itself in the ballroom of the house, the musicians for the evening using the same stage that Bill Boswell had erected earlier.

"I'm not so interested in theatre that I'd drive to thirty separate productions taking place all over the countryside, and as Emily might well say, I wasn't out taking the air, so this may not be the surprise of the decade," Sam chuckled, feeling that he had embarrassed her into deep silence.

Gloria had always found him interesting and she was attracted to him in a way that suggested they could be compatible in marriage. Really, he was all that any woman might hope for, and it seemed unlikely that his wife and family would ever be less than well off financially. But, there was a part of her – a part she considered to be some form of lingering madness – that however pointlessly, went on lingering on the impossible notion of she and Arthur Brewer.

Gloria had felt guilty – the idea that she would steal away the man that Deirdre wanted above all others, did nothing to enhance her self-esteem. But she knew, even as she prepared to give Sam her answer, that had Arthur come to her and revealed feelings similar to her own, she would have dropped everything, every thought, word and idea that she had ever held about Gentile men. Trembling at the enormity of her mind-shift, she allowed that she had fallen in love and that

244

she was in the grip of some form of divine madness. It had been through living with these alien thoughts, and an overwhelming desire to be with Arthur, that she had come to understand her mother's addiction to Jem Riley. As she prayed for Rebecca's peace beyond the grave, she knew in her heart that she was also praying for herself, and her future, her entreaties to a God unknown including even the wild, forbidden wishes that formed her dreams.

Arriving at the cottage, Sam followed Gloria indoors. It was a two-roomed affair, beautifully decorated in the simplest style. The huge fireplace housed a glowing fire, the plain pine table supported a huge vase of freshly-cut flowers, an ice bucket chilled a bottle of champagne and a tray of snacks covered with a fine white muslin cloth awaited consumption. There was also a jug of fresh water, and various glasses and cups and saucers.

"Forgive my silence, Sam. I am overwhelmed that you have been thinking of me as a wife. Please bear with me for a minute. I need to get out of this costume."

She went into the bedroom and Sam opened the champagne. When she came back she wore a light wool dress of pale blue. He sighed wantonly as the shape of her body turned the garment into a second skin. Catching his reaction, she took a cream shawl from the back of a chair and put it around her shoulders, pinning it closed beneath her breasts.

Accepting the champagne, she raised her glass. "Here's to you, Sam. You are a good man."

He acknowledged the toast with a diffident

response, rather anxious about what was coming next. "Have I been very presumptuous?" he asked. He didn't at all feel that he had been presumptuous, and he didn't give a damn whether she had thought him so. He held a realistic view of just how good a catch he was in terms of a marriage prospect, and he could not help wondering just how many marriage proposals she had received this week from a prominent man, someone of substance, who had the power to open the door to – according to what Emily Boswell had told him – the life of wife and mother that Gloria wanted for herself.

"Is your question a proposal of marriage?" She had drunk her glass of champagne and was beginning to relax a little.

As he poured for her he nodded his head. "Yes, it is. Will you marry me?"

"I want to say yes, Sam."

"Then say it."

"And I have no doubt you would make a fine husband. But, I want you to get to know me better." She sipped the champagne. "I need to be a committed Jew, Sam. I need to have a Jewish home, bring my children up as Jews who are committed to all that being a Jew means. I have no interest in the performance, the glamour of the theatrical life. I want to live and die a Jew proud of her heritage." The quiet passion in Gloria's voice caused him to wonder was she trying to convince herself of this, or was it, in fact, how she really felt. The fire was mirrored for moments in her violet eyes as she hammered out the words. He was captured by the rise and fall of her breasts, wanting to have her right there on the spot.

She sipped champagne before she went on. Sam remained silent as she spoke of the death in London of the father she had never known and of the despairing effort to bring her mother to Ireland. He heard of how that dream had turned into a nightmare that ended with the heart-breaking demise of her mother on board the mail boat ferrying them to The Promised Land that was Ireland.

"For my mother and father, for my grandfather Mendel – and for all of them, for all of those that died because they had to walk west from Ukraine and Lithuania and wherever else . . . I want, I want and I need to be what I am. And first and foremost, Sam, I am a Jew."

As she endorsed this picture, she was reminding herself that there would be no room for thoughts of Arthur once she committed to marriage. Being in love was surely a form of madness – she felt sure Jem Riley had been in love with her mother, and all too clearly that state of mind had little or nothing to do with love, certainly not the kind of love essential to the building of a nest that would be home to her husband and children within the traditional values of her race.

Tears came to her eyes, evidence of her mixed feelings as she forced herself to eschew the persistent insane desire for Arthur. Could she come to love Sam as her husband, father of her children?

"You might wish to think about whether you want

to marry a person like that," she told him, grateful for her tears lingering, a blessed diversion since she could not have looked at him in that moment.

Sam felt some surprise as he spoke, since he seemed to be standing some way behind the source of his voice. "I'm a Jew, Gloria. There's no escaping that. I've fought my father's way of life because he never found me interesting enough to even talk to. I want a Jewish home like my mother tried to provide. Why else would I be asking you to marry me? Loving you wouldn't be enough."

As the words dropped from his lips he felt a rent in his self-worth. This is not a nice thing you're doing, he told himself. He shrugged the reservation away. He wanted her, perhaps he even loved her – he was certainly prepared to throw in the Jewish home enticement if it would work.

The truth was that he was unsure how he felt about going all the way with the Jewish thing, but she had aroused him to such a degree that he had to have her. In simple terms he was unable to deny that he was consumed these days by the thought of having her in his bed. So much so, that he was prepared to offer marriage, to even gild the lily just a bit. "I will aim to be the kind of husband you want," he said in honesty. "Can I say more than that?"

He didn't need to convince himself that the marriage was going to go perfectly. Like any relationship that moved beyond the most casual stage, people had to trim their personal sails for an ongoing affair to work out. Marriage was just the absolute ongoing 'till-death-us-do-part affair', made legal by men trying to create some kind of social order. This didn't mean you had to live and die by every tenet that had been laid down. It was claimed that it was all the word of God, which wasn't a bad pitch if you were in the religion business.

"If you really want to marry me, I'll do my best to be a good wife to you," Gloria said, knowing she would honour the commitments she made to marriage. She had no problem in accepting that he was basically a decent man, but something bothered her, something about him didn't ring true.

Sam stepped half a pace closer to look into her eyes. She smiled, as his grin seemed to light up his face much more than the gaslight and the lanterns through the window from the terrace outside the cottage. He held her at arms-length, and then to her total astonishment, he unleashed a yell that split the night like an axe. In that moment, she was delighted with him, and suddenly found herself wanting to be kissed with a hunger she could never have imagined. Without even thinking about it, she took his face in her hands and fastened her mouth on his. As Sam responded, she surrendered totally to the moment, wishing they were man and wife together in their marriage bed. Sam was encouraged by the warm softness of her lips and surprised by the strength of her embrace as she crushed him against her breasts. She had never kissed another man, she had told him this and he believed her. He felt too, that she might surrender to him now that they were unofficially engaged. But something stopped him pressing on with his seduction mode – he felt a dart of annoyance – guessed it was his conscience proving to be a nuisance. In consideration of her innocence he let go of the idea – they had drunk two glasses of wine and it didn't seem right to take advantage of her susceptibility, even if she wasn't actually under the weather.

When he let her go, Gloria felt quite weak in the legs. She sat down by the fire and gathered her breathing. Her heart pounded and there was a glow in the pit of her stomach that seemed to come through her out of the earth. Was this love? Was this it? Was this what all the fuss was about? She couldn't tell, and she wondered if anybody really could. Who could know anything about love, in a world that seemed bent on greed and hatred and lust? Love was what she had felt, still felt for her mother, Rebecca. That had to be love. To feel so deeply, that you would willingly die that the other person might live, surely that had to be love. Was love for your mother any different to the love you might feel for a loving husband? If what she felt for her mother could be linked to the lustful sensation she had experienced in kissing Sam passionately, it must be an altogether shattering experience. If she ever came to a marriage of both feelings about Sam, she imagined she just wouldn't be able to function. She would just want to lie with him, and make love to him at every opportunity – as her mother and Jem Riley had – until she had to sleep and rest so that she could make love again and again, until death came to give her rest from her insatiable need.

"Are you all right, Gloria?" She felt his hand on her own, the caring sound of his voice relieving her of her earlier reservations.

"Thank you," she smiled, "I know very little about life, Sam. I will marry you. You are the best man I have ever met. I don't know whether I love you or not – I have nothing to compare my feelings to. If love can be learned, I will learn to love you. It can't be hard to love someone as good as you."

"We'll be fine," he assured her casually. He almost continued with, 'By marrying me, you are saying I love you,' but he let the thought pass by. He wanted to move his hand to her gently-heaving breast, but he pushed the idea away. It was difficult to do so because he knew by the feel of her, and the strength of her embrace, that she wanted him to make love to her, whether she knew it or not. She just didn't know anything about sexual love – she had no experience of love-making – he rose, thinking what joy there would be in teaching her all he had learned in the arms of some wonderful women whose lustful desires had escaped the prison built from the ideas of little Ten Commandment minds.

He took Gloria by the hand and they left the cottage. He thought it best, afraid that if they went on kissing passionately he would lose his grip on his powerful need to make love, surrender totally to the desire to be wrapped up in her wonderful body. Had he known that she loved the firmness of his chest as it crushed against her breasts, and that she had to fight to resist the powerful demand of her need to press her loins against his rampant erection, he might have abandoned doing the right thing and allowed nature to take its course.

Had this happened, Gloria's powerful desire would have been utterly committed to him – from their coming together the turbulence of wanting would have been deprived of the space to cause pain powerful enough to shatter the lives of generations yet unborn.

As they strolled back to the main house, the moon was bathing a rose garden patchwork of swaying petals in the sea breeze, its light and that of many lanterns adding warmth to the late-night chill.

"Do you have a dark side, Sam?" she asked.

"I'm too simple to be deep," he replied, wondering was this true, "if you know what I mean. Say for example, I feel rotten. I say to myself, so what? Are you the first man ever to feel rotten? I can't stand people who make mountains out of molehills, people who look for a reason or a cause for every little thing that happens. Like, some things just happen and it doesn't have to mean very much when they do. So, though I really don't know, I don't feel like I have what you call a dark side. I can get angry, like most people can, but not that often."

"I feel a dark side to me," Gloria said quietly. "I have a short temper. I'm not all singing and dancing."

Sam found he liked her a lot in that moment and he felt good that they had arrived at an arrangement. Whatever their differences might be down the road he was convinced Gloria was a good woman.

"You've done well," he said with a warm feeling of respect, "to have come this far without going completely mad, I don't know how you and your mother survived as long as you did."

She had allowed him small snippets of her personal story – he knew he would never forget her description of the Jem Riley episode and the passing of Rebecca.

"I will be there as your husband, to help us to come through. Who knows? Even two blind people who love each other, maybe they can make a little light shine where it was just darkness. I won't live in darkness, and neither will you. I saw many marriages in Little Jerusalem that were nothing more than life-sentences. Women consigned to the kitchen and the nursery and the bedroom just because they were women, even the bright ones being allowed no space to indulge any talents they had, because it is a man's world. I won't live like that. We have to come out of the dark ages about women. It suits men to ignore what's right in deference to what is more convenient for them. That will not be how it is for us. Take me on, you won't lose out."

Seamus Byrne appeared, like a man walking on a high-wire. He carried a tray bearing six glasses of champagne above his head, and though the goat-faced man was swaying gently from side to side – 'like an inebriated pendulum' Sam thought with a smile – not one drop of the bubbly was being spilled. Seamus stopped, lowering the tray that Sam and Gloria might take a glass. Both declined, and the servant said in a drunken whisper, "I can let you have a drop of the real McCoy, Mister Sweet. Best poteen in the country," He mumbled with pride and a deal of dignity, his eyes speckled like a bird's egg. "A pint of it inside you, Mister Sweet, you go stone blind," he claimed, his tone suggesting that this was the height of recommendation.

"No thanks, Seamus my friend. It's not often I get a lovely lady all to myself, you understand?" The conspiratorial wink Sam offered was returned by the man-servant, before he bowed carefully and stuttered away, his body movement suggesting that he was made of arthritic elastic.

"My mother would have to live with us, Gloria. I'm all she has left," Sam spoke quietly, almost as though this was an afterthought, watching her carefully as he spoke.

There was no flicker of resistance in her expression. "I wouldn't have expected anything less. Had you not wanted your mother with us, I would not marry you. Mother must receive all respect. She must have all we can provide."

"She can be a tough old bird," Sam chided. "I don't want you to be under any illusion about her."

"Of course, she is tough – you told me she walked from Germany. Have no fear, Sam. I am not made of tissue paper. Your mother and I will find a way to live together, just as you and I will."

Sam turned his head slightly, his smile belonging to the memory of Vicky and her own personal way of avoiding pregnancy. "When will you marry me?"

"I need a little time to accommodate the Boswells. I want to be fair. They are not just my partners. They have been the best friends any woman could have. Without them . . ." She shook her head, dismay glancing over her face, stunned to silence for a moment before she could say, "They saved my life, when I lost Mama."

"Make it as soon as you can," Sam said. "I'll marry you tomorrow, next week, the week after. Just give me enough notice that we can arrange whatever paperwork is involved. I can hardly wait."

Gloria simply couldn't hide her scepticism. "Are you always going to be so agreeable? I can scarcely believe you."

"I'm really not a difficult person," he said honestly. "I'll stick to any commitment I make, I'll provide for us and our children, and I promise to make love to you until my eyeballs fall onto the rug." He laughed and she squeezed his hand as she said, "You'll have to teach me to be a lover."

"Don't worry," he said, swallowing his lust. "I will show you the wonders of the world in our marriage bed."

He took her in his arms and kissed her warmly, but without the urgency they had shared earlier, since his early morning meeting had come again to claim his mind.

"I'm sorry you have to leave, but I'm ready for sleep. I need room to breathe, to get used to the idea of what has happened to us this evening."

"I'm in the same boat," Sam said truthfully. "I've

never asked anyone to marry me before. It's all new to me, too."

"Not even Victoria?" she asked demurely, disarming him for a moment before he replied.

"Vicky and I will always be friends, as Arthur and I will always be friends. Nothing can happen that will change how I care for those two people. As the Boswells are to you, so my twin friends are to me. I would give my life for either of them, and I can't even imagine a time when they will not be an important part of my life."

"They are very fortunate to have you," she kissed him again on the lips.

"I'm the lucky one. On a day when I failed to save the life of a Dublin street-arab, Victoria opened the door to a whole new life for me."

As he was about to leave, she suddenly embraced him, and before he could even wonder what she wanted of him, she began to weep. Not quite knowing what to do, he lied as he said, "It's all right. Let it come out. Better you let it out."

After what seemed to be a long time, she sighed, "How I wish Mama had lived to meet you. She would have been so very grateful to know I was going to marry such a good man."

Again, she wished she were free enough to have invited him to stay with her tonight in the cottage. They were going to be married, after all. Would it have been so wrong to take him into the bed, sleep with him the long night through, hold him close and be held close by him? To perhaps be taken to that place her mother had travelled to with Jem Riley. 'O, God,' she thought as she kissed him goodbye, 'to be made cry out like that by your man making love to you'.

As Sam kissed her lips goodnight, he slid his hand to her breast, his heart pounding in the heat of his returning, burning desire to have her. Things might have moved on from there, but for the fact that Gloria's knees literally buckled under her, and he was forced to support her weight to stop her falling down. She recovered quickly, stunned that his touch had caused such a thrilling eruption in her. She gasped for breath before taking both of his hands and pressing them against her nipples standing out like organ stops.

"I have to go," Sam said breathlessly, knowing he had to get away from her – even if she was willing to go all the way right now. He was not going to take advantage of her vulnerability. He chose to ignore the nagging nudge that the real reason was the meeting that he simply had to attend in Dublin.

He gave her a wave before he disappeared in the direction of his motor car, Gloria even more aware of how much she wanted him to stay.

Wanting to be alone with her thoughts, she walked the short distance back to the cottage. Sitting by the fire she felt hot and opened the doors front and back to let some air in. As she settled down, the night seemed to be enticing her to step outside. She smiled waving at the moon as it painted a silver corridor on the calm surface of the ocean.

A little way off, Dunbla House was like a giant square wedding cake against the cloak of the night around it. Whatever way the light was falling from the windows of Arthur's home, as it married into the lighting provided by the oil lamps and the gaslights and the lanterns along the terrace and about the verandas, it created an effect that seemed so romantic it caused her heart to swell, and fed instantly, the pointless, profane wish to live here.

Feeling lonely now and rather angry, she went back inside the cottage and closed the door. She found she was shivering, and she knew it was not the night turned mild that gave her the shakes. She directed her mind to think about Sam, and she felt better as she contemplated again what a blessed surprise he had turned out to be. She knew that unless he had a change of heart, she would marry him as soon as she could get away from the show. Of course, Bill and Emily would release her tomorrow if it really mattered to her, but she didn't want to do that to them. She knew she was the draw, and she wanted to give them time to find a suitable replacement, before she took off to get married.

They would have to take a short break from the tour anyway, since they simply had to be there at her wedding and they would have to rehearse her replacement for at least a week. She would do things right for them since they were her family.

Restless again, she took a shawl and went out into the night. She walked up the path towards the house, thinking she would have a glass or two of champagne.

A bout of wild inebriated yelling, followed by loud snatches of laughter interrupted her thoughts. She stopped and waited for she knew not what. She was not expecting to see anything nor anybody – it was simply her response to the ribbon of curiosity at whatever evoked that wild laughter in some fellow's breast. A hint of midsummer madness, she said to herself. She felt warm in the wool dress, feeling that her undergarments were sticking to her skin. Early summer madness, given a helping hand by endless bottles of bubbly, and perhaps a tincture or two of what Seamus Byrne had called 'the real McCoy'.

She neared the house wishing she had asked Sam not to go. She stood under an awning, aware that people were waltzing in the ballroom, others wrapped around each other in the shadows at the edge of the lighting. Still others sitting back contentedly as the music reached them. In the moment she knew she wanted to be kissed, that she should have insisted Sam stay. He would not have refused her. She knew that from the bold moment when she had pressed his hands to her breasts.

She knew she had to stop this kind of thinking. She sought out Bill and Emily, but they had probably retired for the night. Her mind was full of Sam touching her breasts in a bed where they lay naked together. Aching to be touched, she wondered would she even survive her wedding night. Surely her heart would burst through the sheer thrill that had been promised earlier when Sam had fondled her for the first time.

She heard another laugh in the night, and she wondered again who it was and what was causing the joyous outbursts? Was someone stealing the heart of another, or was some tipsy rogue attempting to rob a girl's maidenhead with false promises? Was some wayward wife, perhaps, just now being unfaithful to her husband? Was some awful lecher of a husband having his way with someone as innocent as she herself, a servant even, wooed to be left wounded after she had succumbed to his words and the wine? Had the roué followed her down to the wine cellar perhaps, she encouraging him with her slow easy walk to the racks of bottles, stopping for the sound of his determined step, pressed back against a wall wanting him to come and take her, both of them knowing through the exchange of that look that said yes yes, yes! so that below stairs the seducer was being seduced by the serving girl, in the security of her home ground?

Gloria chuckled uneasily at her fanciful reverie, accepted a glass of champagne from Seamus, who was somehow still wandering about with a tray in his hand. He did not recognise her this time, his eyes like amber slates under his heavy brows, his legs elastically supporting him, she knew not how. She drank the wine, emptying the glass and listened to the music for a little while. She took another drink from a table tray, held it in her hand as she decided to go back to the cottage. She stopped for a moment as she heard the ecstatic groans of a young woman as a couple made love in a nearby arbour, emptying her glass, feeling a burst of she knew not what as the champagne slid down. With a tipsy chuckle, she threw the glass over her shoulder and heard it break on the paving path of the terrace.

As she passed through the rose bush fence surrounding the cottage she was startled to find Arthur turning away from the door. "Gloria! How marvellous!" He was delightfully surprised, merry enough to be rather drunk. "I've been checking the cottage to ensure that all was in order for you, and I take it that Sam has departed for the city."

Arthur held three flutes in one hand, a bottle of champagne in the other, but only for a moment. "Won't need that," he said with a chuckle, as he watched the third flute sail from his hand to shatter on the other side of the rose hedge. Gloria could only stand there bereft of speech, nonetheless alarmed by the burst of excitement she felt by being this close to him. He held up the two champagne glasses. "It was my simple intent to toast you two."

"He had to go," she finally croaked.

"Perhaps you and I could share a glass, a toast to you both in my best friend's absence," he said casually, to which she could only nod her head as she moved to open the door, all too aware that he was going to follow her inside.

She left him to pour the champagne, while she entered the bedroom to repair her face. She then found herself biting into a slice of lemon to help her avoid the risk of bad breath. Returning to the living-room she found Arthur adding brandy to the champagne. He handed her a flute with a playfully gallant movement. They touched glasses and he said, "To Sam's lady, the beautiful Miss Gloria Rose, and to the man himself, a friend forever."

Gloria was confused. That he could think of Sam, and yet be standing here alone with her in the early hours of the morning. How could that be? She needed to forget Sam, somehow deny his existence that she might go where this moment might lead.

She watched Arthur down the drink. She sipped her own, clinging to the voice telling her it was perfectly in order. They were only being civil and social and, after all, it was a party. Arthur downed the second drink. Gloria saw his eyes take on a muted hue, so that somehow, instantly, they were the eyes of a total stranger. She was mesmerised as he took the glass from her hand, standing helpless as he simply enfolded her in his arms, everything happening in slow motion. Before she could think, his lips were on hers in an open-mouthed, feral kiss that ravaged her mouth with such passion that she thought her heart would burst in her breast.

Some part of her intended to push him away, bring him to his senses, but he put his tongue into her mouth. She was completely taken by the mad, surging energy of his passion, instead of resisting him she found herself responding hungrily. She met his lashing tongue with her own, pushing towards him rather than pulling away, her stomach aching against the power of his erection as he turned all her ideas and vows and determinations upside down.

He lifted her as though she were a feather. She found herself kissing his neck and his face with a hunger that was new to her. Throwing her down on the bed covers, he simply ripped the clothes from her body, while making contact with some part of her skin with his lips and his tongue and his teeth. She welcomed every move he made, allowing herself to be deliriously lost, her freedom powered by the force of her desire, a wanting too strong to think of fighting it.

Hardly able to breathe, scarcely caring if she lived or died, she felt him prise her legs apart, gasping as his fingers touched her parting, biting into his neck as he stroked her there. Prodding her urgently, making her cry out so that she bit into his flesh again, giving blindly, giving so very willingly to the exclusion of a single thought, even as he pressed his great cock into her.

She endured the initial pressure as he shattered her hymen, knew she was biting into his shoulder again, unable to help it, really needing to cry out as she felt that her head was going to split in two. If Arthur was in any way disturbed by her ferocious response, he gave no inkling of it.

He began to thrust in and out of her, hurting her so that she cried out. He seemed mindless to her discomfort and moments later she felt a rising sensation that took her breath away. Very soon the joyful sensation he was producing ploughed right through her mind, relieving her from the pressure that had been there, taking her out from under all and any of the pressures she had ever known in her life.

He found her mouth again and his tongue pushed against her own, before he tore his lips away so that he could breathe, as breathe he did like a bellows in her ears, while she felt the sweat fall from him onto her skin, her tears mingling with it as she welcomed him and each and every hair on his body, to have her and ravage her and violate her and toss her, and boss her, and do with her whatever he desired for whatever time she had left to live on this earth.

Arthur pulled away from her, and she almost cried out in her sense of loss but then, to her amazement, she felt him move down her body and put his mouth there. In moments she was being driven to insane heights of pleasure by his probing tongue. His lips were then kissing her lips down there as though it were her mouth, and his tongue was torturing her until suddenly, like an explosion inside her mind, her first ever orgasm pumped all over all that she had been and all that she would be and all that she would never be, again in the same way.

Aware that her body had been somehow brutalised, feeling that she could not have got up and walked even a few paces, some part of her sang as though rejoicing in her rebirth. She knew nothing yet she was sure that she would never be the same again. And that seemed like a very special blessing.

Nothing mattered except this, the fact that she was coming out into light and sunshine and joy, feeling shock in the awareness that darkness was merely the absence of light. In the moment she knew no fear or pain or uncertainty, there was nothing to interfere with the bliss so natural to her, and she wept silent tears of gratitude that would not quit.

Arthur returned to probe gently before he pushed inwards and she was opening herself as wide as she could, wrapping her legs around him now, his conspirator in whatever he wanted to do, herself suddenly as aggressive as he had been at the beginning, captured by the need to know again the power of her orgasm as he began once more to take her in that direction.

16

London and Ireland

July 1908

Gloria watched and waited as Sam talked quietly to the official at the registry office in Petty France, but a stone's throw from Buckingham Palace. She saw him give money to the man – the registrar she presumed – receiving in return a whispered response which caused him to shrug philosophically. He then took some more bank notes from his pocket, to press them into the outstretched hand. Gloria sighed in relief. Whatever had been standing in the way of their marriage had clearly been hurdled. All that was needed now was that their witnesses turn up so that the ceremony could begin, enabling her to put the last nightmarish fortnight behind her. Thanks to Sam's never-say-die way of dealing with life, she had come through two weeks of such trauma that, more than once, she had half expected her mind to snap.

The nightmare had started when she felt the

sunlight as it washed her waking in the guest cottage on the Brewer estate, on the morning after she had lost her virginity to Arthur Brewer. She had finally been taken by sleep in the darkest hours before the dawn following their love-making.

When she woke up her head was pounding as she moved to raise it from the pillows, and she felt as though she had been beaten. She was only grateful to find herself alone, until the memory of Arthur's leaving tore open the wound of denial she had sealed off by crying herself to sleep.

She would never forget her despair as she had sat naked on the side of the bed, all her insane hopes crushed to death. She knew soreness between her thighs and inside her vagina, while her mind continued to feel abused by the horrifying conclusion to her night with the man she had fallen in love with. They had made mad, passionate love for over two hours and, though she had wanted every moment as it happened, she had wondered was there no end to his desire for her, his need to fill her again and again and again. Would she ever be able to forget the picture of herself, as she lay in relief while Arthur went to the other room to take drink? Would she forever be burdened by her greed and her lust for his return, for the joy and sensation that seemed to be there just for the taking? When he had erupted inside her for the last time, she had lain there beneath him, wanting to suck him in even deeper, to never let go of him.

Within moments of her lonely awakening, with the

lover who had never been her lover gone from her, she knew there was no escape from this cruel disarming moment. Alone and quite desolate, she had to accept she had welcomed into the most intimate part of her body the penis of a man she had never had a meaningful conversation with, a man who was a total stranger in almost every way. Yet she had become as committed to him as she believed it possible to be, and if this testament to her insanity had not been evident before, it was staring her in the face in the morning cottage after the night of the summer solstice.

She remembered how Arthur had stirred in his sleep. His body was heavy on top of her, her legs ached from holding him there, and yet she felt severe regret when she had to let him go. She wanted to gaze at him, touch him and explore him while he slept, kiss him all over, put her mouth to his great limp penis. She wanted him to wake up, to have him kiss her all over, enter her again, make her explode once more before they set about overcoming the difficulties they would have to face together.

That was the thought she clung to when she considered the pain and heartache to Sam and Deirdre, and indeed Vicky, when Arthur and herself, as a couple, told them of their love for each other. It was a daunting prospect, but she couldn't care. She had been transported up and away and beyond any consideration for others, during the hours spent in bed with Arthur. This was where their new life had begun. Even concern for others could not get in the way of what had happened to them. Their coming together had changed everything, something that could not be stopped from the first kiss, the moment it had started with the intensity of a flash-fire.

Sam touched Gloria's arm, bringing her back to the present. "Everything's *kosher*," he nodded in the registrar's direction. "Bear with me a minute, while I go and find our witnesses." She smiled and, despite her inner turmoil, thought he was the handsomest man she had ever seen in her life.

As Sam left her, Gloria was captured again by the relentless memory of that heart-breaking morning. Arthur had woken up and rolled off the bed without acknowledging her presence. As he walked into the other room, his erection rampant, she had assumed he would return and make love to her again. She heard the tinkle of bottle on glass, heard him gasp as the drink reached his throat, heard him open the back door and step outside to relieve his kidneys, the door slamming behind him when he came back into the cottage.

He came into the bedroom, no longer tumescent, his eyes hidden behind that same blank hue that had imposed itself on him the night before. He pulled his shirt on and picked his coat up off the floor. He put his hand in his pocket and without looking at Gloria he said, "How much? Did we agree a price?"

She felt so confused she simply couldn't speak. She inhaled deeply to still the panic that threatened her, not yet capable of grasping the implication of what he had said. Arthur shook his head as though trying to clear it before he simply threw a roll of notes onto the bedside table, mumbling, "Thank you". With that he lurched out of the room and away from her, the front door of the cottage slamming shut behind him, even as her tears of despair fell on her naked thighs.

Somehow she hauled herself from the bed, shocked sufficiently by Arthur's departure not to be able to think. She was aware of cleaning herself and brushing her hair, in the odd moment when her mind was relieved of its numbness, wondering did life always have to stab you in the back. Was there ever, would there ever be a time when something beautiful happened without a bomb exploding to shatter all the hopes and the dreams that had grown in the experience? She shook away the question, knowing what the answer would be.

Half an hour later, she walked around the rose bushes, her dresses over her arm, her heart so bruised that she ached all over, seeming to come to enough life that the sun shimmering off the morning sea startled her. It was a beautiful day, and this was a beautiful place for anybody to live in, and she wished she could die on the spot. At the same time, she knew that life would never let her off that easily. What she had to do immediately was talk to Bill and Emily so that they could counsel her as to what she should do for the best.

As she passed along the terrace – before taking the path down to the field where the Boswells' caravan was parked close to the wagons of the players, she found Arthur – coffee cup in hand, a brandy balloon in the other – on the verandah overlooking the flowing lawn skirting the drive down to the main gate, looking tired and fragile. She wished she could simply have disappeared before he saw her coming along the path but he came to his feet in an instant, bowing slightly from the waist while she saw that his eyes had returned to something like their normal state. The familiar sparkle was in situ, if somewhat muted. He smiled warmly, and for an insane moment her heart lit up with hope. "I feel rather like a chap who has been having surgery, minus the benefit of an anesthetic. Do join me for coffee and a cure, my dear, but whatever you do, please don't shout at me."

She could see that despite the life in his blue eyes he was severely under the weather, and she began to suspect that he had no memory of what had happened between them. She wanted him to remember, to acknowledge their love-making and the vows that they had poured all over each other. Yes, and she wanted far more than that. She wanted him to want her the way she continued to desire him, wanted him rampant for her as he had been, wanted him, desperately, pointlessly, wanted him.

She sat quite erect on the freshly oven-heated cushion of the wicker armchair he had placed at her disposal, feeling that she needed to throw up. She faced him across a circular wicker table, accepting coffee, declining cognac.

"I'm afraid I failed badly as host last evening, Gloria. Of course, I should never have listened to

Patrick Lote. My friend, the older man with that mound of grey hair, you may have met him during the party. He made one of his special punches laced with pure alcohol. A major mistake on my part – even one of those, and a chap's mind seems to go blank."

He sipped cognac and went on. "I do remember dancing with Dee. After that, well, I'm facing a blank wall. But, that's enough about me and my predicament. Did you have a good party? Did you enjoy yourself after you had entertained us so royally?"

Gloria sipped the coffee, taking her time before she said, "I had a nice time, thank you, and I particularly enjoyed talking to you about your brewery when you walked me back to the cottage."

The coffee and the cognac cure might have been working for Arthur, his eyes seemed to lighten even as he spoke. Gloria had watched him very carefully while she had been speaking, and though she had wished it were not so, no hint of remembrance entered his eyes. "And you dance very well," She laughed as though it had all been rather amusing. "We could hear the music and we had our own private dance-floor in the cottage. It was great fun, Arthur, thank you."

"Just as long as I behaved like a gentleman, I'm delighted to have been party to such fun. How I wish I could remember it." He was clearly embarrassed. "It is a measure of the esteem in which I hold you that I can confide in you. I can remember the earlier evening right up to the moment I touched Paddy Lote's accursed punch. It happens from time to time. Please excuse me for being so remiss," Arthur looked somewhat ashamed. "To have spent time dancing with a beautiful woman and not remember a thing about it. Dear Lord, I will have to look at Paddy Lote's suggestion that my drinking habits are the most likely cause of this confounded memory loss."

Gloria's realised the situation was hopeless. This man was two different people, and the one that mattered, Arthur – as he faced her across the wicker table – had no interest in her. After a moment, she stood up, excusing herself in a formal way, leaving him to continue with his cure. She now fully accepted that her wild hopes were never going to be anything more than that. The truth was that Arthur, while out of his mind – in that he was suffering from some form of amnesia – had taken her the way he took his whores in the fancy houses of Dublin, the leaving of money on the night table being the final nail in the coffin of her dreams.

As she arrived at the Boswells' caravan, she found her friends enjoying an *al fresco* breakfast. Within a matter of minutes, she had told them the story. She sipped coffee, all too aware that Bill and Emily were aghast. "You could be up the pole, pregnant," Emily blurted out. "My God. What a thing to happen to you of all people." She rose and came to stand beside Gloria, her hand on the girl's head. "What should she do?" she asked her husband.

"Put last night behind you, Gloria. Go and find Sam. He wants to marry you. So marry him, and marry him quick. Get him into bed, and keep him there 'til he pleads for mercy. Just in case you are pregnant, he must never have any doubts that your first child is his child."

Within days she had gone to Sam in Dublin. Or rather, she had sent word to his home in Rathmines to let him know she was staying at Douglas's Hotel on Grafton Street, and that she was looking forward to hearing from him. Sam came to her that evening and she kissed him with a passion that startled him. He responded to her open mouth and she felt his tongue come to her own and she broke off the kiss only to say, "I couldn't wait, Sam. I had to see you," this being so true that she didn't have to act it. She gave him her mouth again, and within minutes she knew that he wanted to take her into the bed. But she held off, saying to him, "I want to marry you now. I have to, Sam. I cannot go on waiting to have you make love to me. I want you. I want you desperately, but I have to wait until my wedding night. I promised my mother." She whispered the last words, forgiving herself the lie. What was one more lie on top of the biggest lie of all, that she would not be the virgin he believed he was getting when she allowed him his conjugal rights in their marriage bed.

Before he left her in the hotel, he promised her, "I'll set the wedding bells tolling in the morning."

She asked that they marry quietly in London. "I was born there, and I want a quiet wedding without fuss."

Sam could not have refused her anything, while she hoped that he would organise things quickly, not expecting otherwise since this was his way of going about things. She needed to be married within days. If not, she would have to take him to bed while they waited. This was something she didn't want to do. She wanted nothing to tarnish his image of her as a pure Jewish maiden.

Sam's voice calling her name swept all thoughts of the recent past out of her mind and she turned smiling to greet him across the foyer of the registry office in Petty France. He was beckoning her to come and join him and their witnesses. He had promised her a surprise in this regard, some old friends he had said blithely, and she – so concerned with her predicament – had left the details to him. Now, somehow, she hid the gasp of tortured amazement that momentarily choked her at the first sight of Arthur and Deirdre. Waving cheerily, they stood on either side of Sam, their presence disarming her sufficiently that she almost fainted. Instantly, she drew on all her acting skills, hurrying to join them in a gush of delight, a great smile on her mouth, her heart turning to lead under the blue silk dress that was to be her wedding gown.

"You're a sly one," Deirdre chided her happily. "Thank you for asking us to be your witnesses. We're honoured to be here."

"Yes indeed, Gloria," Arthur had clearly been drinking, but he was to the manner born, a gent, his eyes sparkling in his gladness, his warmth a very real thing as he took her hand while she gave him her cheek to kiss.

In the moment, she was almost dizzy with her response to his nearness, but she had no time to go back

to feeling cheated. Sam was taking her by the arm.
"Come on. The registrar's a busy fella who doesn't like
to be kept waiting."

They celebrated with dinner at Claridges, Gloria
literally applying herself to the occasion as though she
were starring in a play. At one moment she had to dig
deep into the well of her resources as an actress – this
had to do with Deirdre wishing to share her own good
news with the new bride.

"Thanks to Sam," Dee said, touching his hand in a
gesture of gratitude, "thanks to your wonderful husband
and his suggestion that my fiancé should offer to become
a Roman Catholic. And that," Dee was delightfully tipsy
on the cocktail of champagne and happiness, "my
wonderful husband-to-be should give an undertaking
that any children of the marriage would be brought up
in the Church of Rome, lo and behold, Gloria, my father
has come down off his high-horse. He has given his
blessing, and we are to be married on June the twenty-
first." Deirdre finished her happy gushing of the news
and Gloria took them both by the hand across the table,
expressing her wish that they be happy and have many
healthy children, while she gasped mentally to think
that they would marry on the next summer solstice, the
first anniversary of the day on which her impossible
hopes and dreams had crumbled forever.

"It was simple," Arthur said, "since I have been an
atheist all my life."

Gloria bit down on need to question his loyalty to
the religion of his parents and their parents before

them, but it was not her business. Besides, in the moment, she felt the clutching hand of despair grab at her well-being – to be sitting so close to Arthur and yet be so far removed from him, for all time.

"Sam wouldn't tell me who our witnesses were going to be," she said to shift the emphasis. "I am glad now that he did not tell me. Knowing it was to be you both, I would have had expectations. As much as I think of you, they could not have lived up to this, you here this evening to celebrate our wedding dinner with us. I rejoice that my devious husband found a way for your father to get what he needed, at no serious price to either of you. Wonderful news and I have to say, Sam, a brilliant ploy on your part."

Sam grinned happily, and tapped his forehead. "Up here for devious!" he said dramatically. Then raising his foot out from under the table, he pointed at it, chuckling as he added, "Down there for dancing."

Gloria drank more than she would have wished to, but it was the only way she could have come through the dinner party. She played her part, being charming and witty, laughing in the right places, making Sam a promise with every shy glance cast his way over the rim of her wine glass.

The foursome agreed to meet for breakfast in the morning, but Gloria knew that she would beg off. Inside she felt her every smile turn to ashes and she was grateful for the champagne waiting in their suite. She was going to need all the help she could get to make it through this particular night.

"It will be all right," she told herself. "If you can make people weep in a tent as you uttered the ludicrous lines written for poor Lady Isabel, you can convince Sam that he made no mistake by marrying you."

While Gloria refreshed herself in the bathroom, Sam uncorked champagne, sipping the stuff gently as he undressed. When she came into the bedroom he was wearing a silk dressing-gown, a glass in each hand. She came to him, her cream negligée feather-light over her magnificent breasts. Her pale purple eyes seemed alight as they touched glasses, her massive hair in blue-black waves to her shoulders and below. In a moment they were kissing passionately, and she pulled Sam onto the bed, knowing by the strength of his erection that he would be inside her in no time. She felt him pull the nightgown up around her waist and she moved to accommodate him. His face was at her breasts and she urged him on. "I want you kissing my breasts."

His mouth was soon driving sensation right through her and his kisses were hungry and demanding. She opened herself to him, hoping the blood was not showing yet. She kept his face on her breasts and at her mouth, holding his head for moments to look into his eyes as his fingers drew back the lips of her vagina, wanting it to be right, wanting to give him all she could while helping him believe he was getting everything he expected, as he gently pressed the power of his need into her.

"Push hard, Sam. It won't hurt for long," she urged him, kissing him then, and thrusting herself up at him with such force that she felt him gasp. She allowed a short, sharp cry to escape her lips, and as he pulled his head back to see that all was well with her, she again thrust her mouth at his lips and gave him her tongue.

In her mind, she was remembering how Arthur had ploughed through her as though she didn't matter. At the time she had been transported to somewhere beyond her normal thinking mind, but she knew now that from their first kiss Arthur had thought her a prostitute. Now, with Sam thrusting deeper, she tried to give him all that she had given to Arthur. This was all that she wanted for now, seeking no joy, no bliss, no relief for herself. She heard herself saying 'yes', the word coming out of her in sync with every thrust that Sam made. She almost laughed in the joy of relief as she felt him move faster and faster, his breathing tortured at her ears, his pelvis pounding at her own. He arched then as though he had been knifed, his breath exploding out of him as his seed shot into her. She allowed her arms fall away from his body, as though she had no choice in the matter, and she visibly relaxed, breathing deeply through her nose as she felt Sam pull his face up off her shoulder to look at her.

"Are you all right, Gloria? Was it good for you?" His dark eyes were full of his need to have satisfied her, so that for a moment he seemed like a young lad.

"It was so beautiful, Sam, even the little hurt when you deflowered me, all of it. My magnificent man, how you filled me up." She saw him relax and she kissed him full and long on the mouth. As he moved to one side, he came to his knees on the bed and she saw that his penis was spotted with blood. Thank God, she thought, my efforts were not a waste of time.

She excused herself, and went to the bathroom. When she had washed her vagina, she applied a fingertip of cream to the small cut made earlier with the cut-throat razor she had bought in Dublin before taking the boat to England.

Looking into the bathroom mirror, she whispered to her reflection, "You did what you had to do. You went to Dunbla House to do a show. That's all. In your wildest dreams, the Arthur business could never have happened, but it did happen and you are paying for it even now." Applying perfume to her breasts she turned back to the mirror. "And you will do what you have always done, you will survive."

Whispering further to her reflection she sniffed to hold back her tears, "Mama died trying to get us to Ireland. You were saved for something. Now it seems that you have the chance to be a good Jew, make a Jewish home, a Jewish life for your husband and the children you will have. The past is the past – let it go. Many a marriage began without love. You have a good man, work at being a wife as you did at being an actress, honour your wedding vows, go forward with your husband to a long life. Shalom, leave the past to bury its dead. Shalom, Gloria."

Part Two

17

County Dublin

June 1910

When Deirdre realised she was completely lost, she felt a pang of worry followed by an angry reaction to her self-inflicted predicament. "You and your day-dreaming, it won't do. So close to your time, you should never have taken this kind of risk." She spoke in fear, said the words aloud in the hope that the reprimand might just sink in. Besides, she was surrounded by hedgerows so fat and juicy with berries and wild flowers, hemmed in on a slip of broken country road under a pure blue sky, that there was little danger of anybody coming upon her to judge her behaviour.

Her first child was due at any time. She had known this when the urge to walk had demanded her attention earlier in the day. She couldn't have said now that this had happened an hour ago, or two hours ago, because she simply had no idea. She had been wandering along in the sunshine, feeding this incredible urge to go walking even though her doctor, Paddy, Lote, had told her not to go far from the house. "Use the gardens, my dear, the paths on your own land. There is no need for a woman at your time of pregnancy to go outside the gates of Dunbla House."

She had needed in a demanding way, to take walks from the beginning of her third month, and she had tried to follow her doctor's instructions. Now on a country road alone close to her time Deirdre tried to let go of the annoyance she felt at her carelessness, the incipient anger into which she didn't want her child born.

'I am really lost,' she thought, hoping to find a light-hearted response to this because she was genuinely worried that it would be detrimental to her child to come into the world on a beat of anger.

Coming upon a large rock by the roadside, she sat down as though the weight of her situation had suddenly sapped her strength. "Hello, Hello!" she called out, ignoring the idea that it was daft to be yelling on a country road in the middle of nowhere, hoping that someone would hear her.

No leprechaun appeared to offer assistance, no fairy, no angel and no knight on a white charger, and she sighed at the culpability of her own innocence. A moment later she threw in the towel. "Lord, help me. Forgive me for being so stupid. I didn't even tell the servants I was leaving the estate." She felt a dart of pain, and she knew instinctively that her child was likely to arrive at any time. Taking a deep breath, she prayed. "It was thoughtless and stupid to put my unborn child at risk in this way. If you help me now, I promise you I will never repeat this." Another dart of pain forced her to stand up. She had to lean backwards, placing both hands at the small of her back, compelled despite her discomfort to walk on.

Moments later, she came to a curving turn and thought she would faint in relief as the smell of peat smoke reached her on the afternoon air. She moved quicker, the smell got stronger and soon she could see the smoke rising off a tinker's fire by the roadside. Despite her need to reach the fire and whoever had lit it, she knew she had to sit down, take another rest.

Breathing deeply, she thought of Arthur, who loved her as much as he could love anybody – gentle, caring Arthur. She sighed as this picture of him was, sadly, instantly replaced by a fresh portrait of Arthur drinking wine. Regardless of what was going on, or where he happened to be, picture after picture appeared, all of them showing Arthur drinking. Another change and she was looking at Arthur angry – not at her – but so terrifyingly angry with his mother, Constance, who had arrived, unannounced, on the day he had brought Deirdre back to Ireland from their honeymoon in Paris.

Even in her precarious predicament by the roadside, Dee had to allow that, from Constance Brewer's point of view, her son being married in White Friar Street church was tantamount to his admitting he was insane, or at the very least possessed by the devil. All right-minded people knew that only halfwits and beggars and thieves and prostitutes belonged to the unholy Church of Rome.

Arthur has eschewed his mother years before. He and Vicky had never forgiven her over her treatment of a servant girl, Lisa O'Brien, who had loved their father. This much Deirdre knew, and mother and son had only met on that day in June last year because a recently-employed servant allowed the woman into the house without consulting Seamus Byrne beforehand.

Constance had stormed into the drawing-room Arthur used when he was working from home. Time had not been unkind to the once beautiful mother of the Brewer twins, in that she still enjoyed rude good health. Her colour, though, was far richer than nature had intended her face and neck to be, so that she looked like someone who would surely die from heart failure, rather than old age. She wore a powder-pink costume suit, with a pale fur collar, and enough face make-up to ensure that she resembled mutton dressed as lamb,

Most likely, the lady knew that she would get short-shrift from her son, who, had he been given the opportunity, would have made himself scarce before she got within ten feet of him. His mother had afforded him no such leeway, and he looked up startled when, out of the blue, Constance launched into her verbal assault from the other side of his considerable desk.

"Have you lost your wit entirely? You have married a seamstress, a girl who is the progeny of a hackney cab driver, and a pauper from a mud cabin in Wicklow. You have supped with the devil, and become a Papist."

Deirdre was reading in a corner of the huge room but her eyes left the printed page rapidly when she heard Constance Brewer at full flow. Seeing her for the first time – the lady had not been invited to the wedding – she instantly thought how good she would be in one of those melodramas that the Boswells produced with their touring show.

Arthur came up out of his chair quicker than Deirdre had ever seen him move. He planted both hands on the desk, bringing his considerable height down to the level of his mother who wore a mask of defiance, her feet wide apart in her pink and cream shoes.

"Shut up, you silly woman!" he roared. Constance looked for a moment as though she might pass away. She had never heard Arthur raise his voice before, and most certainly she was utterly and totally disarmed by the order to shut up. "You will never again enter any house that I own. To dare talk of my wife, Deirdre, and her family as you just did, well, I am almost speechless in disbelief. You had the benefit of the best education. You have led a privileged existence during times that have been the hardest of times for the Irish people. The Irish people, madam, the rightful owners of the land on which this house is built, and, if the truth be known, all the land of this island. Now, madam, hear me and hear me well. I want you to understand very clearly that from this moment on, you do not address or refer to my wife, Deirdre, unless you do so in an attitude that is suitable to the wife of a gentleman. If I hear that you have repeated one word of your diatribe in any drawing-room, or at any dinner table, I will use every shred of power and influence I possess to have you locked up, put away, incarcerated, for the mean pathetic creature that you are."

Deirdre hardly took her eyes from Arthur's face. When she did so, it was to glance at her mother-in-law who seemed to be facing a monster of unknown origin. Finally, Constance found her voice. "You're really a vicious person, Arthur, something I had not suspected." She shook her head in disbelief. "I really did not know that."

"There is much about Victoria and I that you don't know, madam." Arthur spoke calmly now, but Deirdre heard the regret paining him as he drew this unwanted confrontation to a close. "Regrettably, at the time when we would have been grateful for your genuine interest, from the nursery onwards, actually, you were a very busy person honing your skills as a social caterpillar."

Deirdre's mind was swept clear of this memory by the sound of a rough voice on the roadside nearby. Someone was admonishing an animal, and she turned her head in the direction of the tinker's fire. She was in time to see a stocky figure kicking out at a mongrel hound that yelped as it jumped clear.

The peat smoke shifted on a wisp of a breeze and Deirdre was able to see a makeshift canvas windbreak affixed to the strongest parts of the roadside hedge at its highest point. Nearby there was a shabby caravan, and a dark pony on the wrong end of a hard life. It munched hungrily on the grass along the ditch, its front legs tethered by a short shank of rope. Deirdre smiled as she remembered an Arab maxim she had recently found in an old book. "Trust in Allah, but tether your camel at night."

"Hello," Deirdre said, standing up, dizzily swaying of a sudden.

She was dumbfounded as the masculine figure of an ageing woman holding a milk-can in one hand turned to face her. Deirdre knew just how big she was with child, saw the woman take this in without a blink, before she put the milk can on the ground to come quickly to her. Deirdre was surprised by the strength of the woman's gait, and in the moment knew that she was in safe hands.

The woman wore as a blouse an old flour sack with holes in it for her head and arms. Over this sat an ancient waistcoat. Her tweed skirt had been new twenty or thirty years before, her boots having once belonged to a large man, while her weather-beaten pugnacious face bore windswept blue eyes, under a shock of hair like washed cotton.

"I look a fright, I'm sure, child, but you're welcome," she said softly. Deirdre, moved to tears, made no attempt to shake them off.

"You are the most welcome sight ma'am," she vowed. "I thank God for your presence at this minute. You are the answer to the most fervent prayer I have ever said."

She was called Kelly, and she told Deirdre she was a

tinker, "A sort of mongrel gypsy – nayther one thing nor dother, missus." People like herself were turned away as half-breeds of a sort, she said, as though she was describing the weather, while Deirdre thought 'another race of people treated as less than people'.

This, and more did she learn as Kelly prepared her for childbirth, "With a bitta help from yerself, missus, God be praised."

She had carried much of Deirdre's weight the short distance to the canvas awning by the hedgerow, soothing words and sounds coming from her as naturally as the breath she exhaled. She made Deirdre lie down on her bed of twigs and grass and bits of old carpet, her face at peace. In that moment Deirdre thought of Constance Brewer again, seeing her as she had been on the only occasion they had met – a woman who had a wealth of material possessions, and was tortured by the rules of society, good form, one's duty to one's class, and so much more besides, while this tinker woman who called herself Kelly slept on a bed of detritus, yet welcomed her into it with a heart so open that Deirdre felt blessed.

"It's not what you're used to, missus, but better than either of us was the child born in a manger."

Deirdre now felt free enough to say to Kelly, "If anything should go wrong, if anything . . ." she found it difficult to say the words, drew a deep breath, and managed to express what was on her mind. "If anything should happen to me, my name is Deirdre Brewer, my husband and I live at Dunbla House, and somehow you should let him know, if that's not asking too much."

Looking at the older woman, she saw nothing but calmness and gentle concern in the weatherworn countenance. "Nothin' gointa happen to ya, missus, please God. We're in luck with the hot water, for I had a pot of it boiling to give meself me monthly wash," she chuckled. "Every month, ma'am, I give meself a good scrub, whether I need it or not!" She cackled with amusement and Deirdre laughed with her, until a dart of pain made her cry out, "It's coming."

Kelly helped her to raise her knees, moving into the fork Deirdre's thighs made, her head bent low for several moments. "Aye missus, yer close right enough." She backed out into the sunlight to return with a pot of boiling water. "On the fire for hours," she said as she began rummaging in a corner of the lean-to, to come up with a white flour sack from which she drew forth a clean enamel basin. "I keep this for them havin' childer." She doused it with the boiling water and threw this out into the afternoon. Suddenly there was immense pressure – Dee's vision dimmed for a moment, before she gathered her breathing that she might take Kelly's direction to push.

She could see Kelly's hands then, large hands hewn by the endless work involved in surviving at the bottom end of the social structure, yet feather-light those heavy fingers touched her, the washed blue eyes as steady now as they had been when Deirdre had first seen them.

"Above all, ma'am, try not to worry yerself. It won't be long now."

"Thank God for you, Kelly, and thank God you know what you're doing."

"Oh, now," Kelly nodded to herself. "I long ago quit countin' the numbers. Only yesterday, I delivered a young tinker lassie of a boy child. Yer narrow in the hips, missus. Ah! Yer baby's comin' right enough, so give a push. Push the wee love into this weary worrold. You have courage now, *allanah*. It might be hard on ye for a little while."

Deirdre heard herself say, "What's your name? Your Christian name?"

"Bride's the only first name I ever heard used on me, Missus."

"May I call you Bride?" Dee cackled shortly at the formality of the question.

"Kelly is what I'm known as, but you suit yerself. Now, here," She dipped a bacon bone in the boiling water for a second, holding it until it turned dry in the air. "Put it between yer teeth when the pain comes hard. And ye can pray in yer mind much as you want to."

Minutes later, Deirdre was clamping her teeth on the bone to cope with pain and pressure that almost took her mind away from her. She felt that her body was being forced to release something that wasn't meant to be moving. She thought she would have to die. 'Take me, Lord,' her prayer was a begging letter. 'I cannot survive this.'

"Push, *allanah*. Push hard." Kelly urged, as Deirdre almost blacked out.

The pain was relentless, and she pushed even harder, anything to stop the pressure before it stopped the beating of her heart. Convinced she was about to die, she pulled the bacon bone away, her sweat like oil now all over her body. "Can you see, Kelly? Am I going to have a healthy baby?" She tried to raise her head, but she fell back helplessly. "Please Kelly," she cried out in agony. "Please tell me it's going to be all right."

Dimly now, Deirdre heard Kelly urging her to push. Then, when she truly thought she was sliding into unconsciousness, she found the will and the strength to push again, and to grit her teeth, and to push even harder just this one more time. Then, miraculously, the pressure and the pain were taken away, lifted like mist by the warmth of the day, and Deirdre lay gasping for breath, bathing in her own sweat, tears of gratitude rolling off her face as she gulped another lungful of life.

Kelly leaned in close and said quietly, "You'll have a healthy child at your breast and that's an oul' tinker's promise, given in God's name this day. Just rest a while, till I clean up your son. Rest now child. All is well at the minute."

Some time later, Deirdre knew she had fainted away as Kelly's words relieved her mind, smiling at the remembrance that she had a healthy son. How wonderful for Arthur to have a son. Next time, she winced at the prospect of another delivery, a girl for me.

Kelly was applying a cold cloth to her brow, wiping her face now, gently cleaning the sweat and the snot and the spittle from her nose and mouth. "Your wee wain wants feedin', Deirdre, and he's a lad won't be kept waitin', I'd say."

Deirdre heard a hungry cry and her heart skipped a beat. 'My God', she thought, 'my God.' She got a glimpse of her pinkish-looking son, his face a pulp of tiny features, as his hunger demanded she put him to her breast. For some seconds the only sound she could hear was that of her baby sucking at her nipple. She was astonished – to think that her body had nourished him, sheltered him in the safe lodging of her womb, to send him in its own time into the world, where the same God-given body was now keeping him alive on nature's own milk.

When he finished his first feed, she held him in the crook of her arm. He slept in the cardigan she had been wearing as Kelly found her by the roadside. "I owe you my life, and the life of my son, Kelly," she reached out, and touched the old woman's arm. "There must be some way I can help you. You must let me help you, allow me to show my gratitude, for all you have done for me."

"I'm in need of a clay pipe, ma'am and a bitta tobacco," Kelly said. Then in an instant, tears filled her eyes, and her voice seemed to be addressing an invisible third party when it said. "Times I thought I'd lost her." She looked at Deirdre as though she had just remembered she was still there. "The man above had no room for ye today, Deirdre. He sent you here, and he'll send you away from here, you and your son."

"Promise me you'll let me help you. I have so much and you have so very little." Deirdre recoiled at the injustice of it all. The old woman found a wan smile. "Haven't ye done that already in choosin' me to help you have yer child? That's all the reward I need."

The sound of carriage wheels brought their exchange to a stop. Kelly backed out, and moments later, Arthur, on all fours, found his way to Deirdre in the lean-to.

"You and your walking fits," he said, his voice smothered in emotion, tears running down his face. "Thank heavens you're alive and well."

Deirdre touched his face, and taking his hand she placed it on the head of their first-born child. Arthur's eyes smiled in wonder even as his tears flowed, his mouth fell open, and there on bended knees under the tinker's canvas he took the baby in his arms.

Patrick Lote's professional voice interrupted the moment. "Damn it, Arthur, you said you'd tell me instantly what is happening in there. Is Deirdre all right?"

"I'm fine, Paddy," Deirdre yelled. "I'm not so sure about my husband."

Arthur kissed his son's head, his washed blue eyes all over her face. He chuckled then, wiping his tears as he glanced at the bed she lay on. "What a place to have a child." A wicked gleam appeared in his eyes and he said, "Perhaps I should have my mother come and visit you, before we take you away from all this."

Deirdre found a weak smile, knowing that if she never laid eyes on Constance Brewer again, it would be too soon. "The woman, Arthur. Her name is Kelly. She saved my life, the life of our son. I want a free hand to help her in any way I can."

"Of course, it goes without saying. Whatever we can do to help her. Nobody should have to live like this." Arthur started to back out of the lean-to. Moments later, her doctor, Patrick Lote, was on his knees by Deirdre's side, making no effort to hide his revulsion. When he was satisfied that she was all right, he produced some towels and a fresh cotton gown, and helped her to make herself more comfortable. "Rest for a while, my dear. We'll soon have you out of here."

Deirdre barely came out of sleep as Seamus hefted her into his arms, and backed out into the waning sunlight of late afternoon. She was vaguely aware that her head was resting on Arthur's lap and felt the closed carriage bump along although moving at a snail's pace. Some time after this, she heard her son announce to one and all that he was hungry. She took him to her breast, drifting off again even as he sucked her milk into himself.

"I wish I could see Vicky," Deirdre awoke on her own words. "And if I could see Sam that would make things perfect altogether. And we have to get word to my parents, let them know they have become grandparents."

"All will be attended to, my dear Dee, have no fear," Arthur whispered. "Sam is in town hard at work, but lo and behold, our dearest Vicky arrived here today as we were leaving the house to look for you. She looked quite wrecked – goodness, I thought, how the time has flown since she was home as your matron of honour – what? June last year," Arthur shook his head, his countenance etched in concern. "She doesn't look all that healthy, Dee. I simply told her that I was on my way to collect you. Had I told her that you had disappeared, she would have insisted on joining in, and it was my impression she was in no fit state."

"Can we call him Eddie?" Deirdre asked, starting to doze again.

Patrick Lote, taking the baby in his arms to allow her rest, chuckled, "I'd no idea you had married a royalist, Arthur."

Arthur was more than agreeable. "Whatever name you wish, my dear."

"It is not for Edward the Seventh," Deirdre whispered. "It's for Kelly."

"All right, my love, Eddie it shall be, for Kelly."

Deirdre remained silent now, remembering the old woman's surprise when she had kissed her rough-hewn hand. "I'll be back to see you in a few days, Kelly, just as soon as my doctor allows me to be up and about. Promise me you won't leave the area."

"Don't you be rushing yourself, child. Ye had a hard time today and without God on our side, we might have lost ye."

"I will pray for you every day, every day of my life. And I will see to it that you have a better life. It can't be easy, the way you live now. Is it right? It cannot be right, especially for a woman of your age."

Kelly studied Deirdre's face for a few moments, as

though she was trying to make a decision about something that was important to her. "We'll talk about things when you're up and about. I have something to tell you. Something I feel you have to know, for the future. And if you could fit the name Eddie, Edward like, into the child's name, I'd like that. I never married – I had a son, Eddie. He died a baby."

Deirdre was aware of being carried up the stairs at Dunbla. She heard Vicky's voice, her cooing, ooing and aaahing, as she fell in love with her first nephew, her silken touch then on Deirdre's body as she undressed her. All of it was vague to the young mother, until her son was back at her breast, Vicky laughing at the baby's appetite.

"My God, Dee, he's positively guzzling it into himself. Only been here a few hours and already he's a dairy-man!"

She was sleeping and waking, finding Vicky there applying a warm flannel to her face, and later a cold cloth to cool her down, Arthur joining her as they took turns holding a small jug of liquid to her lips, the twins wrapping her up in love.

From a distance, she heard Arthur calling his sister to dinner, Vicky replying she would stay with Dee. Paddy Lote's voice, then – he was quietly instructing Victoria as to what she should, and should not do, in relation to mother and child. Later, she felt Vicky slip into bed beside her, cuddling her, whispering tales of her time in Paris, wicked and wistful tales that made Dee smile in her half-sleep, the comfort granted her by her sister-in-law's generosity of spirit beyond all riches.

Sam arrived at Dunbla the following afternoon to swallow Deirdre in an embrace before holding her then at arm's length, his eyes brim-filled with tears, the grin on his mouth a torch of admiration and love. "You're an inspirational bloody woman, do you know that?"

Deirdre blossomed at the sight of him, grateful then as she watched him hold Eddie as though he was the most precious thing on earth. She was not in the least surprised that Gloria wasn't with Sam. As time passed, she sensed, more and more, that the couple had grown even further apart, their life having gone off track soon after they returned to Dublin from their brief honeymoon in London.

The two women hadn't seen each other since Dee had called to the house on Leinster Road, the day after Sarah Sweet had entered the world a year earlier. In the absence of Vicky, who was away living in Paris, Deirdre had become Sam's confidante and she knew he was not happy in his marriage.

"I'm the first to admit she gave me warnings, Dee, sort of veiled warnings of things to come once we were married." For the first time Deirdre saw that he felt helpless. "She wanted to be a real and proper Jewish wife, so she kept on saying. She'd be running a Jewish home for me, and the family. In fairness to her, this always included my mother. From the start Gloria was keen to look after her, make her life better." He shook his head in disbelief. "Our family would be committed members of the larger Jewish family, giving our time and our support to the Dublin branch of the diaspora."

Sam reacted with a cynical smile to Deirdre's intake of breath. "That's right, Dee." He snorted a laugh, a short angry chortle, his mouth becoming a hard line. "If it hadn't been for the number of books I read all my life, I'd have had to go and look up the word. But I heard your response to it, the sound of it, and that's how I felt when she said it. I thought, she's going crazy on me, this is fanatical stuff. I tried to slow her down, Dee, get her to see that she had a whole lifetime to come to this. Not her, she wanted to be committed by Friday! The way she's going, she'll end up committed to an institution."

Sam, who was not above enjoying one of his own jokes, didn't find this one amusing. "It's like there's something on her mind, maybe something to do with the life she had to live on the streets of London. I don't know. But, I keep getting the feeling she's trying to make up for something, something that has nothing to do with now, with us, her and me, and the mother, and now Sarah. But, she is killing whatever I felt for her. I warned her about this. She dismissed it as romantic nonsense, told me I was a good man and that a good man would honour his wedding vows, that he would fulfil his obligation to being a Jew in a Gentile world, where Jews had always been, and continued to be, outcasts."

Deirdre, deciding to say nothing held his hand as he sat by her bed. There was more to come, she felt sure, and it was best that he talk it out. She was glad he had come to her. They had a history of being available when one needed the other – he was the architect of the life she now lived and she wanted to help him in every way she could.

"I should have been listening more," Sam was blaming himself. "I was too busy thinking about having her in bed. When she was saying stuff like this, I'd make the right noise and agree in my own off-hand way. I just chugged along with the general sound of the blueprint she presented. I was so busy looking at her breasts rising as she got passionate about how things were going to be. Half the time, Dee, I didn't really hear her words. All I wanted to do was put my lips to her breasts for a start, the rest I'll leave to your imagination. You know," he said ruefully, "the truth is, if I had taken in all that she was saying, I'd have run a mile. Beauty or no beauty, I wouldn't have married her in a million years. I wanted her too badly, Dee, who wouldn't? But I held it down, and I let her think I'd be a good husband, which I think I am. Perhaps I leaned over a bit, that I let her think I'd be the kind of Jewish husband she would need to keep up with her idea of what a Jewish wife has to be, if you understand me."

"Have you tried talking to her about how you feel? Surely, since she loves you, she would want to respect your feelings, consider your needs in your own home?"

"She's not the best listener in the world, no more than I am. It's like she has turned into some kind of martyr to Judaism." His voice rang plaintive, his expression one of discomfort bordering on shock. "It's like she is trying to make up for the fact that she and her mother lived outside the pale for so long, sometimes having to hide the fact that they were Jews – Jew-hating was rife during their years in England. Rebecca's husband, Gloria's father, he was murdered. It's like, I swear it, Dee, it's like she is now trying to make up for all of that by being so bloody Jewish that it's almost funny. The problem is she expects me to feel the same way. And there's not a snowball's chance in Hell I'm ever going to be that kind of zealot."

During the past year, Dee had witnessed the change in Sam's wife. She could still remember how Sam had described how shocked and dismayed he had been when, returning home after a long working day working in business, he was to discover what Gloria had done to her hair.

"She has cut it all off, Dee," Sam was like a man turned numb. "That magnificent head of hair that was like proof there's some kind of God somewhere . . . it's gone, all of it, all she has left is a skullcap." Sam was devastated, a connoisseur needing to weep over a work of art mindlessly destroyed.

Deirdre's disbelief had been etched into her face. "My God, it sounds as though Gloria needs help from a doctor."

Sam had been brutally disappointed, barely holding down the anger eating at him. "She has burned every dress she wore, including the blue silk she had made for the wedding and that cost a fortune. And Deirdre, she now wears some sort of corset that holds her breasts down. She will not even use carmine on her lips, and though she would never refuse me my conjugal rights – her very words – she will play no part in love-making, kissing passionately, touching, caressing. She eschews anything that smacks of enjoyment or sensation. She allows that I am entitled to satisfy my passion through intercourse, but she wants no part of it. To tell you the truth, I wonder if she is not going mad in some way, that's if she isn't already gone gaga on me."

"Despite all this, you say she professes to love you?" Deirdre tried not to judge Gloria, not wanting to fuel a hostile mood towards a woman imprisoned by some power beyond her experience.

"So she claims, regardless of the way she carries on. When I told her I liked her breasts, that I love to touch them and kiss them, and that I liked the look of her when she was wearing a wool top around the house, she told me that this was the very reason she wanted to hide them. As a married woman, she didn't want any man lusting after her in any way, and that, by the way, includes me. She said it was a sin against God, and against love, to lust after your wife."

Over time, Sam and Deirdre had become closer, their long-standing affection for each other what one might expect to feel for a brother or sister. Now that they both had children, their relationship was to be the bond that would ensure their offspring spent lots of time together. Gloria's opposition to this was simply something Sam would have to battle against. "And battle I will, Dee."

"As soon as I'm fit again, I'll invite her to lunch," Dee offered. "I'll meet her in town. We can talk about babies and other ladies' stuff over a meal. It can hardly do any harm." Deirdre was remembering herself coming downstairs from her visit to Gloria and her baby, Sarah, at the house on Leinster Road. She had gone into the front room to say goodbye to Esther – liking and admiring the old woman who had survived her own incredible story on her long journey to Ireland.

The house had been refurbished and decorated before the wedding of Sam and Gloria, and Dee complimented Esther on how beautifully she maintained it.

Esther had disabused her of the notion with a shake of her grey head and a faint smile on her lips. "No, my dear, I'm hardly allowed to do anything. Gloria runs the house – she makes me more comfortable than I have ever been. 'You've worked enough' her very words to me from our first day under the same roof. 'There's no need for it, we have the wherewithal to pay a *shiksa*.' And that's how it has been ever since, though once, when she was waiting for the baby, she let me make dinner for the Sabbath – my gefilte fish. She is so good to me I have to keep pinching myself." The old woman smiled, "You understand, this is not in the nature of a complaint. I will become very good at doing nothing once I keep practising, yes."

Victoria broke into Dee's reverie by exploding into the room with the word 'Sam' booming off her lips, her arms outstretched. He was on his feet in an instant to respond to her embrace. For a moment Dee felt a pang of jealousy, seeing how the easy nature of their passion took them away from her to find some part of themselves in each other. She lay back on her pillows and envied them their involvement, the depth of it illustrated by the fact that in moments she, and their surroundings, seemed to simply disappear. And yet, they felt no need to commit till death us do part, nor did they think they owned each other in any way. They were unique in her, admittedly limited, experience.

When Sam and Vicky lay satiated, they managed to look at each other without either banter or love talk. He could see she was coming out of a lot of pain even though she smiled, her broken eyes fired now with his image, her hands holding his as though she would never let go of him again.

As though reading his mind, she said, "I won't leave you again."

Sam embraced her. She closed her eyes, tears threatening and he said in his 'I'm warning you' voice, "I will be seeing you every day from now on."

She nodded and kissed him on the lips. "You enrich my life, but then, that's nothing new. I'm just happy you still want me?"

Sam threw her a wry smile. "Whatever gave you that idea?" He put his arms about her fiercely and felt her wince for a moment. Masking his concern, he carefully took his hands from her back in a natural way, touching her shoulders and her upper arms as though checking she was all there. He kissed her ears and her face and her neck in a gentle way, while she responded to his tenderness with whispered ululations of gratitude and love. He smiled before he moved to light cigarettes for them both, asking himself was it his imagination, or was the first real love of his life suffering from some malady that could do her in.

18

Dublin

June 1911

"Isn't it incredible, Vicky?" Sam yelled. "The experience of a lifetime?" He was like a jolly schoolboy behind the wheel of his first petrol-driven automobile.

Victoria, quite tipsy in the passenger seat of the open-topped Haynes, leaned closer to him, and brushed her fingers between his thighs. He yelled out in mock remonstration, Vicky laughing flirtatiously as she yelled back at him, "Leaving out being in bed with you, it's pretty damn wonderful."

They were hurtling towards Dublin, and Sam had taken one hand from the steering wheel to point in disbelief at the speedometer. "We're doing twenty-nine miles an hour. Can you believe it?"

They passed through the tiny village of Stillorgan as people stood and gaped at the horseless carriage, Vicky waving cheerily as they sped by. One old woman got such a start that she fainted away as the grey roadster, with green wheels and white-wall tyres flashing, hurtled past her.

Sam was enjoying the same feeling he knew whenever he drank three or four glasses of perfectly chilled champagne. There were uplifting bubbles in his blood, bubbles that made him forget his troubles, friendly burps of air that made him want to chuckle and laugh at the sheer joy of being alive.

"Arthur will be bowled over," Vicky leaned close to yell in his ear. "Nobody's ever given him a birthday present than can move at twenty-nine miles an hour." She offered him the half-empty champagne bottle. "Being a lady, I offer the first swig to the driver."

Sam declined the drink, grimacing slightly as his lovely passenger put the bottle to her lips. He grimaced but said nothing. Vicky had never been one to obey the rules. She had been drinking more than ever since she had come back from Paris, giving him cause for concern. Arthur turning into a semi-permanent drunk was enough for anyone to cope with. But what could you do? Vicky was Vicky and that was it.

Ironically, Arthur had cut down his alcohol intake since becoming a father, and his late night visits to the fancy houses of the Monto were less frequent than before. And he was working harder than ever now, intent on developing the brewery, determined to improve the quality of his product and the working conditions of his employees. But his drinking seemed to be doing more damage than it had in the past – it was as though it was catching up on him, Sam felt.

Arthur's worker-participation scheme was now in operation. Those employees that had been with the brewery from the beginning had received shares in the company; every worker would ultimately own some, as Arthur's expansion plans manifested on the banks of the Liffey at Kilmainham.

Sam was relieved that marriage had turned out to be a good thing for Arthur and Deirdre. He had known of Arthur's habits when he and Vicky had brought the couple together but, because Dee was such an angel, he had believed the big man would change when he took on a wife and a family. So far Sam had been proved right to some degree. He hoped for more of the same, because he believed Dee was a special woman, that Arthur needed her more than he realised.

Sam had seen how Deirdre accepted Arthur, warts and all. He knew that she had never questioned him about the benders he went on, understanding that he had demons that he had to deal with in his own way. He had seen too, how she reached out to Arthur even more as he was recovering from his latest abuse of alcohol, and he wondered how someone so young could be gifted with such wisdom.

'Acceptance keeps you free of judgment.' These words had stuck in Sam's mind during his bookworm days but he had never seen the truism in practice until Dee wore it like a subtle perfume as she served her marriage vows. He had never doubted she would be the right wife for Arthur, his gratitude that she had proven so pleased him greatly – it was also good to know that her ideological aspirations could be pursued the easier because she had married a rich and powerful man. He drew comfort from knowing that her life would be better still now that she had borne two sons to carry on the family name.

On several occasions, when Arthur had gone missing for two or three days, Sam had searched his haunts, found him and brought him home. Dee always received her husband in gratitude – hugging Sam fervently when she had Arthur tucked away in his own bed – with never a murmur of complaint, Dee looking after Arthur as she would have done had he been an invalid.

Dee regularly took the precaution of warning the servants that below-stairs gossip must stay within the house. Anyone found guilty of talking about the ups and downs of the family to outsiders, would be dismissed without compunction.

"Is there another woman in the country actually allows her husband to be however he needs to be?" Sam asked over a cup of afternoon tea at the Shelbourne while Dee was in town shopping. He was thinking of his ongoing struggle with Gloria and his failure to make her see reason in relation to her expectations of him.

"We're all riding on the shoulders of those gone before us," Dee said quietly. "Many are hurt, wounded so badly by family breakdown, hardship, mindless cruelty, that they want to create some sort of protective ring around themselves and their families. Some of us want so desperately to keep out the pain we have known, that we lose all sense of proportion. With your inherent decency and your support, even when she is being difficult, Gloria will surely become more reasonable, given time."

Dee and Sam sat down together – their long-standing friendship more secure than ever – on an evening when he had just brought Arthur home, literally carrying him upstairs. When their beloved charge was tucked up in his bed, they came downstairs and now faced each other across the fire in her withdrawing room. As usual, they had a glass of wine and talked about everything and anything. He would rise to throw a log or a shovel of coal into the flames, replenish her glass, sitting close well into the night. He had always thought her incredibly bright but he could still be surprised by her sagacity which, along with her built-in sense of compassion, was so much a part of her that he took it for granted. "You're like good wine, Dee, getting better with every year that passes."

Sam's mind came back to the present as he approached Donnybrook village. He leaned on the klaxon horn, to warn the driver of a horse-drawn milk-dray that he was about to pass. Moments later he overtook a horse tram, on its way to Nelson's Pillar, giving the driver a wave and an extra blast from the horn.

"I'm thinking Arthur might settle down a bit more, now that he has a second son," Sam yelled. "What do you think?"

"Of course, he will." Vicky was well on the way to

being drunk. "He's a new man since he married Dee. I knew he would be." She smoked on a cigarette, and exhaled a grey ribbon that was eaten up instantly by the gushing breeze about their heads.

Sam smiled to himself – Vicky with her pink specs on! Blind to the fact that Arthur was a confused man, a tortured man at times, but never less than perfect in her eyes. And why not, Sam mused, since the man, despite any fault he might have, was one of the best.

As they drove by St Stephen's Green, he headed for the church where Arthur and Dee had been married. He allowed himself a pat of self-praise as he remembered suggesting to Arthur that he make the gesture that would open the way for Pat Doyle to climb down off his high-horse without losing face. Arthur had acquiesced in a jiffy, creating relief all around – the wedding day had turned out wonderfully well, the Doyle family bestowing its blessing by appearing in its Sunday best to witness Arthur keep his promise by converting in order to marry Deirdre.

As Sam now brought the car to a halt close to the church, Vicky seemed to have sobered up a bit. He felt relieved and took her hand as they stood gazing in some kind of delight at the magnificent roadster. There were other motoring cars parked down the street, but nothing to match his. Many passers-by stopped as they passed, to gape at the sparkling horseless carriage.

"I've written the cheque for my half," Vicky said. "It's on the table in the house. I'm saying this out loud, that I'll remember to give it to you later."

"There's no need, Vicky."

"Of course, there is. It's our joint prezzie to Arthur, and I must pay my share. Now, tell me again those details you mentioned earlier. Later on, I want to flaunt my knowledge of automobiles to all and sundry."

"Well it's a Haines two-seater, with a sizeable bucket behind, quite sporty really for such a classy animal, open-topped though you can pull up the canvas roof. It has a five horse-power engine, a three-speed gearbox. I'm sure it will go up to thirty-five miles an hour, maybe even forty on a good road. Is that enough guff for you to impress people who won't have a notion of what you're talking about?"

Vicky, having failed to take in one word of what he said, hung onto Sam. She was delighted to be with him, to have returned to him, to be rescued by himself and Dee, the pair of them helping her recover somewhat from the pain of her break-up with Michelle in Paris. She doubted she would ever really get over the French-born artist, but Sam's incredible ongoing passion for her helped her to keep going. She was relieved to admit to herself, and to Dee, that she had come some way from wanting to end it all, when Michelle had dumped her for a younger model.

Outside White Friar Street church, she felt it was quite safe to link her arm with Sam. She knew that Gloria wouldn't be at Alfie's christening – that lady was a law unto herself. She shook her head, remembering her first sight of Gloria after her recent return to Ireland. The beautiful young woman had cut off her magnificent hair, looking as though she wore an ebony skullcap that seemed to have been painted onto her head. During the few moments they had spent being polite, Vicky thought Gloria despondent, perhaps even depressed. She had asked Sam why, what was this all about? Why the death-like appearance, why the loose-fitting smock in dark blue, without even a hint of carmine on her mouth. "Why is she hiding all the wonderful gifts nature gave her? Is that what's going on?"

"That's it, exactly," Sam was long since resigned to the situation. "When we got back from honeymoon she cut her hair off within a week. The tent she wears all the time – she has two of them, never wears anything else. I asked her, 'Why would you hide your breasts as though they are something to be ashamed of?'"

"She was incredibly well endowed," Vicky said, "Not that I saw them in the flesh, though I would have adored to." She smiled, giving him a look drenched in pure wickedness. They moved on, but she stopped him short of the entrance to the church. "May we stop for a quick cigarette before we enter this holy of holies?"

He grinned at the ironic tilt to her smile. "When I grow up, Miss Brewer, I am going to learn how to say 'no' to you."

She was already lighting her cigarette. "But not today, I trust?"

"Indeed," Sam conceded, delighted to have her there by his side, three sheets to the wind, or not!

"So what did she say about her beauties, her bosoms?"

"She said God gave them to provide milk for children, not for men to stare at and want to use like playthings when they were sexually aroused. She actually wears a yoke that ties them down, have I told you that already?"

"Are you suggesting that when you two are about to indulge in a wild bout of rumpy-pumpy, that she forbids . . ." Vicky simply couldn't finish the question.

"Gloria would never refuse me what she calls my conjugal rights. But I don't get to kiss her breasts or anything else. When I think back on it, even on our honeymoon when she was very compliant, she seemed to be holding back, as though she couldn't get involved beyond a certain point."

"Perhaps she was raped, assaulted in some awful way. That could account for her, well, being intimidated, I suppose, by the thought of sexual intercourse." Vicky put her Cuban heel on the cigarette, brushing a hint of ash from the frills at her breast. "She sounds like a woman suffering, not like someone born frigid, or perhaps lesbian."

As they took their place in the front pew of the church, Sam returned Dee's welcoming and blew her a kiss. Vicky now took the baby, Alfie, who seemed to purr at his aunt as though he knew she was already in love with him.

Sam waved a smiling silent hello to Kelly, wanting to say, "You look so posh, my dear, I hardly recognised you." The old woman of the roads had been living in her own cottage close by the main house at Dunbla since shortly after the birth of Eddie. "The best wain ever born," Kelly claimed every time the child's name was mentioned. Sam liked Kelly more every time he visited her home, which he did whenever he went to see Dee who had made the mansion at Dunbla her primary residence.

The Brewer family home at Merrion Square was firmly in Arthur's hands. He had found a way to make his mother move out without the kind of disruptive resistance that everyone anticipated, Constance agreeing to leave on the understanding Arthur buy her a magnificent house in London. She now spent most of her time in the English capital, and Arthur sighed wickedly as he remarked to Sam, his tone light as he tried to dismiss the pain that would not go away, "At last, Constance can put to good use the skills she chose to acquire through the first twelve years of Vicky's and my life. At last, the caterpillar can be seen to be a full-time social butterfly."

Arthur now leaned across Deirdre to take Sam's hand. Decidedly sober, Sam noted gratefully, more than surprised that Arthur looked so straight. He had seen Seamus on the way in. The goat-faced Kerryman was leaning in a fragile manner against the wall inside the door at the back of the church. There had been enough life in him to give Sam a sign to indicate that the boss was in good condition this morning. The two men had a secret agreement. They kept no secrets from each other where Arthur's boozing was concerned, working as conspirators in arms, when it came to keeping their charge out of trouble. This they did without demur, on one occasion having broken the law by bribing two policemen who had the great man in custody.

The lawmen were about to throw the book at him for causing damage and mild mayhem in a brothel. Arthur, who had been lost in a bout of alcoholic-amnesia, remembered nothing of the altercation. Since amnesia could not be used as a defence in law, the various charges stood up. A hefty bribe from Sam Sweet caused the police officers to let the matter drop, provided that the damage was made good and all expenses were paid.

Sam, who was one of the godparents, turned to the row behind him and shook hands with Pat and Elizabeth Doyle. They were clearly delighted to see him. Sam nodded to their daughter Mary, a pretty girl with a gentle manner, who was two years younger than Deirdre. He waved a silent hello to her brother, Cormac – a born hothead to Sam's mind, a fella with a hard road ahead of him. He gestured hello to Paddy, the youngest lad, who combed his hair forward to hide his great dome of forehead – at a guess, an interesting and worthwhile fellow.

As the parents and godparents stood around the holy water font, Alfie Brewer started to wail as though somebody was very slowly and very painfully extracting his intestines by way of his big toe, or so it seemed to Sam Sweet. The wailing had such a brutal effect on his tender head – the fourth glass of wine the night before had done him in – that he urgently needed to leave the church, knowing, at the same time, that he could do no such thing. He cursed the little brat for kicking up such a racket, particularly when everybody present was barely breathing in deference to the occasion.

Sam caught Kelly's eye, pulling a face as he playfully mimed the act of choking the life out of the unhappy child. Kelly nodded her head slightly, her own smile allowing him a glimpse of her new dentures. Then he saw her reach across Deirdre, to very gently rub the side of the baby's temple with a fingertip. A few seconds later, the infant's cacophony seemed to slither into momentary difficulty, after which there was silence of the type known as blessed, creating in the small gathering a collective sigh of relief palpable as a round of applause. At that moment Vicky smiled at Sam, tilting her head in Kelly's direction as her mouth formed one silent word, which he read as 'witch'.

Sam had never thought of Kelly as a witch but he had felt from their first meeting that there was something fey about her, this feeling gathering his attention whenever he was in her company. Fanciful as the notion was, he felt that she could have spent time with the little people, the fairies and the leprechauns, that, according to legend, inhabited the face of Ireland. Sam took the folklore with a grain of salt, but there was something other-worldly about Kelly. He had felt this even more since Deirdre had told him the story of being lost on the afternoon of the birth of Eddie. The impact of what might have been had the old woman not appeared through a hedge like a mendicant, a total stranger coming equipped to save a mother and a child that were to be related only by this incredible happenstance. The miracle involved in the meeting of Dee and Kelly had ensured that he was no longer blasé about something he would have scoffed at a few short years before.

Dee had made a revelation one evening as they sat by the fire in her withdrawing room. Arthur was home, in his study, working on another plan for another project, with Eddie bedded down for the night, the house quiet above and below stairs.

They had drifted onto the subject of childbirth, the adjustments that had to be made in a household to accommodate even a tiny infant. He was thinking of his daughter, Sarah, smiling at the way she gurgled sometimes when he leaned over her cot, enjoying the way her light-brown eyes followed his waving finger as though it was some great wonder of the world.

"She has some kind of golden light in her," Sam glowed as he described his baby daughter. "Her skin seems to shine from inside and she has her own looks, not mine, not Gloria's. I find myself wondering sometimes did she decide not to look all that much like either of us, wanting her own look, the look she chose for herself. Fanciful, of course, Dee, but she's such a miracle, well, in her case, anything seems possible."

"I know that you're in love with her," Dee smiled and rose to pour wine. "So I know it doesn't bother you, but . . ." she handed him a glass, "does Gloria feel let down that Sarah is not carved out of her?"

"Gloria is aggrieved about something, Dee. She can't talk about it. I try to respect her privacy even when I feel like shaking her to see if anything gets revealed. She feels Sarah will come to look like her own mother. This seems to give her some comfort. Rebecca remains alive in her life. She keeps a journal, like letters to her mother. I've heard her talking to her at night. As though she speaks the words as she is writing them down. I wish I could help, help her as a human being in pain. They were so close. Quite honestly, I don't know if she's ever going to let go of Rebecca. I certainly have no hope of filling the void her mother left behind."

"My heart goes out to her."

"You and your compassionate nature," he said warmly. "The same lady has not behaved well in your case, or Arthur's."

"What we consider to be inappropriate behaviour usually stems from hurt of some kind – it is no measure of a person's overall worth. I won't give up being open to Gloria. I envy her the facility to write, to keep a journal, to have some place where she can deposit the stuff you dare not talk about." Deirdre sipped her wine and Sam became aware that she was near to tears.

"Dee," he said quietly, "if ever there is the need, you can use me like a journal, please know that. There's no secret I wouldn't share with you. Just know I'd willingly harbour any burden that might ever trouble you. And you know I'd be as silent as a blank page."

Deirdre wiped away a tear. "I need to tell you about Eddie and Kelly and me. I would have spoken before but I knew the trouble you were having at home, knew you were hurting over Vicky's going as well. Much as I love her, I don't think she should have written to you about Michelle and their relationship. What was the point in telling you that? Anyway, I had my reasons for not unburdening myself to you."

"I've seen you as such an oasis, Dee, it never occurred to me you were in pain. I know that Arthur going on his benders hurt you in the beginning . . ."

Dee raised her hand to cut him off. "My feelings for Arthur will get me through any resentment I might feel, now and then." She shrugged, "Whatever he needs to do, just as long as, between us, we can keep him from hurting himself too much." She sipped the wine in her glass. "I'm grateful I've been a source of comfort to you. Now, it's your turn. When Kelly appeared to me on that back road, like a vision really, walking to me straight out of the sun, I was about to deliver my baby. This dear woman of the roads laid me down in her home by the hedgerow, where I lost consciousness through sheer exhaustion, the pressure becoming too much for me."

Dee closed her eyes, tried to gather herself, willing away the tears, not wanting anything to get in the way of the story. "Kelly was coming through a gap in the hedge like a sort of tarnished angel lit by the sun. I saw that she carried an old spade and a milk-can. As I came back to consciousness, she was placing my baby at my breast. I called him Eddie after Kelly's own son, lost some years before. I cried Sam, the pain forgotten. I didn't know, had no idea that I had delivered a still-born baby girl. I didn't know it for some time after. Kelly waited until I was fit and well again before she told me. There was something else, a tragic tale if ever there was one. Eddie's mother, a tinker girl of just sixteen, she had died giving birth to him just the day before. She passed away right there under the canvas where my little darling came dead from my body."

Sam sat still, silenced by the story as Dee went on talking. "Kelly would tell me all within a few weeks, just as soon as she thought me well enough to deal with the truth. I asked her what happened to the young mother, abandoned by the child's father. She had buried her in the ditch behind her tent. She told me that she was praying for help, actually asking God to help her to keep Eddie alive as she came out of the field. Then she found me standing there utterly lost."

Deirdre paused to blow her nose and Sam got a fresh cigarette going. He wanted to go to her, hold her close, let her know how much she meant to him. He remained where he was, waiting, stunned by her revelation.

"As you well know, I've always had trouble with faith in God," she surrendered to a brief rueful smile. "I could talk to you about it, never to my parents. Why disabuse them of their belief that I was the same kind of Catholic as they themselves? That day, as Kelly and I found each other, each of us the answer to the other's need, in Kelly's case my turning up as an answer to her prayers said in desperation, I came to feel that some loving God had touched the pair of us. While I lay there with Eddie at my breast, Kelly placed my stillborn daughter in the ditch grave with the tinker girl – she was called Josie. Later, Seamus and Kelly and I, we went back and we brought the two bodies here to Dunbla. We buried them at night, close by the cottage Kelly now lives in – the same one Gloria slept in the night of the party on that summer solstice. We could not inform the police. Josie died as the result of a beating at the hands of Eddie's father – Kelly might well have been charged with God alone knows what. We wrapped the dear pair in a soft coffin of cotton sheets and buried them under Arthur's old sheepdog, Colly, who had died the day before. Colly lay above them, and we placed a marker with his name on it over the grave. This was how our pet graveyard came to be – an old pet of my husband's to cover up the presence of two very special pets whose presence could not be acknowledged. So you see, Sam, the son of my heart, Eddie, is not the blood child of Arthur and I." She shook her head slightly as though unable to believe her own story. "Seamus, forever loyal and true, asked no questions about that night and I told him nothing. Bless him, he would give his life for Arthur and Victoria, and he gave a lot that night for me. He and Kelly, and now you, are the only ones who know what happened." She touched his hand and looked into his eyes as she said," I have placed a heavy burden on you by sharing this. I needed to talk it out. And who else could I turn to but you?"

He knelt before her in front of the fire to embrace her

silently, simply holding her in his arms, his face against her cheek, allowing her the space to have her tears flow, until he felt it was time to take his handkerchief from his breast pocket and press it into her hand. While she wiped her eyes he poured wine for them both, placing the fresh glass on the occasional table by her seat. Going back to sit down on the other side of the fireplace, he lit a cigarette, and when she was seated again, and sipping the wine, he said, "There will never be anything you can't tell me, for I will never let you down. You will always have me, Dee. Rely on that."

In White Friar Street church, Alfie Brewer slept even as the priest poured the holy water over his head. Sam, relieved to be present again, found Dee's eyes. She gave him a smile, while he admired the off-white two-piece suit she wore, her bearing fine, as she clasped Arthur's hand, the big man unable to take his eyes from the face of his new son, who, obligingly, continued to sleep.

By nine o'clock that evening the christening celebration at Merrion Square had ended, the guests had departed, and the servants had finished clearing up.

Sam found Seamus Byrne sitting by the fire in the empty dining-room. The Kerryman rose to attend to him. "Don't get up, Seamus," Sam protested. The man-servant was already on his feet, a glass of whiskey transferred from his hand to the mantelpiece. Sam could see that he was three sheets to the wind, though this was not as apparent as it had been moments before. "How can I serve you, Mister Sweet?"

"Seamus, I sought you out just to shake your hand, if I may. And to say thanks to you for the thousand services you have rendered me since we met, and me dripping the Liffey, do you remember?"

The flinty eyes lit up, and a broad grin uplifted the goat-like face. "Always a pleasure, Mister Sweet." He took Sam's hand, and shook it heartily, "You have been a great gift to the Brewer family, sir, and thanks be to God, they know it."

"As they have been for me, Seamus, as you have been at every hand's turn." Sam took the glass of whiskey off the mantlepiece and pressed it into the powerful hand. "I remember the strength in that hand."

"I was so impressed, Mister Sweet, by your courage that day that I nearly went in to help you, and me not able to swim a stroke." He stopped and began to chuckle. "Ah, don't mind me, 'tis the Kerry in me, and the whiskey in me, giving out the spoof." He sipped his drink. His expression became contrite. "I couldn't have gone into Anna Livia the way you did that day, not if my Angela's life depended on me. You deserve all the rewards life has to offer a man, Mister Sweet."

About to leave, Sam shook his hand again, nodded his head, deciding not to say the words, 'alongside you, Seamus, I cast a small shadow,' though he felt them. As he went upstairs to Victoria, it was his intention to bid her goodnight and head on home. Arthur was already bedded down. He had said goodnight to Deirdre who was in the nursery with the nanny and her children, and he was ready to retire early.

Stepping into the huge bedroom, he saw right away that Vicky, wearing her most revealing negligee, had other plans. She was sitting on her haunches by the fire, sipping from a champagne glass. As she smiled up at him, she put the glass down and moved to her knees, pausing for a moment with a playful look in her eyes. She came to her feet and stood there looking at him, not moving a hair until Sam, smiled in acceptance of his powerlessness to deny her anything.

Later she whispered to him, "You still do it for me." Her tone suggested disbelief, "It's as though it is the first time every time and that was unforgettable."

"I told you straight that you bewitched me," he said playfully, as her elegant legs caressed his sides. "Whatever you do, don't ever release me from the spell you cast."

Sam had gasped on entering her, surprised at finding her so very ready for him, so completely caught by her need that, within minutes, his orgasm seemed ready to explode.

Feeling him go tense, she pleaded quietly, "Don't come just yet. I want it to go on and on."

Putting aside his own need for an early night, he kissed her mouth to still the annoyance that had risen in response to her order. Knowing he had to do something if he was to prolong his own release, he called to mind Shakespeare's *Richard the Third*, allowing Gloucester to meditate on the death of Clarence – this helping him get his mind into a more manageable state, so that he thrust with less energy and let the words 'Now is the winter of our discontent made glorious summer by this sun of York,' dance across his mind, knowing that all he really wanted here was to give Vicky the time of her life and get on home to bed.

As they smoked afterwards he responded to Vicky's rhetoric without involving more than a morsel of his mind. He found himself thinking of Deirdre and the courage she had manifested in her first childbirth, and its aftermath. He marvelled at the atavistic strength of his long-time friend, the way she arranged the late-night burial of the young mother and her own stillborn girl. He was in awe of the way she somehow found God's good will in the arrival of Eddie – what else but a loving God could have presented the lostling in need of a mother to the mother of the still-born girl who so desperately needed a baby at her breast.

Driving home he had no sense that this was the night before the morning on which he would wake up to the realisation that he and Vicky had become a thing of the past.

As he let himself in to the house at Leinster Road, he was still thinking of what had happened in Kelly's lean-to on the country lane as Dee's first child had arrived still-born. Remarkable really, the way it had happened and the manner in which both Dee and Kelly had played their part in what was almost a biblical parable relating to the power of God.

Sam – who could not believe in God, had long since

found that he was incapable of manufacturing anything like a philosophical concept of a deity – wondered would he ever be lucky enough to have an experience that would help him to feel that there was a God, a loving God. Or would he always believe that man, needing a God to believe in, had created a deity in the image and likeness of himself?

19

Kilmainham, Dublin

July 1911

Sam Sweet drove through the main gate of the brewery with Brendan O'Connor in the passenger seat. He stopped the car close to the site for the new malt-house and lit a cigarette. Brendan was already smoking a John Player. Sam's mind was occupied by the upcoming meeting with Arthur and his board members. These things always put him on edge, had done since his first contract from Arthur, back in the late summer of 1902.

This ongoing reservation had prompted him to say just a few days earlier, "Perhaps you should give this new contract to someone else. It can't be easy fighting a whole board of Jew-haters every time you want to expand at Kilmainham."

As always, Arthur would have none of it. "It's nothing personal, Sam. I thought that by promoting a couple of Roman Catholics to the board, it might balance things up a bit." He was embarrassed and hesitated. Sam helped him out. "Sorry for your trouble, Arthur. The Catholics hate the Jews, I'd say, even more than the West Brits. Most RCs seem to be under the impression that the Jews crucified Jesus, for which they are never going to forgive us," Sam smiled sardonically. "Will you just listen to me? I said 'forgive us' as though it has anything to do with me."

Brendan interrupted the memory. "There was something you wanted to say to me," he said, his forceful tone bringing his boss back to the present.

"There's something up your nose, Brendan, so you better blow it out." Sam tried to sound light, but failed. "Just don't get it on my new suit, right?" As he spoke he was dealing with three other projects in his mind, not least of which was the malt-house he was going to build just yards away from where he had parked the car.

"I've known you a long time. You've been one of the main strengths of the business I'm building. Your info got me the site at Portobello for a song. Your share of that deal bought your house. We have been bold boys with a couple of tarts in the same suite at Claridges in London. You are a close and valuable associate of mine, apart from which I actually like you." Sam exhaled a smoke ring, watching it for a moment. "Ever since I told you about this new contract with Brewer's, you've been giving off the smell of resentment, a whiff strong enough to make me worry about our future. So, tell me the story. Before you do, think about the employment we're helping to create, a lot of work for a lot of men, and all thanks to Arthur Brewer's faith in my ability – which is really our ability – to deliver on time."

"It's all great, and I'm glad it's happening," Brendan assured him. "This contract adds to the positive sound of Sweet Construction."

"So what's this *but* I hear in your voice then?"

Brendan lit a fresh cigarette. "Look, fair play to Arthur Brewer, I respect the man as your friend, and I don't deny he's providing the wherewithal that'll create work for a lot of men who need it. But like, well, this is all happening through money stolen from us in the first place."

"Oh, come on! Jesus! That was hundreds of years ago. And if you say you only heard about it yesterday, I'll punch you in the head." He gave Brendan a tap on the shoulder as though saying 'snap out of it'. "We've enough to do coping with today, and what we have to deal with on the canal. Not forgetting the uproar that I bribed my way onto the Portobello site. Enough to be going on with, I'd say, without delving into yesterday for reasons to be aggravated."

"You'd be surprised at the number of people who think it's time Ireland was run by the Irish, and not the establishment created by the English to keep reminding us we're the poor relations," said Seamus.

Sam was silent, watching a Brewer mini-locomotive pass by on the single-track railway. It carried barrels of stout to the loading bay where Arthur's great shires waited to take it away. Or it might have been on its way to the Liffey landing where flat barges would take it along the river's spine to the docks for export to England and France.

"I thought you were letting go of this revolutionary guff," Sam said, unwilling to hide the disappointment he felt. "You're well on the way to being a man of some substance, Carrots."

"I thought you quit calling me Carrots."

"Sorry," Sam's apology was sincere since he knew that Brendan hated the nickname. "You have a wife and kids to feed, and you like the things in life that cost money. You won't earn them playing soldiers." He raised his hand. "That was uncalled for. Forget I said it."

"What's to stop a bloke from having his own home and whatever, under a government of Irishmen," Brendan said vehemently, "without the Brits having any say in our affairs?"

"Your private life is your own business and you know it. But, the energy you're wasting while you seethe about what the English did and all the rest of it, Jesus, will it leave you enough juice to do your job right? We're growing, so I need you even more than I did."

"Nothing gets between me and what I'm paid to do. I'd never be disloyal to you," Brendan's disappointment was evident.

"The question doesn't arise," Sam threw away his cigarette. "But, and it has to be said, as we've been driving up here, it wasn't this enormous contract that was foremost on your mind. It wasn't the logistics

332

relating to the new brewhouse, was it? It was the guff about the English robbing us and keeping us down all down the years, and all the rest of it. That's what was drenching me like you were shaking your sweat all over me. And you'd better understand, that won't do. It won't at all."

"I thought you might understand it, you being . . ."

"Go on. Say it – you being a Jew, Sam! Yes, I'm a Yid and, yes, I put up with the Jew-haters that are everywhere. But I'm not about to start carrying a banner and spend my days angry because of how Jews have been murdered and raped and expelled for what seems forever. I'm functioning well just now, and part of what allows that to happen is the fact that I get on with my life and mind my own business, and keep my nose out of politics, unless," he couldn't suppress a grin, "unless I'm trying to bribe some honest politician who'd sell his wife for a paper bag full of twenty-pound notes."

"You're a better man than me there," Brendan chuckled ruefully. "And I'm not any kind of gobshite! My paddy rears up every so often, that's all. It takes an Englishman and his money to give us a contract in the town where we were both born and reared."

"Arthur was born here, too, and his da and his ma. Maybe even his shaggin' grandfather for all I know. But it's got nothing to do with you and me as businessmen, right here and now."

"You should be in politics yourself," Brendan said lugubriously. "You could talk the hind leg off a chicken!"

"I need you on top-form for this job, Brendan. That means you have to bury all this Irish Republican Brotherhood stuff while you're up here on the job. Money and prestige aside, I owe it to Arthur to ensure that the work is top quality from start to finish." Brendan attempted to interrupt, but Sam stopped him with his hand. "Nobody must ever have the right to point a finger at Arthur over slack or shoddy work by his jew man friend. Do you understand how important, more than money, more than anything, that is to me?"

"You don't think I've any argument with that?"

"No, I don't. But if you let your dreams of Ireland for the Irish get in the way like you did on the drive up here, it could happen. And if it did, you'd have me to deal with, and your political ideals wouldn't come into it. Like, you're the gaffer on this job, you'll pick the foremen and the tradesmen. It'll be your responsibility, so it's going to need your mind right here all the time."

"You'll have that, I promise you, Sam," Brendan extended his hand.

"Sure about that?" Sam asked, looking him directly in the eye. Brendan nodded his head and Sam shook his hand.

"In my heart I'm on your side, Brendan. But being part of a revolutionary movement has no place in my life today. I've got a half-crazy wife, who hates me for not being the Jew she wanted for a husband. The woman I make love to, she has somehow become dependent on me and I can't help her because she is going to drink herself to death. At the same time, I may have taken on more than I can chew in business. Only time will tell. So you might understand there are no more pieces of me to go around right now."

"So what's wrong with me then?" Brendan said quietly.

"How do you mean?" Sam was genuinely taken by the question.

"Well, I want to be just like you!" Brendan laughed, and Sam gave him a punch in the arm. "Now is there any way you'd have time to step over to the hospitality bar, and let me get a pint of stout into me? Arguing with you makes me very thirsty."

"I've got ten minutes before I meet Arthur."

As they left the motorcar, another locomotive passed them, this one hauling half a dozen open-topped trucks. Sam could see that Brendan was interested in what they were carrying.

"Malt," Sam said, "for the brewing bay. They mix it with some roasted stuff to give it colour. After that they grind it, feed it into huge mask bins where it meets the hot water. From there on the stout is really getting under way."

"It's very like the Guinness down at St James's Gate, isn't it?"

"Arthur'll tell you that himself. He borrowed a lot of their good ideas for the stout, turned them this way and that, to improve them to his taste. Same process, slightly different taste, as good as Guinness some say. My mother thinks it's better. There's room for both, right?"

"Guinness really started it all off, I suppose," Brendan stepped on his butt.

"Not really. We've had breweries in Ireland since the fourteenth century. Some Jews as well arrived back then. Even now, there might be as many as a hundred breweries around the country." Sam closed the door of the car. "So, lesson ended. You enjoy your pint. I'll join you when I've done the business with Arthur."

Arthur's secretary, Miss Roche, a very proper middle-aged lady who spoke as though every word was a pearl dropping from her lips, offered Sam tea. "Mister Brewer will surely be with you in a matter of minutes, Mister Sweet."

Sam declined the tea, his conversation with Brendan very much on his mind. He smoked a cigarette, his mood pensive. Of course, he had known what disturbed Brendan as they drove to the brewery. This was not the first time these rumblings had surfaced, though his right-hand man usually succeeded in keeping his anger to himself. Sam knew all too well that Carrots was not alone in the feelings he had expressed in the car, just as he was well aware that the growing discontent wasn't smouldering merely in the hearts of the underprivileged and the dispossessed. There was a rumbling beneath the accepted day-to-day life in the city, the sound drum-beating the fact that a small army of men were no longer prepared to accept the status quo, men who were working actively to produce a blueprint for the new country that Ireland would be when the foreigner, the Brit, had been driven back across St George's Channel.

For his part, Sam tended to take this revolutionary guff with a grain of salt. Not that he scoffed at the intention of the men who carried the dream, which in every previous incarnation had turned into a nightmare for the idealists. Sadly, these good men continued to deny the evidence of logistics, believing that their belief in the right of their intentions would see them through the task of defeating the trained army of England – a country of such military might and expansionist success, that it was said of it that the sun never set on the empire.

Sam tended not to think about anything that didn't involve himself or his family, his business and his friends. He reckoned this gave him all he needed to be going on with, and if the truth be known all he could cope with. In this context, he thought about Brendan, a man he didn't want to lose at any price.

Brendan it was that had found the land at Portobello Harbour. It was entirely due to him that that pearl had landed in his lap, the Dub having taken the trouble to find, and get to know, the man who had the information that was worth gold. Money had changed hands, Brendan keeping Sam out of any face-to-face contact with Harold Cummins, the civil servant in question. He was a married man, with a gambling habit that would ultimately lead to him cutting his throat in the washroom at the government building where he worked. Brendan had searched the man out, having discovered he would do practically anything to pay off some of his gambling debts. Spending his own money to buy drink for Cummins, he had only come to Sam with the proposition when he was sure of his ground.

There was a prime spot of land on the city's fringe – it was up for grabs at a knockdown price. This situation had arisen because one local government department, keen to sell off land that it didn't want or need, had no contact with another department that had unofficially marked this down for housing development within the next ten years. It was the same old story. Neither section of the Civil Service bothered to let the other know where they stood in relation to the forty-acre site. It stretched along the banks of the Grand Canal and north toward the city centre. Sam had bought it for a fraction of its likely value at any time during the next decade.

He had since learned to live with the hue and cry of those who didn't have the information that enabled him to grab the deal from under their noses. Cries of corruption, criminal intent and backhanders could still be heard eighteen months later. Sam, naturally, paid no heed to the growing pains of the opposition. Had he missed out on the deal because someone else had bought inside information, virtually indulging in what was known as daylight robbery, he would probably have moaned about it himself.

He built rudimentary premises at the harbour end of the property, setting up his builders' provider's company in great wooden sheds with galvanised roofing. Close by, he built offices to service this facility, and to handle the paperwork for Sweet Waterway Services, which was responsible for the running and maintenance of his fleet of canal barges, bought at the right price from a Kilkenny businessman addicted to drink.

His barges ferried much-needed coal and oil to the countryside either side of the inland waterway, returning to the city with wheat and corn, oats, hay and straw, with sometimes a crocodile of barges bringing nothing but sugar beet. This Sam sold directly to sugar manufacturers who picked it up from the boats with their own wagons. By ensuring that the holds of the flat vessels were only ever empty while they were being cleaned of coal dust, Sam was developing a very lucrative business, with a very low overhead cost.

On the day following the signing of the contract at Kilmainham, Sam walked the Portobello site with Arthur for company, his great friend intrigued to visit Sam's most recent acquisition and see for himself what developments had taken place since his last visit two months earlier. Now, dressed as usual in a dove-coloured frock-coat over striped black pants and a six-button waistcoat, a plain black bow at the collar of his ruffled white shirt, Arthur enthused over the new wooden buildings built since his last visit.

"Economical, Sam, but will they last?" Arthur was impressed by the extent of the work that had taken place, understanding that all the while a thriving import and export business was happening around the clock.

"This arrangement fulfils my needs for the present, Arthur, until I am sure and certain that the Corporation cannot break the contract of sale on the grounds that I had inside information. I have no wish to invest the money needed to build premises good for a hundred years."

"Is it likely?" Arthur was genuinely surprised that local government might go to such lengths to cover their own ineptitude. "It was their business to know that another department was selling you land that they wished to buy. You were not obliged to warn anyone that you were stepping in to make a deal."

"I'm prepared to fight them in the highest court in the land," Sam said with feeling. "I can't see they have a leg to stand on, I just didn't wish to tie up a lot of money in case I need it for the best legal brains available."

Every time Sam opened a new business, or acquired another property, Arthur would express his delight at his ongoing success. He laughed now when Sam told him why he had a team of carpenters making doors and windows of a certain specification at a time when Sam had not yet entered the house-building industry.

"The Dublin Corporation is going to build flat blocks, two lots that I know of in Rathmines. They're trying to get people out of the slums which are foul, and a major factor of the growth in infant mortality. The work is about to start and the Corpo are going to need doors and windows. I figure they'll have trouble finding the number of carpenters they would need to make them on site, so I intend to rescue the Corporation by selling them ready-made windows and doors."

"Jolly clever." Arthur was tickled by Sam's effrontery. "But suppose that the housing scheme doesn't happen for some reason. You could be out of pocket."

"Of course, it's a gamble," Sam agreed. "But then I might build a scheme myself, here on the site by the canal. Making sure that the doors and windows fit any plans we might draw up," he chuckled. "You know, Arthur, that's not a half bad idea."

Arthur chortled along with him. "You're incorrigible, Sam, incorrigible."

"I've already bought several teams of fresh horses to haul the equipment and the supplies we're going to need for the malt-house," Sam told him. "My own joiners have made the flat four-wheelers, so as from next Monday my workmen will be into action for you."

Viewing the modern stables, built since his last visit, Arthur was most impressed. "We can stable thirty now," Sam explained. "But I have the feeling it won't be that long before we'll have engine-driven wagons."

"I happen to agree, Sam. The world seems to be exploding all around us. What will you do with the horses then?"

"I'll run a fleet of hansom cabs. Dublin is spreading like bindweed, stretching out on three sides. Or I'll sell them to the French. They eat horsemeat as well as snails," he chuckled. "I have to admit I don't have much time for the Frogs."

"Nor I," Arthur laughed, "though I've had some jolly evenings with Vicky in Montmartre, not today or yesterday, of course."

Later, over lunch at the Shelbourne Hotel, the two discussed Deirdre's work in the Dublin slums. She was now a qualified midwife and gave a great deal of her time to helping the poor. Arthur thanked Sam for the many times his people had come to her rescue when poverty's predators had attempted to rob and intimidate her. Several ne'er-do-wells had set out to rob Dee, and one scoundrel who attempted to rape her had been harshly dealt with by Sam's people, as she went about her service to the pregnant women and children whom she attended – all of this provided at her own expense.

Sam had responded to the need for her safe passage on Dee's first day in the slums by the Liffey. He had not bothered her by saying that he expected she would have trouble. He simply sent a couple of Brendan O'Connor's lads to keep an eye on things, while she went about distributing food and bed-linen to the destitute, applying her skill to women in desperate need, her heart to the good and the bad, the dispossessed.

"My wife inspires me," Arthur's tone was self-effacing. "Dee is a continual revelation of goodness and caring. I can never thank you enough for bringing her into the lives of Vicky and myself. The Brewer line needed her blood and her heart, as I needed her love and her friendship, her understanding. Bless you both."

"You deserved the best, Arthur, and so did Dee. She was special from the first day I met her. Four years old she was, and in all my years I have never met anybody I admire more, though you and Vicky run her fairly close."

"I've been meaning to ask you," Arthur said hesitantly, "if Dee or I, have ever done anything to offend Gloria? She seems to make a point of avoiding us socially, and on those occasions when you have brought her to our home she seemed to be suffering in silence. I'm embarrassed by the question, Sam, forgive me, but Dee had such high hopes that our children might grow up together. Bless her heart, she dreams about Eddie marrying your Sarah. It's a measure of the esteem in which we hold you that we would wish to see more of Gloria and your children."

"I suppose we are the product of our early environment, Arthur," Sam sighed in chagrin. "I don't know if I'm right or not, seems to me impossible that anybody could have had what we might call a happy childhood. Not yours and not mine. I've no wish to make excuses for Gloria, but her early life was little short of horrific. Her mother's life even more so, and, of course, the young girl took on her mother's pain as well as her own."

"I wondered was she unhappy at having quit the theatre. She has so much talent, so beautiful, so perfect for life on the stage." Arthur paused to light a cigarette. "I hadn't considered that her early life had left her scarred."

"She claims that all she ever wanted was to be married to a good man, someone who would be a good father to their children. In fairness to her, she thought that I was much more of a Jew than I am." Sam smoked heavily on his cigarette. "I have never said this to

343

anyone, Arthur, but she is anti-Gentile. She blames the world and his wife for their treatment of the Jews throughout history, her own story something she has to stomach on a daily basis since she won't let go of it. Her experiences have corroded her natural charity. She is a loving, caring mother, a queen to my own mother on whom she lavishes love and caring beyond the call of duty. You've seen for yourself what she has done to her appearance. She runs a kosher household, ritual is more important than my wishes, my wants, my desires. She is sincere to the point of martyrdom, and I am sick to my stomach every time I return to my own house. We have two children, we will have no more, since, and I say this with regret, our conjugality has come to an end. She came to find it distasteful, and I have no interest in making love to her since she is as responsive as a piece of cold fish." He drank wine, needing it to help him hold down the anger that had gathered into a lump in his gut. "I have no idea what is going to happen between us, I remain at home for my children, and for the sake of my mother who is old, and I bury myself in my business life." He found himself smiling, despite his sadness. "That may well be the most long-winded answer ever to a question across a lunch table. Forgive me, my friend, but I keep no secrets from you, which I suppose is one of the impositions of real friendship."

Arthur clasped Sam's hand in his own. "I felt that things were not what they might be, but had no idea you were desolate in your marriage."

"It's partly my own fault," Sam said. "I led her on.

Let her think I was keen to be a practising Jew, that I would welcome life in a kosher household, all of that. I was waffling, anything to get her into my bed. I made the gross mistake of thinking that she was creating for me the picture that she imagined I would like. Had I known she was committed to that vision of life, as she wanted to live it, I would have run a mile, knowing I could never be like that. I want to open up, go out to the world. I will not be imprisoned by the past. So you could say that my missus and I have got problems."

"At every hand's turn, there seems to be an abundance of problems," Arthur sighed. "Sometimes I envy the hermit. Yes," he said with force to counteract the look of surprise on Sam's face, "though goodness knows I have all the material gifts any man could ever hope for, yet at times I envy the holy men, the cave dwellers, those who have shunned society and its trappings. Times I wonder what is it all about, this life that we have had thrust upon us for a few hours or years. Honestly, Sam. I find life quite daunting a great deal of the time, to the extent that the idea of dying holds no terror for me."

Sam killed his cigarette and a waiter appeared to whisk away the ashtray, "Believe one thing, Arthur," he said assuredly. "This world, whatever the hell it is, is a better place for your presence. And that's not any kind of waffle. The fact that you were the only one for Dee proves the point. She responded to your goodness, and who knows, in time she may even manage to help you get rid of your guilt for being born with the silver spoon in your mouth."

"I'd be most grateful if that were to happen. You've been most tolerant, listening to me in my cups, whimpering about the guilt I feel that my forebears had been given land belonging to a man who was given the choice, 'Leave this place or die where you stand'."

Arthur quaffed three-quarters of a glass of wine, like someone trying to wash away a picture that tortured his mind. "That poor man left his home and his land, and the Brewer fortune took its first breath, the gift of a robber baron."

"Yes, all right," Sam said, "But you ought to feel good when you consider the work you create for people. Your shares scheme for your workers is a model of egalitarianism. I don't see that you can do any more, Arthur, and I think you ought to acknowledge the good you are doing. And now with Dee actively working in the slums, it seems to me that the Brewer family is balancing things up, more than a bit."

Sam was remembering his chats with Brendan O'Connor about the haves and the have-nots, the whys and the wherefores as to why sharing was so unequal. He would probably laugh at the idea that Arthur could feel bad about the way in which his family's fortune had found its feet.

"Shag him," Brendan would say in his own inimitable way. "If his wealth and his power and his prestige are such a Jesus imposition, let him wash his hands of it all, give it all to charity and let it be handed out to the needy."

Returning home that same evening, Sam found his

mother sitting by the fire in the front sitting-room, a glass of Brewer's by her hand. As he entered the room, Esther appeared to be taking one of several books from the occasional table where she stacked whatever she was presently reading. In fact, his mother was attempting to hide a book from him, having heard him slam the front door as he came into the house.

He smiled, distracted by the small box of stout under his mother's chair. It was sent each week by Arthur to Esther for medicinal purposes, his mother being devoted to her daily intake of the bitter-sweet stout which, she claimed, was "very good for what ails you". At the same time, Sam wondered did he see one of Gloria's journals in the stack. Of course not, he chided himself, listening to his mother's account of the day turning into the evening of its life.

"Nothing strange or startling," was how Esther put it, telling him that Gloria was upstairs with the children.

He cast another glance at the small stack of books. 'Don't be daft', he told himself. 'Gloria's so addicted to secrecy she'd never leave a journal out of her sight. They're under lock and key in her strong box in what was our bedroom, before I emigrated to the one next door.'

As Sam left the room, Esther gave a sigh of relief, for much as she admired the cut of him, his style and the easy manner he wore like a new shirt, she didn't want him to know she was reading one of Gloria's journals. She was very grateful for the way he had turned out overall, even if he was hardly a Jew any more. He was a good man, a great provider for his wife and family, but with things as they were between him and her, she didn't want Sam to know that she and Gloria had their secrets from him. She would never reveal a word, any more than she would tell Gloria of his womanising. They were poles apart when it came to the things that mattered in a Jewish home, but there were children to be considered, and she wanted the family to stay together.

Esther knew about Victoria Brewer, his shirts in the laundry basket usually carrying the scent of her perfume. She also knew that while Vicky had been in France, the fragrances about his clothes had varied, causing her to accept that 'he's still sowing wild oats at his age. Wouldn't you think he'd have more sense?' Esther knew all this because she made certain to get to the laundry basket before Biddy. The servant was delighted Esther laundered her son's shirts – it meant less work for her. Esther did what she did because Biddy talked a lot. In Esther's opinion, Biddy had a mouth on her like a torn pocket. 'She can keep nothing in it.'

Swigging Brewer's stout, Esther opened the journal again. As she continued reading, her sympathy and respect became mingled with anger as she read on about the efforts Rebecca had made to find the only sister of her late husband, Peter.

Helena Stein had left St Petersburg with an archaeological expedition two years before her brother Peter fled his home city to find death waiting for him in a slum street in London's East End. Esther was soon reading avidly, captured once more by Gloria's words.

20

Gloria's journal, Dublin

July 1911

It occurs to me that I continue believing in some kind of God despite the great cruelties he has poured into my life. I contend that by chastising God, by cursing him at times through the pain-induced dementia, I was not blaspheming. In the attacks I screamed at many an Irish night, I was actually acknowledging his presence. Perhaps I have developed a sense of irony, without which the mind might well shatter entirely under the sense of life's ongoing injustice.

I believe too, that there is a twist in the tail of this tale that I call my life. I read and re-read that God is love. If so, God could not have put my mother and me here simply to go through an endurance course of pain, to no purpose. Someday, he will, I believe, show me why it was necessary that we suffer so much. For Mama and me, life seemed to be practising the art of cruelty and as I turned seventeen in 1905 it seemed to me that we had been chosen to establish how far a human person could be pushed and beaten and battered, without actually going insane. Every time there appeared to be a warm sun rising in the east of our hopes, there was a thunderclap so loud and so brutal that a day could seem like a year before the west opened its arms to the eye of light and gave it sanctuary for the night.

How often Mama and I stood shattered, roped together at the waist in a doorway or under a bridge, old newspapers stuffed under our clothing to combat the vicious cold of another winter. All through the endless months and years of sleeping rough, the coins we earned singing in the streets often torn from us by soulless men, our determination not to be raped and murdered fired by the steel in Mama's spine, until her blood turned to water in the embrace of Jem Riley.

It took Mama two years to find my father's only sister, Helena. I had always known that I had an aunt, if she was still alive, but life was so haphazard for us on the London streets that I seem to have shut out much of those cruel and demanding times.

At times I get glimpses of what I might have been, unsure whether these very images include me, since I might well be inventing a character based on some of the things Mama told me down the years of my persistent questioning.

My father had told Mama that his sister Helena had joined an expedition to Egypt, he never hearing from her again. Mama had hoped to find her, to meet someone who had known Peter, my father, for longer than she had. And then she came to feel that she had to find Helena that she might tell the woman what had happened to her family.

As God allowed us find Aunt Helena, Mama and I were living in a rented room off the Edgeware Road not far from Marble Arch. The letter came from the Anglo-American charity agency in St Petersburg, where volunteers helped loved ones trace each other, taking twelve months to travel from Russia to London.

Imagine our surprise when we found that Helena Stein's last known address was at Gray's Inn Road, which was perhaps two miles from where we were lodging. Once we had an address, Mama and I set about scouring the local markets. Using the pennies we had saved through the spring months, we found inexpensive second-hand clothing that we could alter and improve, my mother having taught me from her own natural skill with needle and thread.

We had been off the streets for a month, sleeping between clean sheets. We were tasting gratitude for the feel of the cotton against our skin, the wealth of a feather pillow under our head. To go to sleep after a good wash, the water heated on the grate in our room being sparse but enough to feel our own cleanliness and laugh aloud as the freedom from our own smells became the norm. I can still feel the sensation of running a comb through my hair again and again just to feel the teeth slide through the tresses without meeting clogged up dirt and lice. It was like being born again, into a world in which only good and beautiful things could happen to a person.

Helena Stein welcomed us into her home, a handsome woman of middle age with the nervous smile of someone expecting things to turn out for the worst. In those early moments, I formed the impression she was a genuine person for whom some terrible hurt lurked behind her brow, distorting her light-brown eyes as she put her head out to look up and down the street, before closing the door behind us.

As we sat down to our first meal in that house on Gray's Inn Road, I said a quiet thanks to God for what was there on the table before us. And though I was surprised that Aunt Helena asked us to join her in saying grace that turned out to be a Christian version, I happily intoned the words behind her lead, as did Mama.

She had prepared a wonderful English dinner of roast beef and Yorkshire pudding, potatoes roasted in the great dish with the meat, the flavour of the juices soaked into them underneath, while the skin on top was simply delicious. There was precious little conversation in those first few minutes and I had to remind myself of the manners Mama had taught me before our lives slipped downhill. At the same time, we had learned over the years on the streets that you must eat when you get the chance, since there was no guarantee of another meal in this lifetime. So I pressed on, eating like the proverbial horse, all too aware that hunger is a great sauce. It is also a barrier to the nagging guilt that you are breaking the laws of grace and etiquette by stuffing the food in without paying it the proper respect.

Aunt Helena owned two houses that had been converted into one great pension for professional gentlemen, and she left us by the fire in her private sitting-room while she checked in an expected late arrival. When she returned she provided us with a drink of cocoa and toasted home-made soda bread with raisins in it, and I stuffed myself again, honestly thinking that I would happily expire on the spot. Then she told us her story.

She confirmed Papa's story that she had joined an archaeological dig to Egypt. What my father didn't know was that she had left home so that she could be with the man with whom she had fallen in love. Joint leader of the expedition, he had fascinated her, stating the passionate nature of his desire for her with such intensity that he swept her off her feet. She had abandoned everything to be with her lover and she was blissfully happy scraping sand from stones buried for thousands of years, until her lover's wife turned up to call her a whore and a home-wrecker. Aunt Helena didn't even protest that her lover had sworn he was a widower, being too shattered to do anything but leave right away. Arriving in England she had worked as a nurse until she married her husband, Mendel Cohen, some fifteen years before we met her. I found myself breathless when I realised that Helena had been in London while my mother conceived me, had been living just miles away, as my father was being brutally murdered. Again it seemed to me that fate had dealt us a very severe hand. It was pointless of me to consider how different things might have been had Helena been available to Mama and me, but I did slip into wondering how much better life might have been for all three of us had we known each other from the time she reached London. I listened over dinner as she spoke of Mendel Cohen with quiet affection, thought of him as a decent and loving man, a solicitor with a busy criminal practice.

He was a man, she said, with some pride who would do anything, including sail close to the wind – without actually breaking the law – to help his criminal fraternity clients to stay out of prison, provided he had been paid in advance. On his death seven years after they married, she discovered that he had left her a considerable amount of money and the ownership of the two houses we were visiting within spitting distance of the heart of the British legal system, known worldwide as Gray's Inn.

She housed and catered to the needs of gentlemen lawyers who weren't rich, providing them with bed and board at competitive prices, her own apartments being sacrosanct. She spoke of the service she provided with little enthusiasm, but you sensed she was proud to be earning a living. Certainly, she was not the kind of person to sit back and spend her fortune while she was fit enough to work.

Aunt Helena spoke of her late husband without sadness, as though she had a facility to take his death in, acknowledge it, and somehow let it go without any need to be seen to grieve openly. I had noticed this earlier when Mama told her of her parents' demise, and the tragic death of my father right there in London, just a short distance east of where we were having a late-night supper.

Although I was tired, I found myself fascinated by this kind, reasonable woman, who seemed to me to be forty-five years old, or thereabouts. But even had my eyes been lead-laden and drooping, they would have popped open instantly when Aunt Helena said, "I want to tell you about changing my identity, so that I can help you both with my conscience clear, for having allowed you the choice . . . well, you'll understand when I tell you what I mean.

"Shortly after Mendel passed on, I changed my name by deed poll," she said in a calm voice, as though playing it down. "Since then I have been known as Anna Coates. When I changed my name, I severed all connections with Jewry. I became a convert of the Church of England, and can admit to being a committed Christian."

It was on the tip of my tongue to ask why she had done such a thing, but Aunt Helena came to my rescue by carrying on with her story.

"I converted because I had endured enough persecution. I will spare you the details, having no doubt that you have your own stories in this respect. No matter what country I have lived in, even while simply passing through, no day passed that I didn't experience some slight, some further example of the hatred of Jews that seems to be rampant worldwide. Direct abuse, brutality and violence have been directed at me almost daily for as long as I can remember, and I had simply had enough of it.

"I make no apology, but I feel it's only just to tell you since you may decide you don't want to work for someone who has turned their back on the Jewish way of life."

"Anna, we have no wish to judge any person," Mama said. "This is your own business and we respect that. And, of course, you may be assured we will not be discussing your business with anybody."

"I'm pleased to hear you say that. I feel warmth for my brother's wife and daughter. I welcome you, and I can provide work and a home. I will give you fair pay, but you must do things my way, and above all, you must respect my wish to live and be known as Anna Coates. The price you pay is that you carry the burden of my secret. When I came here nobody knew me, and today, those who think they do know me only as Anna Coates. What I am leading up to is, perhaps, too big a hurdle for you both. I have to ask you to put your own identities as Jews on a shelf in your mind, in your heart, for as long as you wish to be here with me. If this seems too high a price, believe me, I understand. In that event and I will help you on your way, with clothing and whatever money you need. I have to ask this of you because it's imperative to me that I preserve my new identity."

Mama and I sat like people who had been stuck to their chairs as this brave and resourceful woman acknowledged the dilemma she had placed before us both.

"Perhaps a good night's sleep will make it easier for you to decide if you can fulfill this condition," she suggested.

To sleep in a warm, luxuriously comfortable bed, after a steaming hot bath laced with sweet-smelling salts, is something one can take for granted within a very short time. To taste this luxury, as Mama and I did together, in the bathroom across the hall from our room at Aunt Helena's house, was an experience that I can only describe as sybaritic. Our extreme appreciation was no doubt born of the realisation of just how long it had been since either of us had felt blessed by something so ordinary.

While we had managed to keep a roof over our heads in recent times, anything above what I had christened 'subsistence existence' was out of reach. Work was rarely available, and busking was both demanding and dangerous. The streets were alive with vagabonds of every description, and landlords could charge you what they liked for rooms that were often not fit to lie down in.

That first night at the house on Gray's Inn Road, Mama and I went to sleep with our arms about each other, wearing clean cotton nightdresses that my father's sister provided from her own chest of drawers.

"We don't have to make any decision," Mama said assuredly. "When we wake up in the morning, we will surely know what to do for the best."

Before Aunt Helena called us to breakfast, Mama and I had agreed that we were both weary of the hand-to-mouth existence of the past two years. It was also true that we had never been to *shule* since life turned us downtrodden and unkempt. Sometimes when things had improved for a little while, so that we had been able to buy something half-decent to wear, we might have gone to synagogue. The fact is that we had not. When we were busking we gave the public great value for the coppers that came our way, but how often had I noticed that people I would have identified as Jews rarely threw a coin into the cap before our feet on the pavement. I have to admit that I resented these people, actually thinking of them as tight-fisted yids. So, how Jewish did I feel in those times? How devoted was I to the tradition and the religion that my parents had practised? I told Mama how I felt, and she admitted that deep down she had her own difficulties with her God.

As we sat down to breakfast, I reminded myself we were eating with Aunt Anna and not Aunt Helena, bowing my head in silence while she intoned grace in a rather automatic fashion. In the quiet of my mind I found myself posing the same one-word question to an invisible presence called God. Why? Why this latest hurdle? Are we so bad we need a fence to jump every week of the year?

Aunt Anna seemed relieved when Mama told her that we would like to stay and work for her, and that we would honour her wish. She took both our hands for a moment, before pouring more tea for us both, and urging me to eat up my toast before it got cold. As we finished eating, Aunt Anna – as I was now calling her – warned us of a cult that had grown out of the slums of the East End, which lay on the other side of St Paul's cathedral, and the city, a distance of less than two miles from her house.

"These people say they are striking back at Jews who have converted. They call us renegades and betrayers of our forefathers, and much more of the same colourful rhetoric. They are dangerous. Led by a Jew from Athens, Onassis by name, they have even had running battles with the police. When they target the home of a convert, they intend to drive them from the district. They want to do to the converts what the world has been doing to the Jews since time immemorial. So I warn you to be careful. Beware of Greek Jews bearing gifts!"

Mama and I did wonder was Aunt Anna being paranoid, but she never mentioned it again during the three months we lived and worked together. We forgot her warning, but not her instruction to follow her orders to the letter. We prepared food, Mama cooking while I was making beds, emptying chamber-pots and generally providing comfort for established barristers and indeed, their juniors. Most of the men drank heavily – some of them seemed to take themselves very seriously. The younger ones enjoyed their wine during dinner, and sank their share of port after, often going to bed on legs one wouldn't trust to travel very far.

Mama and I got plenty of time off while we worked for Aunt Anna, and since she had given us clothes she would never wear again, we began to appear on the streets as well-dressed lower-middle class ladies of moderate income. Mama paid for the dresses and blouses by altering garments Anna still cared for, and by making a couple of dresses and a bonnet, that had my aunt chortling with delight.

The British Museum was just a short walk from Aunt Anna's house and Mama and I loved going there. Having my mother as my guide, I was an avid student, as she shared her knowledge of art with me. In the evenings we read to each other, admiring the truth of the street life in the stories of Charles Dickens – the begging and robbing and busking, the confidence tricksters, the street traders and the other hard workers who earned their crust off the highways and byways of London.

Aunt Anna had *The Times* delivered every morning, and she liked me to iron it for her. I thought this a bit pretentious, until I learned that this was done to dry the printer's ink, so that busy people wouldn't need to wash their hands each time they picked up the morning paper. It was on an inside page of that august publication that my eye was captured by a short item describing a break-in at the government office of births and marriages and deaths. According to the short report, some documents had been stolen in a rather mysterious break-in, but as yet no details were available. I thought no more about the story until about a week later when I was returning from the grocery shop where Aunt Anna held her account. Putting it simply, a rather sinister thing occurred, leaving me quite shaken as I continued on my way back to the house.

In the house at Rathmines on the southside of Dublin city, Esther was suddenly irritated by her need to pass water, being very reluctant to leave down the journal at such a crucial moment. She knew she must answer the call urgently. Despite Sam having Dr Berber examine her and give her medicine, her kidneys were not as reliable as they once were. Thinking of Sam for an instant, she considered herself fortunate to have a son whose decency toward her had been constant down the years. Yet she sighed regretfully – these days he always seemed to be under one business pressure after another. Still, they talked most days – more than she could say for him and Gloria a lot of the time. She wondered whether it was their endless discussions of the books they shared down his handcart years that held them close even now. Or was it all because of the dinners she produced for him every evening of his young life? She smiled at the memory of the times he had asked to hear her story. Goodness, how often she had repeated the tale of how she walked her own walk from Zielona, east of Hamburg, to Amsterdam and a boat journey, organised by World Jewry to Ireland.

As she climbed the stairs to the toilet, Esther pondered as to why Sam had kept her close when many sons might have put her in a private residence for the aged. Of course, she had fed him well at the table and in the learning department, never too busy to answer a question or discuss a book, and, of course, she had taught him the German language alongside English, and, of course, Yiddish, passed on to her by her Russian mother.

On the landing she heard Sam and Gloria exchanging angry words in her room. Sam was not speaking German or Yiddish now, but his own brand of English, the grammar perfect when he was not indulging his penchant to the vernacular; the indigenous sound of the streets stitched into his formal vocabulary which he loved for the music in the speech of city people, those he called denizens of the town.

As Esther stepped into the water closet, she suffered a sharp pain in her chest. The attack was enough to send her falling against the wall, causing her to knock a couple of framed street etchings that Sam had hung there onto the floor.

The sound brought Sam and Gloria downstairs in a hurry, her son reaching Esther first. He lifted her up from where she leaned, semi-conscious against the toilet wall.

Gloria hurried upstairs ahead of him. "Put her in my bed, Samuel," she flung the door open, hurried to pull back the covers and stood there, her face drawn, as Sam put Esther down as gently as he could.

"Do what you can," Sam said. "I'm going to telephone Paddy Lote."

"He's an old man," Gloria's protest was muted for the sake of Esther.

"Dr Berber's away and Paddy's one of the best," Sam said, hurrying down the stairs to the hall.

Esther had suffered a heart attack and would have to be confined to bed until her blood pressure was brought down. This was the doctor's view after he had made a thorough examination of Sam's mother.

"Is she going to die on us?" Sam asked flatly. He saw Gloria blanch at the question.

"Your mother could live for years, but like any one of us, she could die at any moment. After half a lifetime spent in the medical profession, I've finally come to believe that we will pass on when God gives us the nod, and not before."

"If you'll tell me how to best care for her, doctor, I will see to it that Missus Green is looked after in the best possible way," Gloria said with sincerity, zealously ignoring Esther's wish to be known as Mrs Levy, since she had reverted to her own name on the death of her husband. Sam noted this but let it go. This was no time for squabbling about something that didn't matter a damn.

The ageing doctor looked from Gloria to Sam. "Your mother-in-law is going to need a fair deal of attention and care, Mrs Sweet. I would recommend a month or two in a nursing home – there is one in particular where the care has been of immense benefit to a couple of my patients, and I'd be happy to . . ."

"That won't be necessary, though I thank you for your consideration. I will look after Mrs Green myself." Gloria spoke softly, but the doctor was left in no doubt that Esther would be in good hands.

He picked up his bag and hat and looked at Sam. "I'll come and see your mother tomorrow, Sam. If you need me meantime, call me on the telephone and I'll come right away. Good evening to you both."

The moment he left, Gloria hurried back upstairs to Esther, who began apologising for being such a nuisance.

"Stop it, Nana," Gloria said softly, a smile on her mouth. "I promise you there will never be a day on which you will be a nuisance to me. In fairness, I believe I can say the same thing for Samuel. So, stop with the sorry, Esther!" she spoke in a conciliatory fashion, her eyes relaxed as she tidied the bed. "You have earned the right to be well looked after, and that is what is going to happen."

"I heard him say about the nursing home," Esther confessed with a sheepish expression.

"How on earth could you have heard that?" Gloria was genuinely puzzled.

"I crept down the stairs," Esther said, somewhat shamefaced now as she witnessed the look of alarm on Gloria's face.

"Nana," Gloria was genuinely horrified, "you might have died on me." She stopped, biting down on her anger, taking a deep breath, waiting until her reaction subsided. She found a wan smile for the old woman who looked worried. "Who am I to tell you what to do? A woman who walked, oh my God, you like Mama, you women! If I were God I would take you early, want you by my side." She came to Esther and embraced her.

"The same stuff that got you through that living nightmare brought you down the stairs and back up again. But listen to me, you wicked woman," she pulled back and gave a short laugh, "there will be no nursing home for our Nana. And she, now that she has proved she is made of cast iron, she will obey the rules that the doctor lays down. Because, and hear me well, Nana, because the children and I, we need you for all the years of our lives. So you must live for hundreds of years, and between us we will find a way to make that possible." The two women fell into another hug, free enough with each other to release their waiting tears.

When Gloria came down to the kitchen, Sam was making a pot of coffee.

"Nana can't have coffee for the moment," she said. "Will you pour a cup for me, while I find my herb book?"

"That was good, what you said to Paddy Lote. I appreciate you being willing to look after Esther." Sam poured the coffee, knowing that he was trying to mend a fence that had been damaged in the row earlier.

"There is no need to thank me, Samuel. Nana is very dear to me. Sarah and Samuel adore her and she has earned her place and deserves all that can be done for her by her family, of which I am privileged to be a member." She took a sip of the coffee and put the cup down. "Now, where did I leave my herb book?"

Left alone, Sam shook his head, a wry smile on his mouth and chagrin riding his mind. To be talked to so politely, so formally, by the woman he had lusted after for months was something he could not have envisioned happening. By the time they had gone to their marriage bed, he felt she was as keen on him as he was about her. What had happened? What had gone wrong on their wedding night? He had no idea. But, two children later, they were like strangers being compatible for the sake of family and tradition. This unspoken arrangement affected the taste of the coffee in his mouth. All had been peace and light just a while before – he had been encouraging his one-year-old son to let go of the day and surrender to the sleep he so badly needed. Sam was singing to the boy, a song he had first heard Gloria perform on the night of that astonishing party at Dunbla House. He remembered how staggeringly beautiful his wife was that night, asking himself yet again if things might have worked out differently had he stayed at the party and made love to her in her tipsy condition, instead of heading off to talk business in the early hours with a bent local government official.

The song was one Gloria had written. He thought it beautiful, the words sticking in his mind though he had heard her sing it just that one time at the party. His son was listening sleepily to his father's low-key singing, Sam unaware that Gloria was fuming in the doorway.

As Sam sang the words

"Joy has been evicted from this heart,
Laughter's gone and pain has moved right in,
Winter's early coming has shut out heaven's light,
Was our passion such a dreadful sin?"

Gloria strode across to where he sat by the bed, hissing down at him, "I told you I never wanted to hear that song again. And how could you possibly think it suitable to sing to our son? Have you lost your reason?"

He managed to hold his temper, waiting until Sam released his first tiny snore before he kissed the rounded forehead, and left the room, Gloria at his heels.

"I'm sorry. I forgot," he began to speak, wanting to hold onto the mood his son's trust had engendered within him. But the lie stuck in his gullet. "No, that's not true. I didn't forget. I like the words of that song. The first and only time I heard you sing it I felt you had written it from the heart." In a moment the night of the great Dunbla party was right there in his mind again. "Although it's couched as a romantic ballad, I thought it referred to your mother's death, she being taken from you. I won't sing it again."

Gloria wasn't able to let go of her anger. "It's just typical of how you are. So busy with your business world and your highly-born friends, your family forgotten, just as you forgot – or didn't care enough about what I asked of you – that you sang a song I hate, to our son."

"Shut up, Gloria!"

Her head was jolted back by the force of his command. She stood speechless as he continued, "You are talking rubbish and I won't stand here and listen to it. I don't know what happened to you at that party. I remember that you sang the song so beautifully, that it helped me propose to you before I left for Dublin." He stopped for a moment before he said, "Perhaps that's it. I proposed to you. And though you played the game, hesitated, asked for a little time, you accepted me as your husband to be." He saw a change take place in her eyes and he felt he knew what had happened to her. "Is it that you didn't really want to marry me? Do you somehow hate yourself for accepting me?" He didn't want to believe this, but he pressed on because he knew there was no love in her for him this night, even though they were close in their caring for Esther. "Is that it? Is that what you threw up between us like a wall of disdain? You seemed to be placating me almost, as I came to your arms in our wedding bed. Stupid Sam Sweet, expecting to die from the sheer excitement of making love to you. What a gobshite!"

Gloria stood there stuck to the floor of the landing, her mouth slack in shock, her eyes wide open despite the terror that he would read her mind, see into her heart. He lit a cigarette and inhaled deeply. She remained silent though he took his time before he said, "If that's it, you never loved me. If that's what caused you to turn from me, turning you into this half-crazy Jewess, cutting off your beautiful hair and strapping down your wonderful breasts. If I'm right, tell me, tell me, and I will do something about it. If your discomfort and pain is caused by some branch of self-hatred because you accepted my marriage proposal, tell me, tell me now, and I will do everything in my power to grant you the quietest divorce in history."

With that he left her standing on the landing, leaving

behind him the last remnants of any hope he'd nourished that his marriage might survive. Though he went softly in his mind, the harsh reality was that the relationship had been a mirage. He had opted to believe in the illusion because she was stunningly beautiful and, so he thought, likely to be grateful for a husband who was wealthy, a man holding a position in the general community that many Jews were not allowed to occupy. What he now thought of as her *kosher* talk, the way she banged on about being Jewish, about how being a good Jew was the beginning, the middle, and the end – he had taken that with a grain of salt, assuming she was playing that role to an audience of one, him. Of course, he knew now, knew bloody well he had made a major mistake since she had meant every word – the evidence was there to see in the manner of her day-to-day living. He couldn't deny that, nor did he wish to. All he wanted now was to find a way in which they could find a level of compatibility that made living under the same roof possible. He was willing to live in a friendly way for the sake of his children and their future, and so that his mother might not suffer any further distress through being exposed to their residual pain.

21

Dublin

July 1911

Sam came downstairs thinking that a couple of glasses of brandy might help him let go some of the angst that was wrapped around his heart and currently kicking his sense of humour into touch. The very idea that he was thinking of going to a public house to buy drink stopped him halfway to the front door. My God, he thought, how close the madness is in whatever goes on between a man and a woman. Something prodded him to quietly turn the handle of the sitting-room door. He went inside. The journal that Esther had been reading was on the floor by the chair she had been sitting in. The pages were open as though she had dropped the book – it lay on the Egyptian carpet he had bought when they had decorated the house for his wedding.

He threw some turf on the smouldering embers and feeling self-righteous enough to be guilt-free he picked up the journal and sat down in his mother's chair. He decided to read from the pages open to him, see if he could follow what Gloria had written without having to go back to the beginning. At first he felt lost – she did like to waffle – but by riffling back through a few pages dated 1901 he came to understand that she and her mother had found a sister of Peter, Rebecca's husband and father to Gloria. She had told the page that her thoughts and her memories were still confused, still bruised from the death of her mother within sight of Ireland, she called it 'our own promised land', but that she had to write about the dreadful tragedy 'that befell Aunt Helena who was so decent, so fair and kind to Mama and me'.

This was Sam's introduction to Gloria's journal. Almost immediately, there arose the nagging thought that he shouldn't be reading his wife's private memoirs. He threw it out with ease, telling himself that even his wife's thoughts were his property, since he was her husband and she was subject, even in law, to his will. He didn't dwell on this long enough to know whether he believed it or not. He began to read.

As this was just a week before Christmas, the shops and bazaars along Clerkenwell Road displayed decorated trees small enough to fit into a living-room. There were great arrays of multi-coloured paper chains, bright, shiny balls with hooks to hang them by, and all kinds of choices for people who liked to dress up their homes for the holiday, ostensibly the birthday of Jesus of Nazareth, upon whose life and word the Christian ethic had been built, with people worldwide believing that this simple fisherman was in fact the son of God.

My mind had been taken by all that was there in the shop windows for the eye to fawn over, so that I was quite shocked when this man with a gruff voice said in what I deemed to be an Italian or Greek accent, "It's a bad thing to work for the convert. You get out from her house before we burn you alive."

The truth is that I almost dropped the basket of shopping, but I turned to face the wretch, almost reeling backwards from the stench of garlic and stale wine emanating from behind his heavy black moustache. He was somewhat taller than I, slight of build, with eyes like black olives, shining with a light that suggested either intoxication or imbalance. He grabbed my upper arm to make sure I understood what he was saying, "Hear me, young woman. You don't work for the convert if you wish to stay alive."

"How dare you!!" I yelled at him, deliberately, hoping to attract help from a passer-by, or at the very least to frighten this horrible person away from me at once. He was not disturbed or in any way frightened. I raised my voice, "How dare you talk to me in that way? I have no idea what you are talking about. Now go away before I have you arrested."

He shook me fiercely by my upper arm, so that some tomatoes fell from the basket. He bent quickly, picking them up with a large hand. He thrust a tomato into his mouth, giving me my final warning as he chewed, his teeth the colour of tobacco.

"You don't get any more warning, miss. Stop now the work for the convert, or go up in the smoke with her."

"You're making a mistake. I work for Miss Anna Coates, an English lady who is a member of the Church of England."

"She is a Jew that converted, you foolish woman. She made the convert and she pay for that. You need not pay. But you stay there working with her, you pay with your life."

He turned then and walked away from me, nothing in his demeanour to suggest that he was doing anything other than having a late afternoon stroll up Rosebury Avenue.

Mama positively blanched as I related the story. Poor Aunt Anna, she almost passed out on her chair. We gave her tea, and Mama fetched a tincture of brandy from her drinks press. The spirit seemed to help her recover somewhat, then as she sipped tea, I realised it was only with great effort that she could hold the cup and saucer. I took them from her and put them on the table.

"Do you think we should call the police, Aunt Anna?"

She shook her head vehemently, "My goodness no, child. That would be a tacit admission that this horrible creature is right about me."

I looked to Mama for guidance. She didn't look in any way inspired. "He may be just a fool or a madman," she offered in a lame way.

"How could he possibly know that I converted? That is private government information, or so I was led to believe." Aunt Anna was like a woman trying to shake off a nightmare, unsure of whether she was in the past or the present.

"I don't know about such things," Mama said. "I was of the impression one could find out such things at the common Records Office. People who wish to investigate their family tree, for instance. I believe you can purchase birth certificates.

"My feeling is that you should go to the police, Aunt Anna," I said. "This man was adamant, warning me to get out or be burned out. He was a dangerous type, not bothered in the least when I yelled at him, not frightened that I might attract attention. Very confident in his ability to deal with whatever happened. To be taken seriously, I would say."

"Please understand, Gloria. I have no wish to have my home and my business burned down around me. But I would sooner die than go back to being a Jew in this country, or any country I have been to."

"We are going to Ireland, one day," Mama interjected. "You could come there with us."

"Ireland?" Aunt Anna's reaction suggested she thought Mama quite mad. "Haven't you read about Turlough O'Connor? He was the high king that set Jews adrift in a small boat off the Irish coast. Cromwell was another hater of the Jews. He wanted to murder the Irish peasants because he deemed them lazy and stupid. Bring in Jews, he said. They had been such

374

wonderful farmers at the time of Canaan. Later, after they had turned the country into an agrarian paradise, butcher the Jews, was his decision. He would then bring his own people in to farm and maintain the thriving industry the Jews had created. What on earth made you think Ireland would be any different to the rest of the world?"

"Peter," Mama said. "Peter believed we could live there without being persecuted for being Jews. I believe that. Peter knew what he was saying and we are going there, no matter how we do it."

Aunt Anna rose from her chair. "I need to go and ask God to help me deal with this awful threat. Please excuse me."

Whoever carried out the fire-bombing of Aunt Anna's premises on Gray's Inn Road had a sense of irony, the first explosion happening as Bow Bells rang out the old year 1901. The second explosion came a breath later as 1902 became the present – my fourteenth year if I live through the madness going on around me – as the world and his wife were celebrating another new beginning. London was rocking with the sound of fireworks. Obviously the fire service would be much in demand so that, even if people had been aware that the twin houses were in flames, little or nothing could have been done.

Mama and I scampered to our room to gather what clothes we could take with us and thankfully I remembered the few pounds we had saved during the past couple of months. As we hurried down the stairs, the top floor of the house had become an inferno. The falling timbers were turning the landing we had just left into something similar. Fortunately, there were no clients staying overnight – New Year's Eve, like Christmas, was a time in the year when both houses were empty of lodgers. When we reached the street we expected to find Aunt Anna waiting for us, but she wasn't to be seen.

Mama and I looked at each other in alarm. Then, as we were about to voice our fear that she was still inside one of the houses, we heard a scream to put fear into a stone. Looking up, I saw Aunt Anna standing in an upper floor window. Her clothes were like a cloak of flames that she had wrapped about herself and in seconds, as she screamed through the final moments of her life, she was consumed, appearing to melt away before my eyes. I turned to Mama and we fell into each other's arms choking on smoke and the grief that the helpless taste all too often in this life.

Because we knew that the fire had been started by a group of people determined to deter Jews from converting, we knew we could not risk being seen as any kind of threat to them. There was nothing we could do for my aunt and so we simply walked away into the night, unnoticed by some drunken onlookers who had staggered along in search of excitement. As we left, I remembered Aunt Anna saying that she would sooner die than try to endure life as a Jew, but the comfort I drew from knowing that her wish had been granted lay cold on my heart.

In our own way, we mourned my Aunt Anna as a member of the Church of England. We knelt in the church she had frequented and we wished her safe journey to a better place, where race or religion was unlikely to be the cause of any further discomfort, anger or death. We wished her to rest in peace, thankful for all she had done to help us when friends were scarce, and charity even harder to find.

We could not get work for most of the sad year that had claimed the life of my aunt, so Mama and I were back singing on the streets, earning enough to pay the rent and buy some second-foot shoes, and then we were struggling to buy food during the endless fierce wintry days of 1902.

We were still dreaming of Ireland, undeterred by the reservations my father's sister had expressed. Our life had once again become hard enough to make the saving of our fares a drawn-out business. We pressed on, singing our best songs, grateful for the ability to earn some money each day. Without the gift of the music, nobody knows what might have happened to us.

Then one night as we walked home with our instruments in our hands and our hard-earned coppers in Mama's purse, both of us ready for sleep, we encountered two men. From which moment, our lives took a sideways turning that went all the way downhill.

I could say more, dwell on how one copes when one is living on the streets, public conveniences being the one place where you can take a bird bath, provided the attendant is in good form, and isn't chasing you out because you won't allow him to chase you into a cubicle as payment for the facility. I could write pages about the dreams I had of Aunt Anna's house with a lovely, clean bathroom across the hall from our room. To what purpose! For all our efforts to remain safe on the streets, one night on our way back to a room in a very run-down house in Camden Town we were accosted fiercely by a wild-looking man. He snatched at the hessian bag I used for carrying whatever food we had bought for our evening meal. I held on as he demanded money, though he was a man who might easily have terrified any woman.

I punched at his face yelling at him, "Get away from us, you hound! How dare you!" Mama was yelling at him too, threatening him with the police. I tried to shove him backwards, make him fall over, but he pulled a knife from his belt and in a moment he was holding it to my throat. "Give me your money, missus," he yelled at my mother, "or by God, I'll slit the girl's throat."

Another man, whose name would turn out to be Jem Riley, arrived from nowhere and punched the thief very hard to the head. The knife dropped to his knees and Jem now kicked the man hard in the stomach. In a moment he lay unconscious into the London gutter.

"Have you far to go, ladies?" Jem was roughly dressed, but there seemed to be a deal of caring in his voice. After the confrontation we had just survived due to his intervention, he seemed to Mama and me, as some kind of angel.

"Not far, thank you, sir," Mama said, her voice throaty, whether from shock or gratitude, I couldn't tell.

"I'll see you home, ladies, make sure you are safe. The streets tonight seem to be alive with all kinds of vagabonds." His accent suggested he was from Liverpool. The swagger in the way he presented himself gave a hint to his Irish heritage. And though the gift of prescience was perhaps the last attribute I would have ascribed to myself, I was uneasy at the ease with which this run-down but affable stranger had ingratiated himself into our lives. He might have looked rather rough but, to my mind, he was somehow too smooth by half.

By the time we reached the lodging house, we knew that our rescuer, who had formally introduced himself, had just recently become unemployed, and that he was temporarily without a place to sleep. There was no hint of the begging bowl in his voice, no seeking of any reward for rescuing us from robbery, even serious injury, and, dare I say it, death at the hands of a desperate, knife-wielding man. I regret to say that Mama seemed taken with Riley and my unease grew stronger.

I could scarcely believe my ears when my mother said, "We have but one room, sir. Since you saved our food, perhaps the life of my daughter, I offer to share our shelter with you for this night. If you wish you may sleep on the floor. We are hard set to keep ourselves alive, you understand."

"You're a decent lady, thank you. Tomorrow I'll be

on my way," he touched his cap to Mama and I wondered had I imagined her preening for just a moment. Need I record that I felt more than awkward in Riley's company as we shared our simple supper with him. His narrow face housed dark eyes above a blade of nose that suggested a violent nature. He was polite, paying compliments to Mama, but I was far from happy. Was it possible, I asked myself, that Mama was flattered by this man's words about her beauty and her elegant hands?

Mama gave Riley her ancient overcoat as a blanket – he seemed grateful for that, and the worn rug on which he would lie for the night. Mama and I lay on the palettes that served as single beds, fully dressed under the sparse bedcovers that came with the rented room.

Without knowing exactly when it happened, I finally drifted off to sleep. All too soon, I came awake, though I could not have said why. I was not left in ignorance for long.

"Oh, please, lady, please," I heard Riley's voice, conciliatory, his words falling along the darkness of the single room. "I hunger for the touch of a woman's body – I've been so long alone."

"Please, Jem," my mother sighed, her voice laden with chagrin and something else I could not identify. "Oh, heaven's, please, don't do that."

I was appalled. Mother sounded like a young girl in love, her voice and her protests like invitations to carry on. Had I heard a grain of truth in Mama's words, in the sound of her voice, I would have attacked the man without even thinking about it. The moon cast a glow across the room and I could see Jem kneeling by my mother's bed.

"A kiss, one kiss, please, beautiful Rebecca." I felt myself go hot with anger. How dare he use Mama's name in that way? "I am so hungry for the kiss of a beautiful woman," he said in a voice that was as dry as a bone. Feeling very confused, I shut my eyes in despair.

Silence followed and my heart sank as I realised Mama had given in, that she was allowing Jem to kiss her. Moments later, I heard the bed creak as the man lay down with her. I was damp with perspiration and suddenly sick to my stomach.

"God!" I heard Riley gasp for breath. "Such lovely big tits! I could devour them – kiss you from head to toe if we were alone."

"Sssshhh," Mama stilled his breathless voice with her lips, but not for long.

"Oh, touch me, lady." He was breathless to the point of incoherence. "Touch me down below, feel what I can give you if only you'll have me." There was some more creaking from the bed and I heard him say as Mama moaned muted exhalations of pleasure, "Feel that, dear lady. Feel me there, there inside you, feel me, beautiful Rebecca."

Mama was murmuring words that I couldn't understand, her voice sounding strange to me. "Be gentle," she pleaded, her tone one of warning as she said, "Don't waken my girl. She knows nothing of life. I must protect her from my weakness."

I lay there feeling nauseous, hearing the bed creak softly then as though Riley was granting Mama's wish. For a long time they seemed to wallow quietly in each other's nearness – the creaking bed an ululation that ended when, for a minute or so, there was a hurried burst of movement, until Riley gasped in some kind of agony while Mama seemed to cut short her own cry of anguished pleasure. I, lying but an arm's length away across the room, felt so very angry, angry with Mama for allowing this stranger to use her and angry at myself because I was breathless, and ashamed of my own excitement at what had just taken place.

I am writing this episode in my caravan home on the outskirts of Athlone in central Ireland. I am sitting alone at the table where I read and eat, and I feel hot and severely bothered by the memory of the love-making between my mother and Jem Riley. I am hoping that by finally writing it down I might exorcise it, that it might never return to haunt me. I have tried to blot out my my own excitement during that event in that rented hovel in Camden Town. But there is no denying it. God! When I think of the times I pointed the cursed finger, the judgmental finger at my beloved mother.

Mama, you should not have given Jem Riley any encouragement, the finger writes. You should have given him some coins as a reward for his good deed, sent him on his way. Never should he have been allowed into our room that night. Never should he have been admitted into our society, into your body.

The times I have had to bite my hand to prevent me

screaming in the agony of the guilt I have known, because I dared point the finger at Mama. In my heart I knew, as I had always known, that she would never blame me for my feelings about that night, any more than she would have judged me had our roles been the opposite of what they were.

No more writing tonight. I want to go on but I am weary. As I am about to go to bed, again I find myself wishing that I could pray, that I could believe, truly believe in God, any God. But it isn't possible for me at this time. If there were any kind of God in the heavens he would not have allowed Mama to be so abused by life, to then die as she did. I know I will toss and turn as I do every night, my thoughts rampaging across my wish for sleep. No peace in the memories of all my yesterdays, no peace in the present either.

Sam put Gloria's journal down on the carpet at his feet, deeply moved by what he had just read. Several times tears had come close as the pictures behind his eyes revealed the dreadful conditions of Gloria's existence up to the time she had written about. While he didn't blame himself for the stance he had taken in the face of her ongoing half-mad behaviour, he couldn't help wishing he'd known what he knew now. A broad idea of the overall circumstances of her life back then had not given him any idea of what she and Rebecca had come through. In reading a small portion of her story, he had found compassion he would not have believed possible alongside the hatred he had felt toward her in recent months. He knew that he had to somehow get his hands on the other journals – not that he could ask her permission to read them. But as his mother was the chosen one in this respect, he would take advantage of the fact. The more he knew, the better he would understand his wife's moods and her flights into madness. He didn't have to read all that she had written. Much of it could be skimmed since he was not interested in her literary style, and he had high hopes that she would have recorded whatever happened on the night of summer solstice party at Dunbla House.

His mind reviewed yet again the moment when he asked her, "Will you marry me?" Even now he could hear the words 'I want to' like the response of a woman with something else on her mind. He would have to find the journal covering that night if he was going to be able to help her, at the same time, helping himself. Whatever had taken place on the night of the party, it would be in one of the books.

Her writing had made him aware of how little he thought about the past, of how little he knew about the Jews and of how sparse was his knowledge about the country of his birth. For a moment he considered engaging in some study of Ireland and the Jews – hadn't there been Jews living in Ireland for many years? He thought so but that was about it. Surely it was time to quit ignorance and gain some insight into the subject? Sooner or later his children were going to start asking questions he simply could not answer. He smiled, accepting that he was a chap that liked to have all the answers. He jotted down a reminder in the notebook he kept with him at all times, actually believing that he was going to find out a little more about the Jews and the Irish, and, he hoped, about himself.

22

Dublin

May 1912

Having watched Esther struggle to breathe during the uncommonly hot summer of the previous year, Sam made up his mind to buy a summer home by the sea at Greystones. He told Gloria the news, knowing she would leave it to him. He made no mention of the fact that he had signed the papers and already owned the magnificent villa on ten acres, just a short distance from the shore and the harbour where you could buy fresh fish every morning of the week for most months of the year. He found it a little sad that neither of them mentioned that it was in Greystones they had talked for the first time after he had seen her on stage.

The house Sam bought opened onto a quite magnificent view of the sea and the winding cliff-face to Bray, which lay about seven miles north towards Dublin. He believed it was the perfect place for the family to spend their summers, while he himself would use it for a weekend here and there in the off-season. Sam knew that Gloria would accept whatever house he bought, once the comfort of Esther was one of his primary considerations. He could acknowledge this in fairness to his wife, finding it less difficult to give credit where it was due, since he'd begun reading her journals.

By now he knew the whole story of her mother's burial, the way in which the Boswells had taken her into their life. He shared the memories she recorded when they returned to haunt her, being gripped beyond belief while reading about the moment when Jem Riley was about to rape her. He was as angry at the man as she had been, identifying with her horror, her virtual acceptance of the inevitable violation, until the abuse of her mother became the catalyst that turned the girl from his victim into Jem Riley's nemesis.

Sam's foot actually moved as he read of her kicking the Liverpudlian in the head, and he identified utterly with her idea of wanting to go back to slit his throat.

As Sam understood his mother's heart condition, the pump itself was strong enough to serve her well for quite some time. Her health problem lay with a blockage in one or more of her arteries – from time to time this caused Esther severe discomfort and pain. The enforced rest that the condition, he thought it was called angina, imposed upon her didn't bother her at all. She had willingly become a lady of leisure when Gloria had virtually adopted her. The women remained close. The younger was so respectful of the old lady who had walked through Germany to the port of Amsterdam, that she treated Esther as she would have done her own mother. Meanwhile, as his wife, she remained good-mannered and civil, playing the role of spouse to the hilt, maintaining a perfectly run *kosher* home.

As Sam had little or no time for the Jewish community, his lack of interest in contributing emotionally to the small colony, mostly Europeans and Russians, was reciprocated. Sam was in a majority of one when it came to commenting that the Jews stayed so close "that they were in danger of festering". He did business with Jew and Gentile alike, and when he needed men to work for him, he left the hiring to Brendan O'Connor, the big Dubliner understanding that no employee was ever to be asked about their religion. RC and Prod alike came and went as tradesmen and labourers. Very few Jews offered to carry the hod since their community, wishing that all Jewish men follow a profession or trade, backed this with money to assist in the education of their own people.

Whenever a zealous Jew was bold enough to take Sam to task for his stance in relation to the community, he didn't retaliate. Sometimes he smiled to himself when he remembered the newly-arrived Viennese Jews of his youth, how they had looked down on the Russians they were expected to sit beside at the St Mary's Abbey synagogue. He remembered how they had shuddered at such close proximity to 'these serfs and peasants'. He thought them blind, these so-called sophisticates who would not recognise the magnificence of people forced to flee from the pogroms, as Rebecca and her father and millions more had done. He admired those magnificent men and women who had lived in the knowledge that they would never own an acre of land in the land of the tsar; people dying while they tried to find a life, after a living death. Their existence had been a far cry from that of the chosen few, those rich and rare Jewish businessmen allowed to live like well-to-do Russians since they made money for the masters of their universe.

Sam had seen the Viennese with their upturned noses, and he couldn't stand their commitment to the politics of appearance and form and behaviour. He could scarcely believe they could be so totally unaware of all that they revealed about themselves when they said things like "some of the women wear shawls to *schul*!".

Many of the immigrants were rough-and-ready people whose very earthiness has helped them survive the walk across Europe to Dublin. Sam resented that they were made the butt of jokes by Austrians that couldn't hide their disconcertion when they realised "they have never even heard of Goethe!"

All in all, Sam carried on in his own live-and-let-live manner, not giving a damn what anybody thought about him, but prodded every now and then into asking himself, 'What do I stand for?' He chose to ignore this dart of enquiry because he had things to do, money to make, beautiful women to entertain in his permanent suite at the Hibernian Hotel, or on the occasional winter night in the summer house at Greystones. But the question, ignored though it was, rarely lurked far from the beaten track.

He also had Vicky to comfort now. He had not made love to her since the night Dee had opened her heart to him about Eddie's true identity, and Vicky's vow to love him forever seemed to have deserted her mind since she had become a semi-invalid. There had been a slow but certain change in her since her return from Paris with, as Sam put it, "her heart in a sling". Her love affair with Michelle, "the only woman I ever fell in love with", seemed to have left her wanting to die in its wake.

When she was well again for another while, she could admit to Sam that she was filled with regret over the extent of Arthur's drinking. He felt that this was due to her sense of having failed her twin, who was now in some stage of drunkenness at all times. Seamus was always at hand, and ever ready to pour a glass of Dom Perignon or Arthur's favourite cognac, a very-superior, old-pale Napoleon brandy, usually just a moment or two before sustenance of a curative nature was urgently needed by his master.

In this way, Arthur remained topped-up and personable, and indeed he appeared to be in full command of his faculties most of the time. But even Seamus had accepted that his boss had long since passed the point where he could face the day and function in his busy life without the company of the booze. Just like me, Seamus thought many a time, as he poured drinks for them both.

This addiction to heavy drinking could only result in a diminution of the high standards of behaviour Arthur expected of himself. He would have been the first to admit and accept this, but he seemed unaware that things had come to such a drastic pass. Sam had made a number of efforts to help Arthur see where his life was heading if he kept on with his present rate of drinking. He never pressed too hard, really thinking with a sense of painful regret that Arthur was a hopeless case.

Meeting with absolutely no success, Sam had more or less decided to let Arthur get on with it, leave him in peace that he might even enjoy the odd moment of his tottering odyssey in search of God alone knew what. A telephone call from Deirdre changed his mind before he had time to allow this notion get set. When he heard her voice on the line his heart warmed up as it always did whenever they spoke to each other.

"I need your help," she said without preamble. "You must be sick and tired of trying to help Arthur see how he's hurting himself . . ."

Sam stopped her right there. "Dee, stop. I'm not fed up, not at all. I'll admit to feeling a bit helpless."

She understood this better than anybody. "But if you would just try once more."

This entreaty took him to Dunbla that same day, a late spring afternoon of such beauty that it belonged in July, and he hoped it was a harbinger of the summer ahead. He smiled as he got out of the Silver Ghost. Giving the Rolls a pat of admiration he opened his arms as though blessing the vast gardens running downhill to embrace the sea where the land turned to water.

Regiments of daffodils and crocuses pulled the eye this way and that, the great trees like soldiers at ease stretching right and left as far as he could see, the limit of the Brewer land to the south and west beyond the range of general sight.

Dee came out of the house and his heart smiled, felt lighter as she stood waiting for him under the wrought-iron-fronted balcony, over pillars in the Ionic style on which the white paintwork shone in the April sunshine. He went up the steps, a spring in his own step, trying hard not to wear his willingness on his sleeve.

She greeted him with a gentle kiss on the lips and a long, warm embrace. She stood back as though she was filling her eyes with him before she asked after Gloria and the children and "Esther, of course! How is the dear heart?"

As they walked inside, Sam enquired after Arthur.

"He's been bad the past week," Deirdre said quietly.

She let him into her private withdrawing room and they sat by the window, he with his arms on his thighs leaning forward on a chaise lounge while she occupied her favourite leather chair which had been given her by Sam as a birthday present the year after she and Arthur had moved to Dunbla.

Dee poured tea for them both, waiting while Sam lit

a cigarette. Then she said, "I'm so grateful you could come this afternoon. Arthur is asleep just now, but I feel he is ready to go on another tear." She handed him a cup and saucer and went on, "Sam if you could keep him from doing that. Is this a grievous imposition?" She sucked on her lips while he wished he could relieve her chagrin. She was close to tears and he felt a strong urge to embrace her, comfort her.

"Dee, please!" He found that he was standing, almost in the act of going to embrace her, reassure her of his devotion to their friendship. "It's my privilege. You never have to worry about things like that with me. I'll be here when Arthur wakes up, and I'll do all I can to." He was at a loss for the right words, so he said with a tentative smile, "Look, let's see how he is, see what happens, and take it from there. Is that all right with you?"

She nodded, and he saw the waiting tears lodge on her eyelids as she pressed them shut a moment, like someone silently praying, his heart lurching so that he was relieved she wasn't looking his way.

Within the hour, he was alone with Arthur in his study, watching him down a flute of champagne before lighting a fresh cigarette. They had been having a chat about a mining venture that Arthur had capitalised in South Africa three years earlier, both of them laughing as Sam, revealing interest in buying some shares, said in self-deprecation, "Your man's losing the run of himself. Shares in bloody South Africa, hmmph! He's come a long way from Little Jerusalem!"

Arthur laughed, and Sam sipped champagne, as he carefully led them into a discussion about booze and his curiosity as to, "Why? Why you have been hitting it so hard of late?" He bit his tongue not to say anything about the last two to three years. He chuckled, waxing amused as he remarked that the fancy houses of Monto might well go out of business if and when Arthur hung up his spurs. From this 'all pals together' mood he gently segued into his growing concern about the times Arthur seemed to lose control, sometimes going missing for days. Arthur didn't comment on this as he poured more wine for himself, first offering the bottle to Sam who declined. He then called for Seamus to bring another magnum, and lit a fresh cigarette even though he had one alive in his ashtray.

"Are you even aware that you are going missing on a more regular basis, Arthur?" Even as he asked the question, Sam knew what the answer was going to be.

Arthur clasped his hands, his expression, like his answer, offered in utter sincerity. "I swear to you, Sam, I have no idea when this kind of thing happens. You know me better than anyone else. It is not in my nature to hurt anything, or anybody. What you describe, goodness, I feel shame strong enough to drown in. When I consider what poor Dee must go through at those times." He was clearly appalled at the very idea.

"When I find you in those places," Sam said, "well, when Seamus and I find you, you have always been with a whore, perhaps two." He found it difficult to simply press on with what he wanted to say, but he knew he had to persist. "Arthur, I feel what I deem to be love for my children, and Esther, and Dee, and Vicky and yourself. I need to speak in this way even though I'm afraid I will alienate you. Clearly, I would hate that to happen, since it would mean that I'd offended you. I'd really hate that."

He smoked heavily, while Arthur held his other hand tightly, rocking ever so slightly backward and forward like a man who could not be still with his own thoughts.

"I've talked to the women I have found you with," Sam carried on. "They say you are looking for a woman, a certain woman, a woman with no name, a woman you spent a night with at some time in recent years. This need, this compulsion to recapture what happened between you and this mystery woman – is that it? Is that the reason why you go off on these tangents? Does that send you like a rapacious madman to the brothels? The whores themselves say you are insatiable at these times, that you seem driven to use them ferociously, as though it will help you find again whatever this woman gave you. Does any of this ring a bell in your memory?"

Arthur shook his head in a gesture of regret, automatically ringing the bell for Seamus. He appeared unsteadily with the champagne even as Arthur drained the flute in his hand. Sam couldn't fail to notice how Seamus, tipsy now at all times like his master, had come to look older than his years.

"And yourself, Mister Sweet?" Seamus stood by in service to Sam, waiting before he would put the magnum into the ice bucket by his master's side.

"Thank you, Seamus, I will. Excuse me a moment, Arthur. I must telephone, since I'm not going home for dinner."

He dismissed Arthur's apologies with an off-hand gesture. "I won't tell Esther, she loves answering the telephone, that I'm enjoying myself," he added slyly, as he crossed the carpet to the door.

Esther answered. Just as well, he thought, as he heard his mother announce in a loud voice, magnified by the acoustics of the hallway at the house on Leinster Road, "Sweet residence, who is it speaking if you please?" Esther always said the same thing and it always made Sam smile. He explained he was in a business conference and that he would not be home for dinner. "This is new?" Esther chortled, speaking, as she usually did, to some invisible third party. "He won't be home for dinner yet. Such a surprise! And how lucky I was nobody fed him when he pushed the handcart! Oy vay! Imagine me in my innocence, thinking he hurried home every evening to make sure his Mama was alive and well."

"Be careful, Mama!" Sam warned Esther in a hushed voice. "The papists use that expression now. You could get a bad name!"

"What expression? Who gives me a bad name, already?"

"I hear they're singing 'Oy Vay Maria' in the churches now. I think Gounod has a lot to answer for."

Esther realised he was making fun of her, and she was having none of it. "Gounod, Schmoonod! You should be ashamed keeping me on my feet to make silly jokes." Esther put the phone down and he chuckled to himself as he headed back to the study to Arthur and this latest effort to find out what it was that made him run to another brace of prostitutes.

So far the evening was a write-off – nothing had been added to what he already knew. The alcohol-induced amnesia took Arthur in and out of his head, so that it was hard to pin him down on anything. Sam wondered if Arthur's life might have been different had his mother been there, as Esther had been for him. Now he smiled again, feeling more than a hint of gratitude that his own tough old bird was still alive and kicking.

Arthur was pouring his own champagne. He drank this in a swallow even as Sam sat down, deciding this was a good time to press on since plenty of drink seemed to make Arthur more accessible, once you didn't lose him all together.

Sam began to speak, but he was brought to a halt when he noticed that the pale-blue eyes had glazed over – they were like fingernails of ice – and that Arthur, the real Arthur, was nowhere to be seen. What happened next caused Sam to perk up sharply. He had been sitting silently for several moments, considering the possibility that Arthur had been captured by one of his alcoholic blackouts. This was pure speculation, but he was remembering the night in Greystones, the night on which he had seen Gloria for the first time and he was forced to knock Arthur unconscious to stop him terrifying everybody else in the overnight hotel. That time, as Arthur ranted and raved and tried to physically hurt Sam, he had seen that same slate-like patina blot out all that was true about the summer-blue sheen of Arthur's eyes.

Certainly, by the look of him as he sat across an occasional table in his study, his mind seemed to have gone missing. Sam would not have been surprised had it drowned to death in the face of Arthur's frighteningly robust drinking, even in the time they had been together this evening. Sam shuddered, and felt fear that Arthur would have a heart attack or some kind of brain trouble if he did not cut down on his daily imbibing. But asking Arthur to stop drinking altogether – that was just too impossible to imagine.

Suddenly Arthur mumbled abstractedly. "I have got to find you. I have got to share your bed again." Arthur was looking directly at Sam, but his mind was clearly somewhere else.

Sam was stunned, but for a moment only. Registering the prescience of his own instinct and all too aware that analysis could lead to paralysis, he decided to just run with the situation. "You've never forgotten her, Arthur. She must have been a wonderful lover." He spoke gently in a soothing voice, wondering was it possible to get through to the man hiding on the dark side of Arthur's moon.

"I have worshipped three women," Arthur spoke in a vague way like someone thinking aloud, not answering the question, seemingly unaware that he was in his private study with the companion he called his best friend. "My twin, Victoria, my great and wonderful

sister, and Lisa who was my first love – my mother-love
I suppose, the first woman I ever ached to be loved by.
She was my soul mother, the balm that made suicidal
days seem bearable. It was Lisa who kept me alive, her
presence helping me to find reason enough to push
away the ferocious need to kill myself. I was able to
think of what my suicide would do to Lisa, and to
Vicky. When Lisa was torn away, ripped from my
existence . . ." His words tailed off as though he could
not remember under the weight of this unwanted
suffering that had been heaped on his life.

"Now I grieve the loss of a woman who granted me
harbour in a way I have never known before. She is a
woman whose face I cannot see, whose name I never
knew. She caused my insane spirit to soar joyfully, so
lost was I in her generosity – I became her as I melted
into her until we were one heartbeat, ensuring I would
never be the same again."

Arthur, in what seemed to Sam to be an automatic
but unconnected way, poured another drink, replacing
the magnum in the ice bucket. This convinced Sam that
Arthur was not actually present. The Arthur he knew,
no matter how inebriated he might be, would never
have first poured wine for himself. He would have seen
to his guest before he attended to his own need, simply
because that was how he was.

Feeling there was nothing to be lost, Sam pressed on,
responding to his own need to help Arthur unravel the
mystery of the woman who had touched him so
significantly.

"Where did you meet her? Was she introduced to you by a friend?" He kept his tone conversational, avoided being pushy, not wanting to interfere by appearing too confrontational.

"We danced the two of us alone. There was music in the distance, a moonlit night, bunting and lanterns and the sounds that lovers create in arbours designed for romantic moments." Arthur drank without appearing to notice that he had done so, while his speech, a monotone, appeared to be happening of its own volition. No response to anything he said was registered in the voice, or the face or the dull, cold, blue-grey eyes of the storyteller. "I do know that she was there waiting, as though she had come to explode onto my consciousness. We ravaged each other. We cried out in the pain of our need to shatter all the barriers society had placed on something so beautiful that only a loving God could have designed it. We ripped each other's clothing off, no word that I can remember being spoken. I was living with such intensity I thought my body would render me unconscious, that it could not possibly withstand the force of the sensations she caused within me. We were like wild things, the desire to devour each other burning up everything else. I buried myself in her body. I have never been so deeply received, never been so imprisoned by a woman. God alone knows if I abused her in my rampaging, I have no idea. But she wanted all I had to offer and more, and I felt utterly insatiable.

"At some stage I went down there, down like a supplicant to the font of all giving. I kissed her with such passion that she erupted as my lips and my tongue drove her to ecstasy and beyond. For a few moments I wished to die since nothing could ever be like this again. I lay then for a while, my lips caressing the creamlike softness on the inside of her thigh. It was then that I saw, for the one and only time, a birthmark, a dark-blue bruise shaped like a medallion." Arthur stopped speaking again, the dull monotonous voice tailing off, as though it had been evicted by the power of the memory.

Sam became rigid in his chair, his breath stolen from him by the revelation of his greatest friend. He gasped for breath for several moments, unnoticed by Arthur, who poured himself a flute of the Dom Perignon to drink it down before pouring another.

Sam stood up and walked unsteadily into the ante-room. Seamus had passed out on a couch, an empty champagne glass on the floor by his limp hand. Sam walked on through and found a bathroom, wondering if he was going to throw up. He ran water into a wash basin and leaned over it, took some deep breaths before he rinsed his face, trying to brace himself before he went back to the study, his mind momentarily numbed so that he could function but not gather a single thought.

Arthur was in a semi-comatose condition in his chair, though not so paralysed that he could not pour himself more wine. When Sam sat he spoke again like someone who had merely paused for breath.

"The only clue I have to the identity of my lady of the night is that birthmark. If I only knew which night it was, I might have been able to trace her. But I remember nothing beyond that. And at this moment, I am gripped again by the urge, some desperate need to go in search of her once more." He threw back the newest glass of champagne and stood up, his legs unsteady, his voice ringing with sudden determination.

Sam had heard that sound before, witnessed the accompanying forcefulness on the hotel landing at Greystones. Feeling now quite weary and knowing that he had no further heart this night to be a facilitator, he simply waited until Arthur put the glass down on the occasional table before he hit him with a fierce punch.

The short right-hand blow caught Arthur on the jaw, snapping his head back. Sam grabbed the lapels of his smoking jacket to prevent him falling backwards and then slowly bundled the big man onto the vast leather couch Arthur slept on when he couldn't make it upstairs. He shoved a cushion under the golden greying hair, before covering the long legs with a tartan rug. Falling to his knees as though his legs had been cut from under him, Sam began to weep and to whimper, his head lying on Arthur's chest as a thousand years of tears denied staked their claim to freedom.

Some time later, he lit a cigarette. He inhaled slowly and deliberately, smoking one after the other until the moment arrived when he could finally accept that it was the hidden memory of his night with Gloria – she was the mystery woman – that was driving Arthur mad.

Sam was shattered by the ring of truth in the revelation of his great friend, who had been so present in the past, that he didn't even realise he was telling the story, and even more significantly, had no idea that it was Sam who was doing the listening. Just as he had no idea of the identity of the woman with the birthmark, the purple medallion blemish that Sam had deemed to be for his eyes only.

He was surprised that instead of wanting to strangle his wife, he felt compassion. Yes, he was hurting, but what was that compared to what she had endured since the night she had trampled all over her own rules. His consideration for Gloria gave him pause. What was going on? Yes, she had crossed the Rubicon while he was bribing a Corporation official on that mad night at Dunbla, and yes she had danced the dance on the forbidden path, and, yes, every madness had been indulged in the search for sensation. But it seemed that sanity and the power to think responsibly had been thrown out with the bathwater, so that two people he loved could self-inflict even more pain into their lives and those of the people they both loved.

The picture of the lovers coupling tortured him for some moments, his blood boiled as he thought of Arthur ploughing through his wife. The image of Gloria with her legs wrapped around his lust, her own giving as wild and wilful as his brutal taking, left Sam fighting for breath. The feeling was of panic, and it took his breathing by the throat. He felt he was choking, scarcely able to believe that his wife had simply been playing the role of virgin on their wedding night.

He almost got hooked into going back there in his mind, part of him wanting to dissect it moment by moment. He got a grip, and gathered his common sense. He stood up quickly – choosing to remember it was something about which he could do nothing. There was more to it though, and he sipped champagne as he willed his thinking to reveal whatever it was. "My feelings," he said quietly to the champagne glass, "just what good are my feelings to me right now?" A thought struck him. "As a matter of fact, what good are they to me at any time, since they are always about me? They always have to do with 'I want, I want'." His eyes opened in the wonder of revelation. "And I only ever hurt, when I bloody well want something. When I want and do not get, I am in pain. And the getting never satiates the wanting for long. Even as I had Gloria, I wanted more, wanted her to want me more than she did on our wedding night. I wanted Gloria to feel with me what she had felt with Arthur. I wanted to dominate her in bed, demolish her with my sexual power, not knowing that Arthur had already taken her to that place that lies beyond imagining."

He stopped the words that made the pictures he didn't need to draw in his mind. There was no point. He could hurt over what had happened, but so what? He didn't have to turn it into a three-act melodrama. Nothing would ever wipe it off the slate of day-to-day living, but he would heal in time. Part of him felt he was settling for cold comfort, but he was feeling easier now that he knew the cause of Gloria's demon Jewess carry-on.

He didn't want to judge Arthur, who – when you

considered his mental condition when he was boozed – had to be blameless. Whether this was true or not, he wouldn't judge. He smoked, his instincts telling him there was more to come, that there was something to be gained from the unconscious revelation of his friend. Arthur would have no memory of what he had revealed, and he wouldn't know that Sam had hit him to ensure that he stayed home this night. There and then, Sam knew it was paramount that Arthur never got to know of tonight's amnesiac eruption, believing that the best man he had ever known would kill himself if ever he came to know the truth of his night with Gloria.

A rueful smile twisted his mouth for a few moments as he allowed that he had hit Arthur a shade harder than was necessary. He forgave himself right away for his violent reaction. His great and gifted friend wouldn't know there had been venom in the punch; he'd been absent since his eyes glazed over some hours earlier.

Sam drank another glass of champagne, tipsy enough to have stopped counting how many he'd had. When he heard his voice again, it seemed to be coming from behind him. "Whenever I want something that is not coming my way, I get angry and want it even more. When I do that, I choose to go one-on-one with the power of the universe. That is what feelings do for me. They make me stupid enough, or insane enough, that I wrestle against all that energy. It's so stupid. I refuse to take no for an answer from the power of life, the very power of life that gave me my life, as though that power couldn't snuff out my individual existence as easily as it granted it to me in the first place. Time for me to go and get a night's sleep," he murmured, much of the energy drained from his body, if not his mind. He bent and kissed Arthur's forehead. "I'll talk to you on the telephone in the morning. Well, afternoon might be better for both of us. And I hope your jaw won't be too sore." He turned back. "I don't mean that. May your jaw give you gyp tomorrow and the next day. Now, good night."

He left. No need to disturb Dee to tell her Arthur was asleep.

23

Dunbla, Co Dublin

May 1912

As the headlamps lit up the driveway at Dunbla, Sam avoided thinking about what he was going to say to Gloria about the night of the summer solstice. But, as he started the car, he could not let go of how she had looked at him as he was asking her to marry him. He eased the motorcar down the drive. Now he knew why she had not been ready, or he believed he knew why. She had been in love with Arthur since the night of the after-show supper, and she had been holding onto a thread of hope that Arthur might have fallen in love with her.

Driving out onto the Dublin road, he remembered that he had seen as much that night, and had denied it because he wanted her, wanted her badly enough to believe that he would turn her around and make her fall in love with him. He almost squirmed in the driver's seat as he recalled the relief he felt when Gloria first understood that Arthur was engaged to Deirdre. He remembered the hotel in Greystones – the after-show dinner party – Gloria admiring Dee's engagement ring, his impression being that she was checking out the lucky man. And, consummate actress that she was, she had, on discovering Arthur was Dee's affianced, handled the situation superbly. But he had witnessed the frisson, an almost invisible sliver of disappointment that the news had engendered as she sat across from him at the supper table in the hotel. Surely, he'd been right about that? Now, as he began the short journey home, he knew just how right he had been. He had sensed it before Gloria had enough time to close the curtain over her feelings.

It hadn't been difficult to believe that he might have been mistaken. The way she banged on about her hatred of Gentiles would have convinced a jury that she could never have responded as she did to Arthur. Sam now accepted that he had only been able to believe this because he had made no allowances for the frailty of the human heart yet innocent enough to fall in love.

He had driven a mile or two from Dunbla, when he had to stop the car by the roadside. He was hurting desperately, feeling so foolish, his mind taking charge again as he stumbled once more over the graphic of Gloria and Arthur in bed together.

Under a waning moon, he leaned back against the car on the Dublin road, smoking with a desperate urgency. He tried to tell himself: "It doesn't matter, now." He said this aloud, moved to tears by some invisible recognition that this was a watershed moment in his life.

He was still resting against the car as he inhaled deeply on a new cigarette, aware of the tube of tobacco resting between his lips, and relieved as he found he was back to the benign emptiness he had experienced earlier. He drew comfort through no longer being angry or afraid, welcoming the peace that had, so silently, moved in. It felt good to be – no need to dismiss facing up to whatever questions were lining up. Questions that were too often shoved onto the back burner because he was busy – had things to do, money to earn, people to see.

He now found himself facing the question – since Gloria had been hesitant about accepting his marriage proposal before he left the party for his business appointment that night, why had she suddenly been so anxious to marry him as quickly and as quietly as possible in London?

Since he already knew that Gloria was the woman who had shredded Arthur's sanity in the cottage near the house, there could only be one answer to the question – she had been terrified that Arthur had made her pregnant. To his amazement he heard himself say, "You poor bitch! Any wonder you carried on like a woman being tortured?" He shook his head in compassion by the moon's light at the roadside, surprised as a motor car hurtled past him, momentarily interrupting his introspection. He could see now that she had to be married to him, in case she had conceived by Arthur, and she *had to be married* to him quickly. A quick marriage would ensure that he made love to her soon enough after the tryst, that any child from the marriage would be seen as progeny conceived on the first night of the honeymoon. Through his reading of her journals, Sam knew about the promise Gloria had made to her mother that she would be a virgin bride. She had broken the vow – another reason to produce another mountain of shame, grief and self-hatred. She was an honourable woman, and, to judge by the record of her earlier life on the streets of London, an unconsciously brave and noble girl. Knowing this helped.

Sam allowed himself to give his heart the freedom to reach out to her, certain that any lie that included the name of her mother would have cost her dearly in the overall scheme of things. So, flatly, he accepted that she had married him in a London registry office, not because she was desperately in love with him, but simply because she desperately needed to cover up her night of insane passion with Arthur.

He started the engine again, about to leave the story there for the moment, when he realised why she had been so neurotic when Deirdre had expressed the hope that Sarah and Eddie would be married some day. Oh yes! Now he understood why Gloria appeared to be going out of her mind. To live each and every day with the thought that Sarah might be Arthur's child meant that a marriage between her and Eddie would be an incestuous one, a case of brother marrying sister.

Sam exhaled in the chill of the night air, feeling uncomfortably hot as he unwittingly empathised with what his wife had endured from the first moments of their married life.

His heart moved compassionately. Any wonder the poor bitch has been going crazy on us? He turned on the headlights and began driving slowly towards the city. He had only just moved off when he saw the figure of a man come through a hedge on the left of the deserted road six or seven miles from Dublin. He saw the man fall down even as the headlights picked him out of the night.

Sam stopped the car and grabbed his torch. Rushing to where the man lay, he bent and shone the light down. He gasped in shock. The face belonged to Deirdre's brother, Cormac Doyle. As he stood there gaping, he heard at some distance several shots fired sporadically, and he was galvanised into action. Without stopping to consider the implications, he hefted the young man off the ground and carried him to the car. Instinctively, he decided against placing him in the passenger seat. He set him down beneath the bucket seat, planning to cover him with a couple of rugs and a pile of newspapers he'd been keeping for four-fingered Louie. About to drive off, he had another thought. Sweating now, as though he was being observed, he undid the wing-nut that held the spare wheel in place. He put this on top of the rugs, and threw the newspapers on top, using the wheel-brace to hold them down. Then he risked taking the time, which seemed endless, to let the air out of the spare wheel's tyre. When he was satisfied that this was flat, he jumped back into the car. Turning it around, he put his foot on the accelerator and headed back towards Dunbla House.

Before he had gone a mile, he observed another car as it became a feature in his rear-view mirror. Sam felt no surprise. Cormac had been involved with the IRB – the Irish Republican Brotherhood – for some time. If he was still alive, he was most likely wounded, shot by police or government agents in the following car.

He had turned into the half-mile driveway of Dunbla House when the other car overtook him, forcing him to stop. He immediately got out, since he had to be seen to remonstrate, and to look like he was prepared to defend himself and his property. He held the torch like a weapon as he yelled, "What the hell do you think you're doing?" at the two men approaching him. "This is private property, you are trespassing, and this family is not without influence."

"We are police officers, sir, in pursuit of a nationalist criminal." The leader flashed his warrant card, which Sam examined in the light of his torch.

"Well, why aren't you following him, Inspector Daragh, instead of wasting time stopping me?" Sam made sure he sounded ruffled, though not totally lacking in understanding that the police had a job to do.

"Is this your home, sir? And would you mind telling me your name?"

"No, it is not my home. And my name is Samuel Sweet with an address at Leinster Road in Rathmines," Sam spoke like a good citizen who was willing to cooperate with the forces of law and order. "But why did you follow me?"

"You were seen to turn your car around, sir, drive

back the way you had come. We wondered had you stopped to pick up a passenger." The implication was obvious, but Sam allowed it to slide over his shoulder. Then he became aware that the second man was beginning an examination of the car.

"Too damned right, I turned around," Sam turned around even as he spoke, using the torch to illuminate the flat tyre on the spare wheel. "I left here a little while ago, heading home after an evening with my friends, Arthur Brewer and his wife. I stopped because my rear wheel went flat. I got out of the damned car, changed the wheel, hence the mud and whatever on my clothing. Here! Take a look." He held the torch to show the dirt he had applied to his cashmere overcoat.

The policeman moved to take a closer look at the spare wheel and Sam said. "Perhaps you'd like to check the tyre for air, or rather, the lack of it."

The policeman pressed the tyre before he backed off. The inspector had one more card to play. "When you changed the tyre, Mister Sweet, why not just carry on home? Why turn around and drive back here?"

"I wasn't prepared to risk the journey without a usable spare wheel, Inspector," He aimed to sound as though he couldn't believe his ears. "This house here at Dunbla is my home from home. I have a summer home at Greystones, but it might as well be in Tralee for all the good it would be to me tonight. I drive nowhere without a reliable spare."

The big detective let it go. "I'm sorry to have inconvenienced you, sir. Please understand we're in pursuit of dangerous malcontents; revolutionaries they call themselves. One or two, here and there, may be sincere in their beliefs, the rest are a ragbag of wasters and criminals. It's our job to find them, and put them where they won't bother honest citizens. I'm sorry for the trouble."

"I understand, Inspector," Sam said in a flat voice, not wanting to sound grateful in case it appeared that he felt lucky to have got away with something.

"We'll pull over to let you pass on up to the house, Mister Sweet."

"Thank you, Inspector. I'll be on my way." Sam gave them a goodnight salute as he passed the stationary police car, grateful that the night was dark enough to hide the sweat on his brow.

When he got to the house, Sam stopped the engine, waiting until he heard the sound of the other car swallowed up by the near distance. Only then did he do anything about his passenger. Even as he removed the spare wheel, the front door of the house opened and a half-jarred, very sleepy Seamus Byrne appeared, carrying a double-barrelled shotgun with the air of a man, albeit not sober, who knew how to use it.

"Put that down, Seamus," he urged in a quiet voice.

"Oh, it's yerself, Mister Sweet," Seamus lowered the weapon as Dee, who was very much awake, arrived tying her dressing-gown tightly about her waist. "Sam? What's the matter? What's going on? I thought I heard cars."

He moved closer to her, and without raising his voice said, "I'll explain in a minute. Right now, I want you to open the kitchen door. I'm going to drive around the back. I have Cormac hidden in the car – he's wounded. The other car was the police. Don't say anything more for now. One of them may be lurking in the bushes along the drive."

He turned to Seamus. "You stay here with the shotgun. And here! Take my torch. Missus Brewer will put on all the lights. If anything moves out there, shout one warning and fire above head height. I'll be back to you in a few minutes."

Seamus nodded his head like a man who was paying for the sin of over-indulgence.

Sam drove the car around the great house, and parked it between the kitchen door and the vegetable garden. As Deirdre appeared from the kitchen, he was removing the wheel he had used to hide Cormac. Pulling the rugs back he was startled to find himself looking into the muzzle of a heavy-looking revolver. Deirdre who had joined him, gasped in alarm before she pushed the weapon to one side. "Cormac, what on earth do you think you're doing?"

Sam was already hauling her brother carefully up from behind the front seats. The stringy-looking youth was clearly in pain, and Dee could see for herself that he had been shot. "You're bleeding. Let me help you."

Sam lifted him from the car, setting him on his feet as Cormac spoke through gritted teeth. "It's not serious, but it hurts like bloody hell." His eyes fluttered for a second and Sam moved sharply to grab him as he was about to tumble to the ground.

When he had set him down in one of the bedrooms, Sam shook his head when Dee suggested they call Paddy Lote to attend to her brother. She looked surprised until he said, "Best if we don't involve him in something like this. Let me make a call. I know someone who knows someone."

Brendan O'Connor answered his telephone like a man who had been surgically removed from a deep sleep. But he was instantly alert, as he heard Sam's voice on the line. "A friend of yours and mine has been injured," Sam said quietly. He had his doubts that a telephone operator would be listening in at this hour of the morning but, nonetheless, he remained circumspect in his speech.

"He is in need of medical attention. I'm at the West Brits, you understand? Can you ask that doctor of yours to drop by here?"

Brendan hung up the telephone receiver, and Sam returned to the bedroom to find Deirdre examining a flesh wound in her brother's right side. He assured her that medical help was on the way. She looked tired and wan, and he wanted to protect her even more than he usually did. He also needed to sit down. "You go back to bed, Dee. I'll look after him 'til the doctor gets here."

She shook her head, her face lined with concern. "Have you any idea what happened, Sam? Obviously, he's been shot."

"He got some kind of miracle tonight, is all I can tell you, Dee. I had stopped by the roadside to think over something Arthur and I had been talking about. I was having a quiet cigarette under a bit of a moon. As I started the car again to head for home, he came blundering through a hedge just yards from where I was, and he fell down. I got him into the car, and threw a few rugs over him. Then I decided to prepare for the worst eventuality, that the police would search my car since I was what you might call, handy to the scene. I released the air from the spare wheel and dumped that on top of the rugs covering Cormac. I messed up my coat and hands to look like I had changed the wheel myself. I was actually in the driveway here when the police caught up with me. Finally, they accepted my account of events, but they are looking for him and whoever was with him tonight. I have to tell you they know he's a member of the IRB."

Deirdre rose from where she sat by the bed, and came to stand by Sam. She put her hand to his face, and she kissed him gently on the lips. "What on earth would I do without you?" She shook her head to dismiss the thought while Sam reeling slightly in his mind wanted to press his lips to her lovely mouth. "Cormac's a fool, Sam, but he is sincere," Dee assured him. "He is passionate, determined to be part of an Ireland free of British domination."

He saw she was near to tears and without ulterior motive rose and embraced her. Her arms went around him and she crushed against him as though it would drive her fear away. He stood still, giving her all the support he could find. He succeeded in keeping his mind out of the moment, so confused by his mixed feelings he simply couldn't have spoken.

"I was already grateful you were here," she said quietly. "You being here stopped Arthur going out tonight."

Sam smiled over her shoulder. 'And a good clip to the jaw!' he thought mischievously. Dee stepped back reaching for his hands.

"That he's safe, asleep on the couch," she went on, "that's something else I have to thank you for."

"You never have to thank me for anything, Dee. We have to have a serious talk though, soon, about Arthur. And I'm going to need your help where Gloria is concerned."

"Of course," she pressed his hands between her own, her eyes warm in her willingness to help in any way she could. "Is she improving at all?"

"She's maintaining a precarious balance just now. And my feeling is that it's got to get worse before it gets better. But, when I've explained all to you, I'm sure that, between the pair of us, we'll be able to help her."

Dee nodded, "I would like to be able to do that. She is so full of pain." Cormac stirred and she went to him. He had fallen back into a dead sleep. Checking that the bleeding had stopped, she turned back to Sam. "The person you called to get help for Cormac, is he IRB?"

"Because I would trust you with my life, I can tell you yes, yes he is. He works for me – Brendan O'Connor."

"My Brendan?" she asked, nodding her head in answer to her own question. "I knew he was an idealist." She touched Sam's face with her hand. "I won't ask about you."

"It's all right," he said. "I'm not a member of anything. You know me."

Deirdre looked relieved. "How many others do we know that are part of the cause?"

"Brendan is my right-hand man, brilliant, hard-working, trustworthy. In him the cause has a good man. With enough like him, who knows what they can achieve?"

Deirdre wasn't that impressed. "Why should this time be different? How can they match the trained army of the greatest military power the world has ever seen?"

"There's no answer to that except one, Dee. As for me, I don't think it's all that bad under the Brits. Bad for a lot of people that are living in poverty, I know. And you with the work you're doing in the slums, you know there's a lot wrong. But a new Irish revolutionary government is not going to fix that situation in a fortnight. In here," he tapped his chest, "I'm with lads like Cormac, but . . ." he shook his head, his expression regretful, "when I think of young lads going up against the force of England, I'd advise them against it. And yet, I find myself admiring them. I never thought you'd hear me talk like this." He stood up and took her by the arm. "Come on. Cormac's not going to improve or get any worse just because we're standing here. Let's get a kettle boiling and a cup of something going. I could live in your kitchen."

As they stood together, fixing a tea tray, Dee said, "I've never heard you talk like that before."

Sam knew exactly what Dee was referring to. He smiled ruefully, aware of some sliver of change in himself. "When I lifted Cormac out of the car I realised he weighs about eight stone. There's not a whole lot of him there." He poured tea onto the leaves in the pot Dee had warmed, while she buttered some home-made bread. "I mean, I could lift him without any bother. A slip of a man, you could say. When you think of the heart it took for him to risk his life tonight – you'd know he has to be quite a man, even if he's not a whole heap of muscles."

Deirdre was adding jam to the bread and butter. She stopped to look at him and she nodded. Sam saw a hint of pepper and salt in her auburn hair, watched it come and go as the electric light caught the movement of her head. By his reckoning she was twenty-six or so now – the dearest heart he knew.

"I know what you're saying. He looked very vulnerable as we left him just now. Like a lad, really, but he has the heart of a lion. He always did. And my only fear is that he will die for Ireland, when I want him to live." Dee took a deep breath and passed him the plate of bread.

"I've got to wake up to what's going on around me." Sam put it on the tray and headed for Dee's withdrawing room. "I'm getting very curious about the Jews. I've been so busy trying to make money, a lot of stuff has passed me by."

He put the tray down, and Dee closed the door. He poured tea for them both, his expression pensive. She smiled at him. "The same thing has been happening to me in the last few years."

"Oh, come on, Dee." He handed her a cup of tea. "You've been doing great work in the slums. You even survived the Church's efforts to get you out of there for showing them up."

"I'm talking about the cause. It was for that Cormac might have been killed tonight."

"Are you saying you want to be involved?"

"I am involved, here," she tapped her chest. "My father would hate the inconvenience of change. I picked up some of that from him. But it was a patina that has faded. Injustice is rampant in our society. Sounds a bit pompous, but that's what I think. And it ought to stop. And I am willing to get involved. Clearly, whether you know it or not, you feel the same. You telephoned Brendan who is IRB, to get a doctor who is clearly a sympathiser or he would not be coming to tend a volunteer. What would you call that if not involvement?"

"What about Arthur? I can't keep anything from him," Sam said.

"You won't have to. He's been guilt-ridden all his life about the robbery of Ireland from its people. I believe that's one of the main reasons he drinks so much. At the risk of sounding fanciful, becoming involved in the cause could be something that might help him to quit killing himself with alcohol."

He went to her, and put his arms around her in the way he had done for years. She hugged him back fiercely for a moment, then as she moved away to pour more tea for them both, she said without difficulty, "I needed that."

24

DUBLIN

Easter Monday • June 21st 1916

Sam knew that if he lived to be a hundred he would never forget what took place on Easter Monday, the horror erupting just hours after he drove Michael Collins up Bachelor's Walk, his nerves jangling just a bit as the sight of so many British army tenders in the Four Courts area, relief surfacing since there was no heavy commitment of soldiers. There was little or no regular traffic, only the odd early morning tram. They motored west, the Liffey by the side of the car.

Back at the corner with Sackville Street, Sam again marked the spot where he had dived into the river after a boy who had died anyway. A street-arab whose name he never came to know. Their paths had crossed for just seconds, moments that altered the entire course of Sam's existence. A couple of minutes from a lifetime that connected him with the life of Arthur Brewer, his long best friend and his secret supporter, along with

Deirdre, in the underground fight to rid Ireland of British rule.

The Big Fella wasn't all that big, but he displaced a lot of air when he moved. He had a big aura, and the size and strength of his heart caused most people to think of him as something of a giant. He snuggled down now into the collar of his greatcoat; they had just left the hotel where Collins had spent the night. In his room, Sam had witnessed the Corkman swear a twenty-year-old Dubliner into the Irish Volunteers, before sending him on an errand that if he wasn't very smart and very lucky could cost him his young life. It was this experience that had prompted Sam to ask why neither Collins nor Brendan O'Connor had sworn him in, even though he was a tried, proven and trusted man in what would come to be known as the Dublin Brigade.

"I've been involved since 1913, Mick. Deirdre Brewer and I went to Berlin that May, and the arms we bought over there were ferried all over the town aboard Arthur Brewer's barges – handguns and small amounts of explosives hidden in bags of bran mash and barley. And how many times since then, I'm not sure, but I've been to America twice, once with Deirdre, again posing as my missus."

"It wasn't my decision," Collins said, "not to swear you in. But when I was told why, it made sense to me. Sorry that I didn't fill you in, tell you the story." He turned to look at Sam, a rueful grin on his face. "I've had other things on my mind this last couple of years."

"I'm not what you'd call bothered," Sam spoke

truthfully, "but I'm bloody curious, and I don't mind admitting it."

"You don't need anybody to give you a reference, Samuel. We've seen your brains and your guts in action, and you get ten out of ten. We were thinking that if you got nabbed, well, we wanted you to be able to say that you were not a member of any republican movement and the Brits know it was the truth. And it was the right thing to do. You've been more use to us outside than you would have been in. I hope that satisfies you," he grinned, "because it's all you're going to get."

"I'm glad I've been able to help out." Sam felt a dart of emotion. It was as though they were saying goodbye, or something like that, which he didn't understand at that moment. "I want to be with you when it's time, Mick."

Collins looked sideways at him. "No, Samuel," his tone and attitude were formal, as they always were when he was about to tell you something to which he would brook no argument. "You will not be with me, but I hope you will be with me and me with you, when this part of things is over."

"I'll be with you to the bullet," Sam said flatly. "If I have to, I'll give my life for what we're trying to achieve. Not that I'm anxious to kick the bucket."

As they headed for the city limits, Collins said, "When this is over, some of us will be dead, possibly a lot of us. I don't want your name on the roll. The country's never going to be the same again."

Sam heard regret in the man he admired most of all, despite what Sam called the Big Fella's tender years – Collins was just twenty-six years old. "If I get hit by a stray bullet or anything, should I be dispatched, there'll be others to contact you, Samuel, aside from Carrots O'Connor. We're making a big statement today, but it could be a while before a lot of us will be out and about again. You don't think we can create a violent uprising, and go out for a pint later?"

Sam nodded, blowing the horn at a mongrel with a death wish. "At least the whole world is going to know we've said 'enough'."

"Do you have faith in God, Sam?"

"Not specifically. In a way, I sort of live as though there's no God, but I have rules for myself that are kind of goddish, if you see what I mean."

Collins smiled, but there was no warmth in it. "Being a bit of a mountain man, simple like, I believe that when there's no way out that you can see, God can make a way."

"I hope that's how it works out today, Mick. Should I head back to Sackville Street?"

"You best so," Collins chuckled. Sam wondered was he nervous? "At the risk of sounding pretentious, I have a date with destiny."

"Pearse and the others, they're very possibly great men," Sam said, "but you're cut from a different cloth. For all their qualities, not one of them has what you have. A lot of wonderful dreams are flying about, but you have to come through this day no matter what.

And you have to be standing, even if you're not free to go for a pint. We can wait for you. We will wait for you."

"I've had to let go of my own wonderful dream," said Collins, "the one that went 'this day the country will pass back into our hands, without a drop of blood being spilt'." He pulled a face, suggesting he must have been out of his mind. "I got a bit carried away. I wanted Ireland, want Ireland so badly to be free. I suppose I'm now saying at 'whatever cost' because I think the cost is going to be severe. I wish people could know about you and Carrots O'Connor and others I could name. But they can't know, for we'll need you again. So no medals, hopefully no bullets either."

Sam turned the car around. As they headed back into the centre of the city he asked, "What exactly do you need from me today? How can I best be of service to you, to the situation?"

"I want you to go home to your wife and family. Keep the head down," Collins said, as Sam stopped the car near the Sackville Street corner.

"I won't lie to you," Sam said. "I won't be able to sit at home. Come noon, I'll be here in the street. So if you need me . . ." he shoved out his hand and the Big Fella held it firm. "You have to survive the uprising, Mick."

"I intend to, Sam. It's only going to be a bare beginning, after all. Even if we won, and that's not going to happen, it'd still be just a start. There's politics here too, right? "

Collins moved to get out of the car. "You're as good

a man as ever I knew," he said with some feeling. "For a Dublin-Jackeen!" he flashed a quick grin. "God bless you, Samuel. I'll be seeing you."

"I hope so," Sam said, as Collins walked away. He was one of the most wanted men the country had ever known, and there he was barrelling along as if he was just Joe Soap on his way to his workplace. "And God bless you, too."

As Sam drove out of town, on his way to pick up Dee and Arthur at Dunbla he knew that he could not honour Collins's wish that he stay away until the smoke had died down. He could not sit still and wait for orders from Brendan O'Connor, or someone else, about what to do next. He would be back on Sackville Street before the rebels made it clear that they were there to fight the might of Great Britain. Even though this meant risking his life, he knew there was no way he could stay away at a nice, safe distance.

Collins wasn't thinking about Sam Sweet, not about any of the men that had helped this day come about. Mid-morning, he was busily marching behind Padraig Pearse, and Joseph Plunkett, and the Labour leader James Connolly. The time was nigh. The uprising could not be stopped now. They were marching into history.

Behind Collins, the column of volunteers marched with Connolly's men. They moved towards Sackville Street intent on taking the General Post Office, while Nelson's Pillar, the monument to England's greatest admiral, looked down on the scene with its one good eye.

Collins believed that British time had come to an end in Ireland. Brendan O'Connor felt the same way. "It's closing time on the fuckers, Sam," had been his last words to Sam the night before.

By this time, Sam Sweet hoped both of his friends were right. "It ought to be closing time, Brendan. Let's hope it is."

As Sam drove south out of Dublin his feelings were mixed but he was hoping that the Germans deliver on time the guns and ammunition he'd bought and paid for in Berlin some weeks before.

He wanted the insurrection to work, wanted the English out – on that there was no equivocation in his mind. Admittedly the Brits had turned the riverside town of mud and poverty and despair, into the seventh greatest city in the Empire, but they hadn't bothered their arses to rid the place of the poverty and disease, nor the despair in the hearts of too many of its people. "A great time for the Brits running the show," he said, quietly bitter, as he tasted the same stew the world had been dishing out to the Jews forever and a day. His recent years of study had turned him inside out. The chap who minded his own business, in the hope that he'd always have a business to mind, had left town, leaving in his place a man who had to be involved in the fight, even if it was going to cost him his life. The sacrifice that Carrots O'Connor and Cormac Doyle, two young men he had come to know very well, made on a daily basis had been the torch that burned away the wick of Sam's resistance.

Easter Monday morning, he found Deirdre more than concerned about Cormac. She gave Sam scrambled eggs and toast and tea and told him her brother had stayed the night, promising her he would not risk his life in the uprising. "When I came downstairs an hour ago, he was gone, Sam. If he dies today it could kill mammy. She's hardly over granny dying. Is there anything we can do to stop him getting himself killed today?" she sat facing him at the table in the breakfast room. "Josie," she said to the maid-servant, "should Mister Brewer come downstairs, would you ask him to join myself and Mister Sweet."

When the girl had left the room, Sam said, "Cormac's committed and very much his own man. He wouldn't thank either of us for interfering. This is probably the biggest day of his life."

"Are we going to be able to help in any way?" Hearing the logic of Sam's reasoning she tried to let go of what she wanted. "It really is happening today?"

"It certainly is," Sam drank tea and got a cigarette going. "I'm going back into town right away. If you and Arthur want to come with me, I'm available. Collins asked me to stay away, but it doesn't sit right with me."

Dee looked at him across the table, concern etched into her eyes. "You could get killed." The thought turned her face to ashes. She rose and came around the table. He stood up to accept her embrace, his heart longing to say something, something he had no right to say. Her nearness, the scent of her perfume filled him with longing and he thought again how lucky he had been to know her in his life. "If anything happened to you," Deirdre cut the thought. "I mustn't even think about it. But why did Collins ask you not to be there when it starts? He was obviously concerned for your safety."

"He says we, the likes of you and me and Arthur, we'll be needed after today. Today will never be over till the Brits are out."

Dee stepped back and like Sam, resisted the recurring urge to say things that ought not to be said between friends, no matter how much they loved each other. "I'm coming in with you. Arthur is very likely going to sleep a lot today. He had a bad night with the booze."

Before they left, Sam got the call he was waiting for from Brendan O'Connor. "All I can tell you is that Roger Casement left Germany with the guns. If he hasn't arrived here yet, it'll be too late. The manoeuvres are definitely on for noon."

This was the agreed code he and Sam used in relation to the uprising. In the previous week, Padraig Pearse, commandant of the volunteers, had let it be known that that the whole force was to be ready for three days of manoeuvres over the Easter weekend, the holiday falling on the twenty-third of April.

The IRB leaders, who had planned the rising, had fixed this date as far back as January. But they didn't get around to telling MacNeill, chief-of-staff of the volunteers and other men prominent in the IRB. This was a conspiracy inside a conspiracy, and it would cost lives and broken hearts – all part of the politics that Collins had mentioned during their early morning drive.

When Sam parked his car at Stephen's Green, he and Deirdre walked down Grafton Street, intent on looking like a couple out for a stroll. Dee had even worn an elegant Easter bonnet to set off her pale-blue two-piece suit. Sam was casually attired, a Norfolk hacking jacket over cavalry twill pants and light-brown walking boots. He wore an apple-pie tasselled cap which he touched over a warm smile for those they met on the street. He swung his cane casually like a man without a care in the world as they headed towards Sackville Street, and what lay in wait for the British authorities.

"I don't see a lot of military about," Dee observed, as they passed Trinity College.

"It's like the whole British Army had a night out on the tiles." Sam was bemused. "In recent weeks the Brits have had a whole team of detectives shadowing James Connolly. They have been practically camped out in Liberty Hall, which was also the active HQ of the entire republican movement. From a Brit point of view, the police were right to want to deprive the volunteers of what weapons we've got. The bloody chief secretary and his team, saying, 'No,' let them be, well it was just amazing! Diplomats, of course, wanting to avoid confrontation and hoping to Christ they can avoid a rising they hope is never going to happen."

"And luckily, they haven't enough evidence yet to lock up the republican leadership," Dee said.

"We got lucky there," Sam said. "Let's hope that

same luck has held out for Roger Casement and the guns we bought in Germany."

"Surely you'd have heard if they had landed."

"Oh, don't remind me. Every bone in my body tells me it hasn't worked out. A bit fanciful, I thought, Casement demanding the Germans provide officers to help us work the bigger guns, asking for a German U-boat to bring the stuff in. There was no way the Jerries were ever going to stick their necks out." Taking Dee by the arm, he drew her close as though whispering, as a pair of RIC constables came towards them at O'Connell Bridge.

Sam was extremely prescient in his assessment of the dilemma facing the forever patriotic Roger Casement. As the facts revealed after the event, this poor man was running close to despair from the moment he began dealing with the people in Berlin. "He discovered too late that the Germans would not send officers," Sam revealed to Dee some time later. "The Jerries needed a year's notice to give themselves a good scratch." He could say this with conviction – his experience in buying of arms over the years entitled him to this. "Are you surprised they wouldn't risk sending a U-boat to Dublin, Dee, because I'm not."

"They sent the Aud," Dee said, "and they weren't in need of something to occupy them, Sam."

"They were already at war when they agreed to help, for money," Sam sniffed. "They could have told us to shag off then and there but they didn't. They saw Ireland as a stepping-stone to England, that's why they pretended they were going to do all kinds of things."

During the weeks following the surrender, bits and pieces of jagged information came to them through one of their spies at Dublin Castle.

Hearing the stories, Sam could see poor Casement in despair, devoid of hope that the arms would get through the British naval blockade. Filled with foreboding, he tried to get messages through to Sam and others in Dublin. The Rising should be called off, he urged. He was convinced it could not succeed and that it would, in fact, end in disaster. Poor Casement – well-meaning patriot that he was, and a thoroughly decent human being – was hanged for treason by the British later in the year, because he had attempted, single-handed, to stop an insurrection by his fellow patriots against the might of England.

As history would reveal, the captain of the Aud possessed enough skill to penetrate the British blockade. He also managed to survive one of the worst gales of the century, sailing into Tralee Bay, where there was no-one there to meet him and sadly no green signal from the shore that night.

British Intelligence knew all about the Aud, and the Royal Navy sailed into Tralee Bay and ordered the Aud's master to proceed to Queenstown. He appeared to accept the order and promptly blew up his boat. In this way, the guns and ammunition turned to powder and then to nothing as the wild waters off Ireland's south-west coast snuffed out the moment, surely a harbinger of things to come in Dublin City on Easter Monday.

This story Sam would only discover later. The same thing applied to the comedy of errors and mismanagement caused by rivalries among the leaders of the volunteers. The insurrection was always on, as far as Pearse and his lot, were concerned.

Not so in the case of MacNeill. He had been kept in the dark originally for fear that he would countermand this decision, and he did have the power to do so. He did agree to let his people take part when Pearse told him that Casement and a huge shipment of arms had arrived in Tralee aboard the Aud. MacNeill promptly turned about once more the moment he knew of the debacle in the harbour at Tralee.

He went so far as to place an advertisement in the *Sunday Independent* newspaper, informing his volunteers that manouvres had been cancelled. British Intelligence was very pleased with this development, their own intelligence telling them that the internecine warfare was in full swing within the Republican movement itself. They were not sufficiently prescient to understand that the conflict in the hearts of the various rebel factions were the seeds of the civil war to come, ambition playing a large role in the saga despite the number of idealistic figures who were anything but self-seeking.

The bravery of men like Padraig Pearse and James Connolly, as well as others in the movement, was far and beyond the call of duty. Pearse knew that his taking part in the rising was the same thing as committing suicide. "The day is coming when I shall be shot," he told his mother. "I will be swept away, and my colleagues like me." James Connolly said, "The odds against us are a thousand to one." He knew in his heart that the rebels had no chance in the battle ahead.

As the noon hour approached, the staff officers and the civil servants at Dublin Castle did not believe that there would be an uprising. At the most, the rebels would have twelve or thirteen hundred men, perhaps another two hundred and fifty members of the Citizen Army who didn't read the *Sunday Independent*. Nobody could be silly enough to go up against the British army with that handful of men, very few of them actually trained to expertly stay alive while fighting to the death. The insiders at the Castle discussed the slaughter at Ypres which had been well covered by the Fourth Estate – the debacle was too recent for anyone to have forgotten it. The battle of Verdun was happening as they spoke, so surely the Irish had too much common sense to throw their lives away on the say-so of a school teacher and a trade unionist and the like.

"Sam, have we any way to find out if Cormac is in the GPO?" Sam felt Deirdre's concern for her brother's safety in the grip of her hand on his arm.

"I'll go in there," he said quietly. "See if he's there. If he is, Dee, I'll do all I can to make him come away with me."

"We might stand more chance if I came with you. I know he respects you – you saved his life that night you picked him up on the road with a bullet in him. But, he finds it hard to refuse me anything," Dee said.

"Is that a fact?" Sam was grinning, glad of a chance to lighten things even for a moment or two. "He has trouble refusing you anything? Imagine that!"

"Stop it, you!" She slapped his arm, linking her own underneath it then, as she went back to being his wife. As they got to the Sackville Street corner, she said, "I can't get over how few soldiers seem to be about,"

"Keeping a low profile," he said quietly. "Don't want to do anything to fuel even the vaguest possibility of an armed uprising." As Sam spoke his eyes were on the columns of volunteers now turning from the quays onto Sackville Street, no more than a hundred yards away.

"Surely they must see that the guts of a thousand men . . ." Dee was clearly puzzled, worried too, as evidence of the conflict to come was establishing itself before her eyes. "Men that are bearing arms and marching as though they mean business . . ." Her voice trailed off, she suddenly was lost for words, her eyes wide as she viewed the columns of men passing them by, their huge presence foreshadowing something that now seemed inevitable.

"Don't forget the Brits have their hands full over in Europe. They lost a lot of men at Ypres, and the Great War is far from being over and done with." Sam played Job's comforter without much conviction in his voice.

"You've heard the rumour they're having a laugh at us, the Brits? 'Marching, the Irish love a good march!'" she exclaimed in a false voice. "They've seen it all too often, to take it seriously, Sam. Is that why we're not seeing so many soldiers?"

"Well, we've had illegal and semi-private armies up and down the country for a right few years now. Where do you think Slattery's Mounted Foot came from?" Sam was referring to a popular song written with a sense of irony in relation to Irish soldiering down the years. "The Brits are still busy laughing at their little joke. So, why would they take today seriously? And, of course, we've been deluging them with false claims of illegal training and armed activity, sending them addresses of bomb-making factories that don't exist. Half the time now they don't know what to think. I'd say most of the regulars, the Tommies, would be happy to get home. The Intelligence mob, we've run them off their feet. As the fella said, too much intelligence produces a cloud of ink."

"Let them laugh so," Dee said as they crossed the road in the wake of the marching volunteers. "We're not as daft as they think we are."

"One or two of them infiltrated the IRB, and the Citizen Army. They were soon spotted. Instead of shooting them, we fed them info, had them hoofing off to check the political situation in Ahascragh and such like. Down to Sherkin Island we sent them; they were going to uncover a huge stack of bombs and stuff," Sam chuckled. "We, the Irish, are like the Jews. You get enough persecution for long enough, the misery handed down along all the years – children're practically born with a talent for secrecy. But, I still say, we're getting off lightly at the minute because Kaiser Bill and his mates are keeping England busy on the continent of Europe, thanks be to God."

Even as they reached the far side of the street and were heading towards the GPO, Sam had the uneasy feeling that this was the calm before the bombardment. England was too big, too organised for too long in the military department. These were the people who invented modern-day soldiering, taking what the Romans had created to then develop and refine it into the model that was copied wherever men were now going to war. And since expansionism was still a growth industry, a man could have a future in his country's army, as long as he managed to stay alive.

"A blind man could see that the volunteers have been pouring into the GPO," Dee said. "Don't tell me the British Army hasn't noticed."

"If they know where you are, Dee, it saves them having to go looking for you. So you're right. But they'll pretend the lads are just out for an Easter Monday parade, showing their mettle. They'll take cognizance of the fact that just by being out there armed and marching, they are saying they're ready to fight to free Ireland. They won't make a move till they have to. The Brits are very skilled – they don't need to fire the first shot."

There was something else that Sam didn't think to

mention. Eoin MacNeill's advertisement in the *Sunday Independent* cancelling all manoeuvres for the three-day weekend would have told the British they had nothing to fear from the die-hards marching the streets. Possibly as a result of the advertisement, large numbers of men had been given leave, and were last seen heading for the Fairyhouse race meeting. As far as the Intelligence section could read it, the part-time soldiers, many of them not even in uniform, were out for the fresh air. Playing soldiers was a safe and relatively inexpensive way to spend a bank-holiday afternoon. Nobody in his right mind would think that these toy soldiers were about to take on the might of the British army. The Irish were quaint in many ways – they could be dashed poetic at times – however, they were not madmen on a suicide mission, not of an Easter Monday!

Since he had first become involved with Collins and the others, Sam had studied pictures of the enemy provided by IRB intelligence. He knew a great many of the faces operating out of Dublin Castle, the main centre of British Intelligence in Ireland. On Easter Monday morning he was looking for some of those faces, searching the crowds gathering along Sackville Street. Seeing not one, he concluded by the time he and Dee reached the General Post Office, that the spies and the Special Branch officers he would have recognised, must have gone horse-racing, too.

He smiled, more than surprised by how well the worst-kept secret of the year had given no pause to the authorities. "The contradictory ads in the paper, the general air of an amateur theatrical show – they were laughing at us, Dee, instead of working out that we tend to come round the houses about a lot of things." Sam actually chuckled as he stopped outside the GPO and began searching his coat pockets for something.

He and Dee stood watching as a thousand paramilitary personnel marched down Sackville Street as if they owned it. "In fairness to the authorities," Sam said out of the side of his mouth, "they're men steeped in military discipline, tradition. Seeing that some of our lads are not even in uniform, they'd think that a bit of a laugh. They'll see the lads as stereotypical Irish types, whiskey on board'd be their assessment – so they view this as us being absolutely out-of-touch, trying to stir up some feeling in the public, but nuts enough to stage an insurrection, ah no, even the Paddie's can't be that stupid."

"So they do nothing unless we actually do something, Sam. It's hard to believe." Dee was looking around her as though expecting some conflict to take place close by.

"If I'd told you there'd be conflicting ads, newspaper ads saying 'It's On', then another ad saying 'It's Off', wouldn't you have enjoyed a chuckle at my expense?" He smiled at the very idea. "I mean, think of it from the Brits' point of view. All right, a thousand men, most of them wearing some kind of uniform – are they going to take on the greatest war machine the world has seen up to now? And for what – to ensure that the world and his wife might understand Easter Monday 1916 as the day the Irish waved goodbye to their second-class citizenship."

Even as Sam was commenting on the events on Sackville Street, the GPO had been taken over by the Rebels, most of the unit present being stationed on the upper floors, so that people could still buy a stamp or send a telegram for as long as possible before the insurgents shut up shop.

When Sam stepped in with Deirdre on his arm, the first person he saw was Cormac. He was acting as though he was composing a telegram, his long, light raincoat covering the machine-gun strapped to his waist. Seeing Sam and Dee, he avoided eye-contact. Sam hung back so that Deirdre could try and reason with her younger brother. Right away he saw that, for all her good intentions, she was not about to have her wish granted. Dee turned, pleading with her eyes for his input. She stepped aside as he crossed the floor and gave Cormac a nod. "I was with Mick Collins earlier. He told me to come and look for you. He wants me, and you and Brendan O'C out of here."

"What're you talking about?" Cormac's left eye twitched nervously, but his apparent resolution to die for Ireland seemed to have turned his jaw to steel. "He's been in here and said nothing to me about it."

"Why would he, when he knew I'd carry out his order," Sam looked about in an effort to remain offhand. "Now, come on, let's get out of here before we get locked in."

"I'm going nowhere, Sam," Cormac seemed to mean what he said.

"All right," Sam said, moving a little closer as

though to whisper something in the young man's ear. As Cormac leaned in to hear what was about to be said, Sam hit him with a short uppercut to the inner edge of his rib cage. Cormac exhaled a gush of air as Sam, already bending down, took him over his shoulder, all in one deft movement. Dee was wide-eyed with shock, but she heard Sam when he told her to go on ahead and keep people out of his way. Near the door, a volunteer stood in front of him until Sam said in a flat, authoritative voice, "I'm taking Cormac to the hospital. His wound from last week has opened up." The young volunteer stepped aside as Sam looked into his innocent blue eyes. All he could see was another 20-year-old going to the slaughter – felt sad that he was unlikely to see the volunteer again. By the time he carried Cormac onto the street, Dee had a hackney carriage waiting, so that in moments they were being driven south along Sackville Street towards O'Connell Bridge.

As they got to the corner of Abbey Street, soldiers were getting down from a truck, rifles at the ready. A stray piebald pony was passing Wynn's Hotel on its way to the corner of Sackville Street. A shot rang out – soldiers dropped to the ground while a sergeant barked orders.

Sam had seen the pony stagger on the gunshot, watched it as it fell dead by the hackney. "Jesus, Dee," he exclaimed in utter disbelief. "The first shot of the Uprising and it kills a shaggin' pony!"

Dee's held Cormac's head carefully on her lap, stunned by the death of the piebald. "I suppose that means there's no going back now," she whispered, as Sam gave her a warm hug of support across the inert body of her brother.

Moments later, Sam found himself having a chuckle at the idea that such a momentous moment should claim the life of a nag that had staked its own claim to freedom by breaking out of its ramshackle stable somewhere down off Abbey Street. "You couldn't make it up," he thought ruefully.

At noon, on this Easter Monday bank-holiday the crowds witnessing the marching Volunteers, and the men of the Citizen Army, had grown considerably. Sam and Dee sat quietly in the back of the cab with the inert body of Cormac between them as a troop of British soldiers crossed in front of them. They were close enough to the kerb to hear street gossip that the rebels had seized five or more major buildings on the northside of the Liffey.

"They've got nine on the southside, too," a man with a know-all type voice said with an inner-city accent.

Someone else volunteered the information "an' they have summa the railways stations," so that Sam could hear as they passed by.

"Do you think it possible, Sam?" Dee was wiping some spit from the corner of her brother's mouth.

"You know what street gossips like, Dee. Take it with a pinch of salt – they'll have us storming the Houses of Parliament in Westminster by teatime."

LEE DUNNE

As the hackney carriage passed over the Liffey into D'Olier Street on its way to St Stephen's Green where Sam had left his motor-car, the rebel leader Padraig Pearse emerged from the GPO to announce the creation of a Provisional Government for the new Irish Republic. As he nailed up the Proclamation outside, inside the building were James Connolly as his military commander, Tom Clarke, Joseph Plunkett – a seriously ill man brought there from a nursing home – Sean MacDermott and others, including the young rebel who was already being spoken of as a future leader, Michael Collins.

As Sam shifted Cormac from the hackney carriage into the back seat of his motor-car which he had parked across the street from the Shelbourne Hotel, Dee's brother came awake and immediately tried to get up and leave. Sam pushed him back against the seat as Deirdre got in by the opposite door.

"Please, please just listen a minute," Dee said.

"You lied to me," he spat the words at Sam, shrugging Dee's hand off his arm. "You'd no right to go along with this, Dee. It's my life and I'm entitled to be where I want. I should be with my comrades." He was deeply moved by his anger, his blue-green eyes glistening with tears, as were those of his sister.

In moments he was inconsolable, his head fell onto Dee's lap, his shoulders heaving over the racking sobs that tore out of him. "O, God!" he cried through the choking wall of pain. "I was so terrified, I could hardly

444

move. I was numbed by the fear that took me over while I was trying to act like a soldier in the post office."

Sam got behind the wheel and started the engine, while Dee silently willed her brother to let out the pain.

"Collins gave me strict orders to get out of town, Cormac," Sam called over his shoulder. "I give you my word on that. He wanted me, and the likes of yourself to be here when all this is over. Those were his very words – some of us have to stand back, just in case we're the only ones left when all is said and done."

Sam drove in the general direction of Leeson Street Bridge. Lorries carrying soldiers shot past the car in the other direction – from Beggar's Bush barracks, he thought, his lips tight as he considered what the men at the GPO and the other occupied buildings were about to face at the hands of British artillery.

"We're all involved," Sam said. "None of us is running away. The fight to set the country free, this is only the start of it. You're going to be needed, and not just to shoot soldiers. We're going to need your brains and the cunning you've developed during your years with the IRB. Nothing you've learned up to now is going to be wasted unless you get shot dead."

He headed out through Donnybrook and onto the road to Stillorgan and beyond, where Dunbla House lay close to Killiney Bay. As he reflected on his chat earlier with Collins, he knew he had been sincere when he said he was ready to die, if that's what it took, "although I'm not anxious to kick the bucket". He could see the Big Fella smile at the old-fashioned expression, and he had no problem in admitting to himself that, despite the hint of nobility in his statement, he was bloody glad to be alive at this minute.

He would later learn on the telephone that the rebels had one of two minor successes on the first day of the Rebellion, the most obvious one being the dispatch of a troop of lancers attempting an attack on the GPO. This charge was quickly repulsed, and the fact that the lancers sustained casualties drew cheers from some of the Easter holidaymakers on Sackville Street, who might well have been watching a game of football at Croke Park.

Sam knew from Brendan O'Connor's reports that the British were taken by surprise. They had placed too much faith in MacNeill's newspaper advert. Once they knew that the toy soldiers were not just out getting the air of an Easter Monday, troops were soon on their way from the Curragh and the other camps outside the city. At the same time, an appeal to London for reinforcements landed in the lap of the unstable Lord French who overreacted by ordering four divisions, that were desperately needed on the Western Front, to be alerted for transfer to Ireland.

What the mass of the Irish people didn't know, or hadn't been able to grasp, was that Home Rule expired on that Easter Monday, taking with it to the grave the hopes and the dreams of John Redmond and his Irish Nationalist Party. Many people though were brokenhearted by this event, some feeling it was just as well that Charles Stuart Parnell – the uncrowned king of Ireland – did not live to see his vision of 'peace in our time' burn up in the flames that were soon devouring the rebel-held areas of the city.

The rebels were not naïve. Many had come to the ball in the knowledge that they wouldn't see another Easter, drawing cold comfort from their belief that the waltz would be extended after this day and hopefully for generations to come. This was the only reason they needed to make them sacrifice their lives to the cause, reason enough so they said, as they prepared to dance to the death.

25

Dublin

Easter Week • 1916

Sam knew for a fact that many Dubliners were laughing and joking about the debacle they deemed the Rising to be. Some people found it hard to believe that the rebels had no wireless links between the strong points they had seized by Monday lunch-time, that Boys of Fianna na hEireann literally ran messages from place to place, this becoming impossible as the fighting got heavier and the casualty list began to grow.

Brendan O'Connor telephoned Joe early on Tuesday to tell him that martial law was declared because of an increase in looting.

"You'd think people couldn't sink that low, wouldn't you?" Brendan's disgust coated his voice. Sam had information that hadn't yet reached Brendan.

"British reinforcements are disembarking at Kingstown," he said, "so keep a low profile. I need you as much as Mother Ireland does." Kingstown was on the southern hem of the city coastline and would gather worldwide press coverage because a mad British officer, Captain Bowen-Colthurst, had three Irish journalists shot, including Sheehy Skeffington, a feminist and pacifist. Clearly it hadn't taken long for the atrocities to begin. Sam was able to pass this on to Brendan thanks to an arrangement he had made some time before with a Dublin journalist who was always in need of a bit of extra cash to support his unquenchable thirst.

"Tha' Bowen whatever he's called, Sam, he must be the same gobshite had the eighteen-pounders brought up from Athlone to bombard Liberty Hall, and nobody home except the shaggin' caretaker."

Wednesday saw the rebels outnumbered by twenty to one. The British now began to attack in earnest. The gunboat HMS Helga began shelling Liberty Hall from its berth on the Liffey.

On his way into town, Sam dropped in at Sandymount for a cup of tea with Lisa. While he sipped the brew in her sitting-room, both of them smoking cigarettes, she regaled him with gossip from her house in Monto.

"Murder going on so there is." Lisa was unusually fired up. "This officer that I see personally," she smiled, free to be open with her old friend, "he told me last night after we did it, few jars on board, relaxed as a pancake he was, said the top brass are up to their ears in red faces – a nine pounder went astray from that gunboat in the Liffey. It killed a sniper near the Castle – the thoughts of what it could've done – they're soiling their drawers in fear of demotion."

"The city's beginning to burn from the shelling. There's no food coming in from outside," Sam told her, wondering how long it would be before the Uprising was brought to its knees.

"Your man last night, he's a decent sort, a real gent, says there's no serious attempt being made to spare civilians. They don't give a shit."

A while later as Sam was heading into the city from Sandymount he had to drive around a huge holdup at Ringsend. He grabbed a news vendor, gave him sixpence. "What's the story? What's going on?"

"De Valera's squad ambushed British reinforcements marching in from Kingstown. Word is they inflicted heavy casualties."

As Thursday dawned, De Valera was still in command of Boland's; Countess Markievicz and Michael Mallin held the College of Surgeons; Eamonn Daly occupied the Four Courts; the GPO remained in the hands of Pearse and Connolly. A quarter of a mile away, Trinity College was a bastion of British occupation.

The rebels were quickly outnumbered, and so outweighed by the sheer volume of British artillery, that they had to consider surrender. James Connolly had been shot twice, hiding the first wound from his men. When he had a foot shattered by a second rake of gunfire, he needed morphia to carry on. Shortly after this he could not walk. Time was already running out for the Volunteers.

On Saturday morning it was all over. Padraig Pearse and James Connolly surrendered unconditionally, their orders to the Rebels passed on by the British military. Soon after, the commanders of the other strong points dropped their guns.

The Insurrection was over.

Sam stood, sickened, as the gallant men and youths who had lived to surrender with their pride and their dignity intact, were jeered, booed and spat at by many in the crowds lining the streets of Dublin. He had known that, generally, public opinion had been against the Rising, but to stand among men and women, who were jeering and spitting and making jokes about the prisoners passing by, made him wish he was somewhere else.

It would take a horrendous and tragic blunder by the British Government to bring about the U-turn of public opinion towards the survivors of the Uprising.

Sam was heading into the slums to check that Dee that safe and sound. He knew she was at some personal risk as she went about helping the poor and the destitute women with too many children.

He was coming for a meeting with his pet journalist, Larry Scott, having bought him a couple of large whiskeys as the newspaperman told him excitedly: "An order directly from the cabinet in London – the leaders will be court-martialled and shot."

"They can't do that; it's inhuman," Sam's reaction caused several heads in the pub to turn around.

"They can and they have, Sam. Unequivocal, over,

LEE DUNNE

kaput. And there's worse if that is possible." He raised his glass and the bartender moved down to serve him. "Only after they are dead will their families be informed."

Sam hurried away from Scott, wanting to get some air into his lungs after his time in the smoke-filled public house . Even more urgently he needed to see Deirdre, make sure she was all right.

"Thank God to see you, Sam," Deirdre was coming down to street level as Sam, prodded by some atavistic instinct, was on his way up the dilapidated staircase of a stomach-turning tenement in Poole Street. This was just one more foul-fever slum that should have been razed to the ground.

"Are you all right?" Sam reached for her hands, seeing that she was trying to hide her distress. Dee threw her arms about his neck and he held her, loving her, willing to hold her for as long as she needed to be supported, while she found a way to say what had just happened.

"The woman above, Milly Clarke, she's close to her time. She had agreed to come with me, let me find somewhere decent for her to have the child. Her man, his name is Denis, arrived a minute ago and won't hear of her leaving the dreadful room. And . . ." she stopped, almost fearful of carrying on.

"What?" Sam said, his hackles rising, as he responded instinctively to his concern for her well-being and safety.

"He exposed himself to me. He's got drink taken. He

tried to grab me – luckily there is no lock on the door. I got out before he could." Her voice trailed off, her breathing somewhat easier now.

Sam moved her up onto the landing. He gave her his hankie, and waited while she wiped perspiration from her brow. She wore a long apron over her dress, her hair was held above her head with combs. Sitting into the circle the combs formed, was a small white hat she always wore when she was in her role of midwife.

"I want you to stay here for a minute." He was deadly calm now, and he spoke to her with great care. "We'll get this woman out of here, have no doubt about that."

He killed the urge to run up the stairs, walking calmly. His chest was occupied by the same kind of the driving energy that fuelled his dismantling of Dinny and Shamey Foran those years before.

He pushed open the door Dee had described to him.

The smell that hit him caused him to blink and step back for a moment. Then he crossed the threshold. The room was a hovel – Dickensian poverty was the term that sprung to his mind.

On the floor a woman lay quite lifeless on the disgusting remnants of what had once been a mattress, her open eyes occupied by fear and pain.

Facing Sam was a large man of about thirty years of age. He sat on a chair, his head thrown back, holding a dark-green wine bottle to his lips.

On hearing the door open, he stopped drinking. Seeing Sam step in, he stood up menacingly, his Dutch courage evident in the way he handled the wine bottle like a weapon.

"We're to take Milly out of here to have the baby," Sam said in a quiet non-confrontational way.

"She's goin' nowhere, Wire. Now take off before I throw you down them stairs," the man assured Sam, his nonchalance suggesting great confidence in his ability to back this up.

Sam moved closer to him, his arms by his sides, his nostrils cringing still before the power of the stench in the room. "You misbehaved with the midwife. That wasn't a nice thing to do, Denis, when she is here to help Milly have her child in cleanliness and safety."

"Just get outa here, and don't annoy me, you." The man called Denis moved the bottle to remind Sam that it was ready for use. "Fuckin' dandy, comin' in here an' the nerve to tell me she's goin' with ye to have the babby. Get out before I lose me rag and mess up yer nice new suit. Get out, ye Jew-faced fuck!"

Denis didn't see Sam's foot move, the pain impacting upon his mind all the more grievous in its unexpectedness. His screech of agony brought Dee crashing into the room even as Sam stretched the big man with a drenched-in-anger punch to the side of his head.

The thought that this oaf should disrespect Dee had added immense power to the expediency of the blow, but as Sam was carrying Milly down the stairs, Dee following, he wondered how much more had been injected by his reaction to being called a Jew-faced fuck.

Having taken the trouble to check that the unconscious man was still alive, Dee had left him several aspirin. "Poor Denis, he's surely going to need them."

"He's luckier than he knows." Sam laid Milly onto the back seat of his car. "He deserves a beating for insulting you – and this poor creature here. What are we going to do with her?"

Joan Ryan, one of Dee's volunteer midwives, came out of a house further along the street and hurried to join them.

"How is Missus O'Keeffe?" Dee asked, as she sat in beside the pregnant Milly on the back seat.

Sitting in beside Sam, who was starting the car, Joan was very matter-of-fact. "She has miscarried, but wanting to get up, if you don't mind! I gave her a sleeping tablet. She won't lie down for long. How can she? She has eight children in that room with her. Thank God, her sister cares. She'll stay and give a hand."

Sam wanted to say something, felt the need to tell them they were mad to be bothering, that it was impossible to stem the tide of poverty that the poor seemed to recreate wherever they were.

"It's all right, Milly," Deirdre softly reassured the young woman who was distressed at that moment. "Hold on, dear. We'll have you indoors, and ready to have your baby in a few minutes." Sam caught her eye in the rear-view mirror. "Merrion Square, Sam, please," Dee said. "We need to hurry, but if you can avoid the bumps . . ."

She smiled at him in the mirror. "Easier for men, to avoid the bumps," she said, patting Milly's enormous tummy.

At four-thirty that afternoon, Milly gave birth to a boy in the bed Dee and Arthur had shared whenever he came to visit her from his own room. When she was satisfied that the young mother and her son were as comfortable as they could be, Dee came downstairs to join Sam for a cup of coffee before he went home to Leinster Road.

"We need a hospital, Sam, a hospital for mother and child. Not just a maternity hospital, a hospital that will be there for the children as they grow, with at least one specialist paediatrician. More children die in Dublin than most people know. We have got to do something."

"You're not thinking of having it here?" Sam said.

"It seems I have made a start in that direction." Her expression changed in response to his startled reaction. She softened, smiled and touched his hand. "What else could we have done with Milly today? Women are delivering babies in the hallways and the corridors of the city hospitals, not to mention hovels like the one Milly was lying in when I found her. Children are being born in the streets, being born and abandoned in the alleyways of this city. It's a national disgrace, and women and children are dying simply because they cannot get into a hospital," Deirdre spoke softly, but there was a glint of fire in her eyes, evidence of the weight of her muted anger. "I want a children's hospital, Sam, and I am going to get it."

"I don't doubt it for one minute," Sam nodded his head, all of his attention captured by the fire in Dee. "And don't ask me quite how, but I'm going to help you. All I meant about doing it here is that you can hardly have it, I mean, in Merrion Square. The nobs won't stand for poor women having babies in this part of town. They won't put up with snotty-nosed kids and their ma's coming here for help."

"What can they do? We own the house. We can do what we like with it," Dee's voice plunged into confrontational mode.

"Sell this place. Use the money to buy something else that's more suitable, in an area that's not this expensive. You could buy two-dozen houses on Cork Street or somewhere, for the cost of this place. And, as you're going to be working with the very poor, they might feel easier about coming to you if you weren't right here in the golden square."

Dee's eyes widened with interest, her brain doing some mental arithmetic. "Buying a number of houses – that would certainly be a start, a real beginning to what might one day become a custom-built hospital for women and children."

"You're an incredible bloody woman," Sam rose to go, and without thinking about it, kissed her gently on the lips. "I've been saying it for years, and you just keep on getting better and better, so I have to keep saying it."

"You're not only my guardian angel." She hugged him close. "You're the spirit that fires me with good feelings." She hugged him again, and he somehow resisted the need to crush her to him. In the moment he wanted that more than anything he could imagine. She looked at him, so that he said, "What?"

"It's probably very unladylike of me to ask."

"That's never stopped you before," Sam snorted a short laugh.

"What did you do to Milly's man, Denis, to make him yell in such agony? Or shouldn't I ask such a question?"

Sam shrugged. "He knew he had me for height and strength – he was tall. So I just cut him down to size."

"Yes, I know. How? What did you do?

"I gave him an unmerciful root in the ballocks, Dee. I kicked him where the sun never shines." He watched her as he said it, not sure how this description was going to land on her.

She simply exploded into a ribbon of laughter, hugged him close until she found her voice. "You're an amazing bloody man. Where on earth did you ever learn to do that?"

"Stuff sticks to you when you grow up on the streets like I did. Nobody has to teach you how to fight dirty – on the street that's the only way. I've got the street in me like another sense."

Back home he closed the hall door quietly behind himself. He checked his watch. It was five-thirty. He was pleased, having promised Gloria that he would make every effort to be home for Friday dinner, even if he would not always be able to observe the Sabbath due to business pressures.

Dancers of Fortune

Hanging his hat and coat on the hallstand, he glanced at the great gilt mirror on the wall facing the sitting-room door. "The pepper and salt is thriving," he smiled at his reflection, patted his washboard stomach, adjusted his watch chain across his cord waistcoat and stuck his head into the front room. As he had expected, his mother was not in her chair by the fireplace. She never was at this time of a Friday. She was a huge part of the household, and she and Gloria worked side by side to prepare the food for the evening meal. He went in and shut the door. He lit a cigarette, and sat down by the tiny fire that burned all day, his heart full of Dee and what she meant to him.

His mind danced with her idea of the hospital for kids, and he thought of how much she had given the country in the three years leading up to the Uprising a few months before. It was clear that she needed help to even begin tackling the problem that existed in the slums of the city. Equally clear to him was the fact of his need to help her help the less fortunate. He had to – he had to be there by her side in the trenches of poverty. For his own peace of mind he had to spend as much time as he could by her side – his heart needed this anyway, and he was all too aware that when he was by her side he seemed more alive in spirit than ever before.

26

Greystones and Dublin

Summer • 1916

Once the children began their school holidays, the
Sweet family moved to their summer house near the
beach at Greystones, the spot where Sam had first laid
eyes on Gloria Rose as she performed in Big Bill
Boswell's tent by the water's edge, while his lover
Victoria had teased him that here was the Jewish mare
to mother his brood.

Sam drove into the city to conduct his business
affairs while Gloria and Esther, Sarah and Samuel
simply lived like holidaymakers for the months of June,
July and August. Greystones, just nineteen miles from
Dublin, had its own railway station and was essentially
a middle-to-upper-middle-class residential town,
where the tradespeople touched their caps to the
residents, apart from those who lived on the wrong side
of the poverty line.

By the early September life returned to normal and

Sam was reading by the fire as he waited to join the family for their Friday dinner. When the sitting-room door opened, he looked up from his book as Gloria stuck her head in. She wore an apron over a dark-blue dress and her hair, which she had allowed to grow somewhat in the last couple of years, was tied back behind her head.

"Just making sure you are comfortable, Samuel."

"Fine," he nodded his head. "I'll be with you all in a minute."

"Take your time. Dinner will be twenty minutes yet," she smiled, "at least."

She was about to leave when Sam asked, "May I ask you a question, Gloria?"

She paused, her eyes opening in surprise. A faint smile came onto her mouth and she bowed her head slightly, "Of course, Samuel."

"I'm curious, about your hair," he said without preamble. "Naturally, I'm happy to see that you've been allowing it to grow again. I'm wondering why."

"There's no mystery, Samuel. It began as a mark of respect for the brave people who risked their lives in the Uprising, who are even now carrying on the fight underground. I did it for them and for me – I am no longer decimated, totally in mourning for the past life. Looking forward is where my interest lies. I have a fire in me, a burning need to do something, to help bring about some change in however small a way before my life ends. We shall only pass this way the once." She allowed her words settle before she said, "Does that answer your question?"

"Thank you, yes it does. Have you a specific project in mind? One to which you might commit?"

"There is something, Samuel, but I'm not prepared to talk about it at present. Should the time come when you need to know where my interests lie outside of the home, I will not hesitate to tell you. Now, I must get back to the kitchen."

He sat there nodding to himself in a vaguely appreciative fashion, not surprised but certainly intrigued. He lit a cigarette, drew the smoke down deep, feeling content that the household was now a peaceful unit that created no more than the usual day-to-day disturbances. The grim dramas of its earlier years were a thing of the past. This was due entirely to the fact that he had let Gloria know about Arthur's alcoholic amnesia and the ongoing insane search for the woman of the summer solstice.

He could see her still as she wheeled to face him, her face a mask of horror under the skullcap of blue-black hair that seemed to have been painted onto her head. She had floundered as she sought for her voice, words that could not come since she was gagging on mental vomit that seemed to have the power to stop her heart.

Sam knew that he had spoken with care, that it was not his tone or his attitude that was causing her to choke on her inability to breathe. He went to her and gave her a flat-handed slap between the shoulder blades, hearing the great burp of air that shot from her mouth as the air bubble burst in her chest.

"It's all right, Gloria. I'm not blaming you, or Arthur.

All I feel now is relief. Now that we know what was has been driving you," He took a breath, not wanting to rub salt into the heart wounded. "We can do something about things, now that we know what's been causing your pain. I'm not here to play judge and jury."

She collapsed into his arms, and he held her while the compounded pain and shame and sorrow pumped out of her. Several minutes passed before she was relieved sufficiently to mumble, "I am so sorry, Sam. You deserved better. You were never less than decent to me. You will never know what I have lived with since that night."

"It doesn't matter, Gloria. Not now."

She stepped back from him, accepting his hankie to wipe her eyes and blow her nose. He stood there silent, wanting only to help her.

"How can it not matter? What I did, it was unforgivable."

"It was life happening, Gloria. If I hadn't been so hungry for the deal I made that same night, you and I might have been lovers and all could have been so different. I'm not blaming myself but I feel I must be, at least in part, responsible for what happened after I left you alone."

"You leaving the party, yes it contributed, but Sam, it had nothing to do with you, not really. I was weak. I drank too much. I was the last person that should ever have done that. I had seen, I had lived with the horror of what drink could do to someone. Jem Riley was not an evil man; when he drank he turned into a demon. I drank that night like someone hoping something would happen to them, for them, I don't know. It was shameful, and all the more so because I thought it was something that it was not, something that it could never have been. My God, I pray that you really can forgive me in your heart. I don't know that I could do the same were the situation reversed. I honestly don't think I could let it go, forgive you, pick up where we left off."

"I'm not looking for that," Sam said calmly. "But you should know that Arthur remains the best friend I have ever had. He turns into some kind of demon when he drinks a lot – there is some sickness there that has the medical profession in a quandary, though Paddy Lote says they are coming to grips with it – alcoholic amnesia due to injury to the brain caused by alcohol. Arthur has no memory of you, your face, from your night together. Surely that's proof of what I suppose they call pathology."

Gloria's eyes were almost grey in the sitting-room light, the violet power sucked out of them by the strength of her distress. "Sam," she said while holding onto the back of a chair, "he threw money on the bedside table as he was leaving. He didn't know me, didn't recognise me, he thought I was a . . . he thought he had been in bed with a prostitute."

"I know." Sam embraced her with care, while she, sensing this and feeling no threat in his generosity of spirit, welcomed his arms. "Arthur told me everything that happened," he assured her, "Next day he didn't even know he had told me. This happens to him when he drinks too much. Paddy Lote says that after many years of heavy drinking, it can happen to people even when they are not actually imbibing. It's a frightening prospect, and Arthur is well advanced, so Lote says. Arthur meant no disrespect to you. Many times since then he has asked me why are you so distant, why have you not wanted our children to play together, grow up together, when he and I are so close and Dee is so willing to be your friend."

Gloria used the hankie again, and found it necessary to sit down. "My legs feel like lead. I am weary, Sam, but I swear to you I will never stop being grateful for these moments. It's just possible I can make some kind of life for myself, be of some use in the world." Her face paled, she seemed to feel a dart of pain as though she'd been stabbed with a knife. "Wonderful as this is," she gasped as though her throat was made of parchment, "it does not help where Sarah and Eddie are concerned. Forgive me for having to say this, but we have no guarantee that Sarah is not Arthur's daughter."

Sam poured a drink of sherry for her, and insisted she sip it. "I have something to tell you, Gloria, and I urge you to please just listen 'til I finish."

Fixing himself a brandy, he lit a cigarette. Then he told her Dee's story of the birth of Eddie Brewer. Gloria sat there entranced, her face registering a gamut of conflicting emotions as she heard how orphan Eddie replaced Dee's stillborn baby, due to the presence of an old woman of the roads becoming at the right moment an administering angel.

"You mean that even if Sarah is Arthur's child, she

is still not blood-related to Eddie?" Gloria articulated the question quietly and firmly.

"That's exactly what I'm saying. And I ask you to believe me. Kelly and Dee and I, we're the only ones who know what happened. And, trust me, Dee doesn't know about the night with yourself and Arthur. She is aware that he goes with other women from time to time. He still goes out there searching for the girl – you – that he found that night. My guess is he will die trying to find her again."

Sam smoked heavily, at peace with the philosophy of acceptance and forgiveness, but somewhat discommoded still. His need to control every situation rebelled against his newly-found live-and-let-live way of being. He allowed a smiling grimace inside himself, 'Always thought all that reading would get you in bother some day.' He let the thought move out, admitting he found it easier to allow life to happen rather than trying to control every moment, every situation, everybody with whom he came into contact.

Rising from the chair by the fire, he made a vow to himself that he would not go back to that night, the revelation to Gloria, ever again. It was water under the bridge, a minor event in the great scheme of things, even if it had wrecked lives with the inevitable pain that came with the words I Want, I Want, which he now regarded as a curse on humanity.

Before going to dinner with his family, he went to the bathroom and threw some cold water onto his face and ran a comb through his hair. As he dried his hands he was captured for a moment – he was back there in the sitting-room reliving the moments when he had felt a little hot and bothered. He rubbed the towel against his hands and found that his connection with the sense of touch set his mind free of all but the moment he was in. He smiled at his reflection in the mirror over the wash basin. "Old habits die hard, my friend. Don't expect a trouble-free journey simply because you want to be free." He held the towel up and rubbed his hands again, slowly this time, again aware that he was just where he was, here and now, in the moment. "Looks like you may have stumbled on a way to quit going mad over the past and worrying so much about the future. So, remember the power of touch – it stills the mind." As he left to go in to dinner he wondered about the other four senses and he made a vow to experiment with them in the days ahead.

Gloria's metamorphosis began soon after that day, but there was not to be a happy, romantic outcome for Sam and Gloria as a couple. They remained friendly and civil, and in every way decent to one another, joined by their commitment to the children and Esther. He accepted that, despite the workable outcome, their marriage had been a mistake and felt no need to try and give it the kiss of life. It gave him pause though – took him to wondering was he to live out the rest of his life as a celibate. He and Victoria had come to the end of their romantic road some four years earlier before turning into a couple of long-time friends. In moments like this he sometimes remembered to connect with the sense of touch. When he did this he found that it worked every time – just the touch of his fingertips to his face or his ear, or his arm, brought him into the present moment. This new-found habit was a real blessing during his visits to Vicky who now lived permanently at her house in Fitzwilliam Square.

He found seeing her hard these days – his once beautiful lover, now in her forties had been turned into a fragile, ageing woman by some wasting disease for which, apparently, there was no known cure. He had not heard the malady given a name by Victoria not did he look for one. He had his own idea as to what might be the problem but since he'd recently had a full medical check-up which included blood tests,

Sam was happy to remain in ignorance of Vicky's precise condition.

He had taken a twice-yearly assessment of his health, compiled by the ageing doctor who was a very agreeable man. "You're fortunate in that you don't drink like we Irish," Lote remarked after his latest set of tests. He paused, seemed momentarily embarrassed, "Sorry, Sam, of course, you are Irish. But your race, the Jews, they seem to have the right approach to alcohol, whereas we Celts rush at it like moths to the flame that takes one's very life."

So, Sam, at forty-seven years of age, got another encouraging bill of health – Lote assuring him that were he to go on living as he was now doing, there was no reason why he should not live to claim his allotted three score and ten.

He had women friends, several attractive ladies with the same needs as himself, and he used them as they used him without anyone being under any illusion that what happened between them was anything more than friends enjoying each other in bed. But he had lost interest in sex for its own sake since he had finally come to accept his love for Deirdre. This had been happening over the years – they had been pals since he was a teenager and she a young girl. When it came to be, when he was able to take in the fact that he was in love with, and indeed, loved Dee, he was astonished and elated all in the same moment. It had burst on him like a summer rain shower that you welcomed with open arms and your head thrown back in the laughter that feeling so good allowed you in abundance.

He knew from then on that had Deirdre been a widow he would have asked her to marry him. In his eyes, she had turned out to be the perfect woman and though he never said a word about his feelings for her, he spent as much time as time allowed in her company. For her part she always seemed delighted that they found so much time to be together, their trips abroad to buy guns and ammunitions for the IRA had been all the more memorable since he found out how deeply he felt – even though there had never been a suggestion that they were anything more than great friends.

He knew without even considering it that he would never have done anything that might have offended her, this being something apart from his sense of loyalty to Arthur. It never occurred to him that his developing feelings for Dee were mirrored by what she now felt for him. He never did or said anything that would transgress on their idyllic relationship, though at times his heart ached to hold her close in that special way, and in time, his dreams included the one where he would wake up to find her lovely face on the pillow next to his own.

Within months of the uprising, Collins was in touch with him through Brendan O'Connor. The Big Fella was incarcerated in Frongoch, the prison camp in Wales, along with others who had survived the bloody carnage that the Insurrection had been.

Being in prison did not mean that Michael Collins was out of action. Far from it – the message being that The Troubles, which he called Troubles for the Brits, were far from over. The Big Fella went on to assure one and all that before long, they would be fighting again for the right to be free.

That same week, Sam dropped in on four-fingered Louie. He now lived in the Long Lane cottage Sam had bought for him a few years before. He had also arranged that Louie receive enough to live on, this reaching him through the post every Monday morning. Louie was getting on now, still bragging that he could pull a handcart, one hand or not, but more than happy to accept Sam's decency even though he reserved the right to go out selling or totting if he felt like it. Sam encouraged this in his old friend. The call of the street never left you, he knew this from his own experience, often seriously considering at various times that he might run a market stall himself on a Sunday, just to be out there again, keeping the knack alive just because it was there.

The problem, of course, was time since his business world continued to expand. He now had assistants – Brendan O'Connor ran a tight ship over the building and construction company, and Cormac Doyle was in charge of the building supplies. Sam reasoned that a young man who could get shot for a belief and survive his own fear was more than capable of running a limb of any business.

"I don't know if I was imagining things, Samuel . . ." Louie said to him, as they sat playing chess and drinking tea that the old man still made in an ancient samovar. "The big man, the one came to Charlemont Street, his name eh?"

"Dinny Foran you mean?"

"Yes, the same man. Big and ugly, his stinking breath something a person would not forget in a hurry. I never got close to a crocodile, this not being a complaint you understand. The smell, it would be appropriate I feel to a crocodile, an alligator, when you consider the diet."

Sam smiled as Louie took his own circuitous route to wherever he was going – he never tried to move the old man along. He loved the ramble every story took, partly in English, partly German with a smattering of Yiddish before the direction and the outcome were revealed. At times like these he felt glad that he could switch off the life and just be with his old mate, if only for a few hours at a time.

"I saw him up near the Four Courts, a few days ago."

The abruptness of Louie's statement took Sam by surprise.

"Are you sure?"

"That Foran, I am not likely to forget. He told me to find a hole and crawl into it, looked at me like I was some kind of maggot. And he said the word Jew like it dirtied his foul mouth. He came that morning to kill Sam Sweet dead. How could I forget him, mistake him for someone else? No. That could not happen. The man I saw was the man you sent packing from Dublin all those years ago with his brother, the stupid one with two left feet."

The remembered anger and hatred that he had felt for the Foran brothers took over his mind for several seconds before he could remind himself to come into the present moment. He licked his lips, sipped a bit more tea, giving all his attention to the taste. His mind became still and he smoked a cigarette. Louie watched him, smiling when Sam seemed to relax. In fact Sam was agreeably surprised to find that he no longer felt angry at the Foran brothers.

This came as relief since he had lived too long while never expecting to forget the killing need that had become part of him on the day he maimed both brothers after they had come to take his life.

The feeling that he could kill, it had stayed,

remained there in his heart from the morning the Forans came to kill him. He was ready for them because he knew when he fired their premises in Ranelagh that he had effectively put them out of business. The physical battle had been a bit one-sided even though they were two to his one. He had been prepared and they paid a heavy price for their evil intent. Later he had banned them from his native city. Looking back he knew that he could not have behaved any differently at that time. He had to kill them or frighten them sufficiently that they would not come back to exact repayment for all he had robbed them of.

Sitting with Louie he shook his head in some disbelief at the memory of his utter ruthlessness. He shrugged off the discomfort. "Nothing to do with me any more," he said to Louie. "I won't bother the Forans as long as they don't bother me." He knew that he meant this – if the brothers had decided to take the risk and come back to Dublin, he knew that he would not search them out. He hardly recognised himself as the man who had carried out such an awful punishment on the brothers from Cork. In a way they were innocent men – hard working, hard–drinking, hard-fisted builders that had been so scared for their business life they were prepared to murder him to protect it.

He could forgive them that, now.

At Portobello Harbour the next day, Sam's secretary, Lily Gaffney, reminded him that he hadn't yet written the cheque for the insurance company, and that he had a lunch appointment with Arthur Brewer at the Shelbourne. "And . . ." Lily advised him, in the voice she used when she felt she might be treading on his toes, "Mister Heffernan from the bank was on twice this morning." Since it was only eleven o'clock, Sam thought that Ally Heffernan must be in a sweat.

"Where's the pile of money from your man in Waterford?" Ally said when they were connected.

"That's a lovely way to open a conversation with the fella let's you beat him at tennis every fortnight."

"Sam, come on! Where is the money? Did your man cough up or not? Tell me the story."

"I am owed money from here to Donegal, Ally. Your man in Waterford is good for the money. He's trying to collect it from the blokes that owe it to him. This is called normal business procedure."

"Sam, you owe us more than is healthy for any of us. You're over-extended, and we are getting very jumpy in here," he sounded unhappy, but that was just Ally.

Sam said, "You sound jumpy. Why don't I treat you to a holiday, for you and Betty?" Sam was half-joking, but whole in earnest, as he made the offer.

Ally, who was not above accepting this kind of perquisite, said fussily, "Quit the messing, Sam. We have to see some serious paper from you. We have to."

"I'll call you back." Sam put the phone down, and then failed to get talking to Bill Mullen in Waterford. Mullen's wife Nuala said he was out trying to collect money and that she'd get him to return Sam's call the minute he came in the door. In fact, Sam had begun to feel he was getting the run-around, something he wouldn't take to with a smile.

"Tell him from me, Mrs Mullen, that I am out of patience with him. That I'll be very put out with him, if he doesn't call me back within the hour."

When he put the phone down he had to gather himself. The urge to jump into his car with Brendan O'Connor in the passenger seat and drive down to Waterford to collect his money – the alternative to that happy outcome was have Brendan chastise Mullen appropriately until he produced it from wherever he kept his little brown jug. He let this idea go, not liking the taste it engendered in his mouth. For now, he'd talk to Mullen, reveal his own position with the bank, and he had no doubt, the money would be produced. The Waterford man wasn't stuck for money. How could he be unless he had a gambling habit Sam didn't know about? He had a busy, thriving business, and Sam believed that all successful businessmen had a nest egg hidden away somewhere.

Sam knew that, despite his change of attitude to people like the Foran brothers, he would do what he had to do to get what was owed to him. He didn't want the bank foreclosing on one of his properties. His plans to go public were under way, and he didn't want anything putting a stain on his chances of being accepted on the stock exchange.

Lily came in to remind him again about the cheque for the insurance company. Sam put her off by telling her he'd attend to it after lunch. He left then for the Shelbourne and his appointment with Arthur. He was not happy that Mullen had left him in the position where he could not pay the insurance premiums for his collective companies, and he had to struggle to let go of his rising angry feelings about the Waterford man. He didn't want them to boil – that would mean he and Brendan would drop down to see Mullen and make him very sorry for not honouring his obligation.

Arthur looked quite strained, Sam thought, and he said so. His friend, languid as ever, put down his drink and lit a cigarette. As he exhaled he said sadly, "I'm afraid it is Vicky. She is not at all well."

"I thought she was sicker than she admitted when I saw her on Wednesday evening. She said she expected to be out and about by the weekend." She had brushed his concern aside in typical Victoria fashion. "Women's problems, Sam. Stuff you chaps simply need not know about." That was all she had given him about her illness, and he had let it go.

She had hardly ever been healthy during the last few years – he had got used to her, put his concerns on the back burner much of the time. At times she had been well enough in her body or her head, but the two didn't seem to find harmony for any length of time. It came to be accepted by those that loved Vicky, that she had paid a heavy price for her involvement with the woman called Michelle, the break-up of the relationship taking its toll on her in every way. At times Sam had felt she was slowly dying, because she simply had no desire to stay alive. In the moment there with Arthur, he simply didn't know what to think.

"The fact that she has lost interest in you, Sam. This is what worries me most of all." Arthur was downcast. "She was never as happy as when you two were close. You were the love of her life."

Sam thought that this accolade probably should go to Michelle. He didn't say so, moving in another direction as he told Arthur about the word he'd had from Michael Collins.

"Wonderful." Arthur's response was whole-hearted and he brightened considerably. "Sam," he touched Sam's hand on the table and said in a quiet voice, "remember, anything I can do – money, transport, anything. You have only to ask."

"I know that, Arthur. I may be touching you sooner rather than later. We've got word about a shipment of arms about to become available in the very near future. Collins believes this is a good time to buy it, if we can manage it. The Brits think that with the leaders dead, we have no active organisation. I expect to go to America in the next few weeks. It could mean Dee coming with me if she can take time off from her lying-in clinic."

"Let me know what you want. A few days' notice is all I will need to get the money together. You can have it in dollars or a bank draft, whatever you need." Arthur was energised by the thought of once again contributing to the cause. "What better way to help out than by spending some of the fortune thrust upon me by men who stole it in the first instance?"

Sam had heard this kind of talk from Arthur several times. He had never reacted directly since he knew how badly his friend needed to unload the cruel memory of an eviction he had witnessed as a young boy. A destitute tenant farmer, his pregnant wife and five children had been forced from a dwelling that was not fit to live in although it was home to the family. Even as they sat nearby in their desolation, the landlord's agents began battering the fragile shell to pieces. The roof was halfway thatched, galvanised pieces of rusted iron forming a partial cover for the other end of the one-roomed hovel, the pauper and his wife unable to look at what was going on as their home fell to the ground. Within a couple of hours, nothing but a pile of rubble remained.

The boy, Arthur, had begged Seamus to allow him and Victoria to stay, wanting, despite the personal pain it caused him, to witness the travesty that had become commonplace in Ireland. When the agent of the landlord and his men were ready to depart the property, they finished their work by driving the wretched pauper, his wife and children from the land he had tried to farm, warning him to leave the area or be punished, and more than likely jailed for vagrancy.

The picture of the woman gathering her children had never left Arthur's mind. He carried a tumour of shame and anguish over the memory of a small girl carrying a scraggy kitten, the child's eyes huge as consumption claimed her lungs, another innocent lamb bound for a pauper's grave as she and her people were forced to move on, and move on again, until they were unable to do anything but die by the roadside.

"I want to put something back, Sam," Arthur often said when he was in his cups. "I have to try and make up in some way."

On the following Friday evening as Sam sat down to dinner with his family, he was all too aware that Gloria was the real head of the household. This was not something they would have discussed outside the family. It would be a cause for scandal amongst those that followed the rules laid down generations before by the wise men of Jewry, but it caused Sam no problem. The truth was that though he was now capable of playing head of the house, he didn't expect to ever feel he was right and ready for the role. Gloria had, despite her own problems, done a very good job in rearing the children thus far. His mother's presence had been a godsend to the young woman but she had put in a willing, consistent effort to do the job right. Sam had seen this, even when he was blinded to her good points by the anger coming from the notion that she didn't want him. So he was pleased that his children had been taught Hebrew by their mother and Esther, and he could admit to them both that he was grateful for them doing his job when he could not be there.

On the evenings when he got home in time to overhear Sarah and Samuel as they recited the psalms learned by heart, he had found himself remembering the words and sounds from the earlier part of his own childhood. He was pleased the children could recite the lines in Hebrew. It had seemed to him, even as a twelve-year-old boy that the poetry was better served by the gritty sounds mingling with the musical syllables of the original language. He smiled ruefully, allowing that it helped if you also knew the English translation.

He almost got caught on the old petard of regret that he hadn't been home more. He let it go, regret being pointless – accepting that he had been driven by his own dreams and demons, that he had provided a fine home and all the money any normal family could need. This had been his chosen way to go, and in this regard he had done well even if he hadn't been a perfect father.

27

Dublin

September 1916

As Sam had expected, since he had promised to be at home for the Sabbath dinner, his mother's gefilte fish was the main dish. This pleased him no end and he saw that Esther, her hair more white than grey now, was quietly delighted to see him sitting at the head of the table. After prayers, as they were about to serve the dish, Esther said to Gloria, "You're very good to have allowed me do the fish for Sam. Thank you, Gloria." His wife was quietly moved. He smiled, happy to see them such good friends.

He saw that Sarah wasn't enjoying the fish. She was now seven and he thought her the most beautiful girl he had ever seen. He wondered what was on her mind – she picked uninterestedly at her food and rarely lifted her eyes from the plate before her. He knew Gloria would talk to her later – she never chastised either of the children in the company of others, not even their father and grandmother. Samuel was tucking in smartly to his dinner, a very bright boy – six now – eating with the same kind of intensity he employed in everything he did. He was not a bad-looking lad, his hair as dark as Sam's had once been, his eyes large and brown and liquid, with a powerful nose and a generous mouth. Basically, he was quiet by nature, liking picture-books better than he liked people. He was advanced for his age, speaking easily to his mother and Esther, adoring of his sister Sarah, and respectful though distant with his father.

Sarah was also extremely bright – she had always been an intelligent child, learning to use the disarming smile nature had provided for her, along with the promise of great beauty to come. Her abundant hair was deep-brown, her eyes darker than when she had been born, black as an eclipse when she lost her temper, bubbling like warm oil when she was happy. She was awkward in that she had not developed the social graces in the way that Samuel had, despite Gloria's ongoing efforts. She tended to be outspoken and impatient when expected to take adults seriously simply because they were bigger than she was.

Sam ate his gefilte fish, his mother's touch transporting him into the memory of his early Friday evening dinners after another day pushing his handcart about the city streets. Recently he had been surprised, even pleased, as memories arrived to invade his mind. He wondered was this a sign that he was growing older, this growing penchant to past experiences, both good and bad. He only allowed pleasant memories to share his time now

– anything he'd didn't wish to entertain was allowed to pass on since he had come to believe that thoughts arising are not necessarily yours – they belong to the universe and you don't have to grab them unless you want to.

His mother had sometimes allowed him to sprinkle salt on the hake she had washed and cut up into chunks in the kitchen in Little Jerusalem. "So, what was it you were saying about the Duke of Gloucester, Samuel?" Esther gave him the attention his curiosity craved.

Twelve-year-old Sam, already buying and selling on a part-time basis, took a moment to make the connection. "Oh! All right, you know when he's meditating on the death of Clarence, and his brother's widow comes along?"

"That's act one, scene one," Esther said, washing the hake again under the kitchen tap to remove the excess salt. "And she doesn't 'come along'. She's walking behind her husband's body, the poor man murdered by the devil Gloucester. What about it?"

"Am I right in thinking that the Duke of Gloucester is serious when he tells her he wants to get into her bed? Why would he want to do that when he had a bed of his own? He was a Duke after all."

"He meant he wanted to marry her," Esther said, with practised ease.

"But wasn't he after killing her husband, so that he could be the king?"

"Yes, that's true."

"Well, look, she knows he killed her husband. Could he seriously expect she'd have anything to do with him after that? And I have to say, Mama, I don't remember the word marriage being mentioned. I'll have to read it again."

"Just you start stuffing the skin with the fish like I'm doing. I'll attend to the tail. Pay attention now, Samuel. I like my gefilte fish to look good, for all the thanks I get from your father."

Sam was smiling at the memory as he finished his food, at the same time keeping an eye on Esther as she enjoyably tucked into her dinner. He saw now that Sarah, who had eaten very little, had something on her mind that was bothering her.

He touched her arm and she turned to look at him. "What is it, darling?" His tone and his attitude were deliberate as he encouraged her to speak her mind

"Daddy, are you going to go and live in . . . what's it called, mother?"

"Palestine," Gloria seemed about to say more but decided to let matters take their course.

"Are you, daddy?"

"If you're asking me am I going to live in Palestine, sweetheart, my answer is no. Of all the things I might do in what's left of my life, I promise you I have no intention of ever going to live in Palestine. Is that a satisfactory answer to you?" Sam gave the girl his full attention, knowing that his heart was going to be very hard-put to ever deny her anything.

To his delight she broke into a huge smile. She beamed his way, and she clapped her hands unconsciously as her joy bubbled through her. "O, Daddy! That is what I was hoping you would say. You have made me very happy, thank you."

Sam looked from Gloria to Esther to Sarah and back again to his wife. "Is this conversation over, or does anybody feel like telling me what this is all about?" He inclined his head towards his daughter, and Gloria shrugged with her face.

"Nana and me, we were talking about Eretz-Israel."

"The promised land, Samuel," Esther said with feeling, "Surely you've read about it in the papers?"

"I might have," Sam said. "I have a problem with it though."

"Sarah," Esther was rising from her chair, "you and Samuel and me, we're off upstairs, all right?"

The girl was still beaming at her father, "you'll come up, won't you, Daddy?"

"Let someone try and stop me!" Sam puffed out his chest, and even Samuel had a short laugh to offer in response to the tomfoolery.

"Is there something going on that I should know about?" he said to Gloria when they were alone. He emptied his wine glass, while he waited for her to respond.

"I'm very interested in the concept of a permanent homeland for the Jews. What Jew wouldn't be? Sarah overheard Nana and I talking about it. She picked up something out of context, thought we'd be moving out by the middle of next week. You know what she can be like."

Sam poured himself more wine, Gloria declining. She never took more than a sip at the Sabbath dinner on Friday evening. "I just don't see how the Jews can call Palestine the promised land. Palestine belongs to the Palestinians, millions of them that just happen to be living there at the present time, people born there, just as their ancestors were there before them, going back quite a way as far as I remember."

"I'd like to go and help Nana with the children. Is that all right with you, Sam?" Her tone was free of irony, and he knew she was simply seeking his permission as master of the house, to leave the table.

"You've no interest in a polemic on the subject of the Palestinian's rights to his homeland, where he has lived for hundreds of years?"

"Sam, it won't be at our dinner table that the pros and cons of the situation will be sorted out. They will probably go on arguing for twenty years of so. So, if you would be so kind as to excuse me, I don't want Nana taking the brunt of their energy at this time of the day."

He acquiesced, though he felt less than agreeable as she left the dining-room. He drank his wine and poured another, wondering why anybody would want to live in Palestine.

Later, as he, for a change, was finally getting Sarah

to bed down for the night, she said through lips that were already half asleep, "Daddy, I really hate Fridays," while Sam stepped on his need to hear more, and stood watching her as she surrendered and allowed sleep to whisk her away from him.

The following Friday, Sam and Deirdre were in New York, once more acting out the roles of man and wife. When he viewed the bedroom in their suite at the Plaza he had the feeling that the trip was going to be even more demanding than they had expected. "There's just the double bed," he said, holding down the alarm he felt at that moment.

"I ordered singles when I telephoned," Dee said, a tut-tut sound in her voice. "You expect better in New York, don't you?" She had started to unpack, keen to hang up her gown for that evening. They were meeting Shane Malone who was currently starring on Broadway in his very successful one-man show based on the life and works of Mark Twain. Sam had seen the show in Philadelphia a couple of months earlier, during an abortive attempt to buy weapons. He had raved about Shane's talent – Lisa O'Brien's son by Arthur Shane Brewer had written the adaptation himself – to such a degree that Dee was looking forward to it with great interest.

Sam was already on the telephone to the reception desk. When he hung up he said, "They'll try finding us another suite. They'll shift our stuff, so go ahead and hang up your gown."

He was on the telephone again immediately talking to a man in New Jersey, setting up a meeting for the next day at one o'clock. "I'll hire a car," he said with a smile. "We'll make a day of it, just in case we are under surveillance."

"What do we tell Shane?" Dee was heading for a hot bath as the thought struck her. "The last time I saw him, I was engaged to Arthur and you were pawing the ground around Gloria." She was smiling at her joke and he stood across the room like a man with his heart in his hand.

"Me? Me, pawing the ground! How dare you, madam!"

Dee chortled and turned to go into the bathroom. "Can you tell him the truth? Can he be trusted with something like that?"

"He's all right, Dee. We spent a good bit of time together during my last trip here. He knows that I'm involved in the struggle, and he's hot under the collar about the Brits shooting Pearse and Connolly and the rest. He would do anything to help us here. Like a lot of American-Irish he waxes romantic about the cause and all that. We're dead safe in his hands, and our story that we are husband and wife on holiday, with me doing a little business on the side, is what we go with. You just act like my loving wife, and I'll respond. I'd say we're getting fairly good at it by now."

"Don't be hard on him for being romantic about the struggle," she said, coming back to sit on the edge of the bed. "Sometimes, when I think of the men, the great and brilliant and brave men, who stood up and said no, no more injustice, even though they had no chance against the power of England, I find myself in tears. I find those men to be romantic figures. I feel great love for them, Sam, love I never truly felt for my own father. Is that silly?" she paused, as though struck by something. "And, of course, you are one of those men."

He heard some part of her reach out to him with those words, but he was so concerned for her well-being that the moment passed. She was moved by her feelings, close to tears, and in a moment he found he was kneeling before her by the bed, wrapping her up in a protective embrace. She responded to his warmth, her arms about him in a loving way, and he heard himself saying, "My indifference to those great men was swept away on Easter Monday. When I think of Wolfe Tone, and what guts it took to lead his band of peasant rebels, dirt farmers armed with scythes and pikes, everything but knives and forks, my heart goes out to them. My mind almost blanks out when I think of Robert Emmet, his poet's body and his lovely mind hanging from a rope in Dublin Castle. When I think of what they went through, I get the feeling I had when I damaged the Foran brothers that time. Madness is what it is, nothing less."

He heard the tears in his own voice before he felt them on his skin and he allowed Dee to move back from him so that she could wipe his eyes with the face cloth from her toilet bag. "In your own way, Sam, you are one with them. They would have made you very welcome in their fight for freedom."

He fell back on his haunches, sitting on his heels looking up at her handsome earnest face, and he knew that his impossible dream to have her for his own was just that, an utterly impossible dream.

"Are you all right, dear heart?" Dee touched his face with her hand.

He turned his head, and kissed her fingers, and he made a show then of giving her back her hand, willing to be amusing, anything to help him down off the petard onto which his desire for her had allowed him to hoist himself. It was daft and stupid, and he knew better, but she had become all and everything to him. He arose to his feet, rubbing his thumb and forefinger together, the connection allowing him some distance between him and the thing he wanted.

"I'm grand. I carry a bit of guilt for ignoring those men. My God, I was so busy as a young man, so busy being angry at my father, taking on the world for giving me such a parent, so caught up with trying to make money that the name Parnell never crossed my lips. Charles Stuart Parnell was alive during my lifetime – he had the backing of a great English Prime Minister, William Gladstone, in his fight for Home Rule. The House of Lords threw it out because so many of those bastard lords owned half the Irish countryside from which they drew rent from starving people, and I never gave Charles Stuart a thought until the scandal when Kitty O'Shea's husband sued him for adultery, and ended the career of a great man." He embraced Dee quietly, and she was happy to comfort him in her arms.

"Sorry for being so dramatic," he stepped back, his face a wreath of apology. "When you learn things late, there's bound to be a bit of self-criticism that it's taken so long," He kissed her forehead. "You go and enjoy a good hot bath. I'm going for a walk in Central Park. I need to walk off some of my own steam."

Walk he did, striding uptown through the park, his mind wondering what would have happened had Parnell managed to get Home Rule passed by peaceful means. He felt that Parnell had been the last man capable of pulling that off. It had taken serious bloodshed and daunting damage to the city of Dublin and its environs to bring the Irish situation to the attention of the world – it would take more of the same to gain another step towards freedom. He knew as he turned back to walk south toward the hotel, that he would be there, every step of the way, even at the cost of his own life.

When he got back to the hotel, Dee was already resting in their new suite, complete with single beds. He smiled as he took a bath. 'Serves you right,' he told himself, 'serves you right for your bad thoughts about your dearest friend.'

As they headed to New Jersey next morning, they were going over some of the funnier moments of Shane Malone's performance as Mark Twain in his successful show on Broadway.

As Sam had watched Shane performing the show for the second time in just a couple of months, he could see how the show had become even better in that short time. He remembered his first impression of Lisa's son when he came onstage in Boswell's tent at Greystones, how he had been very impressed, and convinced right away that this young man could star on the big stages of the world. As he shared this with Dee he said, "It's nice to be right sometimes."

"He was so in love with Gloria that I felt rather sorry for him," Dee said reflectively. "He wasn't man enough for her then, she needed you. By the way, she called me on the telephone just before we left home."

"Was it just a social call?"

"It absolutely was," Dee was elated. "I have never been so happy to hear a voice down the line. She sounded so . . . forgive me, Sam, but you know what I mean – she never sounded so normal, and we agreed to meet and have afternoon tea some time next week."

"I'm glad," he said, not sure that he was. Yes, he wanted Gloria to know Dee better, to hopefully derive some benefit from spending time with her. But, just now, feeling as he did, tasting again the impossible fleeting thought when yesterday, as they had arrived at the Plaza, he knew that any impossible possibility for himself and Dee would be diminished further by any closeness between the two women in his life. He made a point of feeling the steering wheel under his fingers, attending to the sense of touch by using it as his contact point, until in moments the thoughts that were circling, in relation to his impossible impossibility disappeared for the moment.

More than willing to change the slant of the conversation, he told Dee about Sarah, and the way she had dropped the Palestine bombshell in his lap a few weeks before. "I tried to get Gloria to speak about it to me, see how far this thing has settled in her mind. She was having none of it."

"I imagine all that is a long way off," Dee touched his hand in a show of support. "You know how long it takes for anything to happen, too much bureaucracy and not enough action. Gloria made no comment about your answer to Sarah when you said you would never want to live in Palestine?"

"It hadn't cost her a thought, would be my guess. I'm not complaining, but she and my mother are as tight as ticks, thank heavens. That could have been a battle royal. They are like a loving mother-daughter combination, and it has made my life a great deal easier. But, every front has a back – they don't need me."

"I can understand why it might seem like that. After all she has been through its only natural that Gloria will need time to turn back to you as the loving young woman you married. She needs time, Sam."

"I don't want her back, Dee. And I don't believe for one second that she is ever going to want me as a husband. We're married yes, but you know what I mean."

"I'm sorry to hear such hurt in you. I feel hurt myself. Arthur spends most of his time drunk unless he is at the office. We live like brother and sister now, for more than two years. I have come to love him the way a nurse might relate to a long-term patient. I find it sad, yet I'm not unhappy. Compared to the poverty and the degradation I see in the Dublin slums, my situation hardly seems relevant, let alone important."

He glanced sideways for a moment as Dee turned to him, her emerald eyes clear, her intent strong in her voice. "You are the only one to whom I could confess that my children and Kelly, and my work, and being here on this operation with you, your friendship and love, these things support me and help me feel that I am leading a worthwhile life."

Sam suddenly heard himself saying, "Why don't we just forget about going to look at guns for today. Maybe just spend the day on a picnic, forget about our domestic situations. Forget about everything except the day that's in it?"

Dee wouldn't hear of it. "We can picnic afterwards, or if it takes all day to do a deal, we'll picnic tomorrow. At least you can rely on the weather here."

It was a very warm day and Sam was grateful for the open top of the hired car. "All I know is that I'm very glad you're here with me, Dee." The words came straight out – he had no time to shape the sound to ensure that he didn't tread on dangerous ground. Since he couldn't be certain how they had landed, he simply let his concern go. He loved her and he couldn't help it, and he wasn't going to bleed every time a hint of how he felt slipped out before he could censor it.

Dee was glancing at the map, following the directions Sam had been given on the telephone. She used this activity to avoid making any answer to Sam's words. Her heart was beating faster than was comfortable and she ached for she knew not what. Except that she knew exactly what *she knew not what* was.

Sam presented Deirdre as his wife to the man called Slim Levine in New Jersey. He observed how respectful Levine was to Dee. In matters of business he had found that men who behaved well to women were more likely to be honest than those that eschewed females. The American was very average, a man you wouldn't notice unless you were looking for him, but his handshake was firm and dry, and Sam felt he could do business with him.

They followed Levine to a farm at a place called Tom's River and Dee stayed by Sam's side as he went to examine the weapons on offer.

"I thought I was meeting a couple of rebels, revolutionaries," Levine said as he led them into a large shed behind the farmhouse and a huge market garden.

"You were right," Sam said offhandedly. "My wife is the daughter of Countess Markievicz, one of our female leaders, currently in a prison camp in Wales. Some of our women can shoot straighter than the lads."

"I ran your name by a guy I know does business in Ireland." Levine opened another door to reveal a warehouse of weaponry and ammunition. As Sam's eyes opened wide he saw that Dee was equally impressed. "He checked you out, Mister Sweet, seems you're quite a character over there. Anyways, we can do business if you have a mind to."

"I want to buy a large quantity of small arms and ammunition right away," Sam told him. "I have contacts in Manhattan to take delivery of them. During the next three months I want automatic rifles and ammunition, mortars and machine guns. And I have a list of bomb-making equipment that I want. Provided your pricing is fair, I will pay you cash dollars."

"I've got what you need, Mister Sweet," Levine said, pulling a tarpaulin off a long trestle table. Sam was again impressed and he heard Dee's intake of breath as the armoury was revealed close up. There were literally dozens of different types of small arms and rifles.

Levine handed Sam an automatic pistol. "We call these Peter the Painters – a handful of these guys can change the colour of everything," he said with a smile. As Sam took a close look at the weapon, the American slipped a stock against the butt of another and in an instant had turned it into a small rifle. "This is a handy tool. You can carry it in your pocket, put it together in a few seconds, use it for medium range and stash it away again in no time flat. That's a very popular item with bank robbers and people like that."

"I'm sure," Sam smiled at Dee, moving his hand slightly to suggest that she stay calm. The American was showing off to her, and Sam thought that was a good sign.

He accepted a Parabellum pistol from Levine who then handed him a detachable stock. In a matter of seconds Sam had turned the pistol into a small rifle. He was impressed – this weapon was a joy to handle, and easy to conceal.

"Have you got a crate of these?" Sam said.

Levine pointed to a stack of wooden boxes. "Right there, Mr Sweet."

"I want to open a fresh crate and test one of each. And I'd like to choose the ammunition. You have somewhere I can run a test?"

"No problem, sir," the American became affable now that he felt a sale was on the cards.

Sam tested the weapons he had chosen for himself and when he emerged from the quiet room he was deeply impressed by both guns and ammunition. Neither of the weapons was old and he was puzzled as to how the guns had made their way to America.

"They came out of Europe. Some middle-range German officers who don't expect to win the war are cutting their losses. I can sell you other stuff, guns captured from the British, if you want. Be ironic if your rebels were shooting British soldiers with their own guns, wouldn't you say?"

Within an hour, Sam had completed a deal for the hand weapons and ammo, the consignment to be delivered into Manhattan the next day.

The exposure to the weapons warehouse had a considerable effect on both Dee and Sam, and he questioned himself about the wisdom of having exposed her to the coalface of armed resistance. The huge array of guns and ammunition, the practised ease with which Levine had produced one weapon after another, his pen scratching as he wrote down the address of Sam's contact on West Thirty-eight Street, all of it was so normal in its context that Dee felt somewhat sickened by being there. Sam could understand how she was feeling. There was nothing romantic about the cold feel of a deadly weapon, and Slim Levine's warmth as he described how simple it was to fix the stock to the pistol to turn it into a small rifle in moments, was practically eerie.

"I'm sorry, Dee. I should never have exposed you to that. It was selfish of me."

"I wanted to come, Sam. But what do you mean, selfish?"

"Ah, don't mind me." This time he was bothered by the fact that he had overstepped the mark."

"Could you stop the car?" Dee said casually, "I need to stretch my legs."

He pulled onto the grass verge of the open road. There was little or no traffic in the mid-afternoon, the New Jersey landscape anonymous to his eye so that it could have been any one of a dozen states in the country.

He got out of the car and as they walked away from the road he took Dee's hand. He had simply been unable to stop himself doing this and before he knew it said, "What're we going to do?"

She turned to him and put her arms about his neck. Her eyes were cloudy and he felt her tight against the length of him for the first time. "I have a need, a desperate need to know you like I've never known you. I only hope you love me as I love you." She kissed him.

The force of her passion surprised him, but only for a moment. Then they were as one, even though this part of their journey together was at its beginning. When he slipped his tongue into her mouth, she gasped, pushed him away for a second, her eyes incredulous and awe-filled. Then she came back at his mouth with her own, her tongue finding his, her legs wrapping around him as he slid into her in the high wild grass of New Jersey.

They spent hours in the sun of the afternoon on its way to evening. They made love again and again and Dee was fascinated as she handled him, her eyes wide as her fingers induced tumescence, shaking her head in disbelief as he swelled yet again, the helmet of his need turning purple in the waning light.

Later as they lay wrapped up in their loving convalescence, she with her head on his chest, he heard her say, "How long have you known?"

"How long have I known what?" he said in mock sincerity. She was not fooled for a moment by his play-acting. Giving him a puck in the stomach with a fist, she waited for his answer.

"I'm not sure. And if I pick a spot where I think I knew, I was so unbalanced by it that I don't know if it was then or before then, or am I still so shell-shocked that I don't know even now. Can you see my difficulty?" He moved and said. "I need to be looking at you." They moved some more, and they searched each other's face for they knew not what.

"What are you looking for, Sam?

"I don't know, Dee. What're you?"

"I don't know either."

"It's murder, isn't it?, not to be able to find what you don't know you're looking for in the first place?"

"It's very annoying."

"Do you know what I think?"

"Sam, I think we should quit looking, and have another helping."

"That sounds very interesting. Can I ask you something?"

"No. I have to ask you – do women really sit on top sometimes, y'know?"

"No, I don't know. Explain what you mean."

"You do so know."

"Don't start. I've had enough riddles for one day."

"You're a beast. You know what I mean."

"Say what you mean, I'll own up if you're right."

"Do women sometimes sit on top of the man with his . . ."

"Cock is as good a word as any."

"I didn't feel I could say penis. It sounds so nebulous after what I've been experiencing, just not strong enough."

"So, go with cock. See how that sits on your tongue." He grinned like a wicked schoolboy and her heart tilted again. "If you'll pardon the expression," he said

"That's something else I need to know about."

"Get back to where you were. On top, wasn't it?"

"All right," Dee smiled before her expression changed as though something new had occurred to her. "It's incredible. I feel as though a box of nonsense, a box crammed with behaviour patterns, ridiculous images, God knows what else, just dropped off my shoulders."

"I understand. I lost most of that stuff by the time I

was eighteen. But then I was practically living on the streets of Dublin. The corners get rubbed off rapidly when you're exposed to day-to-day street life."

She sounded surprised as she said, "And I thought I was rather emancipated." She paused and kissed him gently on the mouth. "Will you teach me all you know? Help me be a wonderful lover for you?"

"All I can promise," he answered his face straight, "is that I'll give it a good lash."

They began to chuckle and in no time they were lying side by side helpless with laughter, admitting almost in the same moment that they felt more alive than ever before.

"I love you, Dee."

"I know," she sighed and he could feel her joy. "And I love you."

"I feel as if I've been given new lungs, Dee. Sort of released."

"I know. Something important has been added, some impediment has been shifted – I can breathe deeper than ever before."

"All I'm sure of is, I've never felt this before and I'm not just talking about the love-making. But if this is love, I know now that I never loved Vicky or Gloria. I was involved, in-love, sure, and certainly with Vicky I had an amazing sex life."

"She told me you were the best lover she ever had."

"I'm just glad it was good for her." He exhaled cigarette smoke. "Immense though the sensation was, there was no depth to it. It was all to do with sensation."

"After what I've just experienced, there's not a lot wrong with sensation."

"I didn't mean that in a pejorative sense. But sensation for its own sake, it's not enough. And seeking sensation – that habit, desire – it's a voracious character and I'd say it's insatiable, can't be satisfied. It's like money. Much always wants more, and more always wants much more; it's never ending. You can have amazing sensation sexually with people you don't even like a lot."

Dee chuckled. "I'd like to hear more about that. Not now. I want to tell you I like you more than anybody I've ever met. Just in case you hadn't noticed. I've always liked you. I know I fell in love with you that day you kicked Milly's fellow where, as you told me, the sun never shines. And I know that whatever happens after today, you will be the sole tenant of my heart." She moved and came onto her knees. "Now I am going to sit up on you, and you can teach me how to ride the wicked stallion you are. What about that?"

"Sounds good to me," Sam lay smiling up at Dee, as she prepared to slide down on him.

"He's very big, Sam. Will it be all right this way?"

"Don't worry," he said with the wicked grin of a recalcitrant college boy, "Just go easy when he's passing the heart."

She was already moving to wrap herself about him as she started to laugh – and for a moment or two – her breathing sounded strangled, her eyes like lights going on and off as she began to rise and fall. Her muted ululations turned then to groans of delight as his hands caressed her breasts under her bodice.

Driving into Manhattan later, her head rested on his shoulder. "We won't talk about the future 'til we get home, is that all right with you?"

"Absolutely," Dee sighed. "Whatever you say is all right with me."

"Someday, I don't know how or when, I have to live with you, be your man out in the open, wake up with you every morning."

"I want that too."

"Do you want it enough to wait for it, for as long as it takes?"

"I want it beyond wanting. I can wait. But I have to see you, be able to be with you as often as it can happen. If I have to, I'll cheat on the world to get my share of you and your magic limb," she chuckled and her hand touched his lap. "It is magic, to me anyway, to see it come up again and again. And you've put a spell on me. Despite my humble origins, I was brought up to be well behaved."

"What I think, Dee, I think only a loving God could have come up with the whole man-woman sexual thing. But it's got to be right. This is right, in every way, except legally I suppose. Maybe morally, but I don't care."

"I don't care either. And I'm warning you, Sam, I'll never back off what we have finally owned up to today."

"And we're committed to the cause."

Dee nodded, "Absolutely."

"I want to make a bigger input into your dream of the hospital," he said quietly. "Is that all right with you?"

"We'll see," she said firmly. "I have to protect you from now on. You can't do everything for everybody, much as you might want to."

During the following week, following his return from New York, Sam was upstairs in the house, having just seen Sarah off to sleep – Gloria was still reading to Samuel in his room – when Esther came to the door and whispered to him that "the phone call on the phone downstairs is for you. It is from Brendan O'Connor. He told me to say it's very urgent."

"You better get down to Portobello, Sam." Brendan didn't waste words. "We have a serious problem."

"Ten minutes," Sam said, slamming down the phone.

When he arrived at the site by the canal, Brendan and Cormac and a score of onlookers were standing around outside the main gate. This was shut and padlocked. Instantly he saw that a couple of buildings in the complex were on fire. At the same time he heard the bell of a fire engine ring close by even as the Dubliner said quietly, "It's not our padlock, Sam, so we couldn't get in."

Sam felt as though someone had just walked over his grave as Cormac said, "Dinny Foran is inside. He's armed, fired a couple of shots already. He wants you. He won't let us put a hand on the lock without shooting. You, he said, you can open the lock and step inside. Only you, is what he said, Sam."

As Sam looked at him in shock, Brendan dangled a key on a piece of string. "He even told me where he'd left the key for you."

Sam took the key, knowing he had to get inside and quickly. He opened the lock, trying to think of the best way to deal with this. He knew he had to reason with Foran, just in case the Corkman planned to do what he would have done in the same set of circumstances.

"Doesn't take genius to work out that Foran intends to wipe out everything here." Sam's heart had swollen with anger, resentment pushing against his chest plate. "I can't let that happen. But you lads stay here unless I call you."

28

Dublin

September 1916

Stepping inside the gate at the Portobello complex, Sam yelled, "Dinny! It's Sam Sweet. I'm inside the gate."

Turning back to Brendan he asked: "Is his brother with him?"

Brendan nodded his head. "Someone else is there all right. I saw one fella. He went in the wood store. A minute later it started to burn, haven't seen him since."

"That'll be the brother." Sam moved into the yard, jumping in shock as a bullet bounced off the concrete at his feet. "Take it easy," he yelled. "We need to talk. We can sort this out."

"How does it feel, jew boy? How does it feel to see your life's work go up in smoke, ay?" The sheer force of Dinny Foran's hatred for Sam sent a shiver down his spine. It was eerie, listening to the disembodied voice – another bullet bounced off the ground close to his feet and he jumped in shock.

"There's no need for this, Dinny," he called out, forcing himself to stay confident. "We can work this out. I can make it up to you for what happened between us."

He could see Dinny Foran now. The big man was standing in the doorway of the special unit he had built some months before. This was a wooden building of exquisite detail that had cost a fortune to design, build and decorate – the structure was to be the best possible example of the kind of work Sweet Construction was capable of. Any serious punter that wanted a home built, a building designed, a very special one-off creation, all he had to do was see this special unit and the sale was a done deal.

The interior of the building was equally impressive. The most modern convenience of every kind was in place on each of the three floors. The furniture had been made in America to specific designs from Sam's best and most creative home specialists, artisans that were artists, men that worked solely for Sam on specific projects and used the high fees he paid to buy the time to cover canvas with their need to paint.

Foran came out of the doorway, and walked across the complex in the late evening light. 'If this was America it'd be stone dark by now,' Sam thought. Why think that just now? Was he thinking of Dee and himself in New Jersey? Did that mean he thought he was going to die? He rubbed his fingertips on the seams of his pants, walking slowly towards the big Corkman. Dinny carried a rifle that looked like a toy in his huge hand,

and, as he stepped under a lamp close to the office block facing the special unit, Sam could see that he had a revolver tucked into the belt of his trousers.

"You're going to see this place go up in smoke, Jew boy, and then I'm going to blow your fuckin' head off." Dinny pulled a half bottle from his pocket and took a swig of the spirit. "You think you could do what you did to me, and go to your grave having a laugh at my expense? Well, think again, you fuckin' Jew bastard! Shamey," He called out, "come and see the Jew boy."

Shamey Foran emerged from the office block which even now was beginning to display the fire that had been lit inside. "If it wasn't for Dinny here, I'd have taken your life years ago, you stinkin' Yid. He said wait, wait, 'til the time is right. And now is the time, isn't it, Dinny?"

"You said it, brother. Now is the time."

"Why now?" Sam asked, knowing he was in very serious trouble.

Suddenly a voice reached them over a loud hailer. "This is Chief Inspector Daragh of the Royal Irish Constabulary. I'm ordering you people to drop your weapons and out. Come out now with your arms above your heads."

Sam felt a dot of relief that the police had arrived, remembering the name Daragh from the night he had picked Cormac up off the ground with a bullet wound in his side.

"It's Sam Sweet, Chief Inspector. I'm being held at gunpoint by a man called Dinny Foran. He is burning my premises and everything here to the ground, so he tells me, and then he says he's going to blow my head off. So, I'm afraid I can't come to you, not just yet."

"Mister Foran," the policeman's voice made another dent in the late evening, "I appeal to you to stop this right now, before you end up facing a capital murder charge. Put down your weapon and come forward."

By way of an answer to this request, Dinny Foran released a shot into the air. For the moment Daragh turned silent.

"Get on with it, Shamey. You know what to do," Dinny Foran yelled.

Sam realised that the police presence wasn't going to be much help to him. He repeated the question, "Why now, Dinny?" in the hope that he could buy his way out of this situation.

"I've watched you, Jew boy. I paid a fella, a fella knows how to go about these things, a private enquiry agent, he calls himself, a fella that could find out for ye what the Pope had for his breakfast this mornin'. He told me that you were over-extended, that you had been taken for very big money by a Waterford man with a very good act when it came to getting serious credit."

Sam blanched at the reminder that Mullen had conned him – he had taken him for a ride to the tune of fifty thousand pounds. The man and his wife had already left Waterford by the time Sam and Brendan had driven down there to collect the debt. It transpired that Mullen had been renting the property, the lease he had deposited against payment with Sam a forgery. To make matters even worse, Sam's best informants assured him that Mullen and his wife had departed Ireland.

"Mullen wiped your eye to the tune of fifty thousand quid, Jew boy, and I know that for a fact. And you, with your cash-flow constipated, you hadn't the brains to use your own money, the stuff you have stashed, you Yid bastard. Ye were too tight to spend it on your insurance cover. It's nearly three years since you had insurance on this place, and tonight's the night you pay the piper."

"What good is it to you?" Sam called out. "Putting you out of business didn't do me one bit of good. If anything, I've had a guilty feeling about what I did to you. I went crazy after the beating you two gave me. I wouldn't carry on like that today."

The voice of Inspector Daragh, as dry as a ship's siren on the night air, repeated the request that Foran lay down his gun and surrender himself. This time Dinny yelled back.

"You move one step, copper, and I swear to God, Sweet gets shot where he stands. Ye've enough people there around ye to confirm that I warned you. So you make a move and he's gone for his tea, and it'll be your fault." He turned back to Sam, "So, ye poor Jew man," Foran's words were drenched in irony, "ye felt guilty about half crippling me and Shamey, and about deprivin' us of the chance to recover in the only town we could have got a shillin's credit in, to try an' start up again. Ye rotten fucker! Ye screwed us to the door, and

510

now yer goin' to get a taste of the same, and then, on the life of the mother, God be good to her, I swear I am going to blow your Jew head off yer Jew bastard shoulders. Hurry up, Shamey!" he yelled across the complex as his brother appeared at a top-floor window of the special project building. A moment later he threw a chair worth a hundred pound through the window, doing the same thing with a few more before Dinny yelled at him to get the fire going.

Sam wanted to risk attacking the big Corkman, but Foran turned the rifle directly on him. "Not so tough without the weapon in yer hands, Jew boy. You try and take this weapon off me, and I'll break it over yer head. But don't worry if that happens. Ye won't miss anything. I'll throw a bucket a wather over ye to make sure and wake ye before I put a bullet between yer eyes."

The sound of a chair crashing through another top-floor window drew Sam's eyes away from the weapon in Foran's hand. He saw a flame rising behind where Shamey was now standing at the window.

"Get on with it," Dinny yelled. "Do the next floor on the way down and then get out of there." He gave Sam his attention again, "So, with yer overdraft hittin' the roof and no insurance on this place, and countin' the money you won't be able to collect 'cos ye won't be able to complete contracts, yer goin' outa business, Jew boy, goin' outa business in a big way, the biggest ye might say, when you consider ye'll be wavin' bye bye to all this, and the resta the worrold as well."

"Dinny, let someone in to release the horses. No need for them to suffer and burn to death."

"Never mind the horses. Ye should be sayin' yer Jew prayers. Now, you and me, we're takin' a walk across to that lovely structure ye put together. Musta cost a fortune. A hundred thousand or so, am I right?"

"Near enough," Sam said.

"Well, since ye spent so much on it, why don't we use it to save yer wife the price of a coffin? Like, yer goin' to die right here, so why not just burn y'up like them Hindus out in India?"

"I'll give you fifty grand," Sam said. "I'll get you the best legal team in the country at my expense. When you come out, your money will have earned you a lot of interest."

"Are you startin' to beg for yer worthless life, ye Jew shit?"

"I'm offering you a business proposition, Dinny. Why am I surprised you're too thick to take it?" Having accepted that he was wasting his time, Sam was trying to make the Corkman even angrier. He was also looking around for a lump of wood, something he could use as a weapon. But, on his orders, especially since he had quit paying out the enormous premiums for fire insurance, the complex was neat and clean and tidy, with not a stray piece of wood to be seen. He sighed, and wondered if he was really was going to get shot to death right here and now. "And by the way, Dinny," he said with a sneer in his voice, "did you know that everyone in this country calls Corkmen 'the Jews of Ireland'?"

Shamey Foran smashed out another window down on the first floor. As he stood there pushing a chaise lounge out into the night, he was struck from above by a length of burning timber, which not only knocked him halfway through the broken window but set his clothing on fire. He yelled in terror as he tried to extricate himself from the window frame. Terrified at the sight of his own blood pouring from an artery cut by a shard of glass, he tried to shake off the flames eating into his back and his hair.

Dinny half turned, yelling to his brother to get out of there. This gave Sam the split second he needed to kick out with all his might. His leather brogue hit Foran in the knee Sam had attacked in the tenement hallway on Charlemont Street all those years before. The big man screamed in agony, the rifle dropping from his hand as he instinctively reached for the pain-filled area. Sam kicked the rifle away, pivoted and smashed a stiff-arm backhand blow to the side of Foran's head. His face went blank and he staggered backwards, Sam going after him with fists flying, until he managed to wrench the gun from Dinny's belt. He hit him in the forehead with the revolver, and he stood over him, shaking with relief. Then, for the briefest second, he was in the grip of an overwhelming need to empty the chamber of the revolver into Dinny Foran.

Without thinking he licked his lips – tasting wood smoke on his mouth brought him into the present moment – he was instantly freed of the anger and fear and the bitter, bitter resentment of a minute before and all those years before, and free to hurl the revolver onto the ground and into the path of the policemen coming through the gate.

Staying well back, Sam risked a glance at the first floor window of the burning building. He saw the man being eaten by flames, heard Shamey Foran release his last despairing mention of his brother's name. His final cry was a wound on the evening air and Dinny Foran, all else forgotten, tried to fumble his way to his feet. "I'm coming, brother. I'm coming," Dinny's helplessness was heart-rending to Sam who even now deprived him of the chance to get up off the ground.

As uniformed men dragged Dinny Foran away, Sam and Inspector Daragh stood watching the flames eat up the magnificent building, burning it and everything in it to oblivion, even as the fire brigade went about its business. As he turned away from the ruin of another dream, Sam saw Brendan and Cormac shepherding the horses out through the main gate, Dee's brother shifting them onto the canal banks where the soft grass would keep them happy enough until it was safe to drive them back into the stables.

Brendan came running to Sam's side, "Are you all right?"

"I'm not hurt, apart from mentally. Far from all right, though," he shrugged, accepting what had happened, knowing there was something huge to be learned from it.

"I didn't pay the premiums for the fire insurance. Between Mullen conning me and this, I am effectively, as of now, out of business and I'm sorry to say, you're out of work."

"I don't like it," Brendan said laconically, "but I like it better than you being dead."

It was Brendan who came to Sam at the Portobello site – this was being repaired with the last of Sam's *little brown jug* money – bearing the good news that Michael Collins and other Republicans were being released for Christmas.

Brendan poured brandy from a half bottle he'd been keeping in his desk drawer. When they touched glasses, he said flatly, "Lloyd George is still trying to make himself look good to Woodrow Wilson. He needs him in the worst way if he's to end the war in Europe." He lowered the amber nectar in one swallow while Sam sipped quietly the one in his hand.

The time now was five o'clock, and the skeleton staff were gone for the day since the company could only handle so much business – it would be some weeks before they would be back to full capacity, 'if ever', Sam thought more than once. The truth was that his money had kept the place open, alive, but hardly kicking, and unless he could raise money from somewhere, he was likely to finish up in the bankruptcy courts.

Arthur had offered to help but Sam had insisted that this was not a runner – he had never backed off his willingness to be Arthur's best friend, but since he and Dee had become committed as lovers and partners 'til death us do part' he knew that he could not take money from the friend he was cuckolding every chance he got.

Brendan and he talked about the release of Collins in something close to disbelief. "Shows you the pull Collins has in America," Brendan said. "The Irish caucus there leans on the President – he wants their votes at the next election – he has a word in the Welsh Wizard's ear, and dear old David Lloyd George, he who wants to win the war so bad he can taste it, agrees to show the Irish that the English are not as bad as they are painted."

"And you're convinced America will go into the war to help Britain put the boot into the Germans?" Sam sipped his brandy.

"I'd bet money on it if I wasn't out of a job."

Sam smiled at the neat way in which Brendan had read the politics involved in the upcoming release of his hero and the other men lucky enough to be included in the Christmas present to the Irish. "If you put music to that, you could put it on the stage," he said with a grin, feeling good despite the financial downturn that could leave him facing the future without a penny to his name.

When the telephone rang Brendan picked it up and passed the instrument to Sam. Arthur was on the line and to judge by his slightly tipsy greeting, feeling bucked about something or other.

"My dear Sam, I have some news, news that I feel will ensure the worry creases on your brow will disappear in an instant." Arthur then went on to explain to Sam what had taken place that day halfway around the world.

When Sam finally handed the telephone back to

Brendan, his right-hand man sat there holding it in his hands, like a hound salivating over a precious morsel. "It's good news, I know it is, but what, Sam? What's happened?"

Sam swallowed his brandy, gasped and held his glass out for a refill. He opened his cigarette case and said, "First thing I want you to know is that we are back in business, seriously back in business, as of Monday."

Brendan's delight was evident when after he had drunk his brandy down the hatch he danced several steps of a hornpipe before falling onto the chair like a man exhausted.

"Jesus, that's wonderful, Sam, some kind of miracle." He took a box of matches off the table and held one to Sam's cigarette. "I won't ask you how this miracle's came about. When you're ready, you'll tell me."

"I'll tell you now," Sam exhaled smoke in a gesture of such immense relief that he found he was laughing at himself. At the same time, he realised just how wound-up he had been since he had been burned by the Forans.

"To put it in a nutshell for you, Bren, a good while ago, Arthur Brewer was investing a lot of money in a gold mine in South Africa. He mentioned it to me as a very good opportunity for investment – as you know, I'm not bad at doing a deal – I can sell, like, we all have our talents, big or small, but I never bought or sold a share in my life. I said this to Arthur – he was fairly jarred at the time – but he insisted out of his goodwill to me. I gave him twenty-five grand and to be quite honest, wrote it off really – like never gamble with money you can't afford to lose, right. After that there was so much going on I never thought to even ask Arthur if there was any word on the gold mine."

"You're one amazing bloody man," Brendan said with conviction. "You could buy up half of Rathgar for twenty-five thousand quid."

"In the first place I more or less poo-pooed the idea of buying shares. If it hadn't been for Arthur and his belief in the investment, I'd have let the chance pass me by. And if I'd have had even half an interest in what was going on, I could have made even more. Anyway, thanks to Arthur, bless his heart. He sold the shares for me last week – they peaked was his view – today's prices have proved him right, and I am what you might call, quite well off and ready to invest quite a package in Sweet Construction, and you get a rise right away. Cormac too!"

As Sam lifted his drink to take a sip of brandy he tasted the subtle bile that had arrived on his tongue along with the judgment of himself. His criticism – the castigation of himself for not keeping up with his insurance premiums – he had also briefly wished while listening to Arthur that he had given him fifty thousand to invest instead of twenty-five, until he remembered how *much always wants more*. Lighting a fresh cigarette he inhaled and made a mental note to go on practising awareness of the sense of touch as he had been doing in recent times.

For in back of all that had happened – and this included the shares money arriving like the relief of Mafeking – it had been the taste of wood smoke on his lips that had triggered his resistance to killing Dinny Foran with his own revolver. That simple decision meant he was still free, free to take a look at his life and what he wanted to do with the rest of it.

Brendan had a wife and children hence his relief at being back at his job was a palpable thing. When they were sipping the last of the half bottle, Sam said, "You sure Cormac can handle that shipment from New Jersey?"

Brendan had no doubts on that score. "He'll bring the stuff ashore, don't worry about that. Or he'll die trying." Sam accepted this. The weapons from Slim Levine – the second in as many months – would go into the growing stockpile and be there ready for the next time.

Brendan O'Connor's assessment of the politics involved in the proposed release of Collins and others at Christmas would be proved correct. The American President Woodrow Wilson and the British Prime Minister David Lloyd George added a new dimension to the notion of quid pro quo and in 1917 the Americans joined with the United Kingdom to bring the conflict in Europe to an end. This took a little time, before in November 1918 Germany surrendered. This inspired worldwide rejoicing, though hundreds of thousands of families would mourn in their collective broken-heartedness the cruel, desolate waste of so many lives, military and civilian, in the four years since 1914.

In Ireland, untold sadness was engendered in too

many hearts by so much death in such a short period of time. Five hundred had died in the 1916 Rising but was there any word to describe the loss of the forty thousand Irish sons, husbands and brothers who would not be coming home from their first trip to Europe? The green fields of France were littered with the bodies of the fallen, many of them so badly smashed and blown to pieces they were beyond identification, their dog tags the only proof of their existence as soldiers of the Crown. Mostly young men and old boys had gone to war, innocence volunteering to die before it found the legs of living, uniformed children singing as they went to take the King's shilling, their unworldliness costing them and their loved ones dear.

There had been much resentment throughout Ireland as the country's young began going off to wear the uniform of the British army in 1914 and the years thereafter. This was understandable in the context of the times that were in it. Ireland was torn in more ways than one, many pledged their allegiance to England as they were entitled to do, as many again hated the English with inherent passion and wanted the country free of all things British. The latter granted no strength to the argument that Ireland and England was a country broken in two pieces by St George's Channel, that the links had been too strong and too close for too long to ever be completely broken.

Within days of Sam's return, business-wise, from the

dead, Brendan and Cormac had started calling him Lazarus, while Arthur insisted that he join himself and Deirdre for a long lunch in the Shelbourne. "We have to celebrate your good fortune. Perhaps I should say your good business judgment in buying the shares in the first place."

As they took aperitifs before going into the dining-room, Sam scoffed, "Arthur, once more it was you saved my bacon. And I refuse to agree to any description of what's happened that does not read simply, 'once again Sam Sweet got very bloody lucky!'" He heard the words as he spoke, gratified that the sound was one of gratitude rather than self-criticism.

Dee joined them as they were about to sit down, and she and Sam kissed as they had always done. Arthur was already reading the menu. Sam hadn't seen Dee for three days and her eyes twinkled in delight that he was out of the financial trouble he would not allow either her or Arthur to relieve, even as a loan. As he sat beside her, Sam felt that his heart would melt from the sheer joy of just being there.

Arthur quaffed rather a lot through lunch, so that by the time they reached dessert he was well and truly drunk, and feeling somewhat embarrassed about the fact.

Sam offered to take him home. Arthur wouldn't hear of it, apologising profusely to them both. "I really don't know what's happening to me, dears. Not that long ago I could hold the old plonk. It seems I'm losing the knack. Please forgive me, I cherish you both and I am going to take a cab." He made a tiny bow from the waist, and walked quite steadily from the dining-room.

Dee immediately took Sam's hand under the tablecloth. "You really meant it, about taking him home?"

"Of course," Sam was surprised that she had to check this.

"That's one of the reasons I love you so much," Dee was quietly moved by his offer. "You're always willing to be there when someone is in need."

"I'm hearing this," Sam said to some invisible third party who appeared to be hovering just above the table over his right ear, "from a woman who toils most days of the week in the slums of Dublin."

"Oh, stop it," Dee whispered urgently. "I do very little, really."

"It's so bad in the slums that she has to have a couple of minders along, just to ensure she is not robbed, raped, and ridiculed," Sam continued talking to some invisible third party. "The Catholic Church tells its parishioners not to allow her near their wives and children because she is married to a Protestant and an Englishman, even though he converted to the Church of Rome to marry the lady, and this same lady tells me that I make sacrifices." He turned to her with a smile. "I know this probably sounds melodramatic but I'd give my very life for yourself and Arthur. My feelings for both of you enrich me beyond wealth, so you may tell me that I am a man blessed by some loving God, or gods gone laughing that I am a survivor, due to a lot of help and caring from my friends and those I love."

Somehow they resisted the urge to kiss in the dining-room, but, among those still lingering over lunch, it was observed that the well-known friendship between the well-known couple seemed to have become something more.

29

Dublin

May 1919

Driving Michael Collins to the mail boat for Holyhead, Sam was wondering what would have happened had he not attracted the attention of Victoria on that June day in 1902. The thought had been close by for some days, arising, he knew, because his dear friend, his first great lover, was decidedly unwell.

Vicky had actually admitted some weeks before to being under the weather – this in itself a major breakthrough. Sam had been shocked so badly on his most recent visit that he had come away wondering, not was she close to death but, rather, how close to death was she?

Victoria was still some way short of her fiftieth birthday but, seeing her yesterday she looked like an eighty-year-old woman on the verge of death, and Sam would not have been surprised had she passed away in the night.

He carried great sadness that Vicky was almost certainly going to die very soon, and he was worried about what her passing would do to Arthur. His great friend, husband of the woman he loved, was fragile these days. His constant, dangerous drinking habit, and his ongoing forays into Dublin's night town in search of something he was never going to find, were taking their toll on his physical and mental health. Sam was actually concerned that should Vicky die, her passing could send Arthur over the edge.

The more Arthur drank, the more often he returned to the stories of his unhappy childhood. At every turn, Victoria had been the shining light that got him through his darkest early days – she had been the bastion of strength that supported him in his unbearable adolescence, the years after his heart-mother, Lisa O'Brien, had been dismissed from his life.

Arthur ranted his inchoate memories to Sam – repeating himself as his mind failed to keep time in the order it had presented back then. Always, first and always, always there was his sister, his mentor through his first tottering steps into early manhood, the one constant heroine of his heart, always.

Sam had to brake sharply to avoid running into the car in front and this shook him out of his reverie. He put a stop to all this thinking by connecting his mind with the sense of touch. Once again he used the steering-wheel under his fingers, touching this in awareness never failed to bring him into the present moment.

He smiled ruefully as Michael Collins said, "You're

getting very quiet in your middle age, Samuel. I'm not complaining, but you have me curious."

"I got caught in a dose of the 'what might have beens', Mick. Does that ever happen to you?"

"Rumination, introspection, stuff like that, I haven't much time for it. Especially with the pressure I've been under in recent times." Collins spoke in an off-hand way, not a man to dramatise any situation. To Sam's mind, he might have been forgiven were he to do so at the present time.

What had happened in the three years since he had come back from the prison camp at Frongach in Wales was little short of awesome. And there was no sign that the pressure was going to lessen, not for some time to come.

He remembered Christmas 1916, with Michael Collins coming home to find the country still under the thumb of the British. 'Jesus!' Sam thought. He shrugged off the yesterdays and rubbed his fingers together to bring him back into the present moment. Talk about water under the bridge!

They were on a mission right now, just the two of them at the minute. "Can you get your mind back to Easter week and that Monday morning – that car ride up along the Liffey together?" Collins asked as though he was talking about yesterday.

"I remember it well." He spoke the truth – how could he ever forget the very definite way Collins had told him he was more valuable working for the IRB from the outside, this being the reason he had never been sworn in. It left him free to swear, were he taken by the Brits for any reason, that he was not and never had been a member.

His thinking segued into the GPO on the day that Collins, at the age of twenty-six, came of age as an active commander. He held the rank of Captain in the IRB, being second only to James Plunkett.

In fact, Collins had played a relatively minor role in the GPO, Sam smiling at the memory of carrying Cormac Doyle out of there over his shoulder. Collins had been too busy to notice him since he was in serious discussion with Sean MacDiarmada, a man he respected above the heroic, aesthetic dreamer that he believed Padraig Pearse to be.

Bit player or not, Collins had been remembered for his devotion to duty, and for his courage. His ability to keep a clear head at all times had earned him all kinds of praise from the men around him. Some talked in awe of his cool way: "Even when the world around him was having the shit knocked out of it by British artillery intent on wiping him and the rest of us off the face of the earth." This was Brendan O'Connor's cryptic assessment of the Big Fella under fire.

Soon after his return, Collins arranged a meeting with Sam. He admitted to having a good memory of the Dubliner, and the cool head that he carried around on his shoulders. "I'm starting to rebuild the IRB, Sam." Those were his first words as they sat together on the upper deck of a tram to Howth, on a cold blustery February day. Sam had never felt so cold but he made no complaint. No person in his right mind would ride up there on such a day, ergo they had the deck to themselves, total privacy at no extra charge, thanks to the weather. "We need your help," Collins said from behind the lapels of his greatcoat. "Whatever money Arthur Brewer is willing to give us. We'll have funds coming from America, but we need money right away. And since the pay was lousy in Wales, I'm not terribly flush at the moment."

Within a year, Michael Collins had been elected to the Sinn Fein executive. During the months that followed he created an efficient intelligence network. Meanwhile, he had organised a national loan to fund an assassination squad called the Twelve Apostles. On the heels of this, he brought Sam into the picture to get on with the buying of arms, and the stiffer task of smuggling them into the country. "You have some kind of a knack for smuggling, Sam. Did you know that?"

"You could talk the cross off a donkey's back," Sam said laughingly. The joke was based on the Christian fable that every donkey wore a cross that came etched into its coat from the day Jesus rode one into Jerusalem on what would come to be known as Palm Sunday. "Do you mind me asking what the story is this evening?" Sam asked.

"You and I are taking the boat to Holyhead, Samuel, unless you can't join me on this little jaunt." Collins smiled at the irony in his tone. He was way past having any idea or request turned away by the men who had chosen to follow him.

"No, it's all right. I was stuck for something interesting to do, anyway," Sam said this with a smile of his own, knowing that Collins possessed a keen sense of humour, although some doubted this. "I'll make a telephone call from the Royal Marine hotel, if you don't mind. Let the mother and Gloria know, I'm not getting home tonight." What he didn't reveal was his need to speak to Deirdre, let her know he wouldn't be able to meet her later at his house in Greystones.

"Nice enough night for the crossing," Collins said as they went aboard the mail boat. Sam smiled to himself – some of the bravest and toughest men he knew could get seasick on a mill pond.

An hour later, comfortably ensconced in the warmth of the saloon bar, Sam sipped a brandy as Collins bore a hole in his pint of stout. The sea was calm though the boat shuddered from time to time. Collins had his pipe in his mouth when he was not drinking, a floppy cap pulled down low on his forehead, his only concession to the idea of disguise. Sam wore a striped three-piece suit under a long raincoat and a curly brimmed bowler, in his role as a Dublin businessman and builder's provider.

"I wasn't sure I'd live to see the day when we'd have soldiers trained by the British, ready to go to war against the Crown." Collins emptied his glass. "Some good had to come out of the Great War. Next time we will win, Sam, but, if, just if, mind you, we fail, the Brits will never forget what we are going to put them through in the next few years." He leaned closer then.

"By the way, this little jaunt, it's for you and me to get Dev out of the nick."

Later, when Deirdre asked him how Collins and Harry Boland had gone about springing Eamon De Valera from Lincoln Jail, Sam had to admit he didn't know. "I sat with the engine ticking over – Boland had bought a good fast car. I was told to wait, ready to go – that was all I had to do. I waited maybe twenty minutes, ready to put the boot down when they came out of the night and said, 'Let's get out of here'. That was it." He hugged her, happy to have her there in his bed at the Greystones house. "After that it was drive like hell, and keep your head down."

A week after this, Esther had another heart attack, and this time she simply died as Sam held her in his arms. She had been reading in the front room when he brought in a cup of cocoa, her usual night-time drink before bed. Gloria was upstairs with Samuel who was swotting up on his Hebrew. Already, the lad had expressed the notion that he wanted to be a scholar and a rabbi, but it was his deep interest in the Promised Land – Gloria's name for Palestine – that worried his father most.

"I'm ready for a good sleep so I am, I'll make no bones about that," Esther sipped the cocoa. She sounded tired but no more so than she did on any other night when she was about to go to bed.

"Do you want me to carry you up?" He was being

wicked and she knew it, a short laugh crackling in her throat.

"You've never gone short of practice taking women up the stairs," She was amused by her retort. "But I'll make my own way, thanks all the same, Mister Sweet!"

As he smiled at what he called her piss and vinegar, Esther stood up in a startled involuntary way. The cup dropped from her hand and, instinctively, she reached out to him for help. He moved and caught her before she fell to the carpet. Her eyes fluttered and then she released what he would have called her death rattle, life leaving her as she lay in his arms, a mask of calm and acceptance slipping onto her face like sunlight.

In his own optimistic way, Sam found gratitude that she had been left to him and the family for so long. Her presence had given him the chance to make her life as good as he could, and, of course, she had been a mother figure to Gloria. There was nothing he could do about the grief that was part of the package of his mother's passing. His wife would grieve Esther's going, and the children would suffer along with her – and they would mourn her with devotion – which, he felt was only right. Had they not wept and grieved over Esther who had brought her own brand of folksy greatness into Sam's early life, it would have been a sadder world.

Gloria had put her dreams of the Promised Land on hold because it would have meant leaving Esther behind – the task implicit in the idea of making a homeland in Palestine precluded people who were as old as Esther and those in ill-health. Gloria knew that the work and the danger – the Palestinians had been making warning noises for some years now – would have been too much for a woman of Esther's age. She accepted that she had now been set free to get on with doing what had been uppermost in her mind since she had first heard of Eretz Yisroel.

This was a topic that she and Sam did not discuss. In fact, they had both been waiting for something to happen, or for the other to make the first move. Gloria had kept the blue box, in which her ongoing collection for Palestine money was deposited. This blue and white box bearing the embossed letters JNF and the map of Palestine stood on the hall table, and though Sam had a serious objection to this, he put coins in it whenever he remembered, and kept his mouth shut.

In truth, he didn't much mind what Gloria did with her life, but he knew that one day they would have a very serious discussion about what was going to happen to his children.

During the first half of the year, Sam, quietly mourning his mother's passing, made two trips to buy guns on the orders of Michael Collins. He did not take Dee along either time – she was snowed under with her midwifery and the development of some kind of plan to help young mothers. She championed those overwhelmed by poverty and the ever-present pestilence that infested the dreadful living conditions of the have-nots. She went on appealing to the people she had come to know in government circles, trying to find some way to get a national plan put into operation to ease the plight of the poor.

Sam travelled – missing Dee badly though he didn't allow this to distract him from the job in hand. On his return from New York, he discovered that the IRB had been given a new name change, and was now the Irish Republican Army – the IRA. It was led by Michael Collins and Austin Stack and other survivors of the Easter Rising. Sam was not in the least surprised. With Collins in charge, change, and lots of it, was only to be expected.

Some months after Esther's death, Sam got home early on Friday feeling it was time to face Gloria about her Promised Land idea, and the role his children would play in her latest drama. When he got indoors, she was in the kitchen cleaning a chicken for the Sabbath dinner. She was dressed in black, still mourning Esther, and he made coffee, pouring her a cup without enquiring whether she wanted it or not. He lit a cigarette and sat down at the kitchen table.

"Sarah informs me that you're always talking about going to Palestine. Have you anything to say to me about that?" He kept his voice low-key, aiming for a neutral tone, willing to come to this moment without preconceptions, but up to his ears in them. "I have supported you in every way I know how, so don't you think you might talk to me about it?"

Gloria left the chicken to drain, and she wiped her hands on her apron as she sat down and took a sip of the coffee. "I meant no disrespect to you. I know you think of Palestine as what you call an unjust situation. I have no interest in arguing about it. I want to go there, and make a life there."

"I get the feeling you think you are taking the children with you." Sam inhaled on the cigarette, trying to keep his tone neutral.

"Of course, I intend to take my children with me. With Esther's love and care and help, I have reared them. But . . ."

"Sarah doesn't want to go with you," Sam interrupted.

Gloria's shoulders dropped in disappointment. She seemed to feel a dart of pain or something.

"What is it, Gloria?" he was genuinely concerned.

"I want to go. I feel I have to. And I think it ludicrous that a child of Sarah's age – she is just ten years old – that she should have any say in the matter." She held up her hand in a placatory gesture. He saw how difficult she was finding this, and he gave her the floor. "Please, Samuel, just let me tell you what has happened." She took a deep breath, "I have been accepted, I am booked to travel on the trip, the one I have organised on behalf of the committee. Only today did I discover that the children cannot travel with me. Things are too unsettled out there at the present. Later, when things settle down . . ." She paused as though searching for the right words.

Sam stifled the need to tell her to forget this stupid dream. He said then as calmly as he could, "So what are you saying, Gloria? Are you intending to leave the children here, have them join you out there later, or what?" She was nodding her head almost imperceptibly, and he couldn't hide his astonishment.

"And I thought your children meant the whole

world to you," he said, like someone defeated by surprise.

"They do. They do, Sam. Of course they do. But . . ."

"I'm hearing this, and I'm reading it in your face, but I don't believe this is really happening," he said with some feeling.

"I have to go. Can't you understand that? "

"Look, I've done nothing to try and stop you going, have I?"

She shook her head, and he did nothing to hide his incredulity.

"You know we have no marriage, we are able to deal with that, be civil to each other, and you know that I will support you, that I will look after my children as long as I can breathe. So why does it all have to be so dramatic? Why can't you just accept that we are separating, getting a divorce, whatever is to happen? Why do you have to add this Palestine stuff? Aren't things dramatic enough already?"

"You haven't heard a word I've said." She threw her hand up defensively. "I'm sorry. That wasn't fair. You have put up with more than your share of drama, I'll give you that. Now, instead of us having a stand-up row, let me tell you what I need, Sam, and you tell me if you want to help me or not. May I go on?"

He nodded, surprised to find himself feeling a little sorry for her. She looked grateful as she said, "I ask you to keep the children with you. Samuel would be happier if you sent him away to school. Sarah, well, I hardly know what to say."

Sam poured coffee for her, lit a cigarette then and drew smoke in. "Regardless of how intelligent she is, Samuel, she is still a child, and already she has her heart set on marrying Eddie Brewer. Had you not told me the story of Eddie's birth, I would by now be totally demented because I believe that one day they will marry. So once again I must thank you for helping me hold on to my sanity." She drank a gulp of coffee, looking more nervous by the minute. "I believe in the Promised Land for the Jews," she said urgently, "and I am offering my life to that ideal. I don't care about my safety, or my well-being, or my comfort. I want to serve in any way I can and I am going to do that. Let me confess something. Sam, this is not a whim, a fanciful notion to inject some romance or adventure into my life. The truth is I feel I have been called, that this is my destiny. It is what my life has been leading to always. I do not ask you to understand, but if you would continue being the friend you have been through all the times when you would have been forgiven for turning your back on me, I will be forever grateful to you. Please, talk to Sarah and Samuel and say whatever you need to say to each other. Meanwhile, I will go on running our home until the day I leave for Eretz Yisroel. Now, if you'll excuse me, I should get the dinner on. Can you stay home and eat with us tonight?"

Being as honest as he could be, Sam knew, as he had known for a long time, that his son had no time for him. But he knew that the openness that he had fought for, against Gloria's rigid idea on child-rearing, had allowed his son the right to speak his mind without fear of being threatened or beaten for his honesty, however hurtful it might be to his father's ego.

Not that Samuel had ever disrespected him. So, if the lad wanted to go to boarding school, it would probably be best all round. Sam knew already through things Sarah had said, that her brother wanted to go to Palestine because he wanted to be with his mother. In all truth, the lad had been a mammy's boy from his earliest days. This was not a pejorative word in Sam's mind – he had known the same kind of relationship with Esther, eschewing his father with ease, because this rock of a woman was always there for him.

Sarah wanted to stay in Ireland. She was precocious enough to say so, and she believed she knew exactly what she wanted to do with her life. "What I'd like best, Daddy, is to live with the Brewers at Dunbla. Aunt Dee said I could spend part of each week living there, if you would allow it. After I finish my education, I want to join in her work for the poor. After that, Aunt Dee will have me on a part-time basis while I see how I get along. She said that this country is going to need me, and Eddie and those of our generation that are not motivated by success and material possessions. 'You and your fellow students,' she said, 'you are going to provide the backbone for the Ireland that has to emerge from the debris around us'."

Sam could only stand and gasp as his little girl rattled on like this without even pausing for breath. Yes, she was precocious and likely to be a real handful later on, but she lit up his life with her brilliant mind and her quicksilver tongue.

He agreed that Samuel could go to boarding school. He discussed this with his son and between them they settled on Townley Castle School at Ramsgate in England. And he allowed that when the time was right – this to be agreed between father and son – Samuel could go and live with his mother in Palestine. He found his son to be a very brave lad when the day of Gloria's leaving arrived. He knew how close Samuel was to his mother, felt proud of the lad's calm as he said goodbye to her, promising her he would study. Even though he himself was moved by the parting from Gloria and the distance that lay there like wasteland between himself and his boy, Sam had come to terms with his situation, accepting that Samuel would simply be marking time until he could join Gloria.

Sarah was saddened, though not in any way desolated, by her mother's departure. Within days she was packing up certain clothes and the other things she needed, so that she could get on with living part of the week at Dunbla. Trying to imagine what it must be like for his daughter, Sam thought it certainly had the ring of adventure about it. And he knew that once Eddie was close at hand and available to her, Sarah would have no problems. Father and daughter agreed that she would be at home four nights each week. To this end Sam found a housekeeper, a bossy but very capable woman called Kitty Gallagher, who was soon running the Leinster Road house like a military operation.

He also hired a handyman-driver, John O'Toole, a 40-year-old with strong Republican leanings, who would take Sarah to and from her homes, and back and forth to school. John would also attend to maintenance of the house and gardens at Rathmines and run the odd errand for Sam when it was necessary. In this way, within a few weeks things in Dublin soon fell into place, the new routine became the norm for Sam, on the home front anyway. He was surprised by how quickly he came to accept that both his mother and Gloria would not be coming to call him to dinner on the Friday nights he made it home in time. He found himself remembering now and then how touched he had been by his wife's final words before she stepped into the car taking her to the boat. "You have been a forgiving man. I will never forget your compassion, Sam, and all I will ever say about us is that I had the best years of my life living with you and Esther."

"Mind you," he said, trying to be light in the face of her tears, "it was dog-rough before we met."

She laughed and wept at the same time. "Thank you for everything."

"You mind yourself," he said, sniffing back threatening tears. He stood and gave her a final wave as the car moved away from the house. He was remembering something he'd read as a lad. Some Indian guru had written that everything that happens is just that, life happening. That the big emotional moments are no different, it is just life happening. That we are not really decimated by the death or the departure, of people we love, or other traumatic events, it is just life happening. The guru claimed that the pain, and the overt suffering witnessed when a person lost a loved-one was part of man's need to gloss up the ordinary in order to add excitement, drama, depth, or fun, or whatever you liked to call it to give more worth to what could be called everyday events, even if these included living and dying.

As he watched Gloria's car make the left turn onto Rathmines Road for the North Wall of the Liffey and the boat that would take her on the first leg of her journey, Sam was content. And for the first time he felt, through the experience of the moment, that the guru was a very wise man, if not all that easily understood when someone's heart was in a sling over a happening that was the last thing on earth they would have wished for.

Sarah staying at Dunbla several nights a week with Deirdre and the boys, actually suited Sam down to the ground, since he had even more reason to drop out to the house at all hours.

Dee now spent less and less time worrying about Arthur and his drinking. "There's simply too much suffering and deprivation out there. I leave Arthur alone, and he is as content as can be expected," she said to Sam, her attitude and her tone, and he felt sure, her heart coming to the matter in a charitable mode.

She laid down ground-rules for Sarah and Eddie. They were allowed free speech, they could take ponies out as a matter of course, but first Sarah must have riding lessons. They could play tennis and swim – they were both natural swimmers – provided they did not neglect their school work. And yes, Eddie could teach Sarah what he himself learned on the piano, but they had to promise to include Alfie when he needed their company. Eddie wasn't keen on this part of the arrangement, but Sarah adored Alfie, actually enjoying his tantrums and his precociousness, without ever considering that they might be the harbinger of things to come.

Dee was grateful for Sarah's tolerance of her youngest, since she saw less of him than she deemed ideal, due to her work. She spent schoolday nights under the same roof as her sons in Merrion Square, while Sarah was at home in Rathmines, but often she would not get back there before they had gone to bed, worn out by their full days and the homework from their teachers at High School on Harcourt Street.

By early on Friday evening, the boys and Sarah would be climbing into their country duds, as they called their casual clothes, all set to enjoy the privileged life of well-to-do young people.

In this way, Deirdre managed to assuage, if not become free, of her guilt that she was not the committed mother she had planned to be in the days when she had stood around her workshop day-dreaming about life with Arthur. She could smile wistfully in the moments when she managed to forgive herself totally, as she remembered how her own life had seemed immensely enriched when her mother had stopped working alongside her father, especially in the evenings when they had so much fun before going off to sleep.

Sam took lunch with Arthur every Thursday, and never tired of seeing his great friend who sometimes managed to arrive for their midday chat without being three sheets to the wind. Arthur had a new driver now, a man called Tom Faires, who had been a school pal of Brendan O'Connor. Faires was ex-British army and had taken over the duties that Seamus could no longer deal with. Arthur had retired Seamus, without ever using this word. The man-servant lived in his fine cottage with Angela, their home built especially for them close by Kelly's cottage on the Dunbla estate. Seamus had accepted the brief from Dee that he see Kelly every day, just to make sure she was all right – she was getting an old woman now – and not in need of anything.

Arthur had recently contributed generously to the Ireland of the future, his huge donation buying more weapons and ammunition for the IRA stockpile, not that he knew this, or indeed, ever questioned what his money was used for. Arthur preferred to go over old times now with Sam – how they had come together, the first contract at the brewery, Sam's resurrection thanks to the South African shares, and his ongoing success in the building industry. He was always keen to hear the newest plan that his friend came up with and he seemed to be reading more than before. He had begun talking about recent history in quite a knowledgeable way, nothing deep or startling, but his overall attention showed he was genuinely interested in the Irish question, though he appeared to be in some stage of inebriation at all times.

Unlike most of his class, Arthur didn't subscribe to the idea that Ireland and England had been too close for too long to ever successfully be parted. "You would think the two countries were Siamese twins the way some people chatter on, Sam. Just the other day, I heard a fellow say in my club, 'They can't be de-siamesed, not even by the surgery of rebellion'. Did you ever hear such a thing?"

Like Sam, Arthur had been surprised by the general election results. The Republicans were now called Sinn Fein and had won seventy-three seats. Sinn Fein had been the brainchild of Arthur Griffith, an extremely talented journalist – it would be a constitutional, but anti-parliamentarian movement. He never dreamed that it would become Republican. The English translation of Sinn Fein is 'Ourselves Alone'.

The Republican elect soon announced they would not sit in the Westminster Parliament, and to the surprise of the British Prime Minister, Lloyd George, they proclaimed Ireland to be a republic. Soon after this the first session of Dail Eireann took place on January twenty-first 1919.

"Whereas the Irish people is by right a free people . . ."

The opening words of Ireland's Declaration of Independence seemed odd when it was remembered that many Volunteers were behind bars in Lincoln Jail, in England. After his own escape from that prison, De Valera managed to hide out in London. On his return to

Dublin he was immediately elected President of the Republic of Ireland.

Lying with Dee's head on his chest, Sam watched a smoke ring rise in the air above her bed at Dunbla. This stolen time was very precious to them – Arthur was in England on business, the children were in town at school, Dee had taken several hours off before heading for the Cork Street and the twin houses she was turning into a lying-in clinic.

"You can be sure of one thing," Sam turned and kissed Dee's lips. "The lull is well and truly over."

She knew he was talking politics but chose to be wicked. "I'm glad to hear it." She moved her hand to quickly turn him erect again. She moved then, and he shuddered playfully as she slid down to wrap him up in herself.

They weren't seeing each other as much as they wanted. Business and the mental pressure created by his ongoing and developing involvement in the Republican Movement left him needing longer days in order to cope with all that demanded his attention. He longed at times to be free of it all, to simply be able to go off somewhere with Dee.

Deirdre was equally busy. Her midwifery work, the follow-up care she was still trying to develop, had led her into teaching midwifery and the writing of a book about hygiene. She also had a husband and two homes to supervise.

When they made time to be together she was insatiable. "I come, oh God, how I come. But no sooner am I relieved of my wanting, than the demand for more of you and the sensation you pump into me, is knocking on the door. At times I feel I will expire, and at other times I am actually prepared to die, to slither off on a streamer of sensation that leaves me greedily, selfishly, willing to tear flesh to get more of the same. Imagine!" She chuckled at what she thought of as brash and wanton behaviour. "And I was schooled by the nuns!"

For some time, Sam had been aware that his only contentment came when they were in each other's arms. And he felt now, as a matter of course – despite the fact that his home had been broken up – that this was the best and the happiest time of his life. He wallowed in the belief that Dee – with whom he was equally insatiable in bed – gave him this energy to love her in the magnificence that their sexual life had become. It seemed so right, felt so natural, that whatever aggravation snapped at his daily life, well, he simply didn't give a damn. It was just life happening, and when all was said and done, wasn't Dee there waiting to wrap him up in her amazing love.

Even as he lay beside Dee, he found himself again grateful to the Forans for turning him into a bankrupt, something he had been fearful of in the months before it happened. The event had forced him to sell everything that was in his name in order to pay his creditors. Some years before, he had placed ownership of the Leinster Road home and the house at Greystones in his mother's name, the possession of a family home having become more important to him since his children had been born. What money he had tucked away in several safe deposit boxes went to his creditiors and when it was gone he had found that he was all right in himself. He was not afraid.

Going back to the night his bankruptcy had been orchestrated by Dinny Foran, he found there a man who had no fear of starting all over. Up to the fire and the death of Shamey – Dinny was sentenced to five years in prison for his part in that night's events – Sam had no notion that he might have needed the experience. He now believed that he did need it to happen exactly as it had done.

Some months afterward, when the good news about his gold shares came through, he was more than happy to welcome his rescue with an open heart, as he allowed that this fortuitous turn was also life happening. He had no problem whatever, in saying bless you to Arthur for the information about the shares in the first place, and he expected to go on feeling grateful that he had given Arthur the money to invest, even though he had no real faith in the gold mine.

Dee's hand touching his face brought him back to the bed, and he said, "When I think of all the years I knew you before I could see what you truly meant to me, I wonder how I managed to get across the road without getting knocked down by a runaway donkey or something. And there's something else, Dee. As sure as God made little apples, you'll kill me in the bed."

"Listen to who's talking!" Dee pretended outrage, bursting out laughing before she intended to. "I'm bloody lost," she moaned playfully. "I can't even pretend that I'm not carnivorous where you're concerned. And if I do kill you in the bed, I pray to God, please let me go with Sam, whether in or out of bed. Please let me die with the only man I want to live with."

"Be wonderful if we could die together on a mutual orgasm," he said, tongue in cheek.

"Well, yes, but why are you looking so happy with yourself?" Dee was sceptical about where he was leading her.

"Well, if that happened, if we both died in orgasm, well," he held onto his need to laugh, "we'd be sure we were coming, but we'd actually be going!"

She howled through her response, laughter tumbling from her at his wickedness. They shared their hilarity and then she came to his mouth with her own, kissing him hungrily. He pulled his head back and looked at her. "Do you remember how shocked you were the first time I put my tongue in your mouth?"

Dee allowed a gasp to escape the circle of disbelief her mouth had become. "I had never experienced anything like the sensation of that. I honestly think my love life started at that moment. I don't know, but with me, Arthur is so polite and gentle, so sort of antiseptic, if you like, that our love-making didn't do very much for me, though of course it gave us our children for which I will always be grateful."

Sam said nothing, allowing the memory of Arthur's disclosure, and the detail from Gloria's journal about that one night of sexual love to pass by. He had learned that thoughts were best treated like birds – you allowed them to circle overhead but you did not have to give them landing permission. The thoughts you chose to have in your head, that part seemed to be entirely up to you. He knew he had some study to do in this area but he was convinced he was on the right track. All the thoughts you shoved aside, where did they go? He felt they belonged to the universe, like the weather.

He did allow a smile to slide across the screen behind his eyes before he shut memory down completely. From what Deirdre had said Arthur had more fun with prostitutes than he'd had in the marriage bed. Was that part of the reason he kept going back to the brothels? 'I don't know,' Sam told himself, 'and I don't care. I love old Arthur and I would give my life for him.'

30

Dublin

1920

As 1920 found its feet, Sam believed that the Anglo-Irish war could go on for another year or even more, and the prospect filled him with dread. For more than six months now it had been a dirty fight, with atrocities and the inevitable reprisals on both sides, vengeance sending many a man to his death grinding his teeth, his heart screaming out for revenge. Murder was one of the main items on the daily menu, the rulebook having been thrown out of the window, the Irish arguing that they killed selectively, while the British murdered out-of-hand. The British did kill indiscriminately, decimating entire families, destroying entire areas of the city, in their slaying of men, women and children, innocents in the main.

Sam believed the Brits behaved badly, but when he read of an English officer being shot dead in front of his wife and children, he had pangs of guilt.

The money that had helped form and maintain Michael Collins' professional assassination squad had come through him – he had delivered Arthur's latest input into the coffers of the IRA. Facing the result of his service to the cause, Sam found no comfort in rationalisation. Collins, sensing this reservation, wasn't slow to come down on him like a ton of bricks.

"This fight was never going to be Marquis of Queensbury, Sam. And you don't need me to give you statistics. It's got to get worse before it's ever going to improve. So shit or get off the pot. You have the guts, you've proved that, but unless your heart is in the mix, I won't be able to trust you. So, cut this conscience shit, or get out. And by that I mean get out of the country. Go and join your missus in Palestine, the poor bitch. She is going to know what shooting is all about trying to live out there." Collins waited, letting the words sink in. "You're a good man, and I want you in this with me. But if you are not in a hundred per cent, I don't want you. And with what you know, I can't have you around the place. You understand. There's no room here for sentiment."

"Of course, I understand. Sorry for the lapse. It won't happen again."

"I believe that. Would it be easier for you if I swore you in? That would eliminate any tendency to judge what has to be done. You'd toe the line taken by your leaders, or end up with a bullet in the head."

"I'll be all right, Mick."

"Just as well we had this chat. It's out now, so forget

about it. I need your brains as well as the money you bring in. I need your ideas too – direct attack or defence is only an aspect of what lies ahead here. If we can make the Brits redundant in some way – mess up their image, even in their own eyes – put a huge Jesus scare up them. So think about it – whatever you can come up with just spit it out. If we get one really good idea out of a hundred, it's worth the sweat," Collins said. "Between us we must be able to put the fear of Christ into the Brits!"

In time, Sam came to feel good about his part in all that followed, knowing that no matter what was right or wrong in a moment of expediency, the goal would justify the means of its happening. He was now part of a think-tank that held no formal meetings, one of a band dedicated to implementing a policy that while backing up direct confrontation, did its very own damage. The overall plan was to interfere with the ability of the Brits to operate to maximum efficiency. Destroying the structure of their intelligence gathering seemed a good place to make a start. And it soon became clear that though there were daily battles in the streets and on the rooftops of the city, the real struggle was between the intelligence service organised by Collins, and the one that served the British out of Dublin Castle.

Sam got a telephone call he'd been expecting from Dee. "Can you come out to the house this evening? Vicky is back from Paris."

"I take it she survived the trip?" he said in all seriousness.

Ten days earlier, Vicky had informed everyone she was going to Paris to see Michelle. She left out the caveat 'for the last time' but the pause in her waning eyes left nobody in any doubt that this was what she was thinking.

She was terribly frail now, like a very old woman, but she had a will of steel, so that when she made up her mind about anything, nothing short of heart failure was going to stop her going to Paris. Nothing would interfere with her plan to see Michelle.

Doctor Paddy Lote was roped in – how could he refuse her request that he find a reliable nurse to accompany him while he tended to Vicky for her short stay in the city by the Seine where she had spent some of her happiest hours. Lote came out of retirement to grant Vicky's wish. His lifelong respect for her – it was she who had saved Arthur from mental collapse all those years before – left him no choice.

Victoria was transported by coach and train and boat, carried from seat to seat by willing arms, treated with the greatest of care and love and kindness. She made her peace with the great love of her life, and she came home again prepared to die in the warmth of her family's wanting, including Sam.

"She's not at all well, Sam." Dee was all too aware that he knew just how ill Vicky had been before she left for France. She was not ready to let go of her sister-in-law, brought into her life by Sam. "She needs to see you. Be prepared for a shock."

As Dee kissed him and held him for a moment in the

hallway of the great house, he felt the pain in her. "Our dear Vicky is not long for this world, Sam. I'll take you in and then leave you. She has something she needs to ask you. I don't know what it is."

The moment he laid eyes on Victoria, Sam was thankful for Dee's warning – there was no doubt in his mind that Victoria was dying. He recoiled from the idea, trying to keep his expression neutral.

"You brought the paintings, I hope." He got the words out, despite feeling he'd been kicked in the stomach.

"It's all right to be shocked, Sam." Vicky had lost some of her teeth, and her hair was grey and lifeless. Her once lovely face was puckered – riddled was how he thought of it – where the skin seemed to have collapsed inwards as the flesh fell from her cheekbones. He put his arms around her and held her gently, genuinely fearful that he might break one of her limbs if he held her tight.

"What can I do, my old darling?" He tried to sound easygoing and offhand, as though this would in some way lessen the distress her appearance was causing them both.

"I'm dying," she said flatly. "Ironically, I'm not dying quickly enough. I'm booked into a nursing home. I want you to take me there this evening, can you manage that?" She spoke calmly without a shred of self-pity, her sound free of sentimentality.

"Of course, I can take you. Is there anything else you need me to attend to?" He looked at her, despite his need to avert his eyes, his pain buried by sheer willpower. "And I mean anything." He had no idea why he had said this, allowing that it was coming from his desire to be good for her in every possible way right to the very last moment.

"There are twelve paintings – my second reason for going to Paris was to collect them. They have been seen by some of the top people in the art world. It seems that, posthumously, my reputation will far outshine the one I earned while alive. I want you to wait until the time is right, when the work is deemed to be at the peak of its earning power – hold an auction then. I want the proceeds to go to Dee's hospital work. She is to have a free hand to spend it as she thinks fit. Will you do that for me?" Her head was lowered as she spoke, and he saw that her hands were like claws. Her body was emaciated, her lovely face a hideous mask, her nose having receded as her illness devoured her.

"Of course, I'll handle it, love. Is there anything else?"

"I've made you executor of my estate. I have also given Dee a package for you. You're not to open it until after." He nodded, and she nodded gently in gratitude. As surreptitiously as he could manage it, Sam was hauling great breaths deeply through his nose as he tried to stop the tears threatening to spill from his eyes.

"This next request," Victoria has to pause for breath. "Very selfish of me, Sam, but you see what's happening to me. I am being eaten up by syphilis. It can only get worse, and it can go on for some time." She looked up at him, and he saw she was close to tears, the once bright blue eyes that shone to startle him when she saw him enter a room were no more. They had been replaced by broken pellets that looked like frozen mucus. His throat constricted and he stood there silent, simply unable to speak.

"I ask you to put me out of this misery, Sam. Help me by getting me something that I can take, that I might go to sleep before my mind is taken from me completely. Can you forgive me asking you? You are the only one I can ask to do such a thing."

"Don't worry, dearest Vicky. I'll not let you down." His words came through like a willing sigh and he smiled down at her.

"Bless you, my darling." She was now helpless to stop her tears, and he moved close to her again, putting his arms, gentle as feathers landing, about her.

"I know that you would do the same for me, without hesitation. And weren't we always a couple of outsiders, playing the game by our rules and nobody else's? I will come to you tomorrow, and I will be holding your hand till you cross over. I promise you."

When it was time for her to go to the nursing home, he carried her to the car and placed her on the back seat, so that she could rest her head on Deirdre's lap, a tartan rug she'd had since she was a child covering her body. When they got to the nursing home in Bray, he lifted her gently and carried her with all his caring heart into the house she had chosen to die in.

They waited until she was in bed, each holding one of her hands until she had drifted into a drug-induced sleep. They got into the car then for the seven mile drive to his place in Greystones. They spoke just a few words on the short journey, both stunned to silence by Vicky's condition.

Sam knew that Arthur had been missing for three days. So far, he had not made any offer to go and look for him. As he held Dee in the bed, she said, "If Arthur is not home tomorrow, will you look for him? I'm worried because he could be caught up in some of the shooting – it seems to be getting worse day by day."

"I'll find him and I'll bring him home." He resisted the urge to tell her that Arthur's driver, Tom Faires, was no Seamus Byrne, that he went to a prostitute every time Arthur did, attending to his need rather than his master's welfare. Sam held her close. "He may never recover from Vicky's death – you know that, don't you?"

Dee wept silently. He felt her tears on his neck and face, and his heart was sore since he wanted to save her from some of life's body blows.

He took her home at six in the morning and they had breakfast cooked by Angela. She was quiet, clearly upset and saddened about Vicky, whom she had known from a child.

Sam drove into Portobello Harbour for an early meeting. He found Cormac alone in the office. This was a bad sign. If Brendan were on his feet, he would have been in the office waiting when he got there.

"He's not going to die, Sam, but he'll be lying low for a little while. We got rid of two of their top intelligence officers, before a copper got a lucky shot at Brendan. I hit your man, took the car he was driving. I left Bren with the doc – he'll be all right in a few days."

At nine o'clock, Sam called the booking office of the shipping company he did all his business with, and spoke to his contact there. "Just checking on an employee, Brendan O'Connor," he said with emphasis. "Tell me, Mister O'Brian, was it yesterday or the day before that he sailed to Liverpool?"

The man at the other end said, "Give me a moment, Mister Sweet, and I'll have that information for you." Sam shrugged at Cormac, "Nothing beats covering your arse."

"Mister Sweet." The voice of Sean O'Brian was all business. "It was the day before yesterday. His return is booked for two weeks from now. Is that what you were looking for?"

"Exactly, Mister O'Brian. Thanks very much. I'll be in touch."

Sam put the phone down. "The story is that Brendan's in Liverpool. You call Jimmy Hanley over there. Tell him the story, without telling him anything?"

Cormac nodded, and was soon dialling the phone number in Liverpool. Just minutes later, Sam got a call from Michael Collins asking for a lunch-time meeting in the Shelbourne.

When he entered the hotel, he saw Collins sitting in an armchair reading the *Irish Independent*. The Big Fella was wearing a dark-grey suit, and the dog collar of a Protestant minister, causing Sam to smile. It was said of Collins that he never used a disguise – he walked the streets and was never challenged by either soldiers, or the policemen of the Royal Irish Constabulary. In some ways, this was true. Collins never hid his face behind moustaches or beards, but he used the dog collar of both Catholic and Prod to gather the attention of people, this shifting the emphasis off his face, and from time to time he donned spectacles with the same intent.

When Sam sat down he said quietly, "Our mutual idea to neutralise their spies, it has received the highest accolade from the Brits."

"I don't like the sound of that," Sam said, indicating drinks to a waiter who knew him well.

"It's going to cause us some inconvenience. They've sent in the heavy mob." Collins actually sounded pleased by what Sam thought of as a highly questionable compliment.

"They must be heavy when you talk about them like that."

"As heavy as you can get. But, God help them, they have no future. I'm only amazed they have been here for the guts of two weeks and we didn't even know." Collins didn't look at all pleased as he said, "But by God, we know now, and they will pay the piper."

He took a swig from his stout, and Sam told him that

Brendan O'Connor's alibi was in place. "Excellent. He and the other lad, they did the country a great service last night. Now, my reason for asking to see you . . . I need a place, somewhere offside. I have a lot of writing to do. The next phase in our operation has to be planned with great care. As I'd value your input, I wondered about your place in Greystones. Can I have the use of that? "

"You most certainly can," Sam said. "What about I take you out there, leave you, and drop back every day with the grub stakes and such. That way, you won't have to risk any unnecessary exposure. Is that what you had in mind?"

Collins put down his empty glass. "I couldn't have put it better myself, Sam."

As soon as Sam left the hotel, he went to meet the quack Lanigan in St Stephen's Green Park across the road. Lanigan had been a medical doctor, was struck off when his sideline as an abortionist cost the life of a young woman. Only his connections, and the fact that he knew where all the bodies were buried, had kept him out of jail. He now worked with the IRA, tending to wounded men that could not be taken to a hospital. He still carried out abortions for any woman with money, including some of Lisa O'Brien's workers. When Sam had asked Lisa over a sociable glass of wine on one of his visits to her home in Sandymount how come prostitutes allowed themselves to be put in the family way, Lisa had pulled a face.

"Little wonder you'd be asking. It's the heavy

drinkers get caught," Lisa said laconically. "They get pissed without getting the tissue paper in." This remark from his old friend caused him to remember Victoria's answer about a hundred years ago, when he had mentioned the fact that she managed not to get pregnant despite their voracious appetites.

Quack Lanigan was well connected with the seamier aspects of Dublin life, and was never short of work. Yet, in spite of how much he earned he was always short of money, his penchant for backing horses and dogs that most people called rheumatic keeping him in a state of agitation.

"Let her take these before she settles down for the night," Lanigan said, having heard the story of Victoria's condition earlier in the day. "She's right to get out of it as fast as she can. Tertiary syph is a rotten way to go. The poor bitch. I hope there is a heaven. Anybody dying from syph deserves a better life in the beyond."

Sam put the pills in his pocket and slipped Lanigan fifty pounds. He saw the surprise on the doctor's craggy face when he checked how much Sam had given him.

"I'd willingly come with you, give her a jab, Sam. Sooner the better like."

"No, we'll do it this way, David. Let her go off to sleep for good and all," Sam needed to get away from the man. He left and walked in the park, his head full of the once beautiful, vivacious Vicky, the poor duck now ravaged by the shark of all diseases. "I'll sit with her, so she'll know I'm there. But thanks for the thought, David." Those had been his parting words to Lanigan.

Sam smiled grimly as he walked – no longer suffering over Vicky. He had done what she wanted, got what was needed to minimise the pointless gruesome suffering that was ahead of her as day followed day. This was how she wanted it and he would do everything to make her passing as peaceful as it could possibly be.

He thought of how he and the quack had discussed a life and a death in their pragmatic way over a drink while money and medication changed hands. Even as they heard shots in the near distance, he smiled at the way people dealt with the shit that life threw at them every time you looked around. And the feelings of people, they never ceased to amaze him. Like Lanigan over the gunshots.

"That'll be the fuckin' Tans. They're scum," he had said. "The greatest shower of cross-born bastards England ever sent anywhere. Lloyd George should be ashamed to allow them to wear a uniform. I think he's getting his own back, on the Brits, by showing the world what scum they are rearing over there. I don't care if he is the Prime Minister – the little Welsh bastard hates the English as much as we do."

Sam was all too aware that he himself didn't hate the English, or any other race en masse. His hand wrapped around the tiny phial of pills as he walked to his car. He was icy calm in his gut now, relieved that he could help Vicky, his suffering lessened by being able to do her the service she craved. He knew, regardless of what society might think, that it was the thing to do. Vicky deserved to pass over without having to become a screaming mental case.

At the nursing home Sam was met by the nervous nurse he had talked with the day before. "Thank God, you got here for her. She hasn't got long, Mister Sweet."

A nursing sister was wiping Vicky's brow as he entered the sick room. When she saw him, the middle-aged woman nodded her head in commiseration, slipping silently from the room.

Sam moved to the bed and touched Vicky's hand. In a heartbeat, her eyelids fluttered, and to his amazement he saw a hint of the bright blue eyes he had first seen by the Liffey on the day his life had changed for all time.

"I knew you'd come," she whispered. "I waited for you."

He felt her skeleton's fingers tighten on his hand. "I'm all right, Sam."

"I know you are, darling." His eyes spilled tears without restraint, and she sighed quietly. He saw the light go out of her eyes, her fingers fell from his hand and he knew she was not going to be needing Quack Lanigan's pills.

As he drove away from Bray, he was weeping copiously and he cried out a wish, a prayer filled with pain. "Mind her," to whatever power might hear the words. "She was a god's gift to this world."

Arthur was so shattered that he had to be hospitalised

with alcoholic poisoning. Although he didn't know it, he missed Victoria's funeral, as did both her now ageing parents. There were cards and wreaths from both Arthur Shane Brewer and Constance, but neither of them turned up. Sam tried to make allowances for them, "Old people, decrepit through too much rich living, Dee. Travelling would be very hard on them."

Dee, who had never been known to express a judgmental word about anyone, thought they were 'pathetic'.

When Arthur came home from hospital, he seemed quite well, if a little careful in his movements. Sam felt great concern for him, Dee sharing this anxiety. But it stopped there for her – she had long ago accepted nothing could be done, unless Arthur stopped drinking.

About a week after this, Sam was alone in the office. Cormac had been working alongside him up to an hour before. As he'd been about to leave, Sam had asked him if he had plans for the evening. To his surprise, Dee's brother said yes, he had an appointment with a young woman. Genuinely pleased to hear this, Sam said, "I'm glad. You're far too bloody serious for such a young fella. Here," he put a twenty-pound note in the younger man's hand, "buy a bottle of champagne, and drink my health with the young lady."

Cormac was reluctant about the money. Sam had the impression that he seemed to be about to say something, saw a change of heart in his eyes, not surprised as Cormac left with just a nod of his head.

Sam was ready to go out the door and take a spin out to Dunbla when the phone rang. "Sam, I'm really sorry to be such a bother." Dee sounded like someone under stress, and he assured her she could never be a bother. "Dear man, would you mind terribly driving to Monto, see if you run across Arthur. He's been uppermost in my mind all day. I fear that something has happened to him."

"I'm coming out to see you right now. Later on, when the midnight people come out of their coffins, I'll drive in and find Arthur. As early as this, Dee, I wouldn't know where to look."

They ate a roast pork dinner, accompanied by Angela's crispy roasted potatoes and peas from the garden, with an apple sauce touched with wine, the entire meal a joy to Sam's taste-buds. As they were moving into her sitting-room, Eddie came down the stairs with his cramming teacher. He had come down from the city to spend time with this cramming coach, a retired genius who lived in a grace and favour cottage on Brewer land.

Eddie had been waiting for Sam to drive him back to town that he might attend High School in the morning.

Deirdre kissed her son goodnight and he went to get his coat. He was tall for his age and already displaying talent as an athlete. Sam grinned at Dee. "Eddie without Sarah by his side doesn't look like Eddie!"

Sam was home at the Leinster Road house by half past ten, kissed Sarah goodnight, saying nothing about his having to go out again. He would wait until she was sound asleep, before he left her in the care of Kitty Gallagher.

He smiled as Kitty fussed around him – would he like this or that? She was always the same, this buxom, rounded, attractive woman. Sam had been around long enough to see that she had taken a fancy to him. He allowed that, in another time and another place, he would happily have dallied with her, though he could tell she would be looking for more than a romp in the feathers. He smiled, mildly surprised that such days were gone – he was so totally committed to Deirdre – sharing with her a closeness that had been a long time in the coming, and he would never do anything to put a dent in the dreams they had of spending what life was left to them together.

At midnight he drove down though Rathmines village, heading for the city and Monto, particularly Lisa's high-class brothel. You wouldn't know with Arthur – he could well be tucked up there with one of whores that Lisa imported from London and Paris.

When Sam arrived at the brothel, Lisa welcomed him with a bear-hug and a great show of warm affection. In a minute she was pouring him wine in her private parlour and showering him with compliments on his appearance, and his robust good health. "You look tired though, Sam, in need of a good kip, with no hanky panky first." She kissed him tenderly too, and he spent an hour chatting, glad to find her well and content. She showed him pictures of Shane who was now starring in a Broadway musical. She made Sam read the letter, glad when he agreed that Shane seemed a bit depressed. As Sam read on he came to the cause; the showbiz marriage of the decade had come to an end after just two years of connubial bliss.

Lisa, who was tipsy, tut-tutted in her tone as she said, "I never stop saying it. Marriage does awful things to love. That girl, Emily Danvers, was a dote I swear, an absolute dote. I met her myself, and him, he gets better and better, the kindest and most caring lad any woman ever met. And they were over-the-moon about each other, couldn't keep their hands off each other. Here, I thought, I better get outa here before they have to do it with me in the room." She joined Sam as he chuckled at her incorrigibility. "Oh," she said then, as a thought struck her, "you'll never guess what I've gone and done, Sam." She waited as though she thought he might read her mind. When he said nothing, she rose and took her time pouring wine for each of them. "Aren't you just dying to know what I did?" She was enjoying his company, and he went along with the good feeling between them. "Of course, I am, but I'm not going to admit that to you, am I?"

Mollified, she sat down, nodding her head, while he thought her remarkably pretty still, and relatively unmarked by a life that seemed to him to be what a person might well call demanding.

"I wrote to Arthur Shane in America, and I told him that Shane was his son," she said with pride, her posture stiffening as though she was standing for the National Anthem. "It's time he knew. Shane knew anyway from my sister, but I told him from me who his da was. He smiled about being a half-brother to Arthur and Victoria Brewer. He thought she was stunning. He'd have been trying to climb up her leg is my guess, if he hadn't been blinded by Gloria. How is Gloria, these days?"

"You won't believe what I'm going to tell you," he now played with her as she had with him just minutes before. "Aren't you just dyin' to know what I'm going to tell you?"

"I bloody well am, Sam Sweet, and you shut up and tell me." She drank wine and he did the same, warm and content for now, Arthur forgotten for the minute, time enough to deal with that. When Arthur went somewhere for the evening it was his general rule not to leave much before breakfast time. Sam now got up to pour wine for them both, while she did well not to get really vexed with him. It amused him to see her agitated, and he had to allow he was tipsy. "She's gone and joined a kibbutz."

"She's what?"

"She's gone and joined a kibbutz. She's living in Palestine."

"That's good," Lisa said starting to laugh. "Oh, that's very good. If I ever get to meet her, you just watch out. I'm going to tell her you were making up jokes about her."

She got up to answer a knock on the door. "Josie," she said to the servant girl in the hallway, "will you go and check if Mister Brewer is in the house. If he's not, try the others. And if he's not in any of ours, try the nearest opposition. I want to know where he is within the hour, have you got that."

When she came back to sit facing him across the fire, Sam raised his glass. "I'll have another while we're waiting to hear where he is."

"And why wouldn't you, Sam Sweet! Is this any night to get sensible?" She gave a laugh, quaffed the rest of her wine and said lustily, "And d'ye know what? I'll join you, in case you feel lonely drinking on your own."

As usually happened when he drank too much too fast, Sam was beginning to feel sleepy. "You keep a good fire going, Lisa. I'll say that for you." He was trying to stay awake by making conversation.

She handed him another glass of wine. "I doze the odd time in the afternoons at home by the fire. Is it the fire, or is it middle-age? What do you think?" She raised her glass in a toast, "To one of the best, Sam Sweet."

"I give that back to you, dear heart! You were a good friend to me, when friends were hard to find. And you've been the best ever since. God bless you, Lisa."

By the time he finished the wine, Sam had given up trying to keep his eyes open. Lisa sat there sipping her drink, remembering days and nights when she would have settled for him as the only man in her life. He was still a fine thing, no pot-belly or nothing, and you could tell by looking at him that he could still get it up. Shots in the street shattered her moments of recall and she went to the window. Lifting the edge of a drape she saw

men running, heard more shots, saw a number of Black
and Tans on the move, heard a Crossley tender pull up
with a screech of brakes at the corner, more shots, a cry
of pain, and she let the curtain drop. Collins was killing
theirs, so they were paying back on the double, didn't
matter who it was. If they thought someone a rebel he
was gunned down, nobody checking whether he was or
not. They were bastards, a law unto themselves, though
in fairness, some of the officers were decent enough,
and very nice to the girls.

She'd had a couple of officers in during the week.
Toffs. All hoity-toity, the way they talked. Lots of good
manners, standing up when one of the girls left the table
to go for a pee! Very straight men they were. Had it off in
a few minutes, paid up and had a few drinks and went
off without a bother. Quiet they were, careful how they
behaved, but you got the feeling they weren't altar boys.

There was a tap on the door. She checked that Sam
was comfortably snoozing as she went unsteadily
across the room. Opening the door, she put her finger to
her lips and stepped out into the carpeted hall. Shutting
the door quietly behind herself, she said to the middle-
aged maid, "What's the diddly, Josie?"

"The diddly is we missed him."

"Missed him where?"

"Here, he was here, in the house. Had the ride with
Lillian. Then they went into the lounge for a quiet jar.
Fell into talking to that English officer, the one with the
monocle and the marbles in his mouth."

"He was in the other night. I remember him, a gent.

And you're right, Josie. He talks like he's got a mouthful of marbles."

"That's the one," Josie said. "Well, by all accounts, they had a good few, and a good laugh by the sound of it. And then they all went off to Lillian's place. She has that friend of hers staying with her for a while, you know. Your man, Officer Marbles, he wanted to see two lessers having it off – ready to pay through the nose."

"I'll never understand Lillian. She can have any man she wants, gets two and three proposals a month from men that're really heeled, and she falls in love with a fuckin' lesbian. Isn't it gas, altogether?"

"No accountin' for taste is what I always say," Josie shrugged. "Is it true, Miss Stafford, if ye've had it good with a lezzer, ye'd never go near a bloke again?"

Lisa was thoughtful for a moment. "Get Larry to bring the car around. I'm going out. Over to Lillian's."

"Ah, she'll give you your commission, Miss Stafford. She wouldn't cheat you."

Lisa was scandalised by the implication of this. "I am not going to Ranelagh to collect my fucking commission. How dare you suggest such a thing?"

"Ah Miss Stafford, I didn't mean any harm."

"Shut up, girl," Lisa said. "I'm feeling the drink, so don't mind me. I think the world of you. Now, what was I going to say? Yes! I'll leave a note for Mister Sweet. He's snoozing inside there. You put your head in the door in about an hour. Give him the note. What time is it now, anyway?" Absent-mindedly, she looked at her watch.

"Jesus! It's four o'clock, and here I am thinking it was about midnight."

"Ah, Miss Stafford, doesn't the time only fly when you're enjoyin' yerself?"

"Tell Larry, the Rolls Royce. Even the bloody Tans won't bother you in a Roller."

As Sam Sweet napped under the influence of the wine, Lisa attended to her toilette. When she heard Larry give a gentle toot on the hooter, she went out and got into the car. She was feeling tired herself. "I could have done without this middle of the night jaunt over to Ranelagh, but anything to help Sam." She mumbled tipsily into her fur collar. She knew he was anxious about poor Arthur. She was sad for Arthur, too, though she had long ago released the need to talk to him, and had taken careful steps to ensure he never knew who she was. She thought of the times they had talked in one or another of her houses, she in the working wig and behind the make-up, poor pissy Arthur not knowing who she was. 'God love you, sweetheart. The life draining out of you since poor Victoria died. Between losing her, and the booze murdering your mind, ranting to the girls about a woman you can't find, and you riding them half to death. Jesus! Somebody should do a novena for you. That's right, somebody should. And I'll be the one to do it. You never had a chance with that fucking mother of yours. She had a body on her for mortal sins, and she never wanted the ride, Arthur Shane swore that to me, and she had so much hatred in her, you'd wonder how God got the recipe for a person so fucked up, in such a lovely wrapper.

Her driver Larry lowered the glass partition, and said in a familiar manner, "A lot of people are getting shot tonight, Molly love. I'm only hoping your journey is really necessary."

"Don't you Molly love me, you cheeky bastard!" she said, making sure he understood she was not playing games. "Just remember your position."

"Ah, Molly, don't start. You were only too happy with my position last night, if you'll pardon me for bringing it up. You've hurt my feelings so you have." His Dublin accent was quite strong, but he had picked up some English intonation while he was in the British army, so that he sounded phony, even when he was being sincere.

"Did you get paid for your trouble?" she said, dismissing him.

"You gave me a present. It wasn't you paying me. Jesus! You make me sound like a gigolo. Is it no good telling you I love you, and that I want to marry you?"

"If I was mad enough to marry you, I hope I'd still be sane enough to put you in the bank, and sleep with my money. Now, get over to Ranelagh and don't be annoying me further. And put the partition up. I don't like that after-shave pomade or whatever it is."

Not far away from the Rolls Royce motoring along Sackville Street, Michael Collins was issuing last-minute instructions to his team of assassins, Brendan O'Connor and Cormac Doyle being among the men present. "The timing is the all-important thing. What happens in a few hours' time, it has to happen in such a way that the Brits realise they are up against soldiers that will bring them all down, unless they sit down and talk to us."

He reminded them of a lorry-full of Black and Tans driving down a street in Cork shooting anything that moved, burning half the city in their lust for revenge. "It was fear, fear of us that drove them to that. Just like the big shots they brought in to run our country not sleeping so well in their feather-beds these nights. Not since we paid a few visits, tiptoeing through the tulips around their country mansions to blow them to kingdom come where they belong. They have left us no choice. They forced us into guerilla warfare, and this morning they are going to pay a very heavy price for what they have done."

At Lisa's best house in Monto, Josie looked into Miss Stafford's private parlour – Mister Sweet was still snoozing. A decent skin. She smiled. He looked so comfortable she didn't have the heart to wake him up. She'd look in again in a half an hour or so. What's the rush? Won't he be a long time pushing up the daisies?

At Lillian's house in Ranelagh the door was opened by the English lesbian she had fallen in love with. In fairness to the woman, Lisa admitted, she really was a stunning beauty with a wonderful body, and she was very polite. Introducing herself as Karen Williams, she regretted that Lillian wasn't home at the present time.

"They were here, Miss Stafford, for an hour or so. The officer was rather drunk, the gentleman even more so. They were in no fit state to be abroad. In the event, Lillian fetched a hackney cab and, as far as I know, they were going back to the hotel where the officer was staying." Karen Williams spoke with a cut-glass accent, and to Lisa's well-tuned ear, it sounded copper-bottomed real.

"Do you happen to know which hotel it was, Karen? It'd be a great help."

"I wish I could help. It just never came up. Oh goodness, forgive me my bad manners. May I offer you a drink while you're here? I feel I know you. Lillian thinks so highly of you, talks about you quite a bit."

"You're very good, but I'll say no. I've had my share of wine this evening," Lisa was pleased to hear that Lillian spoke well of her. Lillian was an educated woman, she'd been to Trinity, and the Sorbonne and the devil knew where else. "If Lillian gets back in the next while, ask her to ring the house, she'll know which one I mean, and if I'm not back there, tell her to leave the name of the officer's hotel with Josie."

She shook Karen's hand and got back into the car. "Take me back to the house, Larry, and stop looking so miserable. You've a mug on you would stop a clock."

Larry sniffed disdainfully, and closed the partition. Lisa said to herself, 'Hmmph! He's really got the hump. And knowing him he's probably got the horn as well. Let him stew. Just because they know their way around the feathers, they think they can talk to a body any way they like. Well, not this body they can't.'

Checking the time, she saw it was half-past five. She was racking her brains to remember had she heard which hotel Marbles Mouth was staying at. She felt the car stop and, even as she wondered what was going on, the door opened and Larry looked in at her.

"I am devastated, Lisa. Last night, my God, last night you told me I was a giant of a lover, and tonight you treat me like, like a worker. I meant it when I said I love you. I meant it when I said I'd never look at another woman if I could have you for my own."

She sat there stunned as the big brute, a fellow who had survived the battle of the Somme, stood in the open door of the Rolls Royce with tears streaming down his face. Her heart simply melted, and in a moment she had held out her arms to him and he came into the car, pulling the door shut behind him. Even as his tears fell on her face, his mouth was on her lips and she was responding to him like a woman possessed. In moments he had torn off her underwear, she exposing her breasts at the same time, and then she felt him prise her apart as he drove himself in there as though he owned her. Which he did within minutes, so that she could not stop herself gushing her praise all over him, as he pushed and humped her to heights of sensation that drove everything else from her mind. She lost track of time, the urgency and good intentions utterly forgotten, responding to him with all her power of giving and invention, so that by the time he thrust her onto the point of orgasm, she was like a wild and demented woman.

When she woke up, she was cold despite Larry covering her still. She pushed him off her and pulled down her skirt. Tucking her breasts inside her bodice she gave him a kick to wake him up. As he started the car, she told him to turn it around and go back to Lillian's.

Lillian herself opened the door, a dressing-gown thrown on, lipstick smeared all over her mouth.

"Jesus, Lisa. I was nearly coming when you knocked."

"Pardon me, Lillian. I'm quite sure Karen can get you up there again. Now, tell me, which hotel?"

"What?"

"Which fucking hotel is that British officer, the one you and Arthur were with, where's he fucking well staying?"

"Oh!" Lillian was somewhat discommoded, but she rallied and in a moment she said, "Washington Palace".

"I'm serious, Lillian, so stop messing about."

"I told you, the Washington Palace."

"But that's a shithole. A bug palace. Are you sure?"

"Don't you think I mentioned that to him? He wanted to do me up there. I told him I wouldn't go into the place."

"So what happened? You left him there and what did you do with Arthur Brewer?"

"He went in with him. Could have been the Gresham for all he knew. I can't even remember his name. Said he had a bottle of something very special. And you know Arthur."

"All right so, I'm sorry for disturbing you. Go back to your woman and enjoy yourself. She was very nice to me. I'll say that for her."

Telling Larry to take her to the Washington Palace hotel, she was about to tell him to go and fetch Sam from her house in Monto, when he said, "Is that the hotel you were looking for earlier?"

"It is a matter of fact, why?"

"I knew that officer was staying there. He got a bit pissed the other night and I got him a cab, looked after him. He told the driver where to take him. That's how I heard."

"You're a big fucking help, Larry. Are you aware of that?" Lisa was about to launch into a tirade of abuse, but he looked a bit crestfallen that he had not been any help to her. She found herself melting and she shook her head. "Oh Jesus! Spare me from the wrath of my temper. You," she pointed a finger at Larry, "I want you to drop me at that hotel. Then you go back to the house, and get Mister Sweet. Bring him back to me at the hotel. If he's got his car with him, tell him to follow you. He'll need it to get Arthur home."

Behind the reception desk in the run-down hotel, Lisa found the night porter slumped in a drunken sleep on the floor. She pulled a face at the smell as she checked the register. The place was a kip house, a flop for salesmen and whores picked up on the street, along with the pox. The only name that stood out among the

Smiths and the Browns and the Greens, was Semple. That's him she said to herself. No Irish fella with a hard-on ever called himself fucking Semple.

As she walked up the stairs she saw the number thirteeen directly facing her. She turned the handle and the door opened and she stepped in, closing it carefully behind her. The double-bed faced the door, and she knew by the length of him, that the body lying there half-covered by a grotty sheet was Arthur. She felt a flicker of sadness as she remembered that the last time she had seen him in bed, was when he was taken ill just after his twelfth birthday. "God love you, darling." She whispered the words like a prayer.

She heard a tap running in the bathroom, and the sound of a man puking his guts up. "Jesus help you as well, love. You're in a bad way."

She moved the cover from Arthur's face and she saw that he was out to the world, his face that of a much older man. How old was he now? Six years younger than me, so just forty-seven. "You look old this morning, love. You're not minding yourself, so you're not."

There was a bottle of whiskey on the bedside locker, and she took a swig out of it, and then another, needing one more then to stop her tears and still the pain she felt at seeing him so.

"Sweet Jesus! What have you done to yourself, you poor love?" She felt the whiskey hit her, and she sat down on the edge of the bed. "That must be the something special your man said he had." She bowed her head appreciatively to the half-empty bottle

She lay down on the bed and in moments she had her arms about Arthur, and she felt her tears flow, and she kissed his face and wiped his mouth with her sleeve. She heard your man in the bathroom coughing and vomiting, and she thought the room would throw her off if it went around any faster.

Downstairs, Cormac Doyle passed the reception desk without even bothering to look for the night porter. He had fed the man enough drink during the night to keep him out of it for hours yet. He went quietly up the stairs. By the time he reached the top and stood facing the number thirteen, his right hand held a revolver down by his side.

He opened the door as quietly as possible and stepped into the room. He heard someone vomiting so loudly he thought the fella would rip his own lungs out. In that moment, one of the figures on the bed attempted to sit up, and Cormac started shooting.

The second figure on the bed now sat up, and was taken by two of the shots Cormac fired from eight feet away. He knew he had two shots left but there was no need. The two on the bed were dead. He turned, vomiting down his front, and stumbled from the room, terrified by what he had done, unaware that he had dropped the revolver onto the worn carpet.

As he stumbled past the reception desk he heard a car door close outside. Past caring what happened to him, he kept on going and almost fell as he stumbled out onto the street.

Sam Sweet was hurrying into the Washington Palace hotel as Cormac came out like a man who hardly knew where he was going. Sam called his name and when Dee's brother turned, Sam hit him hard enough to drop him to the ground. Sam left him there against the concrete buttress of the railings. Filled with dread, he stepped into the lobby of the run-down hotel. The first thing he saw was the door open at the top of the stairs, and he knew as he bounded up and into the bedroom, what he was going to find.

He vomited at finding both Arthur and Lisa shot to death on the bed. His legs gave way for a moment and he involuntarily slumped to the floor, his hand knocking one of the brass knobs off the cast-iron bed frame. He heard himself throw a mumbled prayer to a god unknown – "May they rest in peace" before trying to get up. He was pushing his hands against the floor, but he couldn't make it. His hand touched something hard and cold and as he looked to see what it was, the door of the bathroom opened and a man came out fast, moving to a chair near the window. Sam saw that he was reaching for a gun sitting there in a holster. In that moment, Sam found he was holding a revolver, and he instinctively raised it as the officer started to spin around, his arm outstretched.

Sam's shot took the man in the forehead, sending blood and tissue splattering all over the window and the faded wallpaper, the body already going backwards to hit the wall.

His adrenalin was now pumping so hard that Sam

was on his feet before he knew it. He put the revolver into his pocket, and moved to the bed. Poor Lisa, she had been shot in the face, unrecognisable was the only word for it. He gave one of her hands a pat. "God love you," he said, as he heaved Arthur's body up off the bed and tossed it over his shoulder. He could hear some movement up on the next floor as he came out onto the landing.

"Stay in your rooms," he yelled up the stairs. "This is the police. There's been a shooting."

Coming out onto the street, he kicked Cormac to bring him around. Dee's brother shook himself and sat up. Sam yelled. "Bring the woman off the bed." Cormac paused, puzzled, and Sam said with feeling, "You shot her, you stupid bastard. Now go and bring her down here, or I'll shoot you."

He placed Arthur on the back seat of his car, covered him with a tartan rug, and closed the door. As he opened the boot of the car, Cormac arrived with Lisa, wrapped in a sheet. Sam helped him shove the body in and slammed the boot shut. A few moments later, they drove away from the hotel, Sam keen to get out of the city as quickly as possible, but driving easily to avoid attracting attention.

As they reached Blackrock, Sam had things worked out enough that he was able to tell Cormac what they had to do.

"The way it happened, nobody needs to know about that," Sam said, nudging him with his elbow. "Do you hear me? Nobody needs to know what happened."

"I shot Arthur."

"Arthur was in the wrong place at the wrong time, and Lisa. We have the bodies, so nobody need ever know what happened. Now stop looking like you want to kill yourself, and tell me you're with me on this, tell me you can understand what I'm saying to you."

"I failed in my mission. I didn't get the officer."

"He's very dead, so you got him, right? Only you and I know how it happened. The other thirteen of these very special English spies are gone for their tea, along with your man. Mission completed." He got a cigarette going, took a deep drag from it and passed it to Cormac. "Jesus knows the extent of the retribution it's going to bring down on our heads." He lit one for himself. "So, you shot him, Cormac. Tell me, say it." He inhaled deeply as he waited for confirmation from Dee's brother.

Cormac nodded but Sam needed more. "Let me hear you say it, Cormac. You have to say it, believe it, come to feel it, whatever it takes. We have to get our story straight and stick to it.!

The young man exhaled a wall of smoke and then he said quietly, "I shot him."

Sam glanced sideways at him a few times, saw him begin to relax a little, starting to shrug off his melancholia, but not yet free of concern. "Arthur," he said finally. "He was Dee's husband. What are we going to tell her?"

"Arthur got hit in a shooting on the street," Sam said firmly. "We only found him because we were looking for him all night. The pair of us spent hours looking for him, have you got that?"

Cormac looked at him, no longer shaking in terror. "You're a cool customer."

"We found him on Sackville Street. That's close enough to Monto for Dee to buy it. Oh shit! I forgot about Faires, his driver. Where the hell was he?"

"He's one of us, Sam. He had a mission just like I had. He knew Arthur wouldn't need him before breakfast. He'll be over at Lisa's house now, looking for him."

"We tell Dee we found Arthur on Sackville Street, between the pillar and the bridge on the east side. You OK with that?"

"Yeh," Cormac was subdued but he was back in control. "What about the body in the boot?"

"It's something I won't be showing around. We'll have to dump my old friend into some wet concrete. You and Brendan, get something fixed for tonight. I'll drive by when it's dark, and we'll give Lisa a midnight burial. The job the bullet did on her – she wouldn't want anybody to see her like that. And she knows I'm doing the best I can in the circumstances. She was a good girl, and I always loved her like a real pal should."

As they turned into the drive of Dunbla House, Cormac said, "You're probably right about reprisals. Lloyd George's piles could explode when he hears about this operation."

Despite all that had happened, Sam chuckled and punched Cormac in the arm. "You hold onto the sense of humour." He saw Cormac nod at him behind a look that told him the lad would be all right now. "You're right there, about the Welsh Wizard's piles. But no matter how heavily they come down on us, the world is watching, and this will bring the Brits to the table. They'll sit down with Dev and Collins after this."

He turned to look as he heard Dee come out of the house. "But do you know what, Cormac? I don't honestly know if we'll ever really be a republic, like we dream about when we're in our cups."

He took Dee in his arms as she turned from the sight of Arthur's body on the back seat of the car.

"We brought him home, Dee. We might be grateful he never knew what hit him."

She was weeping but she knew he was right. "God love him," she said, her tears touching Sam's neck.

"Paddy Lote will sign the death certificate and we can bury him here at Dunbla," Sam said quietly as he took her towards the house. "He's home for good, Dee."

THE END